Calm THE RAGING STORM

TONI WASS

MMH PRESS

A catalogue record for this work is available from the National Library of Australia

National Library of Australia Catalogue-in-Publication data:

Calm the Raging Storm/Toni Wass

978-0-6452641-0-4 (Paperback)

978-0-6452641-1-1 (Ebook)

For Fiona McIntosh – for giving me the kick up the butt I needed to finally get this book written.

CHAPTER ONE

Stewart heard the crunch of tyres on gravel before he noticed a small, cherry red four-wheel drive vehicle pull up outside his front door. He stuck his head around the rounded side of his classic 1950 Circe fridge.

Who in the hell was paying him a visit at this time of the day? With repeated cyclone warnings on all radio stations in the past twenty-four hours, who in their right mind would even want to venture outdoors in this sort of weather? Let alone all the way out here? Bloody crazy!

Stewart tipped out the last of the murky dregs of coffee from his favourite, chipped coffee mug into the sink, rinsed it, then laid it upside down on the draining board. His plan was to see who it was and send them on their way back into town without any hassles at all, hopefully. Whoever it is must be lost or something. Although, come to think of it, this humble abode isn't exactly on the main road.

Stewart took the precaution of checking out his unwelcome visitor from his living room window first, which afforded him an excellent view of his front veranda and the steps leading to his front door. He pulled the Venetian blind slats apart enough to see who it was. If needed, he could disappear around to the back of the house to make out he isn't home until whoever it is gives up knocking and leaves. Stewart could see a woman sitting in the driver's seat.

Why isn't she getting out of the car?

When she did, Stewart exhaled. She was gorgeous. Blonde and beautiful, she was his favourite kind of woman. With moist, peach-kissed lips and all that golden skin, she was a vision of loveliness. Stewart shook himself. *Get a grip on yourself, man. You've been isolated for too long.*

Well, whoever she was, he needed to get rid of her, and fast! He didn't need any more complications of the female persuasion in his life.

No thanks! This woman looks like she could spell trouble for me with a capital 'T'.

Where is he? He would have heard my vehicle drive into his driveway by now.

Peta turned off the engine but stayed in the car deciding on the best course of action in approaching this rather strange, but still intriguing, man.

He's either extremely antisocial or not even home. That would be great, wouldn't it? Figures! I drive all the way out here, sixty bloody kilometres—and he's not even home! Shit!

This man was really beginning to piss her off, and she hadn't even met him yet. Peta had to ask herself now if flying all this way up to Cairns for this one assignment, is worth all this stress after all? Probably not, but she was here now, so she may as well try and fix what's not right. Maybe just concentrating on what needs to be done here, right now, might be the way for her to go. What if he really has flown the coup?

Great! Hang on a minute. I just saw that blind move! So, he is in there! Well, Peta, it's time to just do it!

Maybe she should bite the bullet and knock on his door to see what happened. She was a professional after all—even if having him yell at her could be another thing entirely.

What the heck! May as well get it over with, girl! Here goes nothing!

'Who in the hell are you and how did you get out here?' Stewart said, his voice sharp. 'Don't you realise there's a cyclone predicted for this area within the next twelve hours? Are you mad, woman?'

How does he do that? He actually makes the word 'woman' sound like an insult.

'Whoa! Steady on, Mr. Fletcher. My name is Peta McKenna and I'm with Anchor Publishing, which also happens to be the same publishing firm who publishes the *Today's Voice* magazine. You know, the same one you agreed to do your prearranged interview with?'

Stewart glared at a Peta with undisguised contempt, even more tight-lipped now. 'You mean the interview my agent arranged, not me. It certainly wasn't my idea.'

'You weren't expecting me today? There must be some mistake. Give me a minute and I will call my office and clear this up immediately.'

'Don't even bother trying to call anyone right now as there will be no signal anyway, what with a cyclone approaching. Surely you would have realised this by now? Have you even bothered to look upwards to notice the increasingly greenish-black clouds in the sky at all?' Stewart paused for a moment and fixed Peta with a penetrating stare. 'Well, Mrs. McKenna, you're absolutely right. There has been a mistake and I do believe that mistake is YOU!'

Peta was pre-warned by her boss that some resistance may be forth-coming from her intended subject matter. Even if this interview had been arranged months ago by his literary agent, this man was still being down-right insufferable anyway. Because of Fletcher's aggressive, standoffish behaviour towards her, Peta almost forgot why she was even here and simply couldn't resist reacting with a testy reply of her own. 'Why am I suddenly the mistake, Mr. Fletcher? I am here as previously arranged by your literary agent and the editor-in-chief of *Today's Voice,* Tess Elliot, my immediate boss, to do this interview with you. What is really the problem here? Can't we just calm down and talk about this rationally together? There seems to be some hidden issue at the root of all your anger, Mr. Fletcher.'

'Finally! You've hit the nail on the head! The problem is that you are supposed to be a man. I was expecting a *Mr.* Peter McKenna. If you had taken the time to do some more, well-documented research, Mrs. McKenna, you would already know that I always refuse to do any interviews with *any* women! Period! It would have saved you and your magazine some unnecessary costs, not to mention a wasted trip. Especially during such hazardous, cyclonic weather conditions, too. Like I've already said, if you'd checked more thoroughly first, you wouldn't have come all this way for nothing.'

Stewart continued, his words dripping with undisguised sarcasm. 'Besides, I would have to wonder why any major publishing company worth its salt, would send its journalists out in this sort of weather in the first place? Do they not value their staff at all?'

'It's *Ms.* McKenna, actually. Yes, I did agree to this interview, Mr. Fletcher, but only after Brad Collins, my editor's original choice, had to be with his wife during the birth of their first child. We made a commitment to promote your latest book many months ago and we still intend to honour that promise regardless of any weather conditions *or* your specific request of a male journalist.'

Peta took a deep breath to calm herself before continuing.

'As far as I'm aware, Mr. Fletcher, it's almost impossible to predict any weather conditions anywhere in the world, at any given time. In Cairns, too, I might add—particularly at this time of the year.'

Ah! So, she's not married after all! For some crazy reason Stewart couldn't help feeling secretly pleased about this, but he'd be damned if he'd let her see just how much she's affecting his awakening libido. Not to mention, how much she's trying to disrupt his obvious exile from any species of the female kind. Especially with a vision of splendour such as Ms. McKenna. Ah, ah—No way! He simply must try to get rid of her and fast! The trouble is, she doesn't appear to be the type to back down so easily. Well, he'll just have to nip this potential stand-off in the bud completely now, so she'll have no choice but to accept his final decision: She is not welcome here. Now or ever! He reared up like some haughty stallion in his most intimidating manner in a last-ditch effort to be rid of this annoyingly beautiful woman once and for all.

'So! Let me get this straight, *Ms.* McKenna. I may be wrong, but I get the feeling you and your esteemed magazine are determined to risk life and limb just to get a story. *Please!* Feel free to correct me if I'm wrong.'

Peta smiled at him somewhat sheepishly. 'Well, something like that, I guess.'

'Madness! Sheer bloody-minded madness!' Stewart ran his hands through his already ruffled hair in an obvious expression of sheer frustration. Well, it's not really *my* problem, is it? Nor is it *my* problem that your editor is obviously too slack to find some other male journalist to fill my very reasonable request. If you leave now, though, you'll be back in civilisation before the worst of this impending cyclone unleashes its unforgiving fury on us all. Now if you will excuse me, I need to take immediate steps to protect my humble abode right now and time is a wasting. I do believe our conversation is officially over. SO PLEASE LEAVE!'

Without further ado, he locked his rickety screen door first, then before Peta could even get in another word, he slammed his rough, but solid wooden door, leaving Peta on the outside yet again.

Peta was immediately rendered speechless. Dumbstruck really. If she was to be completely honest with herself now, she felt more than a little stupid. Regardless of the underestimation of her opponent, it finally dawned on her that she had just been ruthlessly and callously left to stand out here to feel totally dejected and at a loss to understand what just happened.

What the! Talk about rude! This Mr. Bloody Stewart Fletcher would have to be the most insufferable man I have ever met in my entire life, bar none! Peta fumed. *Out of all the blockheaded, stubborn and egotistical men in the world, this man takes the cake! The sheer audacity of the man! And all because I am, heaven forbid, a woman! No wonder he seems to have so much trouble with his personal relationships.*

She continued to vent for a few more minutes, all the while trying to figure out where she'd gone wrong and, most importantly, how to fix whatever she needed to fix. Well at least, to get him to open his front door to her again, anyway.

Peta allowed herself a smile of extreme naughtiness now. She admitted, despite all of his thunder and bluster, he certainly was a sexy man. His photos could never truly prepare any normal, red-blooded woman such as herself, for the real thing up close.

He has this irresistible, raw charisma that has me wanting—no craving—to know ALL of him! Yes indeed.

With his curly, ebony hair albeit messy right now, his towering presence and his obviously powerfully broad shoulders. Oh, and those piercing baby blues too. All this blended so beautifully together, equals one compelling, totally male package, that's for certain.

What a damn shame he has to be such a bastard, though! So, what to do?

If she left as requested by the oh-so-famous egomaniac himself, he would have won. She'd have no choice but to go back to Tess with her tail between her legs and no story. She'd probably have no job to go back to, either. Tess was clear with her parting words back in Sydney. 'Since Doug has recommended you, I'm taking a chance in trusting you, Peta, so please don't let me or Doug down either.'

No pressure or anything! Hell no!

That's not going to happen. He's messed with the wrong woman this time.

After much carefully thought-out internal planning, Peta came to the inevitable conclusion. She'd plonk herself down on the uncomfortable, rough wooden steps and refuse to leave until he at least agreed to open his front door again.

I am Peta McKenna and a professional journalist, am I not? That has to count for something, surely?

She knew before accepting this assignment to expect some resistance initially, but Stewart Fletcher's behaviour was beyond ridiculous. She was fully aware he possessed some deeply ingrained hang-ups with women, but his behaviour today, of all days, to a total stranger too, was bizarre and so not funny!

Peta suddenly felt some niggling prickles run up and down her spine. She could sense, rather than see, him watching her from inside.

He's in there by that window! I just know it! I bet he's enjoying my misery right now too. Well, if he thinks I'm going to run away like a frightened little girl, he has another thing coming!

Maybe she should just return his glare for glare so he can't help but be aware she's onto him. After about ten minutes of her decision to give him a taste of his own behaviour, Peta heard the lock on his front door being unlatched.

Stewart Fletcher, the devil incarnated, stormed out onto his veranda and for full effect, dramatically banged his front screen door against the outside wall. Despite Peta's resolve to remain calm and in control, the sudden loud noise made her jump. He glared down at Peta from where she was perched stubbornly on his top veranda step. With pure menace in his voice, Stewart gave her the full force of his viperish tongue. So much more than the last time too, it seemed.

'Why are you still on my front veranda? I thought I made it perfectly clear there will be no interview today, or any other day, for that matter.'

'Sorry, but I'm not listening to you right now, especially when you talk to me like that. I am most certainly not leaving here either. Not until I get what I came for, anyway. It's not my fault if there was a lack of communication between my office and your agent. And it's *not* my fault, if you automatically *assumed* I was going to be a male journalist because of my name. Besides, there are lots of women in the publishing business with unisex names. Anyway,' Peta centred herself, 'it seems to me, you should have checked for yourself if you were so worried about me being a mere woman. And I will tell you another thing too. I was trusted by my editor as a professional journalist to do this interview with you and I will stay out here for the rest of today and all night if I have to!'

'Is that right? What about Cyclone Jamie, which is now moving even closer to us as we speak, huh? What do you plan to do when this cyclone does hit this area with a vengeance? And it will, believe me. Have you ever been out in such weather before?'

'I HAVE been in some bad storms before actually, but no, not a cyclone, I would have to admit.' Peta stuck her chin out with pure defiance. 'BUT a little bit of wind doesn't scare me off that easily, and *you* don't scare me that easily either!'

'A little bit of wind?' Stewart laughed out loud at that little gem. 'That's a classic example of a woman's logic, if ever I heard one. I don't think you comprehend at all, *lady*, just how destructive these cyclonic winds can be. They will probably find parts of you scattered all over North Queensland by tomorrow morning.'

'Be that as it may,' Peta primly interjected, 'I am still not moving from this step until I get what I came for. If I should happen to be blown off the face of this earth, though, it will be *your* fault because you were too mean to let me come inside! How are you going to explain that to the press? Huh? Not to mention all your loyal fans, too. What will they think of you when they find out you're responsible for killing off a perfectly good journalist? And all because I am … Oh no! I'm a woman!'

Stewart inhaled in exasperation.

'Suit yourself then! If you want to stay out here and risk life and limb just to prove a point, then go right ahead. If you think I am going to take pity on you, think again! And as I've said before, if you leave now, you will be back in Cairns before this cyclone unleashes its full fury on you. But by all means, don't take my word for it. Stick around and find out for yourself.'

Stay calm, girl. Stay put! Don't let him intimidate you! It took all of Peta's willpower to rest her hands on her knees and ignore him.

Stewart drew in a few more deep, ragged breaths. This annoying, but beautiful, woman was wantonly, bit by bit, breaking down his resistance to pull her into his arms and crush her delicious-looking mouth against his ravenous lips. *Damn!*

He admitted his efforts to resist her were breaking down. Rather than picking her up and plonking her back in her car as he should be doing, he kept staring. He knew if he were to even to touch her, he couldn't be held responsible for what followed, such was his overpowering desire for her, especially when he just wanted to ravage her body instead. Surely, for his sanity's sake alone, it was well worth one last attempt to be rid of her once and for all.

'You would have to be the most infuriating woman I have ever met!'

Peta remained stubbornly and now silently on his veranda steps, even though the wooden steps' roughness was already applying an unforgiving pressure on her rear end.

'Okay! I can see my warnings are falling on deaf ears. Don't say I didn't try to warn you. Enjoy this *little bit of wind,* then, Ms. McKenna!'

Once again, as her gaze refused to meet her tormenter's, the heavy vibration of his feet stomping on the wooden boards of the veranda reached her. Then came the inevitable resounding thud of his front door as he slammed it, dismissing her from her intended mission once more.

CHAPTER TWO

That went well! Despite her best efforts to inject some positive intent into her dire situation, Peta brushed away traitorous tears of frustration and defeat.

I just can't give in to him. I have to show him his meanness will not intimidate me. Not now, not ever!

She didn't think he would leave her out here to suffer this nasty weather, though. Peta cast a rather apprehensive look out beyond the veranda roof. She noticed the leaves of the banana palms beyond the rusty tin shed bordering Fletcher's gravel parking area were swaying erratically now. Way more than they should for her peace of mind. In fact, every bloody palm tree along the side fence joined in with the volatile force of nature.

Oh shit! Well. Where does all of your stubbornness leave you now, Peta?

Right back where she started, that's where! Oh hell! What had she done? Now she realised Fletcher might be right after all. She could be blown away into the outer atmosphere with this force of wind picking up speed right before her eyes. To make matters worse, she was exposed out here in the open. Not even the curved, wrought-iron roof could protect her once the destructive cyclonic winds hit this area. Soon, too, if the eerie

11

howling wind force was anything to go by. This cyclone was no longer just a warning for Peta, but fast becoming a frightening reality.

Are you sure you still want to stick it out on his front veranda like this?

The problem was, if she failed to secure the interview, Tess would brush her excuses away with a flick of her immaculately manicured hand and say something like, 'That's okay, Peta. You did your best.' But Tess would never trust her again to cover any other difficult assignments. She'd be passed over in favour of some other ambitious and braver journalist than her cowardly self.

But that's just not going to happen! No way!

She could clearly hear her world-renowned journalist father's words in her head right now, 'Quitting is never to be an option when it comes down to chasing a good story, darling girl.' Well, her fear was a palatable thing for sure, but it wasn't an excuse for her to run away from what could well be a life-changing career opportunity for her, despite her current dire circumstances.

No! I will not leave here until I get what I came for! Cyclone or no cyclone!

Peta countered her own inner arguments with another more realistic scenario. Her decision to stay put meant she'd risk her own life for the sake of her career. Was her career that important? She reminded herself it was because of her pride in her own abilities as a journalist, her noted stubbornness, and tenacity by her superiors that earned her this assignment.

From her precarious position on the top veranda step, Peta made an immediate appraisal from a potential survivalist's point of view. She was well aware in Australia alone, cyclones were always treated as a national threat until proven otherwise. What are her chances of surviving this one, then? Probably not very good at all! Well, if she planned to sit out here at the mercy of the elements, she should constructively protect herself more at least. Maybe she could wait it out under these veranda steps, rather than on top of them. Ah-ah. Keeping company with all those spiders and snakes also seeking shelter under these stairs? *Nah, I don't think so! No way!*

She knew one thing, though. If she made it out of this situation alive, she planned on writing a detailed, scathing report about Mr. Fletcher's unchivalrous behaviour for all of Australia and, in fact, the whole damn world to read. He'd be sorry he ever messed with her! *Huh! Brave words indeed. Think, girl, think!*

Maybe she could find a sheet of tarp or even one of those vinyl car covers in that old shed over there? Something to shield her body from these rather nasty winds that already seemed so much stronger than even a second ago. She must do something, though! It was that or stay exposed to the elements.

Before she crossed to the shed, which was only about five metres away—though with the high winds, it may as well be five hundred metres—she needed to secure her carryall bag somehow. She needed to protect her precious laptop, plus the all-important folder regarding Fletcher himself to refer back to if she needed to at any time. If she was ever going to secure this interview, that is.

So far, this brilliant career decision of hers had proven to be a disastrous one. Besides, she was much too young to die today, anyway.

Peta tucked her carryall bag under what she considered a protected site under the veranda steps. Far enough away she hoped, from the full onslaught of these increasingly scary winds threatening to freak her out altogether. It wasn't just her own body at risk, either. These howling, screaming winds, were obviously hell-bent on trying to flatten everything on its unstoppable path of destruction. *God! Please help me! This is no fun at all!*

Desperate, she looked for some kind of bodily protection before heading off towards the shed. That's when she hit on the idea of somehow using some part of a decrepit-looking settee at the far end of the front veranda. With its tattered strips of cane unravelling along the side arms and at both the back and front, the exposed-to-the-elements settee was rather sad looking. However, it had a large and bumpy-looking cushion.

Despite its questionable appearance, it looked like her best option to somehow cushion her body from head to foot. It even had extra padding at the head for anyone desperate enough to stretch out on it.

Peta figured she could hold it up in front of her, vertically along her body length. Given her height was well above average, she might protect most of the front of her body. Peta drew in a few deep breaths and held her nose away from the rank, musty odour of the cushion. She attempted to shape the old cushion around her body as much as she could.

Well, it was now or never! Besides, what choice did she have, anyway? It was either stay here and die or find cover from this nightmare with some degree of safety. She didn't even want to think what sort of creepy-crawlies might be also seeking shelter inside the shed with her. Well, whatever lurked inside would have to get out of her way for now. She was about to make her move.

Stewart stared out of his lounge room window and shook his head in total disbelief.

What the! What's she doing now? What did she hope to achieve with that old settee cushion wrapped around her? Unbelievable! Did she seriously think that mouldy old cushion would protect her from these unstoppable winds? She'd left it too late to drive out of here safely. It looked like he'd have to rescue her after all. *Bloody Hell!*

When she veered away towards his shed and not her car, he figured she was trying to find shelter to protect herself. He had to admire her tenacity. Most woman would have been on the road and hightailed it out of here by now, but not Ms. McKenna. This intrepid reporter was prepared to risk life and limb for the latest story in a magazine, which would end up in a recycle bin one day, anyway. Go figure! Crazy females! Every damn one of them! God love 'em!

Stewart realised he'd no choice now but to rescue her from herself. The thought terrified him, and it had nothing to do with this current cyclone either. Every year during the summer months in North Queensland, he faced a whole range of erratic tropical weather patterns. Nothing new there, except with each new season, this could be the year some hellish cyclone lifted his old shack, piece by rusty piece, and scattered it around his neighbourhood. Maybe even as far as away as Cairns itself. No! It was the thought of having this drop-dead gorgeous woman all alone with him inside his private domain that unravelled his peace of mind. The thought of both of them alone together throughout the night was too dangerous to contemplate.

Why does she have to smell so damn good, too? And those eyes! They flashed like a thousand slivers of exquisite jade. When he considered her overall sensuality, *she is best avoided at all costs.* Stewart's eyes glinted with suspicious thoughts. She might be devious enough to cast some sort of evil spell over him, too. He wouldn't put it past her, either. He'd have to reign in his long-neglected libido tonight. Especially under these forced circumstances and well within the confines of a close, secluded isolation, too.

Man, oh man! Stewart mumbled. *Like I said, Stewart, old son, a dangerous move of yours, indeed.*

Him questioning his judgement and his nagging inner voice wasn't helping his situation one bit.

Upon your head, Stewart. Upon your head.

Interesting choice of words. *Which head am I really talking about here?*

Oh hell! This was his ultimate challenge with this woman. When she came inside, he needed to stay totally detached from her obvious charms. There'd be no escape, not until tomorrow morning, at any rate. Regardless of his obvious reservations about tonight's outcome, she'd left him no choice. His conscience wouldn't allow him to leave her out there one more minute.

Stewart understood the time would come when he'd have to revisit his issues with these complex creatures, especially with a bewitching one right outside. Stewart drew in a deep ragged breath and headed for his front door. It was time to face his inner demon again.

Stewart flung open his front door again with a force that surprised even himself. Peta stopped her inspection of his shed in one startled movement. She expected him to pick her up and throw her back into her vehicle. Then ordering her to be on her way despite the aggressive, persistent slap of palm leaves and the trunk of the palm trees themselves banging against the side of the shed. Various loose and rusted car parts nearby were no doubt about to be turned into flying missiles any second now. She couldn't help but wonder, as she glanced apprehensively all around her, just what a precarious situation she was in. All loose mechanical and gardening items appeared to be stored away in plastic milk crates or in large, reusable coffee tins. Until now, the lean-to at the side of the shed protected them, but Peta suspected they were about to be forcibly removed from their hidey-holes.

Peta had no choice but to acknowledge the forceful winds whipping up even more momentum all around her. Somehow, they didn't seem nearly as threatening as the lord of this tropical manor. He covered the distance between them at full speed, like some huge bird of prey in full flight about to sweep down upon its defenceless prey.

Stewart swept her up into his arms, but not to throw her into her vehicle as she'd imagined. Instead, he headed towards his front veranda and the safety of his four walls and roof.

Yes, he may be letting her come inside, but she didn't think for one minute he would make her feel welcome once he bolted his front door against the threatening elements outside. She bet he'd give her the silent treatment, anyway. Beggars can't be choosers, though. Maybe this deceptively sturdy old shack might at least keep her alive for tonight. If she's lucky.

Once Stewart lowered Peta back onto her own two feet, he opened his front door for her and beckoned for her to enter his carefully guarded, private sanctuary.

Peta's eyes widened as she stared at him, disbelief in her eyes. She shocked him then by pulling away from him and heading back outside again.

'No, no! I can't go inside with you.'

'Unbelievable!' he yelled out to her. 'I've just rescued you from these devilish winds that were about to rip all of your limbs apart, just like you hoped I would, no doubt. Why in the hell won't you come inside now?'

Peta raced across his veranda in some mad frenzy and dove under the front steps like the devil himself was after her.

'You've got to be kidding me!' Stewart shook his head in frustration. 'You'd rather seek refuge under my veranda, then spend the night alone with me. Is that it?'

No answer.

'Look, Ms. McKenna, you won't have to share a bed with me if that's what troubles you. I have a sofa bed you can use for tonight. Ms. McKenna? Why won't you answer me? Oh hell!'

Just as Stewart was about to follow her, Peta emerged from under the steps, clutching her carryall bag to her chest.

'Sorry, but with this storm approaching and in taking steps to protect myself, I forgot I stowed this bag under your veranda earlier. I placed it well back from the perimeter to protect it before heading out towards your shed. I figured it would be better off down there and hopefully safe from any damage for now. Because I'd hidden it so well though, it took me a few precious minutes to find it again.'

Peta pulled back from Stewart's thunderous glare with a sheepish smile. 'Well, I couldn't very well leave it under there, could I? After all, it holds my laptop and all of my important notes.'

'You'll pardon me if I don't comment right now. A woman's logic never ceases to amaze me.'

'That's such a coincidence because I find a man's logic totally baffles me, too!'

Stewart's scathing look was meant to wither Peta on the spot. He held the screen door open for her to enter first, and she breezed past him with a cheeky grin, not fazed one bit. Stewart secured the screen door and locked and bolted his heavy front door.

'Looks like it's going to be a long, long night!' Stewart muttered loud enough for Peta to hear.

CHAPTER THREE

'*Okay, Ms. Mckenna, I* guess you've won this round, but let's get a few things perfectly clear, shall we?'

'This is your house and therefore your rules. I get it! Fire away.'

'You understand, of course, that you will only be allowed inside my home until this cyclone has run out of steam and it's safe for you to leave again. Agreed?'

Peta wisely chose not to provoke him. She merely nodded her head in agreement.

'Unfortunately, this cyclone shows no signs of running out of steam until tomorrow morning, at the very least. I dare say, I could even give you some comfort food as well.'

'Thank you, Mr. Fletcher, and I want you to know, I am very grateful to you for your kind hospitality. I must admit, it was starting to get a wee bit scary there for a while.'

Stewart walked away and secured the remaining window latches on the old-fashioned, slide-out casement window frames around two walls of his living room.

'Don't thank me too soon. I intend billing your magazine later.'

'By all means, bill my office if that makes you happy.' Peta couldn't resist one more tiny but oh-so-satisfying barb though. 'I wouldn't want you to be out of pocket, after all.'

'Yes, well, we will talk about that later, shall we?' He tried to say it in the same gruff voice, but Peta soon realised he didn't sound as nasty as when she'd first arrived at his private home quarters, however humble though it may be.

'Oh, by the way!' Stewart turned around to face Peta, as if he'd suddenly thought of something important he needed to add to his rules. 'While you are in my home as a guest, we will dispense with any formalities, at least until the cyclone blows over and I can send you safely on your way again. For now, I am Stewart, and you are Peta. That okay with you?'

'That's fine with me, Mr. Flet—Sorry, I mean, Stewart.'

'One more thing we need to get out of the way. Just because I invited you into my home, doesn't mean there will be any interview later. Any persistent reminders or even a hint of the word *interview* from you, while you are inside my home and, I promise you, I'll have you out that front door in a heartbeat, cyclone or no cyclone. Have I made myself clear?'

'Perfectly,' Peta answered sweetly. Out of necessity, her mission may have to be put on hold for now, but her underlying professional objectives were still firmly on target.

If he thought she'd back down altogether, then he was kidding himself. In the meantime, for safety's sake, she needed to get her priorities right. She'd an important choice to make now: safety or ambition? On an earth-shattering night such as tonight, obviously safety should always come first. Locked away in a secluded shack with only the devastatingly handsome Mr. Fletcher for company and a big storm—okay, a cyclone—raging out of control outside, who'd protect her from her fast-developing wanton desires for him? She remembered the feel of his arms holding her when he carried her inside. She could still feel the sensation of a million sparks zinging all around her body as he lifted her effortlessly up into his strong arms.

As the esteemed Mr Fletcher said, 'It's going to be a long, long night!' He's got that right, at least.

While Peta straightened out her thoughts in her head, Stewart was busy doing the same thing on the other side of the room. The nearness of this intriguing woman threatened to drive him crazy to the point of total distraction! And why must she continue to taunt him with that amazing kick-ass perfume of hers? If she was only here to conduct an interview, then why did she have to come around here smelling so damn good? His all-too-familiar thought pattern of distrust and cynicism threatened to surface again. Her intoxicating perfume and well-played innocence were obviously meant to be more of an all-to-predictable female trap just to suck him in!

I will just have to avoid the nearness of her scrumptious body as much as possible!

Stewart bustled about as he double-checked every hole in the walls, or any cracks in the windows of his old house. He needed to protect them all from the unmerciful horizontal force of cyclonic winds which could blow apart their only safe refuge. Stewart reassured himself for the umpteenth time that this old house has been here forever, despite its outwardly ramshackle appearance, and would probably outlive him in the end.

'Make yourself comfortable in the living room for now while I find something for us to eat. We will probably lose our power any minute now. I do have a power generator, but I prefer not to use it until I absolutely have to, especially in weather as unpredictable as this certainly is. As for something quick to eat for now, to satisfy our hunger throughout the long night ahead, I think maybe a salad and some tinned salmon might be a good idea. You happy with that, Peta?'

'Sounds good to me! Can I help? I'm not much of a cook, but I can throw together a salad at least.'

'NO!' Stewart said a bit too quickly. The thought of her body being too close to his own traitorous body was too dangerous to even contemplate right now. 'What I meant was, thank you for your offer to help, but everything is under control. I really do work better on my own in the kitchen, if that's okay with you?'

'Fine. But if you don't mind, I need to use your bathroom. Which way?'

Stewart seemed to ignore her at first, as engrossed as he was in his kitchen duties. He pulled out ingredients from his fridge and also from his well-stocked pantry. He acknowledged her finally, though, with a quick offhanded point of a rather large finger to a hallway just to the left from where she was standing at the kitchen breakfast bar. Peta followed the direction of his finger towards the hallway, only to find there were a few other rooms branching left and right off the hallway as well.

'Second door to the left.'

'Thanks, I'll be right back.'

Peta took off down the hallway. She heard Stewart opening and shutting cupboard doors and the refrigerator door in search of the ingredients he needed to prepare their cold, ready-to-go meal. Peta wondered if he was about to create a gourmet feast like on one of those TV reality shows instead of two plates of salmon straight from a can, a bit of lettuce maybe, perhaps a slice of tomato, and even some canned beetroot too. He seemed to be under some kind of intense pressure to be making so much unnecessary noise for such a simple meal. *Jeez! Men and their macho cooking skills!* He obviously didn't need her help, and he obviously didn't want her anywhere inside his precious kitchen space, so she was more than happy to leave him to it.

Peta continued on down the hallway in search of his bathroom, poking her head into any open doorway along the way out of sheer curiosity while the man of the house was otherwise occupied for now. The last room on the right was obviously his, featuring navy blue walls with white door frames. His entire bedroom furniture consisted of a chunky king-sized bed frame, Hawaiian-style wicker chair, chest of drawers and two side tables, all white and all matching, creating a masculine nautical look. The stylishness of his bedroom surprised Peta. She had somehow pictured his bedroom with an unmade bed in the middle of the room, perhaps a bedside table, complete with a lamp, on either side of his bed. Oh, and the usual built-in, two-door wardrobe. This revelation was a pleasant surprise indeed to Peta, with this private domain of his revealing to her yet another side of this intriguing man. She realised she has so much to learn about him still. *Wow! A home decorator AND a master chef in the making. I'm impressed!* After finding the bathroom and, most thankfully, the toilet, Peta spent a few necessary moments washing away the glistening sweat beads from her face, because of the tropical mugginess in the air.

She loosened her messy ponytail and retied her long tresses into some sort of tidy order. As she did all this, she did a quick mental recap of Stewart Fletcher the private man versus the public version. It was surprising how neat this old house really was. Uncluttered, too. 'A place for everything and everything thing in its place.' It was her Aunt Ruby's favourite mantra and she would absolutely appreciate his tidiness, for sure. He must have a housekeeper, though. She couldn't imagine any full-time writer who spent most of his time at his creative pursuits would normally be this houseproud. He wasn't slovenly with his appearance either.

According to his dossier, he was in his mid to late thirties. He was no doubt proficient in using his piercing baby blues to their full advantage, whenever he decided to turn up his sexual aura with the ladies. Works for her anyway, but there was no way she was going to let Mr. Fletcher know just how much he was affecting her, especially with been forced to spend the night all alone with him. Well, she still had her pride and some degree of professionalism left, didn't she?

Forced is hardly the word I would use here, really! After all, I can well imagine a lot of women would give their teeth to spend the night alone with the esteemed Mr. Fletcher. Ha! Eat your hearts out, ladies! Like the actor, Sean Connery, Peta could well imagine Stewart Fletcher ageing just as well and even becoming sexier as he passed beyond his thirties, his forties and eventually into his seventies. That's if his broad shoulders and muscular chest and arms were anything to go by. Not to mention his ebony hair, which revealed faint silver threads at the sides already. Some small crinkles were even forming at the corners of his eyes, giving his already intriguing persona an entirely different perspective—hence the Sean Connery comparison.

Makes me wonder what other hidden strengths he has too. Perhaps I should watch myself tonight. My thoughts are definitely taking another dangerous detour right now. Stay on track, girl!

Peta smiled deliciously to herself. The subject of this paid assignment has delightfully surprised her, even if he has been a reluctant participant in taking advantage of her thus far.

Besides, if he really was as uncaring as her notes said he's supposed to be with women, he could easily have thrown her back into her car, before ordering her off his property, but here he was about to feed her dinner and even offer her a bed for the night. Despite her initial reservations about him, Peta admitted she wanted to get to know more about this intriguing man. Not that she'd get the chance, though. He'd made it clear to her from the start, hadn't he? His offer now was meant only for her bodily protection of being exposed to the possible ravages of a full-blown tropical cyclone. Obviously, his own guilt of treating her so badly in the first place must have made him realise he was also morally responsible for her too. After all, they'd sent her there at the request of his agent and Tess, too. That had to count for something. But absolutely no interviews. Period!

After she'd reached some sort of satisfaction regarding to her appearance, Peta stared at her reflection in the bathroom mirror.

Well girl, you are here for now, so let's just wait and see what happens shall we? In the meantime, I guess it's time to return to the lion's den. This should be fun!

Stewart looked up briefly from his final meal preparations to acknowledge Peta back from the bathroom. He raised his eyebrows in a questioning scowl. 'Well, I'm assuming you did manage to find the bathroom okay? You were in there so long, I was beginning to think you might've got lost along the way.'

Peta smiled sweetly at him, despite his predictable sarcasm. Food was her priority for now.

'Really? I didn't think I took that long in there. Just freshening up, that's all.' Peta forgot any witty comebacks as she eyed off the feast before her. 'Wow, Stewart! This all looks so amazing!'

Peta did a quick double take as she eyed off all the scrumptious food set out on the solid wooden dining table with bamboo placemats at each setting. There were two tempting plates, all ready to go, loaded with chunky pieces of cold salmon, a fresh leafy salad with feta cheese, and succulent, semi-dried tomatoes. There was also the ever-popular Aussie canned beetroot, along with some bread rolls, and a small glass jug containing a creamy salad dressing between the two plates. Simple fare indeed, but to Peta's rumbling stomach, it rivalled any restaurant meal right now. To complete the picture, there were two frosty glasses of beer.

'This is so wonderful! Thanks, Stewart! I have been running pretty much on empty since early this morning. Oh hell! I've just realised, there are still some unwrapped sandwiches in my hire car outside. They must be all shrivelled up and dry by now.'

'Yes, well, even if I do live out here in the sticks, so to speak, I still like to be civilised at least. Besides, you never know when some annoying journalist will turn up, expecting to be fed.'

Peta looked at Stewart's face expecting a scowl but found a grin instead.

'Very funny! You had me going there for a minute. Believe me, I honestly do appreciate the effort you've made with all of this. I never realised just how hungry I was until now. I didn't have any breakfast before I had to catch my flight to Cairns really early this morning. So, thanks again.'

'You mean to tell me, you're not one of these totally obsessive women who starve themselves all the time just so they can fit into today's skinny fashions?'

'Good heavens, no! I have never been that way inclined. I always love to eat. My father comments on my hollow legs all the time—especially during my teenage years. I could eat as much as my father could, but never seemed to gain any weight at all.'

'So are your parents still alive?'

'My father is, but my mother died in a car accident when I was still a little girl, so her sister, my lovely Aunt Ruby, helped my father to raise me.'

'What does your father do, then?'

Peta hesitated for a moment. She took a slow sip of her beer before answering his question. 'He's a journalist and my grandfather was a journalist too. It's in our blood, I guess.'

'Why does that not surprise me? You certainly have the stubbornness and tenacity of a journalist, that's for sure. Runs in the family, no doubt. And with the surname of McKenna, you're obviously Irish to boot! Plus, I'm sure you have a gift of the gab too. Heaven help me!'

'Don't let my Irish surname put you off, Mr. Fletch—I mean, Stewart. I grew up in Australia. Mostly around the Sydney area, so I am as Australian as you are.'

'That may be so, but I bet you still have an Irish temper. I bet you also use those brilliant green Irish eyes of yours to turn on the feminine charm whenever it suits you—right?'

Peta couldn't help smiling at him now. 'Ah! So you aren't completely detached from me as you appear to be then. You noticed the colour of my eyes, at least.'

'Don't be ridiculous, woman!' Stewart snapped defensively. 'Studying people is a necessary skill any author must possess when we create characters. It was merely an observation. That's all!'

The sharp tone in Stewart's voice momentarily threw Peta, but she recovered quickly. 'Yes, of course! If you say so!'

Mmm. Predictably defensive as always.

Peta realised she was about to dive into some deep water with this supersensitive man. If she didn't tread carefully now, he might just throw her out of here after all.

Maybe those blustery outside forces might even be slightly more bearable to deal with than being in here with this cantankerous man. After a stilted moment with Stewart suddenly absorbed with his beer, Peta folded her paper towel a few unnecessary times before she broke this awkward moment.

'Let's change the subject for now, shall we? What's your story then, Stewart? Where do you come from originally?'

Stewart was immediately on the defensive again.

'This is completely off the record, I assure you,' she said in answer to his deepening frown. 'Just a casual conversation between us. That's all! There is no hidden agenda. You asked me about some of my background. Now it's your turn.'

'I guess I can share a little bit about myself since you insist on this whole getting-to-know-you crap! Alright then, Peta. Maybe a condensed version of my early life will satisfy your ever-curious professional mind for now. I grew up in Melbourne, the eldest of two boys. My father, Henry Fletcher, was a solicitor with his own successful law firm in Melbourne and his ultimate dream was for both his sons to follow happily in his footsteps. Unfortunately for my poor father, though, his eldest son had other ideas. The very thought of becoming a solicitor seemed like a slow death to me. As a way of trying to appease my father, I studied law for a whole year before I finally plucked up the courage to tell him I wanted to be a writer instead. Well, I think you can guess how that impressed him. He pretty much disowned me from that day forth.'

'I'm sorry to hear that. That must have been so difficult for you at the time.'

'Do you want to hear my story or not?' Stewart huffed somewhat impatiently.

'Sorry. Please do continue.'

Peta disregarded his snappish words in favour of keeping Stewart opening up to her at last—even if he was still obviously reluctant to do so.

'My younger brother, Matt, fulfilled part of the dream, anyway. Matt became a fully qualified solicitor like Father, whereas I ended up following my mother's career path instead. My mother was a university lecturer in literature and creative writing but is now retired. She instilled in me at an early age the love of reading and writing. That's all I ever wanted to do, really. Not to be stuck in some dingy office in Melbourne wearing a suit and tie every day for the rest of my life. Besides, I have always hated the bleak, rainy weather of winter in Melbourne. It chills my body and soul in more ways than one. I took off for the bright lights of Sydney to start with, and have been roaming up and down the warmer, northern shores of Australia ever since. Five years ago, I ended up here and loved it enough to stay put forever—that's if fate should allow me to.'

'So, did you and your father ever manage to put things right between you over the years?'

'Nope. I'm afraid not. He died just last year, so we never really got the chance to speak again since that last disastrous day together in his office. Father yelled and cursed at me and told me what a great disappointment I was to him. He literally turned his back on me and refused to acknowledge me as his son anymore. I reacted by storming out of his office, and I haven't been back to Melbourne since. Why am I even telling you all this, anyway? I was only supposed to give you the condensed version. At least you appear to listen to me. Most women just aren't interested, really.'

'I am interested, otherwise I wouldn't have asked you in the first place. I'm very close to my own father so I can't even imagine not ever speaking to him again. Your estrangement from your father is all so sad to me. Are you still in contact with your mother and brother?'

'My brother is a lot like my father. Life is business and business is his whole life. In all fairness to Matt, he and my mother have had to deal with my father's seething wrath after I left. Matt and I were very close before I left Melbourne, so he must have found it so hard not even being able to say my name out loud in our father's presence. Luckily, my mother is much more understanding and forgiving. She and I are in touch all the time. She also made it very clear to my father at the start; his issues with me had nothing to do with her and that she would always be my mother regardless of my father's feelings. Thankfully, she also understood my need to be true to myself. And the rest, as they say, is history. End of story.'

Wow! Peta hadn't expected him to open up to her like that. Pity it had to be all off the record. Maybe it was time for her to take the pressure off between them before he shut down altogether.

Fuck! I could still be out the door if I'm not careful!

'Thank you for sharing some of your personal life with me and, I can assure you, this conversation between us will go no further. Okay?'

'Ah, a journalist with scruples! You are a rare species of human, indeed.'

'Sounds as though you have had your fair share of unscrupulous media vultures over the years, then.'

'You could say that.' Stewart sipped his beer slowly while staring her down with one of his most piercing glares.

Reserved exclusively for members of the press, no doubt. Oh boy! If looks could kill!

All at once, she felt like a tiny insect under a microscope. They were both lost for words. They continued to sit across the table from each other and somehow, an undefinable chasm opened up as mere words struggled to fill the gap.

When Peta was able to sneak in a furtive look Stewart's way, she couldn't help but notice, he'd seemed to have developed a sudden fascination for the tiny bits of food still left on his plate, giving her cause to wonder what might be going on in that contrary head of his …

Stewart's barely disguised brooding was meant to be a clever ploy to hide his reluctant attraction towards his delectable—but still unwanted— house guest. The very nearness of her was already starting to mess with his long-neglected libido, big time! How was he supposed to keep his distance from her throughout the night, anyway?

Hell's bells! This situation is too damn cruel for any red-blooded man to be able to resist her.

For the want of something to distract her, Peta somehow found herself staring at the salt and pepper grinders in front of her, totally confused by now of the mixed signals Stewart was sending her way. Even though he was giving her his most effective evil eye, he still managed to radiate raw sexual energy and she was finding it increasingly hard to resist. *What have you got yourself into this time, girl?* A tropical cyclone is about to unleash its fury on this old shack soon and if that's not dangerous enough, she was about to spend the night alone with one of the world's sexiest men alive. Oh shit! An appropriate line from some movie she couldn't even remember the name of suddenly popped into her head, 'Resistance is futile.' It seemed her body was now somehow being controlled by some invisible force pulling her closer and closer to him. Despite this realisation, her secret womanly self shamelessly relished this new enticing outcome a bit too much. In the meantime, she must restore this delicate balance between her and her rescuer.

'Okay then, I can see we're getting nowhere now. Let's change the subject then, shall we? Are there any *safe* subjects we can talk about? Anything that doesn't upset your sensibilities, that is.'

'Nope! None at all because we have no time for any more idle chitchat, Ms. McKenna.'

'Oh, I see! We are back to formalities now, are we? What happened to using first names?'

Stewart didn't answer because, as he predicted earlier, the power suddenly flicked off. His normally sunlit dining area was instantly plunged into an ominous, late-night darkness. Stewart sprang into action. First, he lit the wick of one of the nearest heavy-duty lanterns, each with their light source fully enclosed within its own protective, reinforced glass shield. Stewart had already set up both lanterns and a barbecue lighter earlier to prepare for this anticipated loss of power. He'd also replaced the existing battery in his portable radio for a new one to be sure it wouldn't fade out on him at the wrong time. The screeching winds outside had already started thrashing against the windows with much more force than his outwardly calm demeanour suggested.

'We need to pack this up and lie low for a while. No time to chat now.'

Now Stewart looked really worried and for good reason, too. This whole disaster scenario was fast becoming way more realistic than she agreed to sign up for in the first place. *This is really scary stuff, but Stewart needs my help. Best make myself useful.*

Without any unnecessary words on her part, Peta galvanised herself into action, grabbing one lantern and placing it nearby. She stacked their plates together, along with the glasses, still with the last of their unfinished beer, the salt and pepper mills, and anything else left on the dining table, into the kitchen, in two quick trips. She rinsed and stacked them all into the sink for a proper washing in the morning. She also took the extra precaution of laying a large wooden chopping board over the sink to protect the stacked and rinsed items. Hopefully, the heavy chopping board will protect everything inside the sink, should the kitchen windows—heaven forbid—shatter. Peta also noticed a half-empty fruit bowl nearby and stowed the bowl, along with its contents, away in the fridge. Stewart, busy with his own emergency tasks, gathered some blankets and a couple of pillows and threw everything into his bathtub, much to Peta's obvious puzzlement.

'What on earth are you doing?' Peta stood back out of his way, just outside his bathroom door. She giggled nervously. 'Don't tell me you have some sort of fetish thing about sleeping in your bathtub?'

Stewart stared at her now in disbelief, suddenly all bluster and indignation again.

'No! Of course, I wouldn't normally sleep in my bathtub! What do you take me for, you silly woman? Believe it or not, the bathroom happens to be the safest room in the house during a tropical cyclone. Plus, this solid old bathtub, with blankets under us and over us, should protect us bodily as well.'

'Really? I honestly never knew that.' A sudden unwanted image popped into her head. 'So, what you are saying then, is that both of us have to ride out this cyclone in this bathtub? All night? This should be interesting!'

Stewart ignored Peta's teasing innuendos. The predictable rolling of his eyes made her feel more than a bit silly now.

'Well, at least we'll be more protected in here rather than anywhere else in the house for now.' Stewart said. 'I have also taken the precaution of stowing away any loose objects in here, which can turn instantly into rather nasty, wind-driven flying missiles. As a bonus to your exclusive accommodation tonight, Ms. McKenna, you also have a handy toilet close by in case of another kind of emergency. But if you would rather take your chances outside instead, go right ahead. It's entirely your choice.'

Stewart's ultimatum forced Peta to acknowledge the sound of the wind once again as it howled mournfully—and if possible, even more loudly outside the bathroom window. As though ruthlessly seeking a passage right through these solidly built, but still vulnerable, wooden walls, rather than having to go around its outside boundaries. The old-style casement windows around the house rattled incessantly, loud enough to shatter her already challenged and barely contained self-composure. She didn't have much choice but to share such a close, intimate space with Stewart tonight. How crazy is that? Was she making a terrible choice either way? Seeking refuge so willingly with this rather complicated, but sexy man, instead of taking her chances against the outside, hellish weather elements instead. The thought of his hunky body next to hers all night long, would be a challenge enough on its own. When she considered he hadn't been with a woman for a while, life could become a lot more complicated afterwards. Not just on a professional level either. Despite this realisation, her whole body tingled deliciously at the thought.

The lady in me resists this idea, but the wicked side of me says, 'Bring it on!'

'So what's your decision then? Anytime in the next ten seconds will do, if you don't mind?'

Peta snapped out of her naughty fantasy with the impatient tone of his voice and squinted her eyes at Stewart.

'Mmm. Am I sensing some impatience with my decision right now? In answer to your question, I suppose with your overall concern for our safety in mind, then if it has to be the bathtub, then that's what it must be. Just out of curiosity, though, how long do these cyclones tend to last?'

'Could be hours! Depends on the severity of the cyclone. Then we also have the eye of the storm slap bang in the middle, which often fools the uninitiated tourist or newcomers to the tropics. Just when you think it's all over, the fickle forces of nature are just taking a little breather until the next onslaught of full-force winds. Adding to that, unrelenting torrential rain usually always follows.'

'Oh. Wow! I had no idea.'

'Anything else you need to know? Must I remind you that while you come to to a decision, time is a-wasting and we are still subject to these erratic weather elements *right now!*' Stewart studied Peta's face now before speaking again. 'Judging by your reluctance to get into this bathtub right now, you are obviously weighing up your options whether you should take your chances with the outside elements after all, rather than spend the night alone in here with me. Am I right?'

Jeez! He can read my mind too! How does he do that?

'To be perfectly honest, the thought had crossed my mind.'

Peta, feeling uncomfortable about her decision to comply with this whole bathtub scenario, made the next words that came out of her mouth sound like she was a rambling fool. 'You'll be pleased to know I have come to a decision, which is to follow your advice and stick it out in here with you for now. How do we do this then? Have you ever had to do this before, Stewart? What I mean is. Are you already bathtub-savvy?' She finished her feeble attempt at some humour with a cheeky smile.

'Are you quite finished?' Stewart rolled his eyes again in mock disgust, whilst trying to keep a straight face. 'Yes, I have had to take to my bathtub a couple of times over the past five years, but never with anyone to keep me company until now, that is. If that's what you are implying? The blankets on the bottom should cushion our bodies a bit at least. I think I will get in first—since I am the heaviest—so I don't squash you too much. You will then lower yourself into the bathtub, but only after I have positioned myself to one side as much as possible. You should then try to mould your body to the side of me as much as you can. When we have settled ourselves comfortably enough, I will then throw another blanket over our heads just in case the bathroom window should shatter directly above us and shower us with broken glass. I can't promise the bathtub will be all that comfy, but I can assure you, it will be safe and maybe even a little cosy, for a while, at least.'

'I'll take your word for it. It's the cosy part I have some reservations about at this point in time. Let's just do this, then! Well, Stewart, I guess in this instance, social protocol is reversed for once. Gentlemen first!'

Stewart climbed into the bathtub and positioned himself as far over as he could along the side closest to the wall. The bottom surface of the bathtub was cushioned with a thick cotton blanket and a couple of pillows. He soon realised the hard, unyielding surface of the old enamel tub would play havoc with his back by the end of the night. That was the least of his problems considering the drop-dead gorgeous Ms. McKenna now shared the same small space with him. He wasn't sure how he would endure a forced situation like this for however long they'd have to stay here. He knew only too well that Peta was bound to be worried about protecting her personal honour, and he couldn't blame her. The way he was feeling—even before they'd settled into the barely padded bowl of his bathtub—she'd every right to be concerned. *Yes indeed, Ms. McKenna!*

'Okay! You can climb in now.'

Stewart signalled her with a beckoning motion of his hands. Peta obliged by following each of his hand prompts as instructed, being careful not to stomp on his legs on her way down.

'That's it! Steady does it. Good. Now move your hip a bit more to the right. Perfect!'

'Are you sure you're comfortable, Stewart? I don't want to squash you or anything.'

'We won't have much choice for a while, I'm afraid. When the eye of the storm happens, we can escape the confines of this old bathtub for about thirty minutes or so, to stretch out the achy kinks in our bodies. When the winds starts to pick up speed again, we will have to climb back in here though, to be ready to face the next inevitable onslaught. Which I have to warn you, can often be much more forceful than the first half of the cyclone's fury. Eventually it will pass over us and finally run out of steam and, hopefully, head on out back out to sea again, which should be by early morning.'

'You sound so calm about it all. Don't you worry about your house being flattened, or even worse, have your whole roof blown off? I mean, no offence or anything, but it *is* an old house after all.'

'No offence taken. This old house was built in the '30s, so even though it looks, and is, rough in appearance, it hides a heart of pure resilience and grit. Many cyclones over the years have tried to knock it down, but it's still stands strong and proud. That's why I bought it over some newer, modern homes in this area. Somehow, they always seem to be the ones to be wiped out first. This ramshackle old house will probably outlive you and me, but I still have to be cautious every time. It's not wise to tempt the hand of fate with an it-won't-happen-to-me kind of attitude.'

'No, that's for sure. So, what do you do to keep yourself calm when the winds are at their worst? Do you pray? Recite poetry to yourself? Make up stories? Or even sing, maybe?'

'Yes, I say my own kind of prayer for my home, my neighbours and myself to be safe.'

'What kind of prayer do you usually say?'

'I just say out loud; God, please protect our neighbourhood tonight.'

'I love that one! Simple and to the point. Speaking of prayers, I think those winds are just about to get out of hand BIG TIME!' Peta moved even closer to Stewart's strong protective body.

'Yes indeed! The time has come for us to completely cover ourselves over for now.'

Stewart threw the top blanket over their heads to prepare for the worst onslaught of tropical cyclonic winds.

CHAPTER FOUR

♦

Outside, *the force of* nature, on its furious and unyielding path, seemed intent on flattening everything in its way, including Stewart's treasured rainforest retreat. But then again, he didn't really have cyclones in mind when he bought this place, did he? He just wanted somewhere quiet where he could escape all the media kerfuffle over his divorce.

Besides, unless someone connected to the gargle of gossip hunters —the nightmare factor of his life for too long now—was on a mission to find his ramshackle hideaway abode, they could just as easily drive by and never know which one of the many dirt tracks shooting off from the main road they should take. Which of course, was why he chose to live out here in the first place. He craved complete privacy, but on the other hand, he wasn't fooling himself. He was realistic enough to know that any cyclone, whatever its name, that chose to blow through this area, would absolutely have no trouble finding his humble abode at all. Especially when those Category 2 winds whipped through this normally picturesque rural area at 125-164 kph, Stewart also knew that for the sheer, bloody-minded madness of tropical weather patterns, this latest so-called Cyclone Jamie was obviously hell-bent on flattening not only his own isolated, ramshackle hut to the ground, but perhaps every other house around this area as well.

Inside his beloved old shack this time, however, there was one other person with him who also desperately wished for Cyclone Jamie to blow itself back out to sea and leave them be. Besides, they obviously each had enough troubles of their own right now. Despite his best intentions, being forced to cling together like this, her equally cramped body clung desperately to his in a united effort to stay put in the old tub. Despite the bathtub's claw feet being bolted securely to the floor, those same stainless-steel bolts wouldn't be a match for unpredictable cyclonic winds, should they decide to make a detour right through the middle of the house.

Stewart had seen before how vindictive the full force of these hellraising winds could be. Strong and forceful enough to peel back the whole roof of the house. They had the power to seek any sheltering residents out of their fragile protective spaces, to ruthlessly dump them bodily into some open field somewhere. Perhaps even into some flooded creek nearby. Yet, even though there was the threat to life and limb, he was relishing the feel of her body clinging so close to his, just the same. Even if he chose to enlighten Peta of these potential scenarios, somehow he couldn't imagine she'd be the type of woman to run out of here screaming in fear. After all, she refused to quit this place until she got what she came for. Earlier today, she was even prepared to brave the cyclonic winds outside. All on her own, too!

So, Stewart, my man, why not just enjoy this unexpected pleasure a little longer? Besides, if I am destined to die tonight, I couldn't think of a better way to go.

Peta and Stewart stayed huddled together in the old bathtub for close on two hours, trying desperately not to squash each other, but they really had no choice at all in that regard. With Stewart just under 190 cms and with Peta at around 178 cms, there really wasn't much leg room for either of them in a normal-sized bathtub. As a consequence, they were forced to raise their knees upwards as much as possible.

'I don't know about you, but my legs are starting to cramp up big time.' Stewart tentatively tried to stretch each of his legs one more time to ease the cramping in his muscles.

'To tell you the truth, my bum definitely has gone numb. I can't feel it anymore! How much longer do you think we will be in here?'

'Well, the bad news is, after the eye of the storm has passed and the winds pick up speed again, we'll have to return to this old tub for probably another three hours at least. The second half of this whole cyclone drama could be even stronger than this first half, but the winds do eventually die down after a while, leaving us with lots of heavy rain to follow. Probably for the rest of the night.'

'Another three hours after this? Oh man!' Peta groaned as she tried to reposition herself again. 'I think I will definitely be completely numb by then. So, is there any possibility of some good news to follow all the inevitable bad news?'

'I was just about to tell you the good news if you let me finish.' Stewart answered with his usual I-don't-believe-you-just-asked-me-that tone of voice.

Thankfully for Peta, his gruff expression of impatience didn't sound all that convincing this time around.

'Okay, okay! Please give me some good news then. If you would be so kind?'

'Happy to! The good news is that the eye of the storm shouldn't be too far away now. According to my previous cyclone experiences, when the eye of the storm happens, we should be able to get up from here for however long, to stretch our legs, relieve our bladders, drink some water and for me to check for immediate damage around this old shack. Which from all appearances, it still seems to be upright so far. At this early stage, I can't guarantee the rest of the house will still be standing, though.'

'Why does the eye of the cyclone even happen at all? Right now, I will certainly be glad when it *does* happen. It'll give us a bit of a reprieve for a while, at least. I'm just curious, that's all.'

'I can only tell you what I understand from my own experiences living up in the tropics, mind you. When surface winds all converge together, towards the centre of the storm—called the Coriolis force by the way—it has the ultimate power to deflect the winds away from this whole, highly active vortex, churning away up there somewhere. For a while at least, these mad, crazy winds have no choice but to go around the eye of the storm, rather than through it.'

'I never knew that. I mean, during TV news reports down in Sydney, you hear about the eye of the storm all the time, but I never really knew what that meant until now. Well, I can now tell other uninformed Sydneysiders, I've had a firsthand experience of what cyclones are all about.'

'Wow! When you get back home, the Mayor of Sydney will hold a parade in your honour.'

'No need to be sarcastic just because you're a seasoned cyclone survivor! Seriously though, I've always been in awe of people who live in these areas and who go through dozens of cyclones throughout their lifetimes. Yet, as a team, they pick themselves up, clean up, repair costly damages—and all live to fight another day. Until the next cyclone season rolls around, that is.'

'Well, to be honest, you just don't think about it after a while. It's like your own people down south. They go through droughts and floods every year, but they still stay put, wherever they happen to live. Australia can be an unforgiving country to all of its people, but it's also quick to share its beauty and its abundance too. My lifestyle near the top end of Australia is magic most of the time and I wouldn't want to live anywhere else, really.'

'But what about the humidity? That's definitely an energy zapper for me. Sure, it gets hot in Sydney, but not nearly as much as around Cairns—especially at this time of the year.'

'Most of us locals rise early in the mornings and do as much work as we can manage before midday. Out of necessity, we all tend to lie low during the afternoons, which is usually the hottest part of the day in the tropics, only to come fully alive again in the evenings. Southerners seem to think we North Queenslanders are all a bunch of ratbags, but we are exactly like the Darwinites. You have to be adaptable and more than a little thick-skinned to survive up here. As we locals tend to joke, "If ya can't handle the heat, well then, get outta the bloody tropics, mate!" Well, you get the idea anyway.'

Peta smiled, picturing a bunch of yobbos in a crowded pub some-where up in North Queensland yelling those exact words to some sweaty, complaining tourist who never seem to 'get it' or their quirky way of life.

'You'd have to be an Australian yourself to understand this kind of poke-fun-at-you brand of humour.' Peta laughed along with Stewart.

'That's for sure! Hang on a minute. Listen. Can you hear that?'

'Hear what? What am I listening for! Ah yes! The wind has dropped at last. No howling winds for now.'

'So, let us escape from here right now! As I said before, so let's make the most of un-cramping our frozen muscles while we can.'

Stewart threw off their blanket cover and motioned for her to go first. Peta didn't need any further encouragement. She unravelled her legs first, which were unavoidably interlocked with Stewart's. With a bit of a push from one of Stewart's hands on her buttocks, and by gripping the sides of the tub, she got to her feet. She then gingerly lowered one leg over the rim of the tub to make her first tentative step towards what could well be a slippery wet floor waiting for her. So far, so good. There was no water on the floor, at least. Once Peta was out, she stretched out her hand for Stewart to grab on to it to pull himself out next. Once they were both out of the bathtub and upright, they grinned at each other.

'What I find hard to understand now is with you being so tall and with me being taller than most woman, how on earth did we manage to lay in that tub together for all this time? No wonder your back hurts. Like I said before, I think I've lost all sensation in my bum for now.'

'Yes, I know what you mean, but we did it before and we will do it again. In the meantime, you'll probably need to use this bathroom with some privacy, am I right?'

'I certainly do! I'm busting, in fact. But what about you?'

'Ladies first. I'll wander outside and water a tree nearby, and check for damages, too.'

'Why thank you for your chivalry, sir! What a gentleman you turned out to be, after all.'

'So, I'm not such an asshole after all, Ms. McKenna?'

'I've never called you that, have I? But I'll reserve my final judgement for later.'

'Fair enough! Try not to be too long. Remember—'

'Around half an hour is about all we have for now.'

Stewart couldn't resist laying a playful slap to her backside on his way out. Peta squealed with an equally playful response and even wriggled her bum at him. Stewart left the bathroom laughing, then quietly closed the door on his way out.

Peta stared in the mirror again as the rampant thoughts of her inner self kicked in. *Well, that wasn't so bad, after all. He really has been quite the gentleman so far. Though I wouldn't mind all that much really if he wasn't such a gentleman anymore. Okay, I admit it. I might have shamelessly enjoyed my forced closeness with the devastatingly handsome Mr. Fletcher a bit too much, but hey! Wouldn't any red-blooded woman be the same in this kind of*

situation? Besides, I'm all for seizing the moment, and of course his buttocks too, given half the chance!

The reality of her situation soon hit home. There wasn't much either of them could do about it anyway, all squashed into his bathtub like they were. It was way too cramped in there for starters, and they'd the rest of the cyclone to get through yet. Despite this, Peta knew their attraction was mutual. She had to commend him too, for his gentlemanly attempt to shrink down into the tub more in consideration for her overall comfort— if that was even possible under the circumstances. She could tell Stewart was struggling to avoid touching certain sexual parts of her body too.

But, *if he wasn't in the least bit attracted to me, then surely it wouldn't even be an issue for him in the first place, would it?*

What should she do about this deliciously volatile situation then? She's already stockpiled enough fantasies inside her active mind during their first stint of their bathtub lay-in. Stewart probably wouldn't need much encouragement from her either to totally abandon their unspoken professional boundaries.

Anyway, maybe we should just try to get through this next stint in the tub first, then see what happens beyond that.

Peta was definitely enjoying the closeness of him—for many naughty reasons. She reasoned if nothing had happened between them by morning, then she would know the naughty thoughts she had for him were one-sided after all.

I wouldn't want to misguidedly come onto him and then later, have him angry with me again for my ruthless seduction of him. Definitely not!

Stewart was busy racing around, checking the inside and outside structure of his home. The old house had proved him right again. Solid as a rock. Not too much damage this time around. He would do a full inspection when the cyclone eased. The moment of truth arrived. It was time for him to head back inside again.

Oh hell! I don't know how much longer I can continue to lay so close to her without wanting to ravage her completely. I want so much to kiss her and explore her body all over. Dammit!

If he was honest, this wasn't the time or the place for him to even entertain such erotic thoughts, let alone act on them. *Hell no!* It would be bloody impossible right now, anyway. When this cyclone moved on, then and only then, would he even *think* of making his move.

Yes indeed! Hopefully she wouldn't slap his face or run away screaming. Or worse, write about it and tell all her readers about how he took advantage of her under duress.

Hell! That's all I need! No, Stewart! Until you get the right signals from this sexy damsel in distress herself, you will just have to behave yourself.

Back within the hard, unforgiving confines of the old bathtub again, Peta kept her head way down so she was now resting against Stewart's broad, muscular chest. His tight, muscled arms were once again wrapped around her body, which meant her hands were also squashed close against his body. Despite the ear-piercing, screeching winds outside, Cyclone Jamie no longer seemed an issue to Peta's frazzled nerves anymore—except maybe for her persistent naughty thoughts. This tricky situation she'd found herself in went way beyond the professional boundaries as listed in the journalists' code of conduct. Correct procedures didn't cover what she was supposed to do next when under extreme sexual duress during an environmental disaster.

Boundaries be damned! Admit it. You love it!

Stewart nestled in closer to Peta, his powerful arms wrapped around her to protect them both. He kept trying to convince himself he was protecting her, but that didn't stop him from enjoying the exquisite touch and feel of her so close. He wondered if she might be feeling he same way too, but there was no way he was going to ask her such a thing. Not at this stage anyway, as he accepted his own impossible challenge to try and process his secret thoughts. *Bloody hell! She may as well not be wearing any clothes at all!* He could sense every gorgeous part of her. It was almost like she was somehow physically joined to his own body.

Oh man! I just hope I don't embarrass myself with an enormous erection right now. Especially if her female sensibilities are affronted in any way.

Despite his best intentions, he was determined to remain a gentleman around her. His neglected libido protested over his decision to hold back just the same. It had nothing to do with not being with another woman either. He had to accept that she had affected him from the moment he first laid his traitorous eyes on her. *Wham!* Like no other woman before. Not even his two beautiful ex-wives, which was a strange thing for him to admit. To make matters worse, no matter how rude he was to her this afternoon, she still wouldn't leave.

Man! Talk about stubborn! Come to think of it, she's almost as stubborn as me!

Stewart smiled. She had somehow slipped under his skin from the start, without even trying to. Speaking of skin, her smooth arms and her dainty feet felt so damn soft against his own tough skin.

Hot damn! This is an impossible situation! I never should have let her come inside!

'Stewart? Stewart? Are you okay?'

'What? Yes, of course I am. What's the problem?'

'No! No problem, really. It's just that your breathing sounded a bit ragged. I thought maybe I might be squashing you too much, that's all.'

'Well, as I'm sure you are already aware, dear lady, it's somewhat unavoidable right now … For us both to feel squashed, I mean. Thanks for your concern, though. Much appreciated.'

'You're welcome! Suddenly I feel like some little kid on a car trip—"Are we there yet?" We have probably only been in here about for about an hour, but it feels more like hours and hours already.'

'Yes, you're right. It does feel much worse the second time around, doesn't it? Once these psycho winds eventually die down, we will then be subjected to lots of drenching rain. At least, once we get to leave this old bathtub scene behind, we'll be able to stretch and move our bodies again at last.'

'Best news I have heard all night! My whole body's so achy, as I'm sure yours is too.'

'I would definitely have to agree with you on that. I will make a pact with you though. Let's make a promise to each other for when we finally do escape these cramped confines for good. I promise to give you a full body massage if you'll do the same for me. Agreed?'

'Did I hear you right? You want to give me a massage when we are through here? Then you actually expect me to give you a massage in return? Talk about pushing your luck! But what the heck. Okay, I agree!'

'There you go! Well, I don't know about you, but my body could sure use a bit of help right now to get the kinks out of it. Every few weeks, when I have to go into Cairns for supplies, I sometimes allow time out for a really intense massage—especially when I sit for too long at my desk, typing for hours.'

'Ah! So you aren't so wary of the female touch after all? I was under the distinct impression you were sworn off women for life. So I was wrong then?'

'Ha! You are so wrong. I go to a fully qualified female masseuse at a local gym in Cairns since there aren't any others out this way. As for your assumptions about me, Ms. McKenna, if you dare print that about me in your magazine, I promise I will sue you and your publishing company for damn sure.'

'Oh dear! You've just called me Ms. McKenna again. I guess I must be in the bad books again. I assure you, Stewart, that silly comment about a woman's touch was meant in jest. Of course I wouldn't print anything private without your permission. I do have some scruples, you know.'

'Take it easy, Peta! I do tend to get a bit too serious at times.' Stewart attempted to reassure her. 'I'll tell you what, though. You make good your promise to give me a massage after this, and I might even forgive you for your misguided and rash comment just now.'

'You're on! Phew! You did have me a wee bit worried for a minute there.' Peta relaxed with an exaggerated sigh. She laid her head back down against Stewart's broad chest again as she prepared herself for the next onslaught of cyclonic winds.

Meanwhile, another kind of tremulous storm was running rampant through Peta's mind. She was only too aware she was getting herself into some really deep water here. Stewart was the man she was meant to interview after all. An interview she was being paid to deliver as requested, or else. If she didn't get the interview, she was screwed. Her hard-won professional reputation would have been for nothing. Come Monday morning, her career will probably be null and void. But surely she couldn't be expected to focus on this impossible outcome right now?

Snap out of it! In the meantime, I need to stay focused and get my priorities back into order.

Peta silently thanked the powers that be that if she was meant to die tonight, she'd be forever grateful she were to die in the arms of the sexy, dashing Stewart Fletcher. What an epitaph that would be!

49

CHAPTER FIVE

'*There it is again!*' Stewart whispered.

'Where is what again?' Peta dared to ask, still dreading any further outside changes for the worse.

'I do believe those stroppy old winds have finally packed up and gone home, Ms. Bathtub Companion. This deceptive lull in the storm won't last for long I'm afraid. As I said before, heavy rains will no doubt follow shortly. But for now, my dear, it's all good news! We can finally escape the uncomfortable necessity of this safe haven at last. To finally stretch out completely on a decent bed to get some sleep for the rest of the night.'

'That is good news, indeed. What are we waiting for, then? Let us be away from here!'

Peta was raring to go, but she quickly realised, once again, her legs were still unavoidably entwined with Stewart's. Without realising her predicament, Stewart threw off their cover blanket with one quick flick and motioned for Peta to climb out before him, but not before having to untangle their cramped legs first.

'If you need to have some privacy in here, go ahead. I'll just go water the, ah, palm tree again. I will also need to do a quick check on the house again inside and out before the rain begins.'

'Thanks, Stewart. I certainly do need to relieve myself again. I'll be out soon.'

'That's okay. There's no need to hurry now. You can take your time, for now at least.'

With her urgent personal needs attended to, Peta met Stewart back in the living room within a short space of time. After all their hours spent huddled in the bathtub together, she thought maybe he might be feeling the same sense of intimacy between them too. Apparently not. He definitely seems to be uncomfortable with her again that's for certain. If not, then why is he suddenly avoiding eye contact with her and keeping a safe physical distance from her. Considering their time spent together up close and personal, Peta felt his behaviour now seemed to be too bizarre to be even funny anymore. Maybe the ever-elusive Stewart Fletcher is embarrassed now and feels he was somehow forced into protecting his unexpected guest during the cyclone? Maybe he even wishes he had never even *allowed* her into his humble abode in the first place? He's probably even stressing now that she can't wait to write a tell-all account of the saucy 'bathtub incident' in her magazine as well.

Aargh! All of these maybes and second-guesses are driving me crazy! What am I supposed to do now?

Meanwhile, Stewart has his own doubts to deal with. Not all that different from Peta's, really.

Like, what was she *really* thinking about him, he wondered? Does she regret even coming here, to be scared out of her wits, just to interview him? Which he had also refused to give her too, by the way. She probably would have preferred to have gone back to Cairns just for that reason alone, but no! She stayed put, despite possible injury—or even death—to get the job done as she promised her boss she would.

He had to admire her for that. Now that she had survived her first cyclone up in the tropics, she probably wouldn't be able to resist telling her readers all about how the *famous* Stewart Fletcher protected her from the jaws of death, as well as spending the night all alone with him in his bloody bathtub!

Now that the cyclone has blown over, what is next for them? Did he only imagine that tangible feeling between them, or is it just his own wishful thinking? At least he hoped it wasn't just wishful thinking. He wanted to spend the night alone with her of course, but only if he was positively sure she wanted to be with him as well. If he even tried to kiss her, would she interpret that as him just wanting to have his way with her, before kicking her out the door in the morning? With no interview to take back with her, will she then get her revenge, by telling everyone how mean he was to her, before offering some degree of safety to her, only to take advantage of her in the end?

Bloody hell, man! Where do you go from here? As the saying goes; you're damned if you do, damned if you don't. There was no easy answer for certain in this messy scenario. *Perhaps I should let her take the lead.*

'Everything okay with the house? I mean, not too much damage, I hope?'

'Thankfully, no. A few of the smaller trees have been flattened to the ground and a few sheets of roofing on the side of the shed has also blown off. I imagine they're probably scattered all over the neighbouring properties by now. Apart from the obvious signs of storm damage, everything inside and outside, I think I have fared very well so far. It is more than I could have ever hoped for, really. Hopefully, I won't have too many insurance claims to fill out later.'

'That's great news then, Stewart. I am so relieved for you. I am sure a lot of other houses around here might not have fared as well as what you have.'

'Yes, there will be, you can guarantee it. There doesn't seem to be any rhyme or reason which path the cyclone will take each time. One house might be safe for one cyclone, but the next time, it could be wiped out completely. That's why I never take anything for granted up here in the tropics. You always have to be vigilant and never drop your guard where Mother Nature is concerned. Can I get you anything to eat or drink?' *Good move Stewart! Stick to safe subjects for now.*

'A glass of water, please. My kidneys could certainly do with some relief right now.'

'One glass of water coming up. We'd best get some sleep soon. It's just on 11:30 pm, even though it seems much later, doesn't it?'

'Ah. Stewart. What bed did you refer to before, by the way? Were you suggesting your own bed? You and me together in your bedroom?'

Stewart stopped on his way to the kitchen to turn around and look Peta in the eye. 'The way I see it is, you have two choices, Peta, in regard to sleeping arrangements tonight. You can, of course, bunk down here in the living room. *Or* you could share my own superbly comfortable king-size bed for the rest of the night. After all, we've already shared some rather restricted space together up until now, haven't we? This is my way of making it up to you.'

'Ah but, Stewart, sharing your bed in your own private bedroom is an entirely different matter altogether.'

'Well, let me put it to you this way then. This room is quite comfortable normally, but just not now, I'm afraid. It will probably be more exposed to the constant drum of heavy rain, once it beats down on the tin rooftop above you. Whereas my bedroom is more insulated and, thankfully, more muted from outside noises. Your choice, though.'

'Well now, let me see. There's this perfectly good sofa bed here in your living room, and although it *does* look quite comfy mind you, I do think my poor back needs to be nurtured a lot more right now. So, being totally selfish now, I think my choice would definitely be to go for your great big bed to stretch out on.'

'Good choice!' Stewart held his hand out for Peta to take.

Peta merely gave him a cheeky smile in return, knowing full well what he was implying with his invitation.

'Mmm, I do have to ask you now, Stewart. Let me get this straight first—just so there are no misunderstandings between us later.' Peta smiled a smile now that any wench worth her saucy reputation would be proud of, as she looked deep into his baby blues. 'So, am I to understand, that you would be willing to be share your bed with me then? An interesting offer, indeed. Mmm, what to do? I would probably consider such an offer on one condition; will you *still* continue to keep me safe from this nasty old storm out there?'

'Of course!' Stewart looked puzzled by her question. 'Haven't I protected you so far tonight?'

'Yes, of course you have! But what I want to know now is, will you promise to hold me and keep me safe for the *rest* of the night as well?' Peta smiled at him again with part shyness and part devil-woman in her eyes.

Stewart grinned, finally catching onto to her hidden meaning, his own eyes blazing with a burning fire. He sauntered over slowly, locking his gaze with hers the whole time, making her powerless to resist.

'Well, if the promise of a full body massage can't entice you into my bed, then perhaps this will.'

Before she could even think of pulling away, in one swift movement, he pulled her close. Stewart's lips crushed down upon her own responsive mouth in just one showstopping, toe-curling moment, curtailing any resistance from her sensibilities once and for all. Any spoken words were completely out of place.

Once they finally came up for air, Stewart's only response now was to take her hand in his, silently asking her to trust him now. Peta paused for a moment before accepting his proffered hand, but not without a tiny last twinge of caution from her persistent inner voice.

This is it, Peta! You go into that bedroom with him now, there will be no turning back! What about your work ethic? What about your professional reputation? Is this what you really want?'

Well, yes, I believe I do!

Once in his bedroom, Stewart let go of Peta's hand to throw back his lightweight navy cotton bedcover, along with the top sheet to follow. He climbed over to the far side of his bed and turned towards her, playfully patting the space beside him. 'Welcome to my private boudoir, Ms. McKenna!'

Peta didn't need any further encouragement. She knew full well that once she stepped over the threshold into his private territory, there would be no turning back. Tomorrow was bound to be loaded with harsh incriminations of, 'Are you crazy Peta?' or, 'What were you thinking to do such a thing?' but this feeling felt right and, let's face it, just too irresistible for her to ignore. The overwhelming feeling of wanting to be nowhere else but here, and despite her inner reservations about entering his bedroom, she knew she was going to anyway. Whatever repercussions followed tomorrow and all the days after, she would deal with the consequences of her actions then. A night such as this, only happened once in a lifetime and she wasn't about to let it slip away so easily. Outside, she could hear the torrential rain belting down on the old tin roof, but the outside sounds immediately faded into oblivion once Stewart moved in closer to tease her responsive lips with his own. Before she knew it, their mouths seemed to have welded together, so it was hard to tell anymore where her own lips started and his ended.

Before they could go any further, a sudden urgency persisted within Peta's befuddled mind. It took all her willpower to push Stewart forcibly from her.

It didn't take long for Stewart to realise he wasn't holding her close anymore.

'What the hell, Peta?' Stewart groaned with obvious frustration. 'Why are you pushing me away like this? I don't understand. Are you saying you don't want me anymore? Why are you turning away from me now? *Please!* I need to understand what is happening, Peta?

An uncomfortable silence invaded the room, with Stewart moving over to his side the bed as far as he could go. Peta couldn't see his face, but she was guessing he was hurting real bad by now over her sudden rejection of him. She found herself having to broach a delicate subject, that neither of them had obviously thought about until now.

'Why would you automatically think you've done something wrong, Stewart? I promise you were doing *everything* right, but in case it has completely slipped your mind, as it did with me, does either one of us have some other kind of *safe* protection?—If you get my point. No pun intended?'

Stewart suddenly slapped his forehead. It finally dawned on him as to what Peta was trying to tell him … 'YES! You are absolutely right! Up until just now, my sole intent was to get you into my bedroom in the shortest possible time, so I must confess, I didn't give that side of things any thought at all. Geez! How irresponsible am I?'

'Don't beat yourself up too much, Stewart. I have to confess myself, that I didn't think of it either, but unless we want a mini version of you or me making an appearance in nine months' time, we really do need to take certain precautions to make sure such a scenario doesn't happen at all … Not only that, apart from this one day together, you really don't know me and I don't really know you—Well, not in this way, obviously. So, isn't it worth it, for us to be a little bit more careful now?'

'SHIT, YES!' The full force of their near-miss hit him, Stewart realised too late he had just raised his voice a bit too much. Even after he calmed down, though, he was still berating himself for his foolishness. 'Oh man! Just as well one of us has some common sense around here.' He looked over at Peta now with a sheepish grin. 'Will you forgive me?'

Peta grabbed hold of his beautiful big hand to wrap both of her own hands around it. 'There's nothing to forgive, Stewart. Luckily, we both came to our senses in time, but now we need to figure out what to do next? You wouldn't happen to have any boxes of those little foil packets around here somewhere, would you?'

Stewart didn't answer her at first, as he tried to think whether he did or not. Then it dawned on him.

'Come to think of it, I *might* just have some stashed away at the back of my built-in, here.' Stewart headed over towards his built-in wardrobe and quickly rolled back the door. He took a moment to look up and down the boxed shelving, trying to remember where he'd hidden what he was looking for. All the while he continued talking to Peta. 'I assure you, I didn't have them on hand because I haven't had any other women in here really. There was only ever Felicity in here before you. Way back when she *did* live here that is. She was on the pill—when we were *actively* married, that is. But when she kept coming back into my life again after our divorce, I decided to buy some condoms as extra insurance, just in case Felicity had it in her mind to trick me by getting pregnant. I hated thinking this way but, believe me, she would have stopped at nothing to trap me financially any way she could. From that time onwards, I always insisted on wearing one, for whenever I fell for one of her clever seduction ploys again. Thankfully, she soon tired of my efforts to stay one step ahead of her sneaky plans every time.

Stewart hunted around for a few more minutes more, before he finally re-emerged, uttering the magic words Peta longed to hear. 'Aha! I knew they were still in here!' He triumphantly held up a handful of foil-sealed condoms in his hand.

Peta couldn't help but giggle at the excited grin on Stewart's face, thinking how he reminded her now of a little boy who had at last found his childhood bag of treasured marbles again.

Stewart closed the built-in door firmly and sauntered back over towards her with a burning look.

'So, where were we, you sexy wench! I have my secret weapon now, so you cannot escape me!'

Peta's singlet and light cotton overshirt had ridden up a bit more, free at last from the waistband of her light cotton cargo pants, leaving her back exposed to the feathery touch of his fingers.

After ditching every last piece of clothing from their bodies, he touched her skin with feathery-light fingers in small, distracting circles, gradually moving up and around on either side of her backbone, effectively relaxing any tense muscles along the way.

Peta shivered with tingly pleasure, but lay as still as possible, more than happy for him to continue his delicious exploration of her body.

With such delightful pleasure in store for her, Peta wouldn't have dreamt of spoiling this moment. In fact, she copied his movements, with the same careless circles up and around his back, with light, caressing strokes. Stewart responded with the same involuntary shiver of pleasure. Their responses to each other's caresses set the scene. Neither of them were averse in any way to this natural progression towards intimacy. This very moment was a sensual, heightened feeling compared to the uncomfortable closeness of being locked together in his old metal bathtub.

Stewart pulled her even closer towards him with a firm hand on her buttocks and waited for her to move away from him in protest. When she stayed where she was, he growled a deep, primal sound before taking the next tentative step of kissing her mouth with soft fleeting kisses to each side of her lips. Then with a much more pleasurable pressure at the centre of her delightfully responsive lips.

Peta smiled, responding with some light, teasing kisses of her own. Tit for tat. Whatever exploratory moves Stewart made towards Peta, she responded in kind. When he deepened his kisses, Peta answered his call with a sensual, uninhibited passion to equal his own.

They both pulled back a bit at the same time as the pounding rain belted down outside the bedroom window. Despite the darkness, Peta didn't need any light around her to picture his electric blue eyes, alight with a barely suppressed passion, piercing hers.

Stewart felt totally mesmerised now by the thought of Peta—drawing him deeper and deeper into a pair of bewitching cat eyes, superbly alight by exquisite slivers of jade. When their kisses deepened even more with a heightened intensity, his hands felt free to wander freely, even greedily, over her delectable body to the point of no return. Her body ultimately reminded him of an open, unexplored field of the highly arousing sensations of touch—along with the heady smell of her exotic perfume—the combination was a potent mix indeed. An all-powerful elixir to be captured and stored within his store of treasured memories for all time.

'So, what do we have here?' His probing fingers separated the soft folds at the centre of her feminine core.

'Oh! Sweet heavens above! What are you doing to me?' Breathy desire punctuated her words.

'But Peta, I haven't even started yet! Ah, there it is! Are you ready? Here goes!'

Stewart flicked her hidden button. Fast, then slow. He knew exactly-what he was doing, with Peta in the throes of accepting his pleasuring, she offered no resistance at all. 'Can you feel that? Do you like me touching you like this?'

Peta's only answer was a drawn-out, 'Please! Have mercy on me!'

'So, you want me to stop then?'

'NO! Don't ever stop!'

'I thought you'd say that!'

Stewart obliged, his grin devilish, pushing her closer to the edge. His touch catapulted Peta upwards and outwards on some delicious, never-ending, unfathomable spiral, somewhere beyond her physical body.

'Had enough?'

With her head thrown back and her back arched like some

loose-limbed, languorous cat, as she once again rode the waves of a sweet, torturous ecstasy, Peta was lost to sensation. 'What are you doing to me, you meanie?' With her hands, Peta grabbed onto both of his shoulders and laughed out loud. 'Oh man, you do know how to pleasure a woman, don't you? I think you should be required by law to carry around a warning card with you at all times. This card declares your hands, particularly those nimble fingers of yours, as a lethal weapons. Not the same lethal weapons, I might add, practised in marital arts, though.

'You think so, do you? So perhaps then, if I had have produced a card like that when I first opened my front door to you yesterday, you would have run a mile, right?'

'Well. Maybe not, when you put it like that.' Peta laughed. 'But seriously, Stewart, if I had have left then, I would have been a real fool. It's hard to believe we have only known each other for less than a day. Unbelievable! And to think I could have easily missed out on this moment with you now. What a tragedy that would have been for both of us, don't you agree?'

'Most definitely. I feel like I have known you forever, but if I can be so bold, right at this moment, I absolutely do enjoy getting to know you this way most of all. Having said that, I do believe I simply have to explore your gorgeous body just a little bit more … Just like this.'

Stewart stepped up his sensual intent to extract all the sweet nectar he could from Peta's body, again and again. For the umpteenth time, Peta arched her back and groaned with sublime pleasure, which in turn enticed him to want to pleasure her even more, until Peta climaxed in ever-increasing waves, each one more intense than the last, until she finally collapsed back onto the bed beside him, into a dreamy, ethereal state of mind.

Just when Stewart obviously assumed she had drifted off to sleep, Peta sprung into action catching him completely off guard. 'So, you think you're pretty clever, don't you, Mr. Fletcher? Like I said before, you have bought me to heights of pleasure I've never quite experienced so intensely before. Well, you might not realise this, my good man, but two can play at that game. Ha! Never forget that we women have the power to thrill and excite too. The time has come for me to return the feeling.'

'Peta? Peta? What are you up to?' Stewart stretched out his hand as he searched in vain for the sensuous touch of her body again, that up until now had been right beside him. This was before she'd mysteriously backed away from his searching touch. A tingling sensation of a soft breath, followed by a soft voice, whispered in his ear.

'You can dish it out, ahh, but can you take it? Be prepared to take your own sweet punishment.'

Peta moved on down to his engorged manhood as she already knew it would be by now. Then she stroked him with her fingertip and circled around and around him with the lightest of touches. Stewart bucked his hips with pleasure and reached for her, but she evaded him.

'Oh boy! I think I might be in big trouble. Please feel free to continue, though.'

'Oh, I will! You can be sure of that.' Peta inflicted delicious torture on him with her busy tongue and the feathery caress of her fingertips while she teased him with her own kind of sweet torture as promised.

'Oh Lordy! What are you doing to me, you wicked woman? I don't know how much longer I can hold out if you keep doing that to me.'

'Do you surrender then?'

'Well, within reason. Only if you promise to put me out of my misery, by letting me come you inside right now! Are you ready for me now, Peta? I mean, I'm not pushing you into this too soon, am I?'

'Are you kidding? I want to feel you inside me. In fact, I really do need to feel you inside me. Deeper and deeper. *BUT!* First things first; I think this definitely might be the time to break open one of those little packets we talked about, before we both get too carried away to remember why we needed to afterwards.'

'Absolutely! I'm with you on that one.' Stewart leaned over and grabbed one of the foil packets from his bedside table and with a cheeky raising of his eyebrows a few times, he ripped it open from the corner of the packet, before handing it to Peta. 'Perhaps you could do me the honour now of covering my friend down there with the shield of protection.'

'Why certainly, my dear! Be happy to.' Peta obliged, then dramatically clicked her fingers to declare her job done.

'Come over my way now, sexy lady! I do declare we have now officially been given the green light to proceed and my fine upstanding friend down south says it's all systems go for him, too!'

'How wonderful! Well, let's not disappoint him, then. Peta didn't need further prompting to take her cue, ready for the ultimate reward of Stewart exploring her right to the senders of her most essential womanly core.

'Oh man, you feel so damn good, Peta! You are so unbelievably sexy to me! If I'm dreaming, please don't ever wake me up.' Stewart raised his head to meet Peta's lips. They kissed deeply with hungry mouths seeking so much more with each brand-new kiss.

'Oh, Stewart. I never want this to end, either.'

Their hips moved now without any conscious effort at all. Their momentum and desire now completely in sync with an overwhelming need to reach their ultimate peak of satisfaction. Together like this, they were in full control. Never settling for less, never having to.

'Oh! I don't believe it! I think I'm coming again! What are you doing to me?'

'You and me both, babe! I'm not far behind you.'

Their peak of ecstasy became a pinnacle conquered and at last, released. A whole kaleidoscope of moods, colours, hopes and dreams were at play here tonight and as a result, neither of them would ever be the same again. Inevitably, as they kissed, teased and clung to each other, they realised with absolute certainly, this one night alone would be irreversibly spun into a delicious cloak of saucy memories. Remembered always with an inner glow. Peta collapsed back onto the bed beside Stewart. They were back from wherever they'd been on their sensual journey together. A visible sheen of sweat slicked their bodies as their breathing returned to normal.

Outside, the torrential rain continued.

A smug, satisfied grin adorned Peta's face as she caressed his smooth, firm body. 'I don't think I have ever had quite so many orgasms before. It's so amazing when it happens like that. One after the other. Wow!'

'So, you aren't in any relationship at all right now?' Stewart had to ask, even if he wasn't sure if he wanted to hear her answer. Especially if it turned out to be what he feared—she already had someone waiting for her back home. 'I mean. I would have thought that a beautiful woman such as yourself would have men waiting in line to claim you as their own.'

'Sure, Stewart, I certainly understand why you are asking me this. Yes I did have one meaningful relationship in the past, which ended a year ago now because we both realised we wanted different things in the end. There were also some other not-so-meaningful ones as well, but after one messy, painful break-up in my life, I always tried to make damn sure after that to never to complicate my life in any way anymore, if I could help it. I never wanted to make any false promises I couldn't keep, either. I've somehow managed over the years to keep my head—and my heart—intact, so I could concentrate on giving my career a chance to develop to its full potential. After all, I have undertaken years of study to get where I am now, so I wasn't prepared, at the time, to step away from my career with thoughts of marriage or even starting a family. Especially during those first early years of study and trying to find my own way amongst the thousands of other fledging journalists with exactly the same dream that I have.'

'I understand what you mean, Peta. It's not easy to willingly choose one's career before love.'

'Ain't that the truth! You and I both have chosen the same type of career; the written word.'

'True! Anyway, let's take a quick shower together, then try to get some sleep until morning.'

'I seriously think we'll have no trouble sleeping unless we get waylaid again.'

They did get waylaid again, of course. The heady combination of erotic soap-ups and wash-downs was just too tempting to resist, prolonging their shower much more than was necessary. To compensate for the constant drain on his tank water supply, Stewart kept turning the shower on and off.

Peta, intensely curious by now, just had to ask, 'Stewart, why do you keep turning the tap on and off? I would imagine after all this heavy rain overnight, your water tanks must be full to the brim by now.'

'Yes, I am quite sure my water tanks must be overflowing by now, but old habits die hard. This was one of the first things I had to learn when I first moved up this way. Growing up in Melbourne and later spending time in Sydney, I took simple things like water for granted. Even in the tropics, you still have to be mindful of the level of water in your catchment tanks 365 days of the year.'

As they washed each other's bodies, Stewart kept on playing with the taps. They allowed the gentle droplets of sweet smelling rainwater to trickle over their bodies as they soaped each other up, only turning it on to full force again when it was time to rinse off. All the while, a few large candles helped to create a soft, sensuous atmosphere in the bathroom. There was still no electricity or hot water back on yet, but with the early morning mugginess, who needed hot water anyway. Besides their bodies needed cooling down, not warming up, after their earlier horizontal activities. There was no shortage of soapy bubbles either, to heighten the touch of their bodies, entwined so pleasurably together.

For now at least, they felt safe from any outside weather forces. That is until a new sunrise dared to bare its sunny side over a shaky uncertain horizon. Right now, nothing existed for Stewart and Peta beyond the protection of these sheltered walls. Even if this old weatherboard shack appeared to be humble on the outside, they still felt safe.

'I really do think it was a brilliant idea of mine to conserve water in this way. Even if I do say so myself,' Stewart murmured as his busy fingers soaped up Peta's full, perky, rose-tipped breasts. 'It gives a whole new meaning to that old saying of; save water, shower with a friend—don't you think?'

'Yes, absolutely!' Peta agreed as she traced her own soaped-up fingers over his tanned, sculptured abs. 'There's no limit to our combined talents when you think about it, Fletcher.'

'I thought so too, McKenna.' Stewart quipped back.

'Ah, to be sure, to be sure, my good fellow!' Peta followed up her statement by giggling impulsively.

'Would you like me to wash your hair? At no extra charge for house guests, I assure you.'

'Yes, that would be lovely. Are you sure you don't mind?'

'Not at all. Wow! Your hair is really long, isn't it? It's halfway down your back. The colour of your hair reminds me of silky honey. It's so thick and healthy too. Have you always worn it as long as this?' Stewart queried as he sprayed Peta's hair with water. Then he pulled her hair together in one long ponytail with one hand, while he turned off the tap with the other. He applied the shampoo, then rubbed it into the tips. He massaged her scalp next, emitting blissful sighs from Peta.

'Yes, pretty much. According to my father, I've inherited my mother's hair. I don't have time for short, fussy styles really. Plus when I'm working, I can just tie it back. Why? Do you think I should cut it?'

'No! Not at all! It would be such a shame if you did. It is just so amazing to touch! I really love it!'

'I'm thrilled to hear you say that. *Ahh,* Stewart! That feels so good. It must have something to do with your magic fingers, perhaps. You're making me feel so unbelievably sexy!' Peta sighed with deep pleasure before turning around in his arms to kiss Stewart deeper than before. After exploring each other's lips in a fresh onslaught of erotic exploration, Stewart finally came up for air.

'Ah, but there's more to come, beautiful lady!' he whispered into her ear. 'But before I fulfil that promise, let's rinse you off first.' He turned the tap back on again and rinsed the shampoo from her hair, running his hand sensuously through it at the same time. He followed with conditioner, massaging the creamy liquid in with his strong fingers, sending Peta into a thousand more spasms of delightful pleasure.

'Wow! Like I've already said, your nimble fingers should be registered as a secret weapon.'

'You mean this kind of touch?' Stewart whispered as his hands now moved down to cup her full breasts. Stewart's mouth took over where his fingers left off. He sucked hungrily, first on one highly aroused nipple, then the other.

'What a sneaky man you are!' Peta declared without any need for explanation. 'Oh boy! You certainly have the ability to stir me up so easily again. I have a sneaky feeling you are already aware of this, anyway.'

'That's the whole idea! Being in the shower with you like this is so incredibly sexy to me. I can't help but be turned on by you either. Do you think you can handle any more, though?' He kissed her mouth again, her lips so soft and wet against his own.

'Oh yes, indeed! I can definitely handle it!' and with that, Peta explored his body now with a special touch all of her own.

Her wandering hands strayed down towards his obvious arousal and stayed there for the longest time. She allowed her teasing fingers to do their own kind of sweet magic for a while, sending him an unmistakable message of more pleasures to come. Stewart was helpless to hold back some expressive outbursts of his own as he responded to Peta's delicious challenge to him.

'Like I said before, Stewart, two can play at that game and revenge can be so unbelievably sweet.'

'Okay, okay, you cheeky wench!' he laughed. 'You win! But I'm afraid we will have to hold that thought for now. At least until we have towelled each other down and have added a new layer of protection—If you catch my drift? Believe me, I'm not about to forget any precautions this time around, I promise you that!' Stewart helped her out of his bathtub for the second time tonight, but for a whole different reason this time. 'Are you ready?'

'You have my full attention, Mr. Fletcher.' Peta whispered seductively as she pressed herself even closer to his body. 'Take me back to your bed then. I am completely at your mercy once more.'

'Well now. Here we are back in bed again.' Stewart remarked unnecessarily.

'Amen to that!' Peta sighed. Their bodies spooned together, both relaxed in each other's arms. Back in Stewart's huge, king-sized bed after their soaped-up love play, under the gentle caress of soft, sweet-smelling water flowing over them, then towelling each other off afterwards. Both of their bodies were more than a little achy by now. They knew they would probably pay for all this marathon of horizontal activity come morning. In the meantime, they needed some sleep, for however long, to revive their depleted energies. At least until the morning light seeped in through Stewart's bedroom window, to break their spell at last.

Before they drifted off, Peta turned her face towards Stewart and groaned. 'I think I have re-discovered parts of my body I've forgotten ever existed. Man! I am so ready for sleep right now. What about you?'

'Oh really? I guess that means you don't want to fool around again right now?'

Peta stared at him now like he must be one of those people who could never get enough. 'You're kidding me. Right?' But then she caught the silly grin on his face and playfully thumped his arm closest to her. 'Oh, you are kidding! Thank goodness! To tell you the truth, I don't think I can even move another muscle if I tried. At least for the next few hours, anyway. How are you, honestly?'

'The same as you. Achy all over but in a really good way, though. Why is it that we all tend to neglect our love muscles? We all seem to favour our work muscles or our thinking muscle instead, when our love muscles are so much more fun. The best part, I believe, is how quickly these same neglected muscles can be so easily revived again with the right person and the right chemistry. Wouldn't you agree with that, Peta? Peta?'

Stewart realised Peta had drifted off to sleep while he was murmuring to her.

She's asleep already! Man! What a truly sexy woman she is!

Stewart grinned, listening to Peta's light snoring. How did he ever get to be so lucky to find a woman who matched his own needs so perfectly?

He hoped her sudden need wasn't the selfish kind this time around. He didn't think he could handle having his heart broken again. For now, he intended to make the most of every spare moment he had to spend with her. Who knows what new challenges lay ahead to disrupt his relatively uncomplicated life he'd strived so hard to maintain this past year? Perhaps the fickle finger of fate might have a hand in this after all, playing some cruel game with his wounded heart again.

Whatever happens tomorrow, I'm not prepared to give Peta up so easily, that's for sure! No sir-ee! He reached over to switch off the bedside lamp. It didn't take long for him to drift off to sleep himself, spooned against Peta's sleeping body.

CHAPTER SIX

Peta opened her eyes a few blinks at a time, not daring to open them fully just yet. As per her usual waking process, she luxuriously rolled onto her back, before stretching out her body to its full length, only this time, absently wondering why she felt so achy this morning. Somewhat disorientated by now, Peta was forced to ask herself, *Where in the hell am I, anyway?*

This isn't her bed! Her pillow! Then she remembered … 'Stewart?' she tentatively called out to him, then again a little louder, but it was obvious by now, no response would be forthcoming.

Where could he be? … Probably outside checking on the house for damage—or perhaps watering another tree again.

After accepting Stewart really wasn't around, she laid back down and tentatively attempted to stretch out her long legs again. When she felt ready to roll back over onto her side, though, her body wasn't too happy with this idea at all, but she persisted anyway. Within her languorous, comfy zone once again, Peta's thoughts drifted back to the night before. Right at this very moment, a weird feeling of serendipity took over her. It somehow made her feel like she was suddenly thrust back in time and she was now part of some 1940s movie scene, where her leading man had slipped out of the scene for a moment, to go fight the baddies in a nearby tropical jungle. *Well at least he won't have too far to go for a tropical jungle,* Peta smiled to herself.

Wow! What a night! Was what happened between Stewart and herself last night even real, or did she just imagine it all?

No, it was real, all right. That's what her aching body was strongly trying to tell her this morning, anyway. *It's a good ache, though,* Peta decided with a crazy happy grin.

Absolutely delicious, in fact.

Peta grabbed Stewart's pillow and hugged it close to her body. If all this was really just a dream, then why could she still smell his aftershave on his pillow? She smiled to herself now, reliving the divine sensations of his mouth devouring every tiny crevice of her naked body, his hands working their exquisite magic in erotic places even she'd forgotten about.

Oh wow! I feel like I have died and gone to heaven. I wonder if Stewart is feeling the same.

'Jeez!' Peta was suddenly catapulted out of her dreamy state with a start, her eyes now fully open, as a really horrible thought suddenly popped into her head. What if Stewart was deliberately avoiding her this morning because he was having second thoughts about last night? *Shit!* Maybe that's why he wasn't here when she woke up this morning? *Hell's bells!* He could, at this very moment, be thinking of storming in here any second now and demand that she leave his bedroom immediately! He could even throw her out his front door, too, just as she is—stark-bloody-naked! Peta raised her head up from the pillow then sat up straight. She pulled the top sheet over her exposed breasts, feeling vulnerable and unsure of herself.

It's a bit late for modesty now, girl—he's already seen all of you!

Maybe her first course of action should be to calm herself down and play it cool for now. Failing that, her second course of action—and the most sensible, really—should merely be to go by Stewart's mood when he comes back into the bedroom.

As if on cue, the man himself poked his head inside the bedroom door. Seeing Peta already awake, he entered bearing a breakfast tray of aromatic coffee, hot buttered toast and a small jar of raspberry conserve. Stewart smiled as he placed the tray on the bedside table, then sat on the side of the bed, leaned over and kissed her softly on her still-tender lips. *Ah! All good! He seems happy enough, at least. No need to take flight just yet.*

'Good morning!' Stewart grinned before kissing her again, only much deeper this time.

'Good morning to you, too,' she responded with a few deep exploratory kisses of her own. 'Ah! Breakfast, I see! How wonderful, especially the coffee! What time is it, by the way?'

'It's just going on eight now. When I woke up this morning, you were sleeping like a baby. I just didn't have the heart to wake you.'

'To tell you the truth, I'm still a bit sleepy *and* so blissfully relaxed, but this coffee and yummy toast and jam should be enough to revive me pretty soon.' Peta propped herself up against some pillows Stewart helped to position behind her. He sat down close beside her and handed her one slice of buttered toast, generously loaded with thick, fruity jam.

'What have you been up to while I've been totally slacking off in here?' Peta asked as she bit into her toast with her usual ravenous appetite.

Stewart raised an eyebrow. 'What do you mean by "up to"?' He burst out laughing. 'Do you mean what have I been doing just now, or are you suggesting something entirely different?'

'You know exactly what I mean.' Peta laughed as she whacked his arm in jest, but a shy blush still infused her cheeks anyway. 'Oh no, my good man, I suspect you might have an incurable case of sex on the brain this morning! … Mmm! I wonder why?'

'As you Irish always say, "To be sure, to be sure!" And who could blame me for that? Especially when you consider what happened between us last night.'

'I have absolutely no idea what you are talking about,' Peta primly replied, then ducked away, giggling as Stewart tried to pull the bedsheet playfully away from her. Insanely shy with him again, she tried in vain to keep the top sheet in place. Even just over her exposed breasts for now.

'Come here, you wicked wench! You can't escape me any more!' Stewart laughed wickedly.

Peta's mobile phone rang on the other side of the bed. Still laughing, Peta made a sneaky lunge for it once she was safely out of Stewart's reach.

'Well, at least we have reception again,' Stewart remarked. Serious now, he poured steaming coffee from the plunger into their mugs. 'Go ahead and take that call. It might be your work people trying to contact you. I imagine they must be quite concerned about you by now. Try to make it a quick call though if you can, unless you'd prefer lukewarm coffee.'

'Hello. Peta speaking!' she answered in her best professional tone.

'Peta? At last! I've finally managed to get hold of you. This is Dominic. Where are you?'

Dominic! I completely forgot about Dominic coming here today too. Oh shit!

'*Bonjour!* Listen, can I call you back in about five minutes? Will that be okay?'

'That would definitely *not* be okay. I've been trying to call you all morning so *non!*'

Oh man! He sounds really pissed off with me. Understandably so, too.

'Okay! I get it. Well in that case, could you at least stay on the line for a minute, please?'

'*Oui,* I can do that at least, but please make it as quick as you can.'

Peta put her hand over the speaker of her phone and held it away from her as she whispered off side to Stewart. 'Sorry, Stewart, but I must take this call in private. Work stuff. Would you mind terribly?'

Stewart regarded Peta with a suspicious look but said nothing. He nodded and left the room with his own coffee and toast. Peta waited until he closed his bedroom door before speaking again.

'Dominic! I'm so sorry to have kept you waiting. I am out at Stewart Fletcher's house. As you are no doubt already aware by now, there was a rather nasty cyclone last night in this area and Mr. Fletcher kindly offered me a bed for the night inside his place.'

'Ah! This is good! I am so relieved! I pictured you perhaps stranded or injured somewhere and that's why I couldn't contact you. I have been very worried, as you can well imagine.'

'Yes, I can certainly understand why you were worried, but there was no phone reception at all during the cyclone. I didn't think you would be able to get to Cairns until lunchtime today, anyway. I was about to call you soon, after I've had a bit of breakfast first.' There was an awkward silence at the other end. Dominic was definitely not happy with her explanations, so she changed tack. 'So I gather you are in Cairns right now then?'

'*Oui!* That is correct. I arrived here about an hour or so ago. I am now at our hotel and have been trying to contact you every few minutes ever since. So, *chérie,* is the interview still on? I would imagine you would have talked Mr. Fletcher around to the idea by now?'

Peta paused before answering. A tricky question indeed, but she'd have to play it by ear for now. She hoped Stewart would forgive her after she explained why they still had to go through with this dreaded interview. Dominic, the photographer assigned for this important interview, would not be impressed to know it was a no-go zone for now. *As Dominic is so fond of saying; 'Jeez Louise!'*

'Peta? You still there?'

'Yes! Dominic, of course I'm still here! Just thinking, that's all. Okay! Get yourself out here when you can? In the meantime, I will endeavour to take care of things at my end.'

Sure, no problem! Piece of cake, Dominic. That's if I'm not tossed out of here first.

'*Oui.* Are you sure everything is okay? You sound a little … distracted … for want of a better word.'

'No, I'm fine, thanks. I guess the cyclone yesterday has traumatised me more than I realised. You just concentrate on getting yourself out this way. I'll take care of everything this end somehow. Bye for now!'

Easier said than done! In the meantime, she'll have to do some fast talking before Dominic arrives, or they will *both* be in Stewart's bad books for certain. He might even send them on their way with no photos. Even worse—no story. She couldn't even bear to think about that right now.

Peta reluctantly climbed out of bed and retrieved her clothes from the wicker chair where Stewart had thoughtfully placed them for her. She had this vague recollection of their clothes being carelessly tossed aside the night before. She wasted no time, ducking across the hall into the bathroom and closing the door quickly, before Stewart could return to ask her some awkward questions she wasn't prepared to answer just yet. Judging by the wary look he gave her as he left the room, he was already on guard again.

I need a little time to get my head around all of this. Oh, hell's bells! I can't think straight! What to do? What to do?

Peta used some necessary time in the bathroom to pull herself together. Once in the bathroom with the door securely closed, she washed her face and hands and applied fresh make-up to start her day with some normalcy at least. All the while, her thoughts continued to bounce around inside her head. Instead of some much-needed inspiration, Stewart's bathroom mirror gave out no sympathy at all. Instead, it reflected back at her an unforgiving accusation instead.

This is a fine mess you've got yourself into yet again! her reflexion accused.

Oh really! You think? Well, you know how much I love all this drama in my life! Come on, girl. Think, think!

For starters, she couldn't let Dominic know she'd slept with Stewart, or she'd be in some really deep shit, especially if it got back to Tess, her immediate boss. In the meantime, she'd little choice but to explain to Stewart why this interview must go ahead. Oh hell! She could almost guarantee how it would go down with Stewart this time around! She'd be kicked out his front door, *pronto*. Only instead of a tropical cyclone outside, it would be because of Stewart's stormy wrath seething up close and personal instead.

At this point, I think I might actually prefer the cyclone.

Stewart turned around to face Peta as she walked back into his kitchen to return the breakfast tray. He took it from her before pulling her close. Stewart nuzzled her neck playfully, but when Peta failed to respond, he pulled away with a puzzled frown.

'Is everything okay? You know, with your work people, I mean. You seem so serious all of a sudden.'

He kissed her again. She returned his kiss in a distracted manner, and by the look on his face, she knew she'd set his alarm bells ringing.

'Stewart. We have to talk.'

'Uh-oh! I don't think I like the sound of this. What's going on, Peta?'

Peta didn't answer immediately. Instead, she grabbed hold of his hand and pulled him over towards the sofa. She sat and patted the space beside her for him to follow suit. Stewart didn't oblige. He remained standing, his hackles well and truly on the rise.

'Okay, let me guess. Thanks for looking after me during the cyclone, Stewart, but I have to go now—right?'

'No, Stewart! That's not what I'm saying at all! You jump to conclusions much too quickly! Will you please give me a chance to explain to you what that phone call was all about?'

'So if you're not leaving, then why do you appear to be so serious now? Please do explain then, Peta, if you would be so kind?'

Already he's on the defensive. I have to make him listen—fast!

'I wasn't planning to leave here just yet, but I have a feeling that once I tell you what I have to tell you, it will be you who will be asking me to leave.'

Stewart looked totally baffled now. 'I don't understand. Why would I ask you to leave?'

'Please, Stewart! Come and sit down. I can't talk to you while you're standing up there, glaring down at me. It's very intimidating to say the least.'

'Okay, I will sit down if that makes you happy, but I will sit over here for now.' He sat himself down on the chair positioned closest to her at the dining table, his face suddenly set like a chunk of granite. An attitude of barely suppressed apprehension filled the already muggy tropical air as Stewart waited for Peta to continue.

'You'll remember, no doubt, when you let me come in out of the storm, you gave me an ultimatum at the time of absolutely no interviews being allowed. Right?'

'That's right! And I meant it, too!' Stewart puffed out his chest.

'Well, I agreed to your rather strict conditions at the time because, naturally, I wanted so desperately to come inside. I would have agreed to almost anything. To be safe, you understand.'

'I do understand your fear at the time, but I meant what I said about no interviews, too.'

'So you keep reminding me!' Peta said with obvious frustration. 'The thing is, what with the cyclone and waiting out the worst of it in your house, and making love to you throughout the night, I'd completely forgot about Dominic coming here too. He was supposed to arrive here yesterday.'

'Dominic? Who the hell is Dominic?' Stewart's glare was one of pure thunder by now.

'It's not what you think! I assure you, he's not my boyfriend or anything like that. He is the photographer with *Today's Voice* who has flown all the way to Cairns to photograph you for the interview we were both supposed to do with you. With the impending cyclone, all flights up here were cancelled, so Dominic wasn't able to fly to Cairns in with me yesterday as originally planned. Plus, he'd another job he needed to finish in Sydney first. Naturally, we talked on the phone about what to do. The new plan we decided on, was for me to come out here on my own to introduce myself and to prepare you for the interview beforehand. We—that is my boss Tess, Dominic, and myself—honestly didn't think, even for one minute, the cyclone would be as intense as what it turned out to be. I didn't think you would put up such a stubborn resistance to me being here either. I was a bit shocked, but I'm not one to back down from a challenge, and I was determined to get what I came for, as you already know by now.' Peta smiled sheepishly at him.

'You accuse me of being stubborn! Man, oh man!' Stewart broke in. 'When you dig your heels in, there is no way you will ever back down.' He even smiled at the memory now, despite the unmistakably stubborn set of his shoulders.

'I know you think I tricked you into letting me into your private space for the sake of a story, but if you think back on our stand-off yesterday, you'll realise I'm really not that ruthless.'

'So you say, but due to my past experience with the press, some journalists seem to have no scruples at all when it comes to getting their story. Especially when I was still married to Felicity. Being a TV celebrity, she always craved any kind of media attention. She'd complain openly to the press about them poking into her private life but, unbeknown to me, she would send them anonymous tips of any social or romantic outings with her husband. Every time we went out together, there they'd be with their cameras and, worst of all, their intrusive questions. Do you even have to wonder why I resent the press so much? Even if I know I still have to promote my books.'

'I am fully aware of why you resent the press, and I can certainly understand that, especially after the media circus you endured after your marriage break-up with Felicity. Need I remind you that your interview with *Today's Voice* was already arranged months ago between our publishing company and your agent, even before I was sent here instead of Brad Collins. I would also imagine at some point you would've discussed this upcoming interview with your literary agent too?'

'Yes, that is absolutely correct. I did agree to this interview initially, but in case you might have forgotten too, I quite plainly requested no female journalists! So naturally, I would have been expecting a Mr. Peter McKenna, or so I thought!'

'Yes, that may be so, but it's not really my fault, is it? I was only ever meant to be a last-minute choice. Professionally speaking, though, I was merely sent to Cairns to get the job done. Nothing more, nothing less. If you will now take a moment to think back on our unplanned lovemaking too, it was actually you who seduced me first, not the other way around!'

After a strained and overly long pause in conversation, Stewart and Peta retreated into silence, each into their own defensive corners. This uncompromising stand-off between them could well become a no-win battle, with no chance of a reprieve for either side. At a last-ditch effort to get beyond Stewart's stony silence, Peta was the one to speak first.

'Look, I'm sorry about my rash comment just now. About your seducing me, I mean. It was rash of me to say such a thing and totally uncalled for, I know. I just want you to stop for a minute, please, and try to understand my part in all of this, now, if that's at all possible?'

'I'm sorry too. I probably could have handled your unexpected arrival here a lot more diplomatically at the time.'

To Peta's inward relief, Stewart showed signs at last of backing down. Out of total frustration and also out of sheer habit, he ran his fingers through his already ruffled hair as he tried to get a grip on this awkward moment between them. 'Ha! You think?' Peta smiled at him and comically raised her eyebrows a few times. They stared at each other for a moment until their laughter bubbled to the surface. Any lingering tension in the room was finally broken. They kept their distance from each other for now, though.

'Okay, where do we go from here?'

Peta stood up to pace around the room, as she often did when solving problems. 'You probably haven't even realised this. When I was sent to Cairns on this assignment, the cost of my flight, my hotel and my hire car were all covered by my employer on the condition that when I returned, I delivered the goods in payment for their generosity. If I *haven't* done what I've promised to do, my employers are most likely going to either sack me or cast me out into the wilderness—as far as employment opportunities go, that is. I will never be trusted to interview anybody ever again!'

'You're right! I never gave a thought to your precarious situation in this whole drama at all,' Stewart offered sheepishly. 'I honestly feel compelled to apologise to you most sincerely now for being so damn selfish. I really have placed you in the worst kind of predicament now with your employers, haven't I?'

'Thank you, Stewart.' Peta breathed an audible sigh of relief. 'It means a lot to me for you to openly acknowledge this. Now maybe you can understand why I had to take a stand when you ordered me to leave yesterday?'

'I think it took real grit for you to stand up to my wrath the way you did. In fact, I'm going to request for you and only you to do all of my interviews from now on.'

'Yes, well, let's not get ahead of ourselves.' Peta smirked.

'To be perfectly honest, I'm still not all that wrapped in the idea of *this* interview, period! Please don't misunderstand me when I say that, though. It really has nothing at all to do with you this time. Yes, I know I have to go through this tiresome process of promoting myself as an author in order to promote my books. It's this whole intrusive thing of probing into my private life that I don't like. I find it very difficult to bare my soul even to friends and family, let alone the public. Do you know what I'm saying?'

'Yes, of course I understand. You have been put through the wringer with your divorce from Felicity. News of your failed marriage turned out to be a real media circus for a private person. That must have been very painful for you.'

'Yes, it was. In fact, it was a bloody nightmare! I don't ever want to go through that again.'

Peta didn't answer him for a few moments. She needed to think about what to say next.

'Let me reassure you. I don't work like that. I don't believe it's right for me to pressure you—or anyone for that matter—to reveal all of their juicy gossip. Especially when it comes down to sharing any private details you may be sensitive about. My approach would be to make up a list of questions I'd like to ask you, then let you read them through first. If there are any questions you don't feel comfortable with, I'll either remove them or ask you in some other way, so you feel more comfortable with me. If there is anything else you'd like to add at the end about your book, then we can certainly include your own input. No surprises, I promise.'

'Believe it or not, I want to trust you professionally. It's because of some sneaky editors that I don't always trust easily. They can change simple statements into something smutty. It seems to me, these kind of real-life stories are really all about selling lots of papers or magazines.'

'I promise you that Tess, my editor-in-chief, is not like that at all. She is ethical and aboveboard, otherwise I wouldn't want to work for her. By example, she inspires great journalism within us all. Her staff are extremely loyal to her and have been with her for years.'

'Fair enough. I believe you. So this Dominic who is coming out here this morning, is he the same as you? Ethical, I mean.'

'Let's put it this way. Dominic is an independent photographer who works for most of the major publishers, but if he was ever to step out of line with Tess, she just wouldn't hire him anymore. End of story. I can assure you that anyone who steps out of line with Tess—they're gone! There are no second chances with her—including me!'

'Okay, okay! Enough already!' Stewart chuckled, and held up his hands in defeat. 'You've totally convinced me. This editor of yours really should use you in advertising. You could probably sell palm trees to an islander.'

Peta had the good grace to smile and nod her head, while not necessarily agreeing with him completely.

'I give up!' Stewart threw up his hands in mock defeat. 'I guess that now you've sold me on the idea of this blasted interview, the least I can do now is to give you my go-ahead.'

Peta stared at him in disbelief. 'Did I hear you right? You're happy to do the interview? I don't believe it!'

'That's what I just said.' Stewart shrugged his shoulders offhandedly. 'It's a done deal!'

'Oh Stewart! How stupendous! You are so wonderful!' Peta jumped onto his lap and just about toppled them both off his chair. She rained kisses all over his face, finishing up on his lips. 'I am so, so very happy. You won't regret this, I promise!'

'Wow, I can't help but wonder now, if I'd agreed to this interview yesterday, and if you'd kissed me like this to start with, we'd be kissing each other a lot sooner.' Stewart came up for air from Peta's new onslaught of kisses. 'Nah! I think I like it better this way. It's so worth it for me to have kept you waiting just for these grateful kisses alone.'

'Ah! So my kisses sealed the deal, huh? Damn! Why didn't I think of this before? But then we would have missed all of those getting-to-know-you moments in your bathtub, right?'

'Damn right! Hold me closer, you sexy woman! This deal needs to be sealed some more.'

'Ah, I hate to be the one to put a damper on our sexy intentions right now, but let's not forget Dominic is supposed to arrive here soon. Don't you think he might be a wee bit suspicious if we don't open the door for him, with us still wrapped up in each other's arms?'

'Ah, yes! I did forget that for a moment. Damn it! Hang on a minute! Why did you tell Dominic to come on out here, when you knew I wasn't going to be happy about it?'

Stewart lifted her off his lap, fixing her now with one of his predictable piercing glares.

'Believe me, it wasn't my intention to be underhanded with you, Stewart. Please think about it for a minute. I couldn't very well tell Dominic not to come at all, could I? He would have been really pissed off with me, especially after flying up to Cairns for nothing. I just figured maybe I could work things out with both of you once he was here. Or something like that, anyway.'

'I must say, you took a real chance in doing that. What if I'd still refused to do the interview?'

'Of course I had no way of knowing if you would or not, but I was kind of hoping you would. And you did.'

'Yes, I did, didn't I? Lucky for you I'm not the ogre you made me out to be then.'

Peta smiled gratefully at Stewart. 'Lucky for me, indeed. Thanks again for being so understanding, and for trusting me enough to go ahead with the interview after all.'

'It's okay. I guess I'll just have to take it out of your hide later though.'

'Oh you will, will you?' Peta laughed happily. 'Hold that thought! In the meantime, though, I need to use your bathroom. I'll be back shortly. I promise.'

'Go ahead. I'll be in here, clearing away breakfast.'

Stewart stopped in his tracks and turned back before Peta disappeared from view. 'I just had a brilliant idea. Before this Dominic fellow gets here, we might just have time for a quickie.' Stewart hoped for Peta's enthusiastic response to his amorous idea, but she must have missed his last words since she was already in the bathroom with the door closed.

What was I thinking just then? That sexy minx has me so bewitched, I can't think straight anymore. I must be losing my mind! Whether I am though, I'll just have let her make it up to me later then. Man! Will I ever!

Stewart tidied his kitchen with a gleam in his eye and some wayward stirrings below his belt.

CHAPTER SEVEN

'*Morning, you must be* Dominic,' Stewart greeted Dominic at his front door. He even added a friendly smile to go with his firm, businesslike handshake. In turn, Stewart observed Dominic was much shorter than he imagined, but stocky in build, with a rather sparse covering of unfashionably long brownish hair crowning an already receding hairline. Stewart put his age at around mid-forties. Despite Dominic's rather outdated hippy appearance, he projected an air of professional self-assurance. If Stewart was not mistaken, he also detected Dominic's accent to be of a French-Canadian background, which he assumed attracted most women to him like a moth to a flame. Including Peta, perhaps? Stewart made a mental note to keep an eye on him.

'Yes, I am indeed, Mr. Fletcher. Delighted to meet you at last.' Dominic answered with a barely concealed look of surprise. He hadn't really expected Stewart's friendly greeting, especially considering his ongoing difficult reputation with the press.

'Please come on in. I've just been going over the questions Peta will be asking me during the interview. But where are my manners. First things first. Would you like some coffee, Dominic? I've just made a fresh pot.'

'That would be most welcome. Thank you!' Dominic enthused as he crossed the threshold, sidestepping Stewart, who held the screen door open for him. He spotted Peta with her laptop open on the dining table and headed straight towards her. Peta looked up as Dominic entered the room and stood up to greet him.

'Dominic! You made it! Did you have a good flight this morning?'

Peta gave him a quick friendly hug, but she withdrew when she noticed Stewart's outward appearance of friendliness towards Dominic's arrival managed to also project a piercing observation of the newcomer.

'I did have a good flight, thank you, Peta. Not too much turbulence this time, anyway.'

Stewart bought over a ceramic mug and the coffee plunger for Dominic. The plunger was full to the brim, emitting a strong, kick-arse aroma of freshly made coffee. Stewart prompted Dominic to sit, then filled his cup. 'Here you go, Dominic. Milk? Sugar? Help yourself.'

'*Merci*, but I always drink my coffee black and unsweetened.' Dominic took a careful sip of his steaming coffee. 'Mmm. This coffee is amazing! Hot and strong too—exactly the way I like it.'

Stewart waited until Dominic took a few sips of coffee before sitting down beside him and waiting for the right time to continue. When he could wait no more, he started questioning Dominic for answers he anxiously needed to ask. From across the other side of the table, he saw Peta stiffen and heard her quick intake of breath. Perhaps she anticipated an irate verbal attack towards Dominic, but Stewart could imagine her surprise when he spoke.

'Dominic, I hope you don't mind me asking you a question. It has nothing to do with the interview, but I'd really like to know—If you don't mind me asking, that is?'

'Certainly! I'll be happy to answer any questions you wish to ask,' Dominic replied in a friendly manner, but he threw a guarded look towards Peta. Dominic couldn't help but notice the anxious look on Peta's face. He didn't quite understand why yet, but he made a mental note to ask her about it later.

'I must say, Dominic, you being here has reassured me that your flight at least, was still able to land at the Cairns airport. I know you've been in Cairns for only a short while, but I'd like your honest opinion. From what you've observed already yourself, what do you think the overall damage of Cairns and the surrounding areas might be so far? Being an anxious local of this area, I'd really like to know.'

Peta's body relaxed almost immediately. She was able to finally release tension, which created havoc within her churned-up stomach; but at least she was able to put her mind at ease as to the real reason Stewart suddenly wanted to ask Dominic about something totally irrelevant to the interview.

This was hardly the time to sit on her laurels, though. There was still the interview to get through yet and even if Stewart *had* agreed to let it go ahead, he could still call a halt to it if he chose to. This was his home territory, after all.

'I can certainly understand your concern,' Dominic sympathised. 'Cairns City fared rather well I think, going on first impressions only, of course, and from what I could see below from my aircraft window. There were quite a few roofs that had been lifted off completely in some areas, but these were mainly beyond the city. Obviously, any buildings directly in the path of the cyclone have been affected the most. I also noticed quite a few vehicles have been lifted up and carried away, only to end up in some creek or waterway, far away from where they belong. Large trees seemed to have survived well, in and out of the city, but the smaller, unestablished trees looked to be flattened completely by the force of the wind. I'm no expert, but I think they will probably survive. Also, on my drive here, there was a lot of plastic garden furniture scattered all over the place too. Thankfully, I didn't see any dead animals at all. In one area, there were some Energex trucks diverting traffic on the main road, just beyond the city area, no doubt securing some loose power lines. From what I can see of your own place though, you seemed to have fared pretty well overall,' Dominic paused now to sip his coffee again, uncomfortably aware now of Stewart watching him intently. 'Did my answers help you at all?'

'What?' Stewart's answer was a bit snappish now. Despite his need to hear of storm damage on his property and beyond, Stewart found himself listening to Dominic's charming French accent instead and the effect he probably had on women overall—including Peta. Stewart snapped out of his brooding thoughts as if they'd never happened. He'd been caught out staring at Dominic and he knew it. The only thing he could do now was to brush off his embarrassment and move on. 'Yes well, thanks Dominic. It can be a challenge for most locals to face the cost of damages the morning after. From what you've just told me, we've managed to survive the negative side of our so-called idyllic, tropical lifestyle once again. Anyway, I do believe I have an interview to get through this morning, so let's just get this over with then. Shall we?'

Stewart threw his words back at Peta and Dominic in a clipped, businesslike manner as he headed casually over towards the kitchen with the depleted coffee plunger and empty mugs. He then set upon his task of rinsing off everything for now, crashing the mugs down on the dish rack with more noise than Peta thought necessary. She suspected

Stewart was deliberately making his presence known, so Dominic and herself knew without a doubt he wasn't too far away to hear their conversation.

Peta couldn't help but notice an undefinable knot of tension in the room again and sensed Stewart was once again on edge. He still wasn't too happy at all about this interview being set up in his home. Perhaps Dominic's arrival also reminded him he won't be able to worm his way out of the interview this time. She and Dominic looked towards each other while Stewart's back was turned. Dominic affected a silent groan, then rolled his eyes. Peta had no choice but to stifle a giggle before Stewart turned around again.

Despite his barely concealed displeasure, she realised any interview was always going to be a fearful process for such a private man, and she didn't want Stewart to think that either she or Dominic were making fun of him behind his back.

'Let me assure you both, I will be refreshing our coffee again in a little while.' Stewart sounded more lighthearted. 'You can never have too much coffee in the mornings. By the way, Dominic, I have set up a cleared space over here for you and your equipment. Will this work for you?'

'Please do not worry yourself about that, Mr. Fletcher. It's perfect. I can always add or take away any artificial lighting whenever I need to, anyway. I'm used to it. But speaking of equipment, if you will both excuse me, I still need to go grab my gear from my vehicle now. Be back soon.'

'Sure.' Peta nodded in agreement. 'Dominic, you and I can collaborate with any last-minute details together soon. Okay?' Dominic gave her a thumbs up and disappeared out the front door. 'Stewart, we'll go over your questions one more time now. You happy with that idea?'

'Now that you mention it, I'd like to discuss one of the questions with you, if I may?'

'Yes, of course. Let's sit down together and do this then while Dominic sets up his own equipment. Shall we sit in here or go out on the veranda?'

'I think the veranda would be better. It's not like I have anything better to do!'

Oh man! He's not happy at all. I just hope he doesn't walk out on me after all. That's all I need right now.

Stewart led Peta out onto his back veranda, which extended from just outside his kitchen window, all the way around to just beyond the bathroom and laundry door on the other side of the house. As Peta stepped out onto the veranda, she noticed with much delight, there was more than lush green tropical foliage all around her. There was also a stunningly plumed parrot nearby. It's feathers immediately captured Peta's attention with their vibrant tones of electric blue, verdant green and crimson red. The bird was perched on a rough wooden perch at the corner of the veranda, totally engrossed with its meticulous, daily ritual of cleaning one glorious feather at a time.

'Oh Stewart, what a gorgeous bird!' Peta inched closer to the bird, not wanting to frighten it away. 'I've never seen a wild bird up this close before. Male or female?'

Stewart came over and scratched the bird's head. 'Meet Oscar. My best friend, faithful companion and confidante all rolled into one. I named him after Oscar Wilde. He's a king parrot. Notice how much larger he is compared to other wild parrots. There's no need for you to worry about him flying away, though, is there, Oscar? He has never shown any signs of returning to his other fine feathered friends or to the call of the wild, so to speak. I rescued him from a heavy, thrashing storm a few years ago. He was a real mess and close to death at the time, but I somehow managed to restore him to his usual good health.'

Even though Peta knew she had to get this interview underway before Stewart changed his mind, she was still curious enough to question

Stewart more about Oscar now, 'So what happens to birds like Oscar during a tropical cyclone like I've just experienced for myself, Stewart? Do you keep him a cage somewhere safe during a cyclone?'

'No way! I tried keeping him in a cage once, but he became so stressed locked up inside the cage, I never tried it again. He is still a wild bird, after all, and always will be. I've noticed for myself, that most birds always know where to seek shelter from severe weather when they need to, which is usually deep down hidden within thick foliage, low leafy trees, or right up under roof eaves. Verandas, such as mine, help to keep them away from the direct force of the wind as well. Anyway, long story short, at the end of his convalescence, he either decided to stay put with me out of gratitude or he'd become so accustomed to a constant source of food that he decided to stick around with me for the long haul. Oh, and he loves wine too, by the way,' Stewart laughed.

'You're kidding me, right? A parrot that drinks wine? That's hilarious!' Peta laughed as well. 'How did that happen? I mean, when did you first notice Oscar going down this path of self-destruction?'

'At night I like to relax with a glass of wine before bed and often leave a small amount of wine in the bottom of the glass, which I'd forget to rinse out until the next morning.'

He grinned as Oscar leaned into the scratch.

'Oscar's natural curiosity must have got the better of him, so after I'd go back inside, he must have decided to check it out for himself. I never even realised he was into the dregs of my wine glass until I caught him red-handed with his cheeky beak in the glass. I don't think it does him any harm really and I wouldn't intentionally leave it here for him. I did try to warn him about the pitfalls of alcohol abuse, but he still continues to do it anyway. Wretched bird!'

'What a funny bird you are, Oscar.' Peta crooned to Oscar as she scratched his head with her pearly fingernail. Oscar responded by dipping his head so she could prolong his bliss even more. Oscar had no hesitation whatsoever in prompting this perfect stranger to continue his ecstasy by nudging her hand with his beak each time she pulled her hand away.

'Uh-oh! You fell for it! You might have to stay here forever now.'

'Funny bird! Funny bird!' Oscar loudly squawked and bobbed his head up and down.

'Ah! So you talk too, do you?' Peta laughed again. 'Oh, Oscar! What a big show-off you are!'

'Parrots are natural mimics, as you probably already know. He has another habit, which I have to admit, isn't at all that endearing to me. If I've been writing late at night when I can't sleep, Oscar still wants his breakfast at the usual time, so he starts pecking at my ears to wake me up. It can be so annoying at times!' Stewart chuckled. 'On the other hand, he is a damn good listener. When I'm in the editing stage of my manuscript, I always like to read it out loud. This way I can usually pick up on any obvious mistake I've completely missed.'

Stewart extended his hand towards Oscar for him to move onto his forearm.

'Oscar here, perches himself beside me and either listens intently or uses this time to preen himself. He never, ever interrupts though, do you, Oscar?'

'Good bird! Good bird!' Oscar screeched as he bobbed up and down again on Stewart's arm.

'You certainly seem to have a wonderful rapport with each other. As you said before, I imagine Oscar would have flown away long ago if he didn't like it here anymore. Who looks after him when you have to go away?

'I have a neighbour who looks after him for me. Leigh lives close by, and as a bonus, she also cleans my house for me once a week. Oscar really loves her, don't you, Oscar?'

Oscar bobbed his head in agreement, then without any apology, moved back over to his lofty perch where his seed supply awaited him. 'I think he's had enough of us humans for now. As I said before, he still is a wild bird in lots of ways. Anyway, enough of this crazy bird distraction for now. While Dominic is outside, we just have enough time for this,' Stewart pulled Peta in close against his hard body to tease her with a kiss deep enough to curl up her toes.

'Oh man! It's such a temptation for me not to rush you off to my bed and make wild passionate love to you. You must realise, sexy lady, that you're like a powerful sex drug to me now. I can't seem to get enough of you!'

Peta returned his kiss with equal passion, but then her sensibilities jolted her back to reality. She needed to be the one to pull away first, pushing her hands against his broad chest with much regret.

'Much as I would love to return to your bedroom with you, Dominic might be back any second now. We don't need him to see us in a passionate embrace, for now at least. To be perfectly honest, I really don't think we should tell anybody about what has happened between us. Not just yet anyway. Wouldn't you agree?'

'Unfortunately I have to agree with you, but that doesn't mean I have to like it,' Stewart groaned and immediately moved over towards the veranda railings with his back to Peta. 'I'll have you know, Ms. McKenna, you have created a very embarrassing predicament for me. Do you realise that I now have to hide an enormous hard-on from Dominic when he does return?'

'Oh dear!' Peta smiled wickedly. 'That *is* a problem for you, isn't it? But I promise I'll make it up to you later. In the meantime, I'm off to the bathroom to fix my make-up before Dominic catches on to what subject has really come up between us since he's been gone.' Peta ran a playful hand over Stewart's firm buttocks, then teased him with a featherlight kiss upon his mouth. Breathlessly, she whispered in his ear, 'Later, Mr. Fletcher. That's a promise.' After taking only a few steps away from him, she stopped and turned back again. 'By the way, what was that question you wanted to discuss with me. You know, in regard to the interview, I mean?'

'I lied.' He grinned. 'It was just an excuse to get you on your own. Will you forgive me?'

'That was very sneaky of you! But yes—I forgive you. Gotta go! See you back here soon, handsome.'

Stewart let out a ragged sigh and walked over closer to Oscar. While he attempted to adjust the bulge in his pants, he whispered, 'It's hard to believe, my feathered friend, that I've only known this woman for a day and already she has me tied up in knots. Hard to believe, isn't it, mate?'

Oscar turned his head sideways now. All the better to tune into Stewart's voice.

'I have to wonder now, what all the other days I spend with her will be like. Whatever happens though, mate, I think I'd like to stick around for a while to find out.'

By way of an answer, Oscar affectionately nipped at Stewart's ear in his usual approving way.

By the time Peta returned from the bathroom, she could see Dominic sitting at the table, already switched into work mode. Still in the process of signing into his laptop, Dominic looked up briefly to acknowledge Peta and gave her a quick wave before he continued logging in. His various selections of cameras and lenses were laid out beside him on the table, ready to go.

'Ah, Dominic! You're already back, I see. Shall we go over our individual notes first before I start the interview?'

'Sure thing. Come and sit beside me and we'll do that now. It shouldn't take too long. After all, we've both done this kind of procedure before, in one form or another.'

'Yes, absolutely.' Peta noticed Stewart was nowhere to be seen. 'Where's Stewart, by the way?'

'I've been out on the veranda,' Stewart answered her as he entered the room. 'I'm just heading into my office for a moment or two, then maybe I might even make us a fresh brew of coffee, if you like. I thought I'd also leave you two some space for about fifteen minutes or so while you go over your notes together. Will that be long enough for you?'

'Wonderful! Thanks, Stewart.'

Peta gave him a grateful smile, but he could tell she was already distracted by their task at hand. Stewart realised he'd have to get used to seeing a whole different side of Peta this morning. The professional side, that is. Regardless of what might happen between them, though, or what future they may have together, he needed to be damn sure of his feelings beforehand. He was determined to be extra careful this time around—not to give himself away so completely. To keep part of his heart intact for now, just in case. Stewart walked past them on his way to his office but stopped for a second to tell them, 'Just give me a hoy if you're ready for that coffee any earlier.' He didn't really expect any replies from either of them, and he was right. Peta and Dominic were already right into their technical discussion, so he left them to it. On his way out, though, Peta stopped him in his tracks.

'Oh, before you go, I forgot to give you these before.'

She handed him a few sheets of printed paper.

'These are the questions I will be asking you during the interview. If there are any questions at all that you have concerns about, put a question mark next to it and we will go over them together before we start. I meant to give them to you on the veranda before. That okay with you?'

'Sure thing. At least it will give me something useful to do while I'm in my office, won't it?'

Peta watched Stewart's back until he entered his office. His body was wired for a quick retreat. The moment he disappeared and was no longer within hearing range, Dominic stopped what he was doing.

'Correct me if I'm wrong,' Dominic whispered. 'But I seem to be getting this curious vibe from you and the mysterious *Monsieur* Fletcher. I'm not quite sure what to make of it.'

'What vibe do you mean?' Peta asked him in an offhanded, too-busy-to-talk tone.

'I could have sworn I sensed some kind of strange vibe between you.'

'Why on earth would make you think such a thing?'

'You did spend the night together after all, and my highly sensitive romantic radar is heading progressively faster towards the red danger zone. Tell me to mind my own business if you like, but I can't help but detect something sexual between you.'

Peta scoffed, 'You are being totally ridiculous and way out of line. Even if you are as intuitive as you say, you really are reading way too much into this. There is nothing between Stewart and me, so please can we get back to our work?'

Dominic persisted. 'If there is nothing going on between you, then how come you are calling Fletcher by his first name?'

'Well, if you must know, he asked me to. In case you've forgotten, we were forced to spend the night together alone in this house because of a raging cyclone. It would have been much too formal under the circumstances and at such a stressful time too, I might add, to still refer to each other as Mr. Fletcher or Ms. McKenna. Wouldn't you agree?'

'Yes well, I guess so, but I'll have you know my radar has never let me down in the past.'

No spoken words were necessary, by way of Peta's response to Dominic's so-called sexual radar. The sudden glare she fixed him with, followed by the stubborn set of her shoulders, was all the warning Dominic needed to back off. He had seen that look with Peta once before and knew without a doubt, there would be no more answers forthcoming. That didn't mean he'd give up entirely, but he was a professional and there was work to be done.

Stewart re-entered the room just as Peta and Dominic were wrapping up their side of things.

'Okay people, it's time to pump up our bloodstreams with more caffeine. Any takers?'

Peta and Dominic both put their hands up.

'Thanks for your understanding, Stewart.' Peta walked over towards the kitchen. 'Whenever we work together, Dominic and I always have to be on the same page, so to speak. Don't we, Dominic?'

'*Oui!* Indeed we do,' Dominic answered offhandedly, still distracted by his work.

'Not a problem. By the way, Dominic, I'd much prefer it if you could call me Stewart from now on, while you are in my home, at least. I don't believe in standing on formality out here in the country.'

Peta caught Dominic's eye with a smug, silent message. *I told you so!*

'*Merci,* Stewart. So I will from now on then.'

'So, Stewart,' Peta jumped in attempting to keep things on schedule. 'Are you are feeling more relaxed now? Are there any last-minute reservations you need to discuss with me?'

'I will always have reservations in regard to interviews, as you well know by now. Being a very private person, I'm never going to be comfortable with this whole process of baring my soul to *any* member of the press. But I know I have to if I want to promote any new book of mine. I feel sorry for my agent too because she has to always remind me of this fact. I must admit this time, though, I do feel a lot more comfortable with you. You both seem more like friends this time around, rather than the enemy. Until you hit on any touchy subjects, that is.'

Stewart's piercing stare made Peta squirm uncomfortably in her chair. *I'd better not stuff this up, then!*

One more glaring look from Stewart was enough to remind Peta that despite the memory of last night's loving, there were still some boundaries with Stewart she must never, ever cross.

'I get the message.' Peta flashed him a reassuring look of her own before continuing, 'I assure you, I am taking your initial reservations on board. Anyway, you already know what questions I'm going to ask you, so I hope our little talk beforehand has helped to ease your mind somehow. Besides, it can be a much more pleasurable experience for everyone concerned when we're more relaxed with each other to start with.'

'Before we do start,' Stewart said. 'I do have a concern about Oscar being just outside this room. He can let out a sudden loud squawk sometimes. Will that interfere with us taping this interview? I can throw a cover over him for a while, so he thinks it's night time. Until the interview is over, at least.'

'No, don't worry about Oscar outside. Even though I'll be taping this interview, it's mainly so I can go back over our questions and answers later. For legal reasons, too. The recorded tape will protect both you and I from any legal action down the track. I can also assure you that whatever I record here today will be kept strictly confidential. To ease your mind about Oscar, though, he can squawk as much as he likes because it won't make any difference. Do you think Oscar might distract you too much, maybe?'

'No, I don't think so. I'm used to him by now. Usually I can tune him out at any time.'

Peta breathed a sigh of relief. It was all systems go at last!

Dominic said, 'Pardon me for interrupting, but who is Oscar, if you don't mind me asking?'

Peta turned to Dominic and laughed. 'Sorry Dominic, while you were out at your car, we were on the veranda. Oscar is a gorgeous king parrot, who happily lives here, by choice, with Stewart. I'm sure Stewart will be happy to introduce you to him after the interview.'

'Ah! I will look forward to meeting him then. Please, let us continue with the interview.'

'Excellent! Then let's get started, shall we?' Peta looked over towards the sofa and back at the dining table. 'Stewart, would you prefer to sit over on the sofa or here at the dining table?'

'I think I'd prefer the sofa. These wooden chairs can be a bit uncomfortable after a while.'

'Yes, I agree with you. I can set up my laptop on the coffee table in front of me.'

'I have a long lead you could use now that we have the power back on,' Stewart offered.

'Yes, that would be the way to go. I'll take you up on that offer. Thanks.'

'No problem. I'll be right back,' Stewart said as he headed off to his office to get it.

Peta was on a roll now. 'Dominic, are you ready to go after I finish with the interview?'

'Absolutely! I'm happy to just sit here and enjoy this excellent coffee for now.'

Stewart was back with the power lead within minutes. In no time at all, the laptop was set up on the chunky wood coffee table, ready to go.

Here goes, girl! Peta pepped herself up one more time. *It's now or never, but if he should happen to get up and leave the room during this interview, I'll know I've failed miserably.*

Peta patted the empty space on the sofa beside her now and gave Stewart a reassuring smile. Despite Stewart's responsive smile and his sudden willingness to cooperate, Peta still found she needed to take a few deep breaths to help steady her already rattled nerves.

Why do I get the feeling Stewart suddenly looks like some helpless animal caught in the headlights of a vehicle?

CHAPTER EIGHT

Peta began her recorded interview with a quick recap for those readers who might not know who Stewart Fletcher is, or even what kind of books he wrote.

'When you think of famous literary action heroes what comes to mind to you as a reader? If you immediately think of Tyler Jackson, then you are just one of millions of readers around the world who have already discovered the adventures of this tough, loveable Aussie hero. Enthralled readers can't wait to devour each heart-stopping adventure of Tyler and his daring escapades, especially when Tyler rescues yet another strong-minded damsel in distress from the clutches of the wickedest villain around. At each journey's end, despite his no-frills, kick-arse brand of heroism, Tyler still wins our hearts so easily. Of course, any damsels in distress would only be too happy to be swept off their feet and into his bed without a moment's hesitation.

'What makes Tyler Jackson so different from all of the other action heroes out there? It seems even our own famous Crocodile Dundee or America's Indiana Jones can't compare to Tyler Jackson's smart quips or no-nonsense attitude once he springs from the pages of your book and right into your heart. Maybe the thought of a great page-turning book is what entices you into buying your first Tyler Jackson adventure.'

Peta grinned.

'According to popular opinion, the *Tyler Jackson* series is guaranteed to keep you turning those pages well into the small hours of the morning. That's if all of those positive book reviews are anything to go by. Two reviews that instantly come to mind are, "You simply cannot put it down until the very last page," and, "The literary prowess of Stewart Fletcher never fails to thrill my adventurous soul."'

Stewart shifted in his seat.

'*Today's Voice*'s exclusive feature story this month is all about Stewart Fletcher, the sole creator of the *Tyler Jackson* adventure series. We'll be taking a look into what it takes to stir up those way-out ideas within the creative soul of this author. What does the man himself like to do in his spare time when he's not busy creating another nail-biting *Tyler Jackson* escapade? Stewart Fletcher lives up in Far North Queensland, with Australia's Great Barrier Reef practically at his doorstep. He could live the high life anywhere in the world if he chose. Yet he prefers to live a quiet, uncomplicated life, happily hidden far away and surrounded by lush, tropical rainforest most of us can only ever dream of. So why does he, then? Well, why don't we let the man himself answer that question for us.'

Peta turned to Stewart, secretly relishing the fact that sitting beside her was the very same man who devoured her body throughout the night.

Do try to focus, Peta.

'Stewart, you pretty much have had the world at your feet for some time now with your highly successful *Tyler Jackson* series. So why *do* you prefer to live up in Far North Queensland, in such a remote area that is undoubtedly considered to be one of Australia's most inaccessible areas?'

Momentarily intoxicated by the nearness of Peta's body next to his, Stewart suddenly finds himself forced to somehow switch off his amorous thoughts back to the subject at hand, which in this case, unfortunately, was all about himself.

How is he supposed to concentrate on Peta's questions anyway, if all he wants to do is to carry her back to his bedroom and make mad passionate love to her?

'Stewart? Stewart? … Are you still with me?' Right at the very beginning of the interview, Peta already found herself having to bring back Stewart's attention from wherever he drifted off to just now.

She noticed immediately Stewart now appeared to be sitting somewhat awkwardly on the sofa. Finally, after a bit of an adjustment here and there, he was finally able to wriggle his body into a more comfortable position. Coincidently, a little bit closer towards Peta each time … She narrowed her eyes at him suspiciously, but he merely offered her a smile of pure innocence in return.

'Sorry! Just getting myself comfortable. Would you mind repeating that last question please?'

'Certainly!' Peta conceded, while giving Stewart the benefit of the doubt. She gave Stewart a suspicious look just the same, to let him know she was onto him. 'With my last question, I was just asking you, what sort of work ethic do you have for yourself and what's important to you when planning your daily creative hours at home?'

'Well, Peta, for most authors, myself included, to be seriously focused on their writing, they need an unlimited time frame in which to create a book from start to finish. We also need an unconditional personal space as well, with no interruptions during the writing process. I've discovered this for myself the hard way. Personally, I find it impossible to write freely within a noisy city environment. I've been there and done that in the past, but it doesn't work for me at all. My career as an author is very important to me. It's not just some job to make some money for myself. It *is* my life's work and my passion, so if it means shutting myself away for months at a time, then so be it.'

'I can understand where you're coming from. Stewart, you've been married twice before. Do you think the isolation you insist on contributed to you being single again these days?'

'Without a doubt. My first wife, Samantha, who is a very independent woman, has her own career as a highly valued art valuator to focus on, so she needed to be in constant touch with art galleries and independent artists. Sadly, we were both too caught up in our own careers for our marriage to work,' Stewart replied as he sneakily moved his leg over closer to Peta's, who in turn, was forced to move away imperceptibly to maintain her focus.

'Stewart, you've remarked in the past about how your first ex-wife took advantage of you right around the time the publicity surrounding your second marriage was happening. Do you still believe that to be true?'

'Well, it certainly hasn't done her any harm!' Stewart chuckled. 'To be fair to Samantha, though, she would have made a success of her career without me, anyway. She is a very talented lady in her own right.'

Stewart sneakily positioned his leg back against Peta's and smiled innocently at her. Every time Peta moved her leg away, Stewart still somehow managed to inch himself closer again. The warning flashes in her eyes for him to try and behave himself made no difference at all.

Damn it, Stewart! You're not making this easy for me!

'Yes, quite right, Stewart.' Peta cleared her throat before fixing him with her best, don't-mess-with-me look before continuing with the next question.

'So, Stewart, that leads us to your second marriage to well-known Australian actress, Felicity Cambria. Are there any thoughts you'd like to share with our readers about the demise of your marriage to Felicity?'

'Well Peta, I am sure you and your readers are fully aware by now of my very sordid, highly publicised divorce from Felicity.'

Stewart became serious now. The hidden, unspoken pain of his divorce fought to stay hidden.

'She and I have somewhat different memories of what went wrong with our marriage. I foolishly hoped my second marriage would work out better this time around and Felicity declared my isolated "shack" as she always called it, would be perfect for her privacy. However, she soon learnt that romance and reality are two entirely different things when it comes down to living up here on a day-to-day basis. In the end, she really came to hate it out here with a passion.'

'What about her claims to the press that you were, in fact, cruel to her?' asked Peta.

'Ha! I loved her very much, so there was no way I could have ever abused her physically. As for emotional cruelty, Felicity cited this as a reason for our divorce. I probably did seem cruel to her. After all, I did keep her isolated up here, away from her promising career, for a whole year. Felicity realised she was never going to be able to talk me out of leaving here. When I refused to move back down south again so she could pursue her lost career, that was pretty much the end of our marriage.'

Stewart stopped talking, suddenly realising he might be baring his soul a bit too much now. Perhaps even making himself out to be guilty of mistreating Felicity after all. He had completely forgotten for a moment that it wasn't just Peta he was talking to here, but all of her readers too. It was time to regain his confidence and get this interview back on track again. He paused to take a deep breath before continuing.

'In my own defence, I did try to be completely honest with Felicity. I foolishly believed she understood my need to have my own career, separate to her own highly publicised career. I am not trying to put myself in a good light here, but I truly believe Felicity was the one who is delusional when it comes to pointing the finger of blame. But I don't need to go there right now. I am fully aware Felicity currently resides in the United States and is presently in pursuit of her new overseas career connections as we speak. I do wish Felicity the very best for her latest adventures and I do hope she finally makes it on Broadway, Hollywood or whatever her current dream might be. End of story.'

Peta noted the change in Stewart's voice. He went from a casual chatty tone to a much sharper, uptight Stewart. If she hadn't witnessed his quick change of moods over the past twenty-four hours, she might have missed the signs altogether.

He's about to pull the pin on this interview any minute now.

If she didn't change tack soon, she'll lose his full participation altogether. It was time for her to steer him back into calmer waters for now. Besides, she now realised that the press have done this whole nasty Felicity saga to death.

'Let's move on then, shall we? So what's next for your reluctant hero? Will there be any more exciting adventures in store for all of Tyler's avid followers?'

'I am sure Tyler will have at least two more adventures in the future to keep his loyal followers happy for a while yet. I am presently pursuing an idea for another book series, which I hope my readers will find equally exciting. The protagonist will be completely different from Tyler of course, but rest assured everyone, Tyler will always stay my number one man.'

'Why do you feel the need to move beyond Tyler Jackson? After all, it was Tyler who made you famous, wasn't he? I mean, why not stick with what your fans are happy with?'

'As much as I truly appreciate what Tyler has done for my writing career, I firmly believe any writer worth their mettle should constantly try to reinvent themselves to stay ahead of the competition. To think creatively beyond our own self-imposed boundaries, to forge into the future and keep one step ahead of outdated ideas all the time. I think that goes for most people really, no matter what career path they take.'

'Speaking of the future, what of Stewart Fletcher, the man? What do you see happening in the future for him?'

'Ah yes!' Stewart's eyes lit up with enthusiasm. 'I suddenly do have some exciting plans in the pipeline.'

Stewart made sure he caught Peta's attention now as he gazed at her. She couldn't help but notice a glint of something undefinably mysterious in his eyes.

'I am really starting to believe life has taken a turn for the better, with maybe some new changes about to happen for me personally. I can feel it in my bones, so stay tuned for further developments.'

'That's wonderful, Stewart. Our readers and I look forward to reading about this next chapter in your own life. Perhaps this time next year, we can catch up with you again?'

'I feel confident enough to say for now, you can count on it!' Stewart fixed Peta with a knowing look, leaving her with no reason for doubt as to the true meaning of his last statement.

Heaven help me!

Goosebumps were suddenly on a rampage up and down her body. This complicated man now had her under his spell, and there was no escape. It left her wondering if she could ever go back to being the woman she was yesterday. The Peta of yesterday would have been immune to his obvious charms. This new Peta, however, tingled with eager anticipation over his slightest touch. Peta sent him a silent message of her own.

Looking right back at you, lover. The feeling is definitely mutual!

But first, she needed to focus on her task at hand and wrap up this interview.

'Thank you, Stewart, for talking with us today. It's not always easy for anyone to open up one's private life, let alone someone in the public eye all the time. Our readers are well aware you are an intensely private man and for good reason too, considering what you've just shared with us. From my own professional point of view, I know our readers always prefer to know the real truth behind any newsworthy headlines. Unfortunately, fabricated rumours are far too common within the social media network of today. We at *Today's Voice* believe it is our responsibility to inform our readers of both sides of someone's personal story. Especially when they have been unjustly and unfairly portrayed as the villain by the media in general.'

'Thank you, Peta. As you already know, I have had some rather heated run-ins with some rather unscrupulous journalists in the past. I appreciate your understanding of my previous reluctance to cooperate fully with any representatives of the press.'

'Thank you again for your honesty and candour today. I'm sure our readers will all agree with me on that point too. Thank you also, for allowing Dominic, our photographer, and myself into your private sanctuary today. With Stewart's kind permission now, we're going to share with you an exclusive glimpse of Stewart Fletcher's own writer's retreat right in the middle of a tropical rainforest. It doesn't get any better than this. Having said that, I hope our readers will understand why we can only show you a glimpse of the inside of Stewart Fletcher's home. As you are all fully aware, with Stewart being such a private man, we still need to respect his personal wishes at all times. Before we finish up, was that a definite "yes" for a further update of your life this time next year?'

'I don't see why not.'

Stewart answered her with his devilish trademark smile, guaranteed to curl up her toes. He continued on as if he was totally unaware of his effect on Peta.

'Anyway, who knows what might happen between then and now? A lot can happen in just one year, wouldn't you agree?'

He looked directly into her eyes now with a hidden promise meant for her only. Peta faltered for a moment but managed to regain her professional composure just in time.

'Yes, I'd have agree with your last statement wholeheartedly. You just never know what surprises might lie ahead for each and every one of us.'

'Whew!' Peta smiled at Stewart and breathed an obvious sigh of relief. Whatever rampant sexual feelings she might be experiencing, she still needed to maintain her professionalism. Regardless of Stewart's powerful effect on her, she was fully aware that Dominic was still in the room, looking over her way with a knowing smirk on his face.

'Thank you so much, Stewart. I know it can't have been easy with some of my more challenging questions towards the middle there. Do you feel better now that it's all over?'

'It wasn't as bad as I thought it would be,' was Stewart's reply.

Stewart, still aware of Dominic nearby, pulled himself together with no outward hint of his inner turmoil. He wanted to take Peta in his arms and kiss her madly, so he concentrated on answering Peta instead. 'I must say, your overall sensitivity and your professionalism certainly did help to create a much more relaxed atmosphere for me. I find myself somewhat in awe of the way you handled the whole experience as you did. You are my idea of the consummate professional.'

'Thank you, Stewart. Your encouragement means a lot. I don't know about you, but I am just so relieved it all went well right to the end for you and me both. Having said that, I still need you to hang onto those good feelings for just a bit longer. It's time for Dominic to work his own kind of magic now, before we're finally able to pack this whole interview process away, for another year at least. He still needs to capture a few random natural shots of you. It won't take that long, I promise. Then you'll be free to relax completely. You okay with that?'

'Sure, I just need a make a pit stop first.'

'Of course, go ahead.'

Stewart walked awkwardly when he headed for the bathroom. As he passed by her, and with Dominic distracted with his cameras, Stewart whispered into Peta's ear, 'I seem to have a problem in my pants again, thanks to your closeness on the sofa. I find myself having to hide my very obvious erection from Dominic again. I hope you're satisfied, you sexy wench. Look out when I get you alone again!'

Peta stifled a delighted laugh as she compulsively pinched his buttocks as he walked away. Peta looked to see where Dominic was before whispering back, 'I'll be ready and waiting!'

Stewart re-entered the room, all relaxed again. His previous dilemma obviously a thing of the past. 'Now that we have the first part of this whole interview process out of the way, how about I go make us some fresh coffee? You both up for that?'

'*Merci,* but honestly, during the interview, I finished off the last of the coffee in the plunger, so I think I am all coffeed-out for now. I wouldn't mind a glass of water instead, if you would be so kind.'

'I feel the same, Stewart,' Peta broke in. 'A glass of water for me too, please.'

'That's fine with me. One jug of water and some glasses coming up. Be right back.'

While Stewart was in the kitchen, Dominic took this opportunity to sidle on over towards Peta.

'I was right! There is something going on between you two isn't there?'

Peta glared at Dominic now, reducing his whispered suspicions to mere ashes of burnt rubbish with one look.

'Once again Dominic, you're way off the mark and I'll thank you to leave it at that. Do I need to remind you that we are both professionals? So any sordid suspicions of yours at this moment are totally inappropriate.

After we are done here, Dominic, I'll be more than happy to talk to you about other things, but we have a job to finish off first.'

'*Oui,* Peta. You are right, of course, and I'm sorry if I've upset you. I promise I will back off for now.' Dominic lowered his head with mock shame, but then smiled slyly as he added, 'I must warn you though, Peta, my dear, this conversation is far from over. Regardless of you how you try to convince me otherwise, I know I'm right!'

Peta ignored Dominic's obvious threats by changing the subject back to their task at hand. 'So, how do you think the interview went? Was there anything I could have done better? Were the questions appropriate enough for Stewart, do you think?'

Taking the hint, Dominic switched back into work mode at last, 'No, I don't think you missed any important questions at all. Overall, I think it all went very well. You sounded very professional and I'm sure Tess will be more than happy with the end result.'

'Do you really think so? You know I always value your professional feedback. I'm sure Tess will be happy with your side of things, too. I guess we won't know for sure until she has a chance to go over everything more thoroughly back in Sydney.'

'I don't think you have anything to worry about, Peta. She's going to love it!'

'Thanks, Dominic.' Peta smiled gratefully. 'You've eased my mind considerably.'

'Well, I always try to speak the truth—especially from a professional point of view. If I thought you could have done better, I wouldn't hesitate to tell you so. When you stop to think about it, Peta, if you should happen to mess it up, it also reflects on me, too.'

'Point taken. So getting back to our joint venture, I think I'll leave you with Stewart to work your own kind of magic now. In the meantime, I think I'll head out onto the back veranda for a short while to relax and keep Oscar company.'

'Ah yes, Oscar the bird!' He glanced towards the back of the house, to catch a glimpse of him.

'You are indeed in for a treat. Follow me.' Peta headed for the back screen door, already talking about Oscar as she walked past Dominic. 'Stewart rescued Oscar from a rather nasty storm a few years back. He's still a wild bird, of course, and could fly away any time he wants to, but he seems to prefer to stay here these days. It probably has something to do with the red wine, I suppose,' Peta laughed. 'I still can't get over that!'

'You mean the parrot drinks wine? You're making a joke, right? I've never heard such a thing!'

'Well Stewart says so and sometimes, he even gets drunk, too! Who would've believed it?'

'Interesting!' Dominic mused. 'I wonder if he would like to try some champagne then?'

'You wonder if who would like champagne?' Stewart asked as he joined them on the veranda, bearing a pitcher of iced water and three glasses, intrigued by Dominic's question.

'Your parrot. Peta has just told me about Oscar liking red wine. I was wondering if perhaps he would like to try some champagne too?' Dominic explained with a questioning smile.

'He probably would, being the featherbrain that he is!' Stewart laughed. 'Unfortunately for Oscar, though, apart from a little red wine or even some chilled beer at sunset, there's never usually any champagne out this way for him for him to even try, really.'

'Well, Oscar's sobriety can wait for now,' Peta said. 'It's time for Dominic to work his magic now. In other words, it's time for you two to shoot some photos.'

As Dominic directed Stewart into various poses all around the old house,

Peta took this opportunity to study Stewart without fear of being caught out by Dominic.

What a sexy man Stewart is!

It was hard for her to believe he'd been single for over a year. She wondered if he knew just how good looking was. He seemed oblivious to his latent sexual power. She didn't think he was even aware of the hungry looks from women who unashamedly drooled over him. Or even how women, regardless of age, fantasised about him shamelessly—about what they'd like Stewart Fletcher to do to them, or even if he was available to 'park his shoes under their bed'. Well, she could assure those other women Stewart Fletcher is the real deal. His latent sexiness is not just on the outside. She could vouch for that. Nor would she add such a personal revelation into print. This will remain her own delicious secret forever. He knows how to satisfy a woman, that's for sure. She could vouch for that, too. Peta wondered why Felicity Cambria could have tossed him aside as easily as she did. Stupid woman!

Peta sighed. What will happen once this interview is over? Will he want to see her again or will it just be, 'Thank you, Ms. McKenna, for a wonderful time.' Or maybe, 'Thank you, Ms. McKenna. I had a really great time last night. We must do it again some time.'

She might just shrivel up inside if Stewart was to dismiss her so easily from his life after last night and early this morning. Maybe she *was* just a playful diversion to him. Merely a welcome distraction from a raging storm outside his tropical hideaway. Whatever excuse he might come up with to push her aside, Peta realised Stewart doesn't really need some desperate, clingy female in his life. Maybe she should be the one to pull away first. Let him get back to his solitary life after all. That really might be for the best.

Peta snapped out of her confused thoughts when she spotted Dominic and Stewart shaking hands, signalling an end to their photo shoot. Despite her reservations about Dominic's threats to get the truth out of her, she can't help but be amazed at Dominic's ability to get his own job done so efficiently once he got started. She always admired the way he made beautiful people become even more beautiful through his magical lenses.

Peta drew in another sharp breath and squared her shoulders. It's reality time! Time for her to go back inside, pack up and say their final goodbyes. Such a pity! She would have liked to have known Stewart a whole lot more.

But her resolve to end their short-lived affair was the only way really.

'Peta? Are you still out there? We're finished,' Dominic said from the living room.

'Yes, I'm coming!' Peta called back as she re-entered the room. Her eyes locked briefly with Stewart's. It was hard to read what was on his mind just now, but hopefully they might get a chance to talk alone at least. Maybe once Dominic has left the house to pack his gear into his hire car. 'How did it go, Dominic? Did you get all the shots you think you'll need at this time?'

'*Oui!* Of course! I am sure we both have everything we need for next month's issue. I think it all went very well on the whole. What about you, Stewart? Do you have any other concerns?' Dominic replied.

'No, Dominic. It was all relatively painless for me, as interviews go. Much better than what I have endured in the past anyway. Especially when some TV reporter sticks a microphone in my face and rattles off a whole heap of personal questions for me to answer on the spot. I hate that sort of thing with a passion! Peta, your way of letting me go through the questions beforehand will always be a much better process in my mind. No hidden surprises for all concerned.'

'I'm so glad, Stewart.' Peta gave him a relieved smile. Their eyes locked together across the room. It was Stewart who broke their connection first this time.

'Dominic, would you like one last coffee before you go? I'm just about to make a fresh brew?'

'*Merci*, Stewart, but I really must still say no again unfortunately. I still need to pack up my gear and head on back to the hotel to go over my shots for today,' Dominic paused for a moment with his packing up to turn to Peta standing directly behind him. 'What about you, Peta? Will you be ready to follow me back to our hotel soon?'

Peta was momentarily lost for words. How could she find even five minutes to talk privately with Stewart, if Dominic insisted she follow him into Cairns right now?

While she struggled to come up with some sort of excuse to stay, Stewart intuitively came to the rescue.

'Oh, I see. You both plan to leave at the same time then? Damn! I missed my opportunity to ask Peta if she wouldn't mind hanging back a bit longer, so we could go over some parts of the interview one more time. Just to make sure I'm completely happy with my answers.'

Stewart looked directly at Peta as he waited for her reply. His eyes reflected a look of anticipation that perhaps, maybe, she *might* want to stay behind. Peta could have kissed Stewart for rescuing her, but with Dominic still hanging around, there was no way she was going to do that. Instead, she merely nodded her head with a decent level of professional enthusiasm.

'Oh. I suppose I could stay on for a bit, if you really need me to. After all, I did say we could do that if you had any concerns, didn't I?' After what Peta hoped was a convincing pause for thought, but still avoiding direct eye contact with Dominic, Peta gave Stewart her final answer, 'Okay, let's do it then, while it's fresh in our minds. So Dominic, would you like to go on ahead and I will follow you back to the hotel as soon as I finish up here?'

Dominic glanced from Peta to Stewart with a suspicious look, 'Yes, of course, Peta. By all means, do what you have to do. I'll head off now and leave you to go over those questions with Stewart.'

The look Dominic directed towards Peta spoke volumes, but luckily his carefully spoken words sounded harmless enough to Stewart.

'Great!' Stewart smiled innocently at them both. 'I'll leave you two to sort through your gear together and in the meantime, I think I will just head into the kitchen and tidy up a bit. By the way, Peta, would you prefer a glass of juice instead of coffee?

'Yes, I would love that. Thanks, Stewart.' Once Stewart was back in the kitchen, Peta whispered offside to Dominic, 'I'll try to be as quick as I can.' Peta threw Dominic a tentative smile, hoping he'd be okay with her staying back for whatever reason. Dominic barely nodded his head in acknowledgement, but he never smiled back.

'Sure! You do what you have to do, Peta.'

Peta stared at Dominic. Why was Dominic looking so despondent all of a sudden and why did she get the feeling he was acting like a wounded little boy? *Strange!*

Within fifteen minutes Dominic was packed and ready to say goodbye to them.

'*Merci*, Stewart, for allowing us into your home today. It's been a real pleasure.'

'Likewise, Dominic. Have a safe trip back to Cairns.' They shook hands in polite friendship.

Lastly, Dominic turned to Peta now and gave her a quick hug. 'I will see you soon.'

'Yes, you will, Dominic. I promise! Bye for now!'

Without warning, Dominic whispered slyly into her ear, 'Please behave yourself and do try to remember your professionalism at all times … while you still can.'

Dominic drove off, leaving Peta with a niggling, guilty feeling over his parting words. It was clear nothing got Dominic's attention more than undercurrents of the sexual kind.

CHAPTER NINE

'*Ah, at last he's* gone!' Stewart grabbed Peta from behind as she stepped back inside his front door. He spun her around playfully to face him. 'I never thought he'd ever leave.'

'What on earth do you mean?' Peta questioned innocently as she attempted to duck out of his way. 'I didn't think Dominic took that long to leave. You were just impatient to be rid of him for your own reasons, that's all,' she evaded his outstretched arms, then somehow managed to escape his clutches at the other side of the dining table as well.

'Why are you trying to avoid me, woman?' Stewart laughed the laugh of an evil, diabolical villain, then lunged for her across the table, but Peta was too quick for him yet again. 'You cannot escape me, luscious lady. I have you in my power!'

'Stewart! Stop!' Peta flitted away from him for the third time, all the while laughing at his mad antics to chase her around the room.

Oh boy! If only his loyal fans could see him now.

'We really do have to talk!' She needed to make him see sense before it was too late.

'Talk? Who wants to talk? There's no time for talk. I just want you in my bed. You've kept me waiting long enough. Come to me, you temptress, you!'

'Stewart!' she squealed as she ducked out of his way again. 'What's got into you? You're crazy! Oh man! What have I got myself into?' Peta couldn't help laughing despite her need to get serious. Dominic could make things difficult for her if he had a mind to contact Tess with some damaging report about her unprofessionalism. Distracted, she was caught off guard when Stewart lunged for her again.

'Ha-ha, got you, you slippery wench!'

'Stewart, you sneak!'

She chuckled as she struggled to escape his firm hold, but couldn't resist asking him her next question despite already knowing the answer, 'So, what do you plan to do with me now that you finally have me in your clutches?'

'That's easy to answer. This is what I have in mind.' He found her lips and kissed her with a passion to melt every last shred of resistance from her body.

'Oh, Stewart. Damn it! You really shouldn't kiss me like that,' Peta gasped after she managed to come up for air. 'What are you doing to me? I literally feel all weak at the knees.' Despite her resistance, she still continued to respond to his kiss with equal fervour.

'Stay with me this afternoon,' Stewart whispered seductively in her ear. 'You know you want to.'

'No, I can't!' Peta declared quickly as she finally came to her senses. She pushed hard on his chest to get his attention. 'We really do have to talk. *Please.* It's really important you listen to me now.'

When Stewart caught the serious tone in Peta's voice, he stopped kissing her and pulled right back. He definitely didn't look happy with this sudden turn of events. Not at all.

Oh boy! He's really pissed off with me now. Hell's bells!

Peta knew she needed to lay all her cards on the table, say what she needed to say, then see where they went from there. Either way, she'd be in the bad books with him.

I may as well just get it over with.

'Alright then, I'm listening!' Stewart moved away from her to the other end of the sofa and folded his arms defensively. 'What could be so important that we have to put a stop to whatever is happening between you and me? You were okay with our kisses up until now. You led me to believe, before Dominic arrived, that everything would be fine between us again if I agreed to do the interview after all. I did that, and now you're telling me it's goodbye?'

Suddenly rendered speechless, Peta stared at him for a moment and drew in a deep breath, 'Do you honestly *still* believe I had already planned to seduce you when I came here? Just for the sake of this damn interview? Give me a break! Do I have to remind you that less than twenty-four hours ago, it was *you* who seduced me first!'

'True,' he conceded sheepishly. 'But as far as I could tell, you were definitely willing to meet me all the way at the time.'

'Yes, I most definitely was, Stewart. You already know that. I wanted you just as much as you wanted me. What's the crime in that, anyway? We both know by now it was a mutual attraction from the start. We can both agree on that at least … Right?'

'Yes, I can, believe it or not. So, what's your point?'

'The point I am trying to make is that if I stay here with you now, I could lose my job just the same as if I went back home with no interview at all. Not everything is all about you!' Peta stopped for a minute when she realised her voice had risen somewhat in frustration now. She took a few stress-saving breaths and continued, 'You seem to have forgotten I was *paid* to interview you today. My boss put a damn lot of trust in me, when she gave me this assignment too—as you well know! In return for her trust and faith in me, I made a promise to her that I could be relied on to get the job done. What kind of message would I be sending to her if I stayed on here with you now? It would be like me telling her, "To hell with you, Tess! This opportunity you've handed me on a silver platter means nothing at all."'

Stewart's face flushed with guilt. 'Okay, okay! Point taken. I'm sorry I jumped to conclusions so easily about you. I realise now I've been behaving like a real bastard. You're absolutely right, it's not always about me. I was selfishly expecting you to choose between me and your job and it isn't fair of me at all to put you in this position at all.' Stewart moved back closer to Peta and reached out for her hand, 'I really am sorry, Peta. Can you ever forgive me?'

Peta's eyes glistened with tears. Her tense shoulders sagged at last with a real sense of relief. Stewart was happy to see her smile again. He hated seeing that miserable and torn look on her face. Especially after he'd verbally attacked her yet again.

'Of course I forgive you, Stewart. This feeling between us has been like a roller-coaster ride so far and totally unexpected for both of us. I do want to stay with you—believe me, I do—but I know I wouldn't be able to live with myself later if I gave into my own wanton desires for you now. The reality for me is I really do have to go back into Cairns *very* soon. If I don't, Dominic will report back to Tess that I failed to follow through on protocol with our assignment as promised. My professional reputation won't mean a thing anymore and I have worked too hard to allow that to happen, without a second thought of the consequences, if I should decide to follow my heart instead of my head right now.'

'Yes, I fully understand what you mean now. As you already know, I too have had people in my past who have tried to manipulate me and try to bend me to their will and I didn't like that feeling one little bit.' Stewart entwined his fingers through hers.

'How do we get around this problem? You know I want to stay with you, but you also know that I can't. Well, not today anyway.'

Stewart slapped his leg and stood. 'I think I may have a brilliant idea.

In fact, I think it is so brilliant, you'll probably be kicking yourself that you didn't think of it first.'

Stewart grinned and raised his eyebrows a few times, like a magician about to reveal his most amazing trick ever. Peta chuckled at his wackiness.

'Well, perhaps you could share your brilliant idea with me now. Then I can tell you whether I think you really are as smart as you *think* you are.'

'Oh I will, my dear, I promise, but to make this work, I have to ask you a question first. When do you have to be back in Sydney?'

'I have to be back in Sydney by tomorrow at the latest. Why's that?' Peta answered, intrigued as to what Stewart was up to. She still hadn't cottoned on to his brilliant idea yet.

'My idea all rests on your next answer now. Were you supposed to fly back with Dominic on the same flight?'

'No. Dominic operates under entirely different rules to me. Being a freelance photographer and even if he is under contract with *Today's Voice*, he works for other publications too. He has to leave here tonight to be in Canberra to start his next job first thing tomorrow morning.'

'Perfect! Which means you will be all alone at the Ocean Breeze tonight then?'

Peta's face beamed as his idea finally took hold. 'Oh! You sneaky man!' She laughed out loud, 'I understand what you're up to now, no pun intended. There's only one problem. My room is booked under my name only, but an invoice will be sent directly back to my employer probably the day after I leave. Don't you think my editor-in-chief might be a wee bit suspicious when she sees another person added onto my itemised account for tonight's stay?'

'Ah, but this is why my idea is so brilliant, you see? What if I was to also book into your hotel for tonight, in a separate room, of course, and as close to your own room as possible? Which means for appearances sake, you still get to keep your private room as arranged, but it also gives you the option to come and visit me during the night. If you still want to, that is?'

Peta squealed with delight as she stood to hug Stewart. 'I take back all the doubt I ever had about your absolute brilliance. As you said before, I'm kicking myself I didn't think of it first. Anyway, it doesn't matter whose idea it was, because I do believe we have finally found a solution to our immediate problem, haven't we?'

'Yes, we have indeed!' Stewart kissed her deeply now until, with a twinge of guilt, they both pulled away at the same time, aware at last that time had slipped away since Dominic left them.

'I have to go,' Peta said. 'Dominic will be suspicious if I don't turn up soon, and I know for a fact he already is. He hinted to me as much when he left, so if I don't make an appearance soon, his romance radar will peak into the red danger zone.'

'Well, you'd best go then, you wicked woman! I will not allow you to tempt me anymore. Begone with you before I change my mind and ravish your body until there's nothing left of you.'

Giggling like a schoolgirl now, Peta attempted to squirm out of his arms again. Despite their pact to cool their passions for now, Stewart still couldn't resist trying to waylay her just a bit longer. When she realised his sneaky plan, she laughed with glee and triumphantly managed to escape his strong, muscled arms before rushing into the bathroom and closing the bathroom door.

I swear he really is a bloody genius!

Peta smiled to herself as she washed her hands and freshened her make-up. Hopefully, his plan would work, and they'd have one more night together. Who knew what will happen after that? She needed to be completely honest. This new relationship with Stewart seemed almost too good to be true. She couldn't help feeling something would burst their bubble. It had happened to her before, and she didn't want to go through that again. Memories of her previous relationship sprang to mind. Yes, she'd been hurt before but realised there was no contest between her ex and Stewart. Justin was too much of a wanderer in more ways than one. Justin was so damn immature, whereas Stewart, being only five years older than her, was so much wiser than Justin could ever be. He tried to recapture what they had at the beginning of their love affair when he realised he was going to lose her, but for Peta, it was already too late by then. There is a lot to be said for maturity in a man. Even though they parted as friends, it left a sour taste in Peta's mouth just the same.

Her feelings for Stewart over the past twenty-four hours promised to be like a brand-new start for her at last. As Peta stared at her reflection, she knew for sure in her heart, as impossible as it sounded, she was already deeply in love with Stewart. What she wasn't so sure about was how can they possibly find time for each other, let alone continue following their own careers? If that isn't enough of an obstacle, the fact that he lived here and she lived in Sydney made their relationship damn near impossible.

What was I thinking of, even getting involved with Stewart in the first place? Bloody hell!

She scoffed at her reflection, stopping her runaway thoughts dead in their tracks. Despite all these complicated pitfalls with Stewart, she was still willing to give this new feeling a go, anyway. If there is one thing Peta knew for sure, there are no guarantees with any relationship. If she was to be gifted by fate with one more night of loving with Stewart, then what a fool she'd be to waste such an opportunity.

Peta took one last look at her rearranged hairstyle. She'd tied her long tresses into a tidy ponytail, which trailed down her back, then finished up with a light touch of a soft pearl-toned lip gloss. Satisfied, she opened the bathroom door, then paused to take one last look around before leaving, remembering with a smile their forced bathtub retreat from the horrors of a full tropical cyclone. This room saved their lives last night, and apart from its obvious protective value, it also allowed hidden passions between them to surface. On her way out, Peta grabbed her carryall and computer bag off the dining room table and headed for her hire car.

Before heading down the veranda steps, Peta turned around and took one last look at Stewart's front door. The same door that had almost barred her from her intended mission of passing through the door to get what she came for.

How can it be that within a space of nearly twenty four hours, her life has completely changed course?

Later tonight, she plans to be entwined with Stewart's body, behind another kind of closed door at the Ocean Breeze Hotel in Cairns.

Life sure can be a wonderful mystery at times.

Peta laid her laptop bag and carryall on the back seat of her hire car. On the front passenger seat, she picked up the now stale remains of yesterday's lunch of wrapped sandwiches and handed them to Stewart to dispose of for her. She was all ready to go. Professionally, at least—but when it came down to it, she found it almost impossible to leave Stewart now that she'd finally found him. One simple goodbye peck on the mouth led to many deeper, meaningful kisses from Stewart, as his hands wandered tantalisingly from the middle of her back to settle on her full breasts. Stewart fondled her breasts by slipping his hands inside her open-necked shirt while they kissed. Peta groaned with intense pleasure as Stewart tweaked her nipples—just in case she hadn't got the message by now that he was once again raring to go.

Peta was only too aware of his sneaky plan to entice her enough to stay here with him instead. His plan seemed to work because she felt completely powerless to stop him. She could barely resist his kisses anymore, let alone try to push him away. Not that she wanted to. If she was honest, she wasn't trying hard at all. Despite not knowing how to stop this tide of passion between them, she fixed him with a knowing smile, letting him know that the feeling was mutual. Like two irresistible forces coming together, they couldn't seem to keep their hands off each other and both were reluctant to let go of this feeling, even for only a few hours. After many, many teasing kisses later, Peta finally broke away.

'This is ridiculous, Stewart. I really do have to go! You are making it impossible for me to leave, you wretched man!' She thumped his chest as she half-heartedly pushed him away from her.

'But I don't want you to leave at all. I feel like you have already been in my life forever. How will I ever survive until tonight?' Stewart reached for her, but Peta dived into her car before he could waylay her one more time. Peta smirked, 'I'm sure you will manage perfectly well without me, for a few hours at least. Speaking of tonight, what time do you think you will be in Cairns?'

'Can't wait either, huh?' Stewart leaned playfully into the car towards her lips again.

'Really, Stewart, please tell your friend down south to behave himself if he can,' she laughed. 'Now, if you will be so kind, please answer to my last question,' Peta demanded.

'Okay, okay! How about I get into the passenger seat next to you? Then I can give you my full attention. I am sure you remember that old line, "All the better to hear you now, my dear."'

'Oh no! I don't think so,' Peta scoffed. 'No way! I know what you're up to. Listen, I think Dominic will leave for the airport around eightish at the latest. You could plan to arrive at the hotel sometime after 9 pm maybe?'

'I shall be there, come hell or high water, hopefully with no more cyclones either.'

'Heaven forbid! Okay, that's all settled then! I'd better go before you can distract me again.'

Peta started the engine, blew Stewart a quick kiss, and headed for the main road. Whatever happened tonight would be in the hands of fate.

What she failed to remember, though, as she happily sang along to a song on the radio, was how fate could be so cruel sometimes.

CHAPTER TEN

As peta drove back into Cairns, her mind was abuzz with the activities of the past few days. She listened to the radio as she drove closer to the palm-lined city of tropical Cairns. When some twangy country and western song started playing, she switched it off, no longer in the mood for any kind of music or some radio DJ babbling on. Her own thoughts zinging around inside her head were more than enough to keep her occupied. Yesterday, there'd been a raging cyclone. Last night she'd embarked on a love affair with the sexiest man on the planet who happened to be *the* author of the moment, if not for the whole year. AND there might be a career-changing interview with this man, too.

Once Dominic was gone, they'd spend some more quality time together. It was almost impossible to believe it happened to her in such a short time. If these life-changing events could happen in just two days, imagine what the rest of her life might be like? In the meantime, she hoped she was ready to face the invasive onslaught of Dominic's less-than-subtle innuendos and inevitable prying questions back at the hotel. She was ready for him, though. She was even prepared to stare him down if needed. Like they say in those spy movies; fear is not an option.

Peta knocked on Dominic's door once she'd showered in her own room, her intention to wash away any lingering scent of Stewart's aftershave on her skin. Dominic opened his hotel room door wide for Peta to enter.

'Ah Peta, you're back at last!'

'Hi Dominic!' Peta breezed past him. 'Before we get into work mode, do you have something cold and refreshing to drink in your fridge? Nothing alcoholic.' With her intention to keep her conversation with Dominic light and breezy for now, Peta made a point of glancing around his suite. 'Great room, by the way. Similar to mine in its layout, but somewhat different in its colour and decor.'

'*Oui!* It is a wonderful room, I must say. A lot bigger than some of the rooms I have stayed in, that's for sure. Not that I will have a chance to stay here now, mind you. Especially with this latest photographic assignment in Canberra first thing tomorrow morning. Life is never dull for me, that's for sure. But that's all part of the job, isn't it? You go where you're needed in the shortest time possible. Travelling the world and photographing famous people certainly isn't nearly as glamourous as people imagine it to be. Most of the time, it's all just a lot of jet lag. Anyway, enough of that. I believe you asked me for a refreshing drink and so you shall have it. How about some fruit juice?' Dominic peered into his small fridge over by the mini bar. 'Now let's see, perhaps some cheese and crackers to go with that? Or I have some fresh fruit salad if you'd prefer that instead?'

'No, just some fruit juice will be fine, thanks. I'll wait until dinner before I eat anything. We're still going out for a bite to eat after our work is done and before you have to leave for the airport, aren't we? I'm absolutely famished.'

'*Oui,* of course, and I do believe I might have the perfect place where we can dine together. I noticed when I booked in this morning, a sea-food restaurant not far from here. Out the front there was a chalkboard advertising their specials. Tonight, they have all-you-can-eat gourmet seafood smorgasbord for a very reasonable price. How does that sound?'

'Perfect! Let's do it, then! The sooner we get the technical side of our work out of the way, the sooner we can be out of here,' Peta beamed what she hoped would be considered a friendly smile over Dominic's way before immediately switching back into her professional mode. Before too long, Peta's computer was set up on the small dining table with her handwritten notes beside it, ready to go, giving Dominic no chance at all for small talk or any other probing questions either. She was suddenly all business, but she was determined not to give Dominic any opportunity to trip her up with any trick questions he might have up his sleeve. He wasn't looking too happy about it, but tough! She had a sneaky feeling this little victory of hers to stall Dominic was only temporary anyway. Before long, they were both switched onto their tasks at hand. Together, they made a good work team. They spent their first hour going over every detail of Peta's taped interview looking for the slightest flaw regarding any obvious misinterpretations of Peta's questions or even Stewart's surprisingly cooperative answers. Luckily, they didn't have too much editing to do. Stewart's voice came through loud and clear. Tess would have no trouble picking up every word of Stewart's answers throughout the interview, nor of Peta's questions.

'You did it, Peta! You really did. Fantastic! You covered all of the written guidelines set down by Tess in your own unique open way, too. I am sure she will be more than happy with the results,' Dominic explained.

'I can't tell you how relieved I am to hear you say that,' Peta grinned. 'After meeting Stewart and observing his obvious reservations first-hand, there was no room for error from the start. Can you imagine me going back to Stewart later and asking him to do it all over again? That was never an option, so I was determined to get it right the first time around.'

'You most certainly did! Especially with this being your first major interview. In the end, I truly believe you passed this test with flying colours and I am certain Tess will think so too.'

'Thanks! Coming from a true professional such as yourself, I value your opinion,' Peta replied. Dominic's enthusiasm really did mean a lot to her.

'My pleasure. Now it's time for us to go over my photos if you don't mind.'

'Yes, of course! Please show me what you have. I can't wait to see them.'

Dominic had already downloaded his photos from his camera onto his laptop, ready for the editing process. 'What do you think of this shot? The camera really does love Stewart, doesn't it?'

'Wow! What a great shot, Dominic! I love it!'

It was a shot of Stewart out on his back veranda, with the lush rainforest as a spectacular backdrop behind him. In his cornflower blue, open-necked shirt, with a generous hint of his deeply tanned skin underneath, Stewart's startling vivid blue eyes seemed to pump out his sexuality for all to see. It somehow felt like he was looking directly into her hungry eyes. Peta took a deep breath to recover herself before expressing her anticipated observations of Dominic's work.

'This particular shot really does capture his ruggedness and his obvious magnetism.'

Stewart's sexuality hit Peta with a force she now found hard to hide from Dominic. Her nipples responded by hardening at the thought of those same mocking lips teasing them exactly the way they did last night. Lucky for Peta, she was in front of Dominic so he couldn't see her fully aroused nipples poke out under her soft, tropically flowered shirt.

'So I think maybe Ms. McKenna is not immune to his charms either,' Dominic commented with his barely concealed jealousy held behind his carefully controlled facial features.

'Come off it, Dominic! You'd have to admit any woman would have to be practically near death not to notice this about Stewart Fletcher just from this one photo alone. Really, you could almost blame yourself for capturing such a great shot in the first place. He has this raw sexuality most red-blooded women would respond to. His magnetism seems to jump right out at you. Mind you, I speak only from a woman's point of view, of course.' Judging by Dominic's suspicious sideways look at her, Peta immediately backed off when she realised Dominic's intuition could tune in to her hidden feelings for Stewart all too easily. 'Anyway, speaking from a professional point of view, I really think your photos of him alone are going to help sell a hell of a lot of magazines next month.'

'You think so? I value your opinion too. Like you just said, coming from a woman's perspective, of course.' Dominic went quiet on her, not nearly as enthusiastic about his photos of Stewart as he was a few minutes ago. 'What do you think of these shots on the next screen?'

Peta scanned his photos with an outwardly professional interest, but all the while, her insides are busy doing crazy loop-de-loops. It was hard for her to believe the man in these photos was the same man who would be making love to her later tonight. For Peta, the sexual energy emulating from Stewart's photographic image could never reveal the true sexiness of the man beyond his carefully promoted professional image. Peta knew that 'what you see is what you get' with Stewart. He wasn't just sexy on the surface, but also so very sexy in the flesh.

'Great job!' Peta broke away from her insatiable desire to be ravaged by Stewart to avoid Dominic inevitably tuning into her unprofessional thoughts.

Back to business, Peta!

'They're all amazing. I am certain these photos will impress Tess for sure. So let's see. What do we have left to do now? We've gone through the recordings, my notes, and your photos. Ah yes, now I remember. I must send a quick email to Tess. Then I believe we're finished for now. Wouldn't you agree?'

'*Oui!* I would most certainly agree with you on that. Besides, we will have to go over it all with Tess early next week for her final approval.' Dominic replied.

'Before I send this email to Tess, may I use your bathroom, please?' Peta asked.

'Of course! Since our rooms are pretty much the same, I don't think I need to show you the way, do I?'

'No, not at all,' Peta acknowledged as she headed in that direction. 'I'll be right back!'

Unbeknown to Peta, while she was taking her sweet time in his bathroom, Dominic quickly and quietly rang down to reception for the seafood restaurant's phone number to secure a table for them both for tonight to avoid disappointment. As an extra treat, he also ordered a bottle of champagne ahead of time.

He particularly wanted to impress Peta tonight, as he planned to ask her something that, for once, didn't involve work. After seeing Peta's delighted response to his suggestion of the seafood smorgasbord after their work was done, he felt smug enough now to believe this sexy pussy would be his tonight. *She just doesn't know it yet, that's all.*

Once inside Dominic's bathroom, Peta breathed a sigh of relief. Thank goodness she made it to the bathroom in time. Any longer and she might have embarrassed herself in front of Dominic. As Peta washed her hands, her mind drifted back to her persistent thoughts of a potential disaster with Dominic finding out about her secret affair with Stewart. So far, Dominic seems to be holding back with his curiosity and wasn't asking her any awkward questions.

Not yet, anyway. Thank goodness!

Give him time, though. Peta knew from working with Dominic last year, he could be a bit of drama king. When it came to sniffing out any kind of scandalous secrets, he thrived on it. If he senses a hint of romance in the air, especially where Stewart is concerned, he won't be able to resist pestering her for the juicy details.

But I have your number, Dominic. You won't be getting any juicy details from me!

After returning from the bathroom, Peta was all efficiency again. 'Right, I'll get this email away to Tess first, as promised. Then it's time to reward ourselves for a job well done, which of course is food! What about you, Dominic?'

'*Oui!* I could eat a whole table full of food myself,' Dominic joked, while flourishing a chivalrous hand, letting Peta go first through the doorway before him. 'You first, beautiful lady!'

Upon their arrival at the seafood restaurant, their attentive waiter showed Dominic and Peta to a table over by an impressive water fountain.

'The relaxing ambience of water is so much more pronounced here. Wouldn't you agree?' Dominic says.

The unexpected sight of the water fountain, featuring an alabaster sculpture of three dolphins leaping gleefully through the water, was a complete delight for Peta. The fountain was strategically placed right in the middle of a timelessly classic, cobblestoned outdoor dining area.

'Oh yes, it's all so beautiful! What a delightful setting for a seafood restaurant.' Peta replies.

'It is indeed *magnifico!*'

As if on cue, their waiter arrived with a chilled bottle of Moët champagne on ice. Peta gasped when she realised the waiter was stopping at their table, 'Is this for us? I had no idea you ordered champagne.'

Dominic merely brushed away her surprise with a quick flick of his hand, like it was nothing at all really.

To Peta though, Dominic's underhanded sneakiness definitely suggested pure mischief. *Champagne? Why do I get the feeling Dominic is trying to tell me something? I can't help but be suspicious of his intentions now.*

'But what about your flight later tonight? Is this really such a good idea?'

'Do not worry yourself about it. Besides, I am part French, so to me, it's really just like sipping water,' he reassures her.

Any conversation between Peta and Dominic ceased for now as their smiling waiter popped the champagne bottle with a flourish and poured the bubbly, pinkish liquid into their fluted champagne glasses. Without another word, the waiter re-corked the bottle and laid it back in its bed of crushed ice before leaving them alone again.

'I have always been well aware of your impeccable tastes in food and wine, so why shouldn't I trust your choice in restaurants too?'

'*Merci!* I particularly wanted this night to be a very special one. This champagne calls for some special toasts from both of us. I'll start first if you don't mind.' Dominic raised his glass, 'This first toast must, of course, go to you, *chérie*. Congratulations on the completion of your first major interview for *Today's Voice*. May there be many more major interviews to follow.'

'Hear, hear!' Peta joined in as they clicked glasses before taking their first sip of champagne.

Peta giggled as the bubbles burst open on her tongue all at the same time. 'Thank you, Dominic. My turn now. The second toast must go to both of us for a job well done! Oh, and for good team work, too!'

'To a job well done!' Dominic added as they clinked glasses together once again. 'I have one more toast to offer to you now!' Dominic said in a more serious tone. 'Here's to me spending this magic night, for the next few hours at least, with you. I could never have imagined sharing this moment with anyone more beautiful than you, Peta. I think I must be the envy of every man in this restaurant tonight.'

Peta hesitated before answering Dominic. She made a show of slowly sipping her champagne while gathering her tremulous thoughts together.

Oh hell! I was right! I've obviously sent him the wrong message already it seems.

Her instincts were right! It took only a heartbeat to realise she'd entered a danger zone with Dominic and it had nothing to do with her secret love affair with Stewart. She couldn't believe Dominic could so carelessly dismiss his professionalism in favour of pursuing something so inappropriate with her. She'd always accepted his kind of flirting as harmless before, but this?

Shit! What am I supposed to do now?

She didn't want to be cruel, but she mustn't give him any false hope either. She would be careful about what she said to him from now on. Before Peta could respond to Dominic, though, they both heard the vibration of a dinner gong nearby. It was the maître d's call to dinner.

Ah! Saved by the bell and not a moment too soon. It might be best to just leave the heavy stuff between us for now. I need food first!

If Dominic was even aware of Peta's reluctance to respond to his feelings for her, he didn't let on. He merely smiled with relish at the thought of the feast to come. 'Ah! If I am not mistaken, I believe dinner is now being served. Bring your plate with you, *chérie,* and just follow me.'

'Oh really? Where are we going?'

Peta looked around and noticed other diners doing the same thing. She didn't need any more prompting as she tucked herself in behind Dominic and other eager diners. They all formed an orderly queue, chatting to each other as everyone moved towards an extra-long table loaded with scrumptious food.

'Wow! This all looks so amazing! What an incredible selection of seafood to choose from!' Peta exclaimed as she eyed off the food on display when they reached the smorgasbord table after what seemed like a long time waiting in the queue. There was every kind of seafood imaginable. Some she already knew about, but a lot she hadn't tried yet. Along with the vast fresh seafood, there were also creamy soups, endless salads, and warm, crusty breads. Another cloth-covered table past the main table was empty for now. Dominic noticed Peta's curious look.

'That table is all set up for the desserts later,' he explained.

'Desserts too? Oh man, so much food! I can't believe it. This is all so amazing. I feel like I have died and gone to heaven.'

'You first, *mademoiselle,*' Dominic prompted her to move in front of him in the queue. 'A word of warning, it is always best to start off lightly and then ease your way into a feast such as this. If I were you, I would start off with a small amount of soup such as the clam chowder over there. If you really like it and want some more, you can always come back later. Just because you have an empty plate or bowl to fill up, it doesn't mean you have to do it all at once. You can come back as many times as you like. Try to pace yourself carefully. This way you get to try a small amount of everything without feeling bloated. Believe me, your digestive system will thank you for it afterwards.'

'What about these long queues, though? I think that's why most people tend to grab it all in one go, because they don't want to have to get back into the long queue again,' said Peta.

'Ah, but this is only the beginning. There will always be a long queue at the start, but usually when you're ready to come back again, most of the other diners are still eating their first plateful. Which also means no long queues anymore. You can usually return to exactly where you want to be along the table.'

'Great advice! Thanks, Dominic. I've been to a few smorgasbords in the past, but as you say, they can be a bit overwhelming at times,' Peta took a few moments more to take a closer look at the selection of seafood at the far end of the table. 'Oh man, look at those prawns, they're so huge! I'll definitely come back for some more of those. Maybe some of those delicious mud crabs too.'

'*Oui!* I drool just thinking about them. And what about those oysters and mussels?'

'I must admit, I'm not at all that keen on oysters or mussels really, but I will definitely be back for some of the grilled barramundi, too. It's been years since I've seen barramundi so plump and fresh looking, especially these. They look so thick and juicy as they obviously must be. They're more like fish steaks, really, aren't they? I can hardly wait to sink my teeth into all of this delicious fare!'

'Absolutely!' Dominic enthused with a happy gleam in his eye.

Peta took Dominic's advice and slowed down her impulse to load up her plate right from the first course. After filling a small bowl with some clam chowder and grabbing a crusty bread roll, she headed back over to their dining table. A smiling Dominic followed along behind her with his prized plate of oysters. Once seated, Dominic clinked his champagne flute against Peta's to offer another toast.

'As you Aussies always say, "Let's tuck in."'

After devouring her third helping, Peta licked her lips for the umpteenth time. 'Oh man! Even though I did try to pace myself like you suggested, I think I have consumed way too much food.'

'So that means you won't be having any of their dessert selections then?' Dominic couldn't help laughing uproariously at Peta's answering groan.

'You are kidding, right?' Peta responded. 'I've made a real pig of myself tonight. Why didn't you stop me? Shameful! When I leave, I'll probably have to waddle out of here.'

'There is no way I could have stopped you, because I was too busy stuffing my own face at the time,' Dominic sighed with deep satisfaction. 'More champagne?'

'No way!' Peta placed her hand over her glass before he could pour any more in. 'I think I'll just stick to water from now on, thanks. You may be used to a constant flow of champagne, but not me. I don't want to end up with a massive hangover tomorrow morning.'

'I must say, dining with you tonight has been the highlight of my trip to Cairns this time. You have totally enchanted me with your beauty and your very presence tonight. I wish for this night to never end.'

With a champagne-infused twinkle in his eye, Dominic reached over across the table and tried to take Peta's hand in his. Peta anticipated his change of mood from lighthearted and funny to being serious and intense. She moved it quickly out of his reach.

He continued to speak anyway, 'I think you already know how I feel about you, Peta. In fact, I think you'd have to be blind not to notice my feelings for you. I was hoping you could feel the same towards me. Is there any chance for me that I could, you know, have a future with you?'

'Dominic, that's enough!' Peta's firm voice stopped him from saying anything else. 'As much as I've enjoyed your company tonight, I think you know only too well that I can never be any more than just a friend to you. I honestly don't think I have ever tried to give you any reason to believe otherwise, have I?'

'Ah! But you are such a beautiful woman, *chérie*. What man wouldn't want to believe you could be attracted to him in return? How could you be so cruel and insensitive to my feelings now? I don't understand. After all I have done for you, too.'

'After all you have done for me?' Peta questioned, now shocked by Dominic's bizarre reasoning. 'You really think I'm being cruel and insensitive to you? Huh! Apart from you giving me some very valuable feedback with my first major interview today, I can't for the life of me see what you have done for me. I'm sorry, Dominic, but how can you even say such a thing?'

'Well, for starters, I could ring Tess and tell her about you sleeping at Stewart Fletcher's place last night. I don't believe you slept alone last night either,' Dominic sneered at her. 'I know my instincts are absolutely correct on this one. Otherwise, why would you reject my love for you?'

'You're unbelievable! I never realised until now what a pompous ass you really are, Dominic. In case you have completely forgotten, Dominic, there was a cyclone about to happen at the time I had arrived at Stewart Fletcher's place?'

Dominic at least had the grace to lower his head in either guilt or acknowledgement of his failure to remember this fact. He still said nothing in his own defence.

'So, Dominic, do you think I should have rejected Stewart's invitation to come into his home, in favour of braving the cyclone outside by myself—just for the sake of following the correct protocols?' Peta stopped for a moment to take a few deep breaths by way of calming herself before continuing.

'Quite frankly, Dominic, it's none of your damn business if I did or did not sleep with Stewart Fletcher last night. Even if I did, you'd be the last person I would confide in. But by all means, ring Tess with your suspicions if you feel the need to do so … Just who do you think you are anyway, Dominic?' Peta countered angrily.

With a few more deep breaths to fortify her as she prepared to leave the restaurant with her dignity still intact, but not without trying to make Dominic see reason first, 'Look, up until now we've had a fun night, haven't we, Dominic? I appreciate you buying me dinner too, but please, let's not go and spoil it all now with all of this unnecessary seriousness. You'll be leaving Cairns for your flight to Canberra soon, and I'll be heading back to Sydney tomorrow. Do we really need to part company now with all of these silly misunderstandings between us? I'm all for letting bygones be bygones if you are? Dominic?'

The next words to come out of Dominic's mouth only confirmed for

Peta that he hadn't listened to her at all, because all he could offer her by way of a compromise was, 'Only if you admit that you *do* have feelings for me too.' Dominic tried once again to reach for her hand, but Peta yanked it away fast. 'I know you love me but you just don't realise it yet.'

'What! You're unbelievable! Sorry to burst your bubble, but I definitely do *not* feel anything for you at all and, rest assured, I never will. And on that note, I think it's time for me to leave.' Peta grabbed her handbag from the back of her chair. 'Thanks for dinner, Dominic, even if it sits in my stomach like a lead balloon now. Please don't bother to get up. I can see myself back to my room. And don't bother to knock on my door before you leave. We can say our farewells now. Enjoy your flight!'

Oh man! What an arrogant asshole he turned out to be!

Peta fumed inwardly as she headed back to her room. She'd come so close to slapping his smug face. Lucky for him, she held back her fiery temper. She would've liked giving him a piece of her mind. Peta entered the waiting lift, still fuming. She pushed the button for her floor with more force than was necessary, but it made her feel good. Thankfully, she reigned in her temper before saying something more to Dominic she might regret later, especially if he carried out his threat of telling Tess his suspicions. Her chances of keeping her job as of next week would be zilch by now. *Fuck!* She didn't have time to stew over Dominic. She needed to focus now on getting herself ready for Stewart.

At his name, Peta switched her thoughts away from any impending disasters to unleash her naughty intentions and create an erotic fantasy or two instead. She had some serious loving in mind for them. Once she reached her door, a new fire lit below her belly. She'd no choice now but to go with this delicious feeling.

To hell with the consequences of what may or may not happen! What's happening to me lately? Suddenly, I have sex on the brain. Damn right I do, and I'm loving it!

She couldn't get enough of Stewart and intended to take full advantage of his extra special skills.

Yes, indeed!

Back in her room, Peta rushed around clearing away any unnecessary clutter. She dimmed the lights to a soft, seductive glow, humming happily to herself the whole time.

I should give him a quick ring to make sure he is still coming.

But first things first. The two glasses of champagne she'd drunk tonight were wreaking havoc on her bladder. After a quick trip to the bathroom, Peta hurried back to the bedroom to grab her phone from the bedside table. Happily humming, *I'm in the mood for sex, I mean, love,* she dialled the private number Stewart gave her. But the voice who answered wasn't his.

CHAPTER ELEVEN

Stewart whistled happily as he threw a few of his best casual clothes, along with his toiletries, into an overnight duffel bag. He was much too preoccupied in his task to hear his front screen door creak open. Maybe the fact he was so absorbed in some erotic fantasy of spending the night with Peta at the Ocean Breeze could have something to do with it. So absorbed was he of their erotic night ahead, he didn't hear the creaky floorboards as footsteps move on along his hallway and stop at his bedroom door until it was far too late.

'Hullo Stewart. Can I come in?'

Stewart knew that voice only too well. He hoped he would never have to hear that voice in this house again and now here it was, inflicting a heap of emotional pain on his heart all over again. Stewart stopped in his tracks. He looked over towards his bedroom door to glare at his unwelcome visitor with barely disguised animosity.

'Felicity! What in the hell are you doing here?'

Stewart took in the unwelcome sight of his ex-wife. She was dressed in her usual signature outfit of closely moulded shorts and a tight-fitting halter top highlighting her ample bosom as always. Felicity smiled at him in her usual coquettish way. It was like she'd never really left him at all.

Even if she'd initiated the divorce, she seemed oblivious to the pain she inflicted on him time and time again. Stewart knew damn well her sudden appearance could only mean one thing for him—more emotional pain, and lots of it. He was being sucked back into some bizarre time warp. Their eyes immediately locked onto each other in an all-too-familiar, emotionally charged battle of wills, but with an inevitable conclusion for Stewart.

From her shocked expression, Stewart could tell she was uncomfortable with the scathing look he gave her. But if Felicity was feeling more than a little rattled by his unwelcome response, she hid it well. With her practised, easy-breezy attitude, it didn't exactly help to calm Stewart's rattled nerves at all.

'Really, darling! Why so cold?' At last, Felicity realised she would have to the one to speak first, since Stewart fully intended to give her the silent treatment. 'Is this the way to treat your wife after not seeing her for so long? Don't I even get a welcome-home kiss?'

'Make that ex-wife if you don't mind and no, you definitely will not be getting a welcome-home kiss from me. Not now—not ever again! You were the one who left me without any thought for my feelings. You do remember our past conflicts, don't you, Felicity?'

Felicity backed away as Stewart advanced. He stopped in front of her, close enough to touch, and pierced her with an ice-cold glare. He wanted so badly to verbally unleash some of his pent-up anger, but he spoke in a deceptively calm voice now, which he could see unnerved Felicity even more.

'Do you even remember ruthlessly stomping on my feelings? Or telling literally the whole world about me? Let's see. How dreadfully boring the *real* Stewart Fletcher is? Oh, and how I was responsible for holding you back from your true destiny in life. I have to wonder now if you even remember saying such things at all.'

Stewart didn't give Felicity a chance to defend herself. He was just getting warmed up.

'Probably not. Oh, and if that wasn't enough, you also tried to bleed my finances completely dry in the process. Do you have any scruples at all? I'd very much doubt it. Come to think of it, why are you even back here, anyway? It's money again, isn't it?' he spat.

Stewart eyed her suspiciously, and his instinct was confirmed when Felicity averted her eyes away from his penetrating look. He continued, 'If it's money you came back for, then I'm afraid the money supply is permanently non-existent where you are concerned, right to the end of eternity.'

Felicity pretended to study her manicured, cherry red nails for a moment and even tossed her platinum blonde curls dramatically before replying in her usual honey-sweet voice, 'Oh, but Stewart darling, that was so long ago now. I've changed. Really, I have! Why are you still holding onto all of this unnecessary soppy stuff? Especially after all this time?'

'To tell you the truth, looking back now, I can't believe I could've ever loved you at all. Love really is blind, I guess. Thankfully, though, I have finally come to my senses. I see you now for who and what you really are.'

'Oh, really? Tell me, what am I *really*, then?' Felicity bit back, running her tongue over her glossy, matching cherry red lips.

No doubt she hoped she could still use her feminine wiles to win him back. After all, her well-practised methods always worked with him in the past.

'To be perfectly blunt, I see you these days as being a rather sad, deluded, self-centred, self-absorbed, money-grabbing harlot.'

Felicity stared at him and looked completely shocked now, his harshly spoken words finally hitting home.

'Come on, Stewart! You know you don't mean that! What about all the good times we've shared in the past together? Doesn't that mean anything to you anymore?'

Felicity tried to embrace him, but he stiffened and stepped away from her. Awareness crossed her pretty features and her true self-centred side finally resurfaced, along with her quick, volatile temper. She let loose with a few choice expletives, but to no avail.

'I'm afraid my feelings for you have all dried up, Felicity. What's more, there will be no possibility of reconciliation this time either. Just out of curiosity, what happened to your plans to take on the world or, more specifically, Broadway and Hollywood with your so-called brilliant acting talents?'

'Oh, it wasn't what I really wanted, after all. I soon learnt those Hollywood directors were only interested in sharing a bed with any beautiful woman, really. Especially any new fresh overseas talent that's always available these days. It doesn't matter what gender you are. Besides, with some of those studio heads, they wouldn't even know true talent anyway. Even if it hit them smack bang in their puffy, silicone faces.'

'So when you say some of them, you really mean you did the rounds of the casting couch with *most* of them?'

Felicity's only answer now was to shrug her shoulders, as if sleeping around with any influential studio head was a perfectly natural thing to do under the circumstances. 'To quote one totally stumpy, slimeball Hollywood producer I met a few months back, "A gal's gotta give out if she wants to make it in Hollywood, sweetheart." So who am I to argue with that?'

'Like I said before, you have no scruples at all. You obviously haven't learnt yet that these Hollywood bigwigs are also using you as much as you are them. Once you lose their respect, they'll merely laugh behind your back. Then when they tire of all you starry-eyed, eager hopefuls, they won't hesitate to chew you up and spit you out like you never even existed. Besides, there are plenty of other talents out there, ready to take your place in a show business heartbeat.'

'You don't have to be so cruel!' Felicity huffed. 'I'll have you know, darling, I've worked very hard this past year to break into the movie business, but I've just had some really bad luck, that's all.'

'That's because you thought being an Australian TV soap star with your own fan club meant you'd be able to break into the USA scene so easily. I hate to say it, but you were delusional when you left Australia and you are still totally delusional back in your own country. The same country that made you famous in the first place, I might add.' Stewart offered Felicity his observation with a chilly smile. 'I have an idea for you, though, Felicity. Maybe you could approach your past employers at the TV studio. Maybe they could find a way to resurrect your soap opera character from death somehow. They've done it with others before you. Any storyline can be open for re-interpretation within the prime soap opera world, I hear.'

Stewart ducked out of the way, just in time to avoid a predictable slap on the face from Felicity. He'd hit a nerve.

'Ha!' Stewart smiled, which infuriated her even more. 'The truth hurts, doesn't it?'

'I never would have believed that you, of all people, could be so heartless and totally unsympathetic towards my obviously desperate circumstances,' Felicity sniffled loudly for effect. 'I find myself returning to Australia completely destitute, and do you know what's even worse? You don't even seem to care about what happens to me anymore.'

Felicity's beautiful baby blues teared up all too easily. She watched to see if he reacted to them the way she hoped he would. When her crocodile tears didn't have the desired effect, Stewart knew she'd bring out the big guns. The big mama of manipulation was about to make its play—open threats!

'Well, I can promise you this, before this day is over, the Australian press will hear all about your questionable behaviour towards me once again. Your new book will be marked in the bookstores as "unsold, return to author". The press will eat up any titbits I have to say about you. My loyal Australian fans will be only too happy to hate you all over again and they'll also be infuriated to hear of how cruelly you have kicked me out into the dirt, and penniless too. You'll be sorry you ever messed with me, Stewart.'

'Believe me, Felicity, I am already sorry I even have to listen to your rubbish again. A year ago, I probably would have reacted to your threats and your fake tears, but not anymore. I owe you nothing! You may have managed to suck me dry with your emotional blackmail in the past, but I'm done! I think it's time for you to leave now. Please go!' Stewart stood his ground.

'But this is my home, too! You can't kick me out just like that! My lawyer will hear of this!' Felicity was desperate now.

'More threats? Hell! You don't give up, do you? This is just so typical of you and I don't know why I never realised it until now. Go ahead and do your worst, Felicity. I don't really care. By all means go back to your lawyer with your pathetic sob story. But I am damn sure he will tell you that your part-ownership in this house ended when I paid you out during our divorce proceedings. I guess you forget that bit too, huh?'

Felicity finally realised she had pushed Stewart too far this time. Maybe some timely grovelling wouldn't hurt at this point. 'I'm so sorry, Stewart. I should have never tried to threaten you like that.'

Without even realising what she was doing, Felicity's lightning-fast change of mood suddenly revealed to Stewart her all-too-familiar tactics to win him over to her way of thinking. Her cunning tactics at play were totally obvious to him now, as her facial expressions suddenly switched from anger to seduction in the blink of an eye. How could he have been so blind not to have noticed this before?

'Please forgive me, Stewart. I didn't mean it!' Felicity continued to plead with him, even as he placed one hand under her elbow and escorted her towards the front door, while she tried unsuccessfully to plant her feet firmly onto the floor. Her desperate tears flowed more freely, now with one part total disbelief and many other parts sheer frustration at her obvious failure to squirm her way back into his life again.

'Stewart! Before you throw me out of here, listen to me, please! I still have some clothes and shoes of mine in your office. I left them here because it would have been too expensive for me to ship them over to the States when I left. Could you at least let me sort through them and take what I need with me? Maybe you could pass on the leftovers to some charity store in Cairns. I don't really care what you do with them.' Felicity then added offhandedly, 'If you were to mention to the charity store that the items once belonged to me, they could even make a lot of money from my exclusive and very expensive hand-me-downs.'

'That's so very kind of you, Felicity. I guess I would also be contributing to those charity stores too because it was my credit card that helped you to buy those same very expensive and exclusive clothes in the first place, right?' Stewart threw back at Felicity with just the right amount of sarcasm mixed in to raise a tiny degree of guilt in her.

'Whatever!' Felicity huffed with a dismissive wave of her hand. With a quick readjustment to her attitude, she continued more sweetly this time, 'We don't really need to go there this time, do we? Haven't you said enough to crush my heart into a million pieces already?'

'Give me a break!' Stewart rolled his eyes at Felicity's attempt for sympathy. 'Go ahead, sort through your boxes then, but you only have ten minutes to do so. I have to be in Cairns for a meeting shortly. While you're doing that, I'm going to take a quick shower, so I want you to be ready to leave here by the time I'm finished in the bathroom. Is that clear?'

'Can't I just stay here until you get back? You obviously don't realise it could take me a while to sort through everything. You're being perfectly unreasonable to expect me to go through all of these boxes in just ten minutes!'

'Well, you had better move fast then. Ten minutes is all you have. Take it or leave it.'

Stewart brushed past Felicity with indifference and led the way into the spare room across the hall from his bedroom. It was meant to be a spare room for guests before he turned it into an office. The sweeping view of the back garden, lush with rainforest vegetation, was a bonus. He opened up the sliding doors of the built-in wardrobe, which took up the entire back wall of his office. Felicity pointed out the four large boxes she'd left in there. He pulled them all out and placed them on the floor, side by side.

'Okay, here are your boxes. Knock yourself out. Remember, ten minutes.' With nothing more to say, he left her to it. On the way to the bathroom, he grabbed the clothes he'd planned to wear. He closed the door and breathed a sigh of relief. The worst was over. He'd stood his ground. Soon she would be out of his life forever.

Felicity stewed, mumbling to herself as she sorted through some outdated fashions, shoes and accessories she'd almost forgotten about herself.

That bastard! Who does he think he is?

She didn't even want these things. These boxes were merely an excuse to stall. Not that she would want to live back here in this godforsaken hellhole anyway.

Stewart still has that damn noisy, smelly parrot out the back, too. That stupid bird never really liked her anyway, plopping bird shit all over her good clothes every time he flew past her on the veranda. She most certainly didn't like him either. No love lost between them where Felicity was concerned.

Stewart and that bloody bird really do belong together. The perfect combo, a scrawny featherbrain and the psycho, featherless man-bird. Ha! Good joke, Felicity.

Each time Felicity left Stewart before, he had been only too happy to have her back again. Until now, it had always been a cinch to win him back. So, what changed this time? *What happened to the love-struck husband I used to know?*

She couldn't put her finger on it, but she'd figure it out. Besides, she had no choice but to win him back. She was desperate, and desperate times called for desperate measures. Admittedly, she could hardly expect Stewart to welcome her back with open arms after their divorce. Why, she could even recall a time when he never wanted her to leave *ever*. He'd always beg her to stay whenever she drove out of here, especially after the last of their many fights.

It seemed he'd moved on. Right into the arms of another woman, too. Felicity could almost guarantee this was the real reason for his heartless rejection. How else could he resist her charms once she turned them on to their full wattage? What man could, really?

Mmm, I wonder who she is?

Whoever she was, maybe she should try to get together with this new competition. She could tell her a thing or two about the *real* Stewart Fletcher. She bet she could even come up with a few untold, creatively nasty stories that would have this mystery woman running far away from him in double quick time.

Stewart's landline rang, the sudden ringtone jolting her out of her erratic thoughts. After a few rings and with exaggerated impatience, Felicity yelled out, 'Stewart! Your phone is ringing!'

When he didn't reply, Felicity concluded he was in the shower already.

'What am I? Your bloody secretary or something?' Felicity shouted again, but still no answer was forthcoming. Felicity groaned in frustration when she realised, that in order for her to grab the phone from where she was sitting cross-legged on the floor, she'd have to stand.

'Perhaps I should go ahead and answer it for you then, shall I?' she yelled out again, but still no answer. 'It's not like I have anything else to do!' She exaggerated a sigh for full effect.

Despite Felicity's intention to ignore this annoying interruption, the phone just kept right on ringing. In a huff, she threw aside the items on her lap.

Oh, for some peace and quiet!

'Hullo? Hullo? Is anybody there?' Felicity was greeted with only silence on the other end. 'Be warned whoever you are; if you don't answer me in the next three seconds, I'm hanging up.'

'Sorry! I was just about to hang up. I thought I might have a wrong number for a moment there. Thankfully, I heard your voice just in time. My name is Peta McKenna, a journalist from *Today's Voice* magazine. I was just wondering if Mr. Fletcher will still be heading into Cairns soon to finalise the interview Dominic, our photographer, and myself taped this morning?'

The unknown woman's hesitation spoke volumes, and Felicity immediately picked up on the reason for Stewart's indifference towards her.

It's her! This woman on the other end of this call is why Stewart wants me out of his life. I'll bet my life on it.

Felicity smiled wickedly at her reflection in the mirrored cupboard doors.

'Sorry, Ms. McKenna, but Stewart is in the shower right now. We were just talking in bed before and come to think of it, he did mention a meeting he had to go to shortly. He assured me, though, that he would try to get back here later tonight.' Felicity placed her hand over her mouth to stifle her giggle. 'As you can understand, being separated for far too long, we've had such a lot of catching up to do,' Felicity could barely stop herself from laughing out loud now.

'Oh, I see.' There was another pause, as though the woman was struggling to respond. 'Well, I guess I can understand then why he doesn't really need to drive into Cairns after all … So, who would you be?'

'Sorry. I didn't introduce myself, did I? How silly of me! I am Felicity Cambria. Technically, his ex-wife, but not for long. Soon I hope to be living back here permanently again,' Felicity paused now for full effect. 'We've decided to give our marriage another go and try to work things out between us. Can I confide in you, Peta? You know, from one woman to another? I must say, Stewart and I have certainly got off to a great start already.' Felicity's perfectly effected giggle tinkled down the phone line.

There was a predictable silence at the other end, as Felicity suspected there would be. She was right about this woman. Her silence said it all.

'Would you like me to get him to call you back when he gets out of the shower?' she asked sweetly.

'No! That's okay.' A sharp intake of breath sounded. 'Please tell Mr. Fletcher not to bother with this matter any further. I should have enough material anyway to wrap up the interview without him. If we need anything else from him, my editor-in-chief can contact him later. Sorry to have bothered you.'

'Oh, okay then. I'll be sure to tell him you called. Bye!' Felicity ended the call.

Five minutes after the phone call, Stewart emerged from the bathroom, looking all spruced up and ready for action. The kind only Peta could give him. Felicity was still in his office, sorting through her boxes. There were various items scattered all around her. He'd been so caught up in reliving the delicious memory of himself and Peta in the shower together early this morning, he'd almost forgotten the reality of his current and awkward situation.

Felicity is still here! Hell's bells!

How could this have happened? Stewart paced the room now with obvious agitation before confronting Felicity again.

I need to hurry her along faster before she guesses what I'm planning to do in Cairns tonight. Yes, there will be a meeting, but certainly not a boring business one, this time anyway.

Stewart spoke in a clipped tone, 'Why are you still going through those boxes? I thought we agreed you'd be finished and ready to leave by the time I was out of the shower.'

'What? Sorry, I didn't realise you were speaking to me. Did you say something just then?' Felicity feigned ignorance.

Oh man! Her stall tactics are at work again. If I try to rush her, she'll go even slower. This calls for some heavy tactics of my own.

'I just asked you why are you still sorting through those boxes? I thought we agreed on only ten minutes for you to go through them?'

'I don't remember agreeing to anything of the sort. Besides, you can't possibly expect me to have all these boxes sorted in just ten minutes. It's impossible!'

'Have it your way. I'm not going to get into an argument with you right now. I don't have time. By the way, I thought I heard my phone ring while I was in the bathroom, or did I just imagine it?'

'No, it did ring.'

'So, what happened then? Did it go to voicemail?' Stewart's patience was wearing thin.

'No, I answered it for you,' Felicity appeared to be completely absorbed in her task.

'And?'

'What? Oh, it was some journalist on the phone. She said her name was Peta McSomething. Peter? Is that really her first name? Peter is more a masculine name, isn't it?'

Stewart's patience was almost non-existent by now, but somehow, he maintained a sense of calm.

'Felicity! Could you give me a proper answer, please? What did this Peta say then?'

'She just asked me to tell you that the meeting for tonight has been cancelled.'

'What? You're kidding me, right? Did she say why?'

What in the hell is going on here?

'No, she just said to tell you there was no need for you to come into Cairns after all. She also said if you have any concerns at all about the interview, to contact her editor-in-chief instead.'

'Are you sure that's all she said?' he snapped.

'Am I supposed to take your messages too, while sorting through all my boxes? All in ten minutes, too, I might add!'

Stewart could have cheerfully choked her, but he ignored her for now. At least until he had a moment to get his mind back on track.

While Stewart struggled to make sense of it all, Felicity smiled at her reflection.

Stewart swore under his breath.

Man! Felicity can be such a bloody infuriating woman without even trying.

He'd a terrible feeling about this call, but if he were to let on to Felicity that Peta meant something to him, she'd milk it for all it's worth.

'If you must know, she said that you don't need to contact her directly anymore.'

Now he knew something was definitely wrong. Felicity was acting way too smug for her not to have had a hand in this change of plans. The only plan of action he could think of was to drive into Cairns and sort this all out, face-to-face with Peta.

'Well, I am afraid your time has definitely run out, along with my patience. It's time for you to leave!'

'But I haven't even finished yet!'

Stewart ignored the sulky tone in her voice. 'How did you get out here, anyway?'

'I have a hire car outside. What do you care?'

Before Felicity could get up from the floor to stop him, Stewart grabbed a box she hadn't opened yet and carried it down the hallway and outside towards her car. Once he reached Felicity's little red Getz, he plopped the box on the ground and headed back inside for the other boxes. Despite Felicity's desperate ranting and raving, he grabbed all the loose items scattered around the room, threw them all into the nearest box, and headed outside with this one too. On the third trip, he carried two boxes, with each one balanced on his shoulders and his arms stretched around each box. He'd no intentions of letting Felicity know just how heavy her boxes were, either.

Felicity followed close behind on each of his trips from his office to her hire car. She even tried to grab one box out of his hands along the way, but to no avail. Stewart had a firm hold on them and wasn't letting go.

'Like I said, Felicity, it's time for you to leave. Open the hatch at the back and I will put the boxes in the back for you or you can do it yourself. Either way, you are leaving here NOW!'

Felicity opened the hatch for Stewart and stepped back. She couldn't resist one last threat. 'I meant what I said, Stewart. I will be in contact with my lawyer first thing tomorrow morning. You're going to be very sorry when I finish with you!' she screamed the words at him.

'Go for it! In case you've forgotten, you no longer have any legal claims where I'm concerned and you know it. Our legal settlement is already done and dusted. I don't feel the least bit sorry for you either. You've bought all of this so-called bad luck on yourself. Please don't bother to come back here anymore. I mean it this time, Felicity. We're done!'

CHAPTER TWELVE

Stewart, although completely devastated his rendezvous with Peta was now cancelled, was determined not to let Felicity see how upset he was. Once Felicity drove off in a raging temper, kicking up the small stones from his driveway with her spinning tyres in the process, he collapsed onto the steps of his front veranda. He lowered his head in abject misery, his erratic thoughts spinning even more out of control. Caught up within some crazy whirlwind, he struggled now to try to understand why Peta cancelled their clandestine night together. Was this meant to be some cruel joke? Any minute now, the jokesters responsible would pop up and laugh their silly heads off at his expense, 'Sorry, Stewart, but you've just been roasted!'

What the hell is going on here? None of this makes any sense. Why would Peta cancel their planned rendezvous? Whatever her reasons were, he knew he still needed to drive into Cairns to sort it out—if it's not too late, that is. Regardless of her sudden change of heart, it was more important to dispel this miserable confusion.

Felicity? Did she have something to do with Peta's change of plans? He wouldn't put it past her. What damage could she have come up with on the phone by just taking a message from Peta? Oh hell! Something must have happened to change Peta's mind, and he was determined to get to the bottom of it before she left his life forever.

Forced now to be completely honest with himself, though, at this stage in his life, he really didn't think he could handle having his heart broken three times in a row.

There is no way he'd be able to stay here alone tonight. His erratic thoughts would never allow him to sleep anyway. He needed to find out what happened since he kissed Peta goodbye. The fact was, now he'd found her, he wanted to be with her all the time. It was like he needed her now in the same way he needed to take every breath he'd ever take from now onwards. Not only that, his traitorous body still ached to be with her again. Even amid all of this confusion. There was no way he'd let her fly out of his life when he had only just found her. If fate will allow it, he wanted to be given a chance to explore the possibilities of this new relationship more thoroughly, well into the future.

Maybe he should ring her first, but his trusted gut feeling acknowledged it wouldn't do him any good. Regardless of her thoughts about him, nothing could be put back together if he continued to waste time, sitting on his fast-numbing rear end, on these hard, unforgiving wooden steps of his. *Peta was sure right about that.*

So, why was he still here then? He needed to be outta here, *pronto!*

Time for action, Stewart, old son. Get moving!

In one crazy, hell-bent burst of energy, Stewart raced into the house, grabbed his overnight bag, threw it into the seat of his four-wheel drive. Backing out of the garage, at least he stopped long enough to lock the garage door. Without caring, he kicked up even more gravel than Felicity had done before him, as he spun the front wheels around to point the Rover towards Cairns City like his arse was on fire.

Peta sat quietly amongst the other passengers, waiting for her flight back to Sydney. Her red, blotchy eyes were covered by an oversized pair of dark-tinted sunglasses. She was well aware some nearby passengers were intently looking her way, some with their not-so-subtle stares. Some with open curiosity that said, 'Why is this woman wearing her dark sunglasses inside the terminal and not outside where she needs them the most? Such a strange woman, indeed.'

Yes, that's me! So let them stare.

Peta always took pride in her personal and professional appearance, but just not now. She was beyond caring at this point. Peta tucked her body even more defensively within itself, just to prove it to those watching her she meant it, too.

No, that's entirely not true. How stupid did she feel at this moment and now here she was, getting all soppy over a man she's only just met. And in a busy airport, too, of all places?

Totally pathetic, Peta!

Despite Peta's obvious I-don't-care attitude, she could understand why people were staring at her. After all, being an enthusiastic people-watcher herself, she often wondered where all of these interesting-looking people came from. What's their life story? What do they do for a living? Do they have a family or are they alone and miserable, just like her? Have they had their hearts broken because they gave it away to a lying cheat, just like her? *Same old story. Blah, blah, blah.*

So why didn't she just ring him back and give him a piece of her mind? The old confident Peta would have done that and probably felt a whole lot better for it, too. But it seems that old confident Peta has flown the coop and left her to her own miserable pathetic self.

Was it really only this morning? How can one's life, filled with so many new possibilities in the morning, turn into absolute shit by the end of that same day?

Anyway, what would she have achieved by calling Stewart back? His wife was obviously back in his life again. He'd rather return to his long-lost love than take a chance with her. The sexy man who women fantasised about all the time.

Yeah right! He turned out to be a weakling after all. No backbone at all. I'm better off without him!

Ex-wife, she reminded herself for the umpteenth time. So what? She's back in his life.

In his heart, she was still his wife, wasn't she? He was a broken man for a long time after she left him, so why wouldn't he want her back in his life? Apart from these past few days, she and Stewart didn't have any history together, did they? How could she even think he would choose her over Felicity? It was a no-brainer, really. It looked like the annoying journalist was out of his life for good and the glamorous soap star was back in. She should've seen that one coming.

Peta retrieved a wad of tissues deep from in her bag to wipe away fresh hot tears. For good measure, she pulled out a few more crumpled tissues to blow her sniffly nose yet again.

Crap! I must look a real mess. Jeez! How dumb am I to fall for his sexy, lovey-dovey act?

Who would have believed the elusive Stewart Fletcher could capture her heart so easily? She was a strong, independent woman. She'd worked hard to get where she was today. So how could she so stupidly drop her guard only to become so unprofessionally involved with this cruel, heartless man in the first place? And so willingly, too! She truly believed she and Stewart had a special connection for a while there. How wrong was she?

Not to mention deluded, too. Don't forget that one. Especially when he has been ruthlessly deceitful to her the whole time, and without any remorse whatsoever.

Bastard! But I suppose it's better to find out now rather than later.

Yep! When Peta took time to think about this whole mess now, Felicity probably did her a huge favour. Bless her giggly heart.

In the meantime, she really should go and splash her face with some cool water and at least make an attempt to put her outward appearance back together somehow. Pity she couldn't put her broken heart back together again too. Peta took herself, along with her misery, off to the ladies' restroom with her shoulders slumped down, wheeling her carry-on case behind her.

Unbeknown to Peta, two passengers who had been sitting either side of her watched her leave, each wondering what could have happened to that poor woman for her to be looking so sad.

Stewart frantically scanned the airport crowds for Peta, but there was no sign of her. Upon his arrival at her resort hotel in Cairns, the hotel receptionist informed him in her most diplomatic way, without actually revealing any private information about her guest, that Ms. McKenna was no longer a guest at the Ocean Breeze.

Stewart attempted unsuccessfully to shake off this sudden feeling of total confusion. Glancing at his watch, Stewart now had to make the choice of deciding what to do next. Plan A: Was to drive back home and accept defeat *or*, Plan B: Head for the airport anyway. If he headed to the airport immediately, he might still catch her before her flight departed. So Plan B definitely seemed like the way to go. If his memory served him correctly, he recalled she was originally booked to fly out around this time tonight back to Sydney. That was, of course, before they had conspiratorially agreed on their rendezvous at the Ocean Breeze after Dominic left Cairns.

Mentally berating himself for allowing her to slip away so easily will just have to wait for now. He had a plane to catch, or rather to try and stop a beautiful lady from leaving on that plane—there was not a moment to lose. Stewart bolted back to his Land Rover, screeched out of the hotel car park. Since he had already started to pick up too much speed, he was forced to remind himself to slow down. He'd never make it on time if the police pulled him over for speeding.

Now here he was, wondering how he was supposed to find her amongst all these people with only minutes to spare.

She must be here somewhere. Hell! I just hope I'm not too late.

Stewart concluded it might be a good idea to check the information screens. Even if he didn't know which airline Peta was with, he could discover which flights were leaving Cairns for Sydney tonight. Locating one, he rushed over to study it. His gaze anxious, he spotted one flight due to leave for Sydney within the next twenty minutes. It probably wouldn't give him much time to try to talk her into staying, but he was here now, and he wasn't going anywhere, not without knowing where he'd gone wrong.

Let's see. Gate 4. That's a good a place as any to start.

Everyone along the way became a blur as he sprinted past them on the way to gate four.

Peta emerged from the restroom facilities looking and feeling more refreshed, although she hadn't ditched the dark glasses yet. There wasn't much she could do about her weepy eyes at this point, but maybe she could ditch the glasses on the flight in favour of an airline-issued face mask. It might even help to stop any curious looks or persistent questions from other passengers. Worse, some eager-to-please flight crew member hovering over her.

Shit! I feel like death warmed over. Probably look it, too.

Peta couldn't wait to get back home so she could collapse on her bed. Free at last to let go and bawl her eyes out for the rest of the night and all the other empty days and nights to follow. Caught up in her misery, she knew only too well all she could do now was wait for her flight to be called so she can escape this living nightmare.

At least with nightmares, you get to wake up from them.

She sighed miserably. There will be no waking up from this one, though. It was here to stay.

Peta sat down and, just like before, wrapped her arms protectively around her body in a vain attempt to comfort her wounded heart. Surprisingly, it was beating strong, despite all of this pain and misery inflicted upon it.

Is there a time limit for one's broken heart to heal?

Stewart stood off to one side of the boarding area, watching her from a safe distance.

Oh man! She looks really pissed off!

Stewart studied Peta. He realised it wasn't just because of those silly dark glasses she wore, either. Her body language spelled out she was obviously in defence mode. The optimistic Peta, with her quirky sense of humour he'd come to know and love in the past day or so, was nowhere in sight. This new Peta worried him. He wasn't sure how he could possibly reach her through this new closed-off demeanour she was projecting to all those around her, warning them to back away and leave her alone. She was a picture of absolute misery. Despite that, Stewart was determined to reach her somehow. He wasn't exactly sure how yet.

I'm here now and I have to try. Or risk losing her forever.

Despite her defensive body language, she looked gorgeous. He found it hard to believe what an impact she'd made on his life already. That's why he couldn't let her fly out of his life without first finding out why she was so damn upset with him.

What could Felicity have said to plunge Peta's normally cheerful optimism all the way down into such a miserable state? Whatever the reason, he was determined to find out.

Well, here goes nothing!

Stewart took a few deep breaths and headed over towards Peta, expecting the worse. He stood before her with his hands in his pockets for a moment before speaking.

'Peta! Why are you leaving like this? Why the sudden rush to get back to Sydney?'

Peta looked up at the sound of Stewart's voice, not registering at first who he was. Peta didn't answer him straight away, but he could tell by the way she stared back at him, that several thoughts were frantically racing through her mind all at the same time. Peta slowly raised her head to look up and acknowledge him. For too long a moment for Stewart to bear, she suddenly appeared to be fixated with the silver belt buckle on Stewart's hip-hugging beige pants. Her eyes, still framed by a ridiculous pair of oversized sunglasses, wandered ever upwards, to finally settle on his own anxious eyes, fully exposed to her final judgement of his recent character change.

'Well, well! If it isn't the famous Mr. Fletcher in the flesh! What are you doing here? I thought you and Felicity would be all cozied-up in your ruffled sheets by now.'

'Felicity? What has she got to do with you leaving so suddenly?' said Stewart, a bit stunned by her harsh words.

'Well, since you asked, *Mr.* Fletcher, when I spoke to her earlier today, she informed me, ever so nicely, about how you spent the afternoon in bed together. And how you were both going to work things out together. Lastly—and the most exciting part of all—about her moving back in with you again.'

'She what? THAT BITCH!' In shock at what he had just heard, Stewart realised he spoke louder than he should have, but he didn't care. 'Bloody hell! I can't believe she told you such blatant lies. I can fully understand now why you took off the way you did.' Stewart collapsed onto the nearest chair. 'I can assure you, Peta, what she told you is news to me, too. You have to believe me when I tell you that any kind of reconciliation with Felicity is definitely *not* an option for me!—Now or anytime in the future, I'm very happy to say, at long last.'

'What are you trying to say?' questioned Peta with an equally shocked look on her face. 'So, what Felicity told me earlier isn't true?' Peta shook her head in confusion, not sure what to believe anymore.

'Please, Peta. Can we go off to the side a bit and talk in private? We don't really need to let everyone know our private business.'

'I don't know, Stewart. My flight is due to leave soon, as you no doubt already know.'

'Yes, I am well aware of that fact, which is why I had to bust my arse to get here in time to stop you. Even if I didn't quite understand at the time why you were leaving so suddenly, I had to try at least. I figured I could deal with the consequences later.' Stewart took a deep breath and continued. 'It's really important for you to hear me out now, especially in regard to these nasty, vindictive lies straight from Felicity's lying mouth.'

Peta took off her dark glasses for the first time since this whole miserable drama escalated out of control. Could it be, she now asked herself, that perhaps, *maybe* she might have been a bit too hasty, beating a fast retreat to the airport, before even taking the time to hear Stewart's side of the story first?

In a way, she had been just as guilty as everybody else in misjudging the *real* Stewart Fletcher behind the professional image—by automatically believing all the bad press about him. She really should have taken the time to check the true facts first.

Peta was somewhat surprised now to see a genuine hint of sincerity and regret in his eyes, laid bare right at her feet.

'Okay, let's talk then. You have ten minutes to convince me of the real truth in all of this.' Peta looked around and spotted a deserted boarding area across the hallway. 'Over there looks like a good place for us to have our private chat.'

Peta led the way at a brisk walking pace, wheeling her carry-on behind her, leaving Stewart no choice but to follow her or be left behind. Stewart willingly obliged until they were both standing face-to-face in the deserted, darkened area.

'Indulge me for a moment please, if you don't mind, Stewart. What you're trying to tell me then is; you and Felicity are *not* getting back to together after all?'

'Pardon me for what I am about to say, but what my ex-wife told you is absolute bullshit!' Stewart drew a few ragged breaths in, as he thumped the back of a nearby chair a few times in obvious frustration. 'She sneaked inside and waited outside my bedroom just as I finished packing my overnight bag to drive to Cairns to be with you. Felicity implied—and not very convincingly, I might add—that she was down and out and needed to come back here to live and to be with me.'

He thumped the back of the chair again. 'I finally realised at that point, just how much she has been manipulating me all these years, but I was always too damn blind to see it until today. I knew only too well from past experience the only reason she was coming back to me is because she must be flat broke, yet again. In the past, I'd always weaken and give her more money and you guessed it; let her back in. Predictably, though, she'd always up and leave me again. That is, until she finally flew off to America. The very last time, however, I had had enough! I finally asked her to leave permanently and never come back.'

'How did she get to answer your phone then, if you had already asked her to leave?'

'She asked me if she could grab some of her personal things, which were packed away in boxes in the spare room. This room also happens to be my office now and where my landline is. I honestly couldn't see any problem in letting her do so at the time. My housekeeper had stored the boxes for me, inside the built-in wardrobe in my office. I told her she could go ahead and grab them, but she had to be ready to leave by the time I was out of the shower. She even asked me if she could stay there while I was in Cairns, but there was no way I was going to allow that. I then had to remind her once again, of her ten-minute time frame or she'd have to leave without any of her stuff.'

Stewart placed one hand on Peta's shoulder. With the other hand, he raised her chin gently, so she looked directly into his eyes.

'By the way, just for the record, Felicity never stepped foot in my bedroom or my bathroom at any time. Please believe that!' Stewart held his breath as he waited for Peta's answer.

'It seems to me,' Peta said, 'from what you have just told me, Felicity Cambria is one very sneaky, underhanded woman. Especially when it comes down to getting what she wants, in whatever way she can. Being an accomplished actress, it would have been all too easy for her to convince me she really was back to stay again. *Plus*, she'd just been given the perfect opportunity to ruthlessly wreck revenge on both you and me! She just happened to be in the right place for herself, but predictably the wrong time for us. She was probably laughing at me all the time. I can understand exactly what you mean now. What a conniving bitch she is! Unbelievable!'

'Please don't mess with me, Peta,' Stewart paused to draw in a deep breath before continuing. 'I need you to be completely honest with me now. Are you saying you really do believe I'm telling you the truth?' Stewart awaited her final answer with an undisguised look of hope reflected in his eyes.

'I must admit, I had my doubts for a while there!' She chuckled in-between happy tears. 'But I know in my heart, where it counts, that you *are* telling me the truth. Otherwise, why would you be here at the airport trying to talk me out of leaving? You must also understand, though, Stewart, that for me—if you hadn't of done anything at all to try and stop me from leaving—it really would have been forever. Back home in Sydney, I probably would've blocked any further contact from you *forever*!'

Peta smiled at last, much to Stewart's relief. The Peta standing before him right at this moment was more like the easygoing Peta he'd come to know these past few days, especially when she jokingly poked him in his ribs.

'I hope you realise, *Mr.* Fletcher, how very lucky you are that you've managed to catch me when you did! It was touch and go there for a moment.'

Stewart didn't wait for her to finish. He grabbed Peta and kissed her with a deep passion, not caring about the gathering crowd of people now at her boarding gate nearby, leaving Peta with no doubt at all of his true feelings for her.

'Dare I ask?' Stewart smiled tentatively after they resurfaced. He held her close, before pulling back a bit, to look deep into her eyes. 'I need to know now if there is any hope for us at all?'

Peta stepped away from the warm cocoon of Stewart's arms to give him the answer they both needed to hear.

'Right now, that's not an easy question for me to answer without some careful consideration for both our sakes. Having said that, I now find myself truly ready to believe we might just have a promising connection between us. After all, right from the start, we've had this instant attraction going on, haven't we? Even if neither of us would have admitted it at the time.'

Peta and Stewart laughed out loud, as they were reminded once again, of their first fiery encounter with each other.

'That was definitely true for me. When I opened my front door to this drop-dead gorgeous woman and when I looked into those brilliant green eyes of yours, it was like WHAM! I was totally smitten with you from the start.'

Peta looked somewhat doubtful now, as she raised her eyebrows with a you-must-be-kidding-me kind of look before continuing.

'Oh come off it, Stewart! You really are getting carried away now, but anyway, the first thing we need to consider right now, is that I live down in Sydney and you live up at the top end of Australia. I have my career and you have yours. Since our careers are important to each of us, how can we possibly make this work between us over time? From my own understanding, long-distance relationships are notoriously known to fail miserably within the first few months. That is, if all of those talk shows and magazine articles on the subject are anything to go by.'

Stewart nodded his head in acknowledgement of what Peta had just said, but he quickly added, 'Yes Peta, I do understand all the pitfalls of long-distance relationships and even though I know what you're saying is *supposed* to be true, I also happen to believe that any kind of mutual attraction that sparks up between two people is never going to be easy initially. Especially when neither of them have been actively looking for any kind of love interest in the first place.' Stewart sat down again on one of the nearby chairs and gently pulled Peta's hand down in an attempt to encourage her to do the same, but she resisted his insistent tug of her arm to remain standing.

'I can't sit down with you now, Stewart. As you know, I have to board my flight soon.'

'Just for another minute or two. *Please?*'

'Okay! Just a few minutes more then.'

'Look Peta, I was just wondering if there is any chance at all that you could still stay here in Cairns with me tonight after all. You could cancel this flight and I'll be happy to pay for your return flight home. You must admit, we do still have a lot to talk about—among other things! Please, Peta, say you will?' he begged.

'Believe me, nothing would make me happier than to stay with you tonight, Stewart.' Peta sighed with frustration. 'I just can't though! I had a bit of an awkward episode with Dominic at dinner tonight, so who knows what his report to Tess will be if I don't go back to Sydney tonight.'

'You had a run-in with Dominic? Why? What happened?'

'Dominic admitted he has feelings for me that aren't of a professional nature. I rejected him, so he's probably feeling maybe more than a little upset with me right now. He might even be tempted to hint to Tess that it was me who came onto him, not the other way around. It was obvious to me when I left him at the restaurant that his ego was somewhat bruised. So who knows what he will do?'

'Really? He would do that? He seemed like such an agreeable man when I met him earlier.' Stewart frowned.

'I already knew Dominic was a bit of a flirt, but I just put it down to office gossip. I even defended him at times. Now he's proven to me that all the rumours about him are true. By the way, he also picked up on the sexual vibes between us, too.'

'Ah! I get the picture. So you think he might try to jeopardise the trust that your boss has in you?'

'It's very possible at this stage, but either way, I have to go back to Sydney tonight.'

'Yes, of course! You definitely do have to go back,' agreed Stewart. 'But I refuse to let you leave just yet, without extracting a promise from you first.'

'Promise?' Peta questioned with a quizzical smile. 'What sort of promise do you mean?'

'Well, since you insist on flying out of here and leaving me all alone to return to my very lonely bed, the least you can do is promise me it won't be the last time I ever see you.'

'Oh, Stewart! Please stop! You're going to make my waterworks act up again.' As if on cue, a single tear rolled down her cheek unchecked. 'You must know by now that I would stay if I could.' As she paused to reach for a crumpled tissue from her bag, Stewart gently removed it from her grasp to wipe the tear away for her. She looked up into his sexy baby blues and in the process, damn near lost her resolve to still fly away from him. In an attempt to re-gather her momentum before continuing, Peta was forced to move back just out of his reach. 'Of course I'll promise this definitely won't be the last time we see each other.'

'I'm sorry, Peta. I'm not making this easy for you, am I? Don't mind me. I'm just feeling pathetically sorry for myself. It's just that now that I have found you, I'm reluctant to let you go. I can be a selfish bastard at times.'

'No, it's okay.' Peta leaned forward to touch his hand gently to reassure him. 'Believe me when I say this, Stewart, I was so looking forward to spending tonight alone with you too, so naturally it was a big let-down for me also when I realised our secret rendezvous wasn't going to happen after all. To be perfectly honest with you, before you came here to find me tonight, I didn't think we would be together again *ever!* Believe me when I say this, Stewart, but I am just as disappointed as you are that I have to leave you now, with so much between us still unsaid.'

'I don't know how to reassure you about where we go from here, Peta, but I do feel absolutely certain in my heart that this feeling we have between us is real. And worth hanging on to ... Wouldn't you agree?'

'Oh, Stewart!' Peta sighed and held him tight. 'Yes, you're right. I can't deny that something amazing has happened between us, whether we are ready for it or not. I think at this stage, though, each of us needs to allow some time alone in the next few weeks to fully process our feelings for each other. Maybe this way, we can come up with some sort of workable solution.'

'As much as I hate to admit it, I think you are absolutely right. We do have to take a step back and figure out where we go from here. It won't be easy for me to watch you walk away from me so soon when I've only just found you.'

'I feel the same way, and thankfully, we've both come to the same conclusions on our own without any pressure from either of us. Any minute now, I'll be asked to board my flight and you will go back to your little shack in the rainforest to sleep in your very comfy bed without me this time. Our careers must be taken into consideration too, for both our sakes. I just know we can work this out together if we take it a bit slower to start with.'

'I agree with you in a way, but we mustn't let our careers rule our lives either. In hindsight, I realise now I did that with both my ex-wives. Each of us ended up emotionally empty and resentful at the end because we foolishly put our careers above all else. This time around, I truly want this new feeling we have for each other to be the prime mover in our relationship. Complete honesty between us has to play an important part, too, otherwise there is not much point in being together in the first place.'

Peta smiled in agreement with him. 'Yes, Stewart, you are absolutely right. Honesty is the only way to go, isn't it?'

Stewart moved forward, with no resistance from Peta this time, and kissed her lightly at first, but their gentle feathery kisses soon turned into deeper ones until they were interrupted by an announcement over the loudspeaker.

'Will the passengers travelling with us tonight on Tropical Airways Flight 204 to Sydney, please make your way immediately to the boarding gate.'

'That's my cue, I believe.' Slightly breathless, Peta broke away first.

'Probably just as well, otherwise those other passengers might be soon yelling at us to, "Go get a room!" They'd be right to say so, too. Man! I am so tempted to drag you back to the Ocean Breeze now,' Stewart murmured in Peta's ear.

'Oh, how very naughty, Mr. Fletcher, but I fear if don't return to Sydney tonight, come Monday morning, I might not have any career to speak of at all. I really must go!'

'Mmm.' Stewart tried to pull her back, but she resisted him until he finally backed off and let her go.

'Yes, I know. Okay, I have to let you go, but reluctantly too, I might add. Please call me when you get back home tonight. It doesn't matter how late. Promise?'

'I promise! I really do have to go now!' Peta grabbed her carry-on and hurried over to join the other passengers. Peta turned to wave to him one last time before disappearing from his view.

Stewart had beamed her a happy smile as he waved back, but on the inside, he felt lonely already.

How will I ever exist without her now? I feel like my heart is flying away with her tonight.

But at least, he reassured himself, there was still a chance of them reconnecting again—in more ways than one. Even though Peta was flying back to Sydney tonight, she still talked of wanting to see him again.

It could have been a whole different story, though, if he hadn't taken the chance to at least try and put things right between them. Staying home feeling sorry for himself just wasn't an option for him anymore with a woman like Peta.

CHAPTER THIRTEEN

fter her flight touched down in Sydney, Peta was happy to be on the move again. She wasted no time in collecting her luggage from the carousel, then was off to the airport car park to pick up her zippy little Suzuki hatch. 'Hello Suzi! I'm back!'

Before long, she was pointing Suzi towards home, sticking as always to her tried and true evasive route around the outskirts of the more erratic, heavily trafficked areas within the pulsing heart of the Sydney Harbour area. Home these days was a roomy granny flat in the quaint Lavender Bay wharf area, which on work days, usually gave her easy access to the city's water ferries.

Peta let herself into her home and threw her keys into their usual basket by the front door. 'Hello home! Have you missed me? Hello plants! Has Alison been looking after you while I've been away? Judging by the moisture in your potted beds, I can see that she has. I am so lucky to have a landlady like her, aren't I?'

Not expecting any answer from her home or plants, Peta talked to them anyway.

'You're not going to believe what's been happening with me these past few days. Unbelievable! Some challenges with the job of course, but some also mind-blowing—and even some totally unexpected—pleasures, too, I might add.' Peta smiled, remembering the erotic touch of Stewart's lips and fingers on her skin. 'In the meantime, I need to settle in for the night and find something to eat. First things first, though. I need to call to a certain sexy guy up at Cairns or he'll think I've forgotten him already.'

Peta retrieved her mobile phone and dialled Stewart's number. While she waited for him to answer, she wedged the mobile phone under her chin as she unpacked some of her clothes into her quaint chest of drawers positioned along the side of her queen-sized bed. As for her laundry, she merely emptied the contents of her travel laundry bag into her compact washing machine. Out of sight, out of mind until tomorrow morning.

'Hello! Stewart Fletcher speaking. Is this who I think it is?'

'Spot on, lover! Well, do you miss me yet?'

'Nah! Not at all!'

'Yeah right! I'll have you know that I miss you enough for both of us then.'

'Not possible. More like fifty-fifty really. To tell you the truth, I feel like you have been gone for months already, instead of mere hours. Since you've gone and left me up here all alone, I now have some serious doubts about my sanity for letting you go at all. It's such a harsh fate indeed, for us to be so cruelly forced apart when we've only just found each other.'

'My, you are being melodramatic tonight.' Peta sniggered down the line. 'I do understand what you mean, though. I honestly don't know how we're going to last for even one night apart, let alone several months. I ache so much for you already. It seems like forever since you made mad, crazy, passionate love to me. We really must be a pathetically obsessed pair.'

'Don't care! Return to me now please! I want you back in my bed immediately!' Stewart demanded.

'I wish! Like I said before, if I could be up there with you now, I would be. You know that.'

'Yes, I do. Well, my friend down below certainly does, too. He's shot up, ready for action, just by the sound of your voice. He says to tell you he's ready to party with you anytime, baby!'

'Is that right?' Peta giggled with girlish delight. 'If I was up there with you right now, he would be well and truly satisfied, I promise him. Not just him, but *all* of you, too.'

'Oh, I don't doubt that. You really are as sexy as you look, Ms. McKenna. Heaven help me!'

'And you, Mr. Fletcher, are the real deal, too. You're not just another handsome face either.'

'I hope you're not going to tell your readers that about me, are you?' teases Stewart.

'Not a chance! Your secret is safe with me. Besides, I want you all for myself now.'

'Good answer! Anyway, perhaps we'd better veer away from this phone sex, for now.' Stewart groaned for effect over the phone line. 'I have such a hard-on now thanks to you, and you're much too far away, sexy lady, to ease my obvious discomfort, aren't you? Maybe we really should change the subject for a while?'

'Point taken. Oops! No pun intended. Yes, I agree. It *is* time to change the subject.'

'How do you think you'll go when you return to work on Monday morning? Do you think your boss will be happy with the interview?'

'I think she'll be happy with the interview side of things, but she may not be very happy if Dominic should happen to let on to her that I have been unprofessional with the subject matter.'

'All jokes aside, you really are worried, aren't you? Do you seriously think Tess will fire you because of whatever Dominic may say about you and me? Surely, he wouldn't be that vindictive, would he?'

'No probably not.' Peta sighed. 'Maybe I am just blowing this whole scenario out of proportion. By the time I go into work on Monday, hopefully my fears will prove to be completely groundless after all.'

'Everything is going to be okay. My advice to you right now would be to always trust your own professional abilities, Peta, especially now. Don't let Dominic rattle you with his verbal or written accusations—whatever they may or may not imply. Show no fear in the face of opposition and, above all, don't openly admit to anything to your boss or Dominic. If you look visibly upset, your boss will know you're guilty for sure. Be cool!'

Peta smiled, despite knowing he couldn't see her response.

'To be perfectly honest, apart from Dominic's ego being crushed of course, I thought you conducted my interview in a totally professional manner and I am sure your boss will see that too,' Stewart offered by way of encouragement. 'Anyway, getting back to Dominic, he has no real physical proof of any wrongdoings by you. Besides, he only has his own suspicions to go by, really. If you have any doubts about what I say, take a minute now to think about this, then, if you will. You really had no choice but to stay alone with me that first night. Because of the cyclone and all the weather reports at the time, you shouldn't have any problem proving that to Tess, right? Apart from that, you behaved professionally with me at all times. Well, most of the time anyway and most definitely while Dominic was in the same room as us.'

He chuckled wickedly. 'Naturally, I will defend you one hundred percent if your boss should happen to ask for my side of the story.'

'You are so sweet. Yes, I did need to hear that. Thanks for the pep talk too. It helps so much to know you're on my side. I'm sure everything will be okay once I talk to Tess face-to-face. It's just this silly fear that has me tied up in knots right now. Just for tonight anyway, I think I need to get a good night's sleep.'

'If I was there with you right now, I could promise you I'd help you to sleep like a baby.'

'Yeah right!' Peta snickered, feeling more lighthearted now. 'You conveniently left out the part where we keep each other awake for all of those hours beforehand, which also involves some very intense horizontal activity.'

'Yes, well, that's true. I cannot deny it, but I promise you will be totally relaxed afterwards, though. But I do understand that I have to let you go to bed without me for now. Have you had anything to eat yet?'

'No, but I'm just about to cook up a speedy noodle and vegetable stir-fry. Easy-peasey.'

'So, you love to cook then?'

'Are you kidding?' Peta scoffed. 'I'm a terrible cook! I can cook some basic, everyday, tasty meals to get by with, but don't ask me to cook any of those fancy meals you see on those cooking shows. What about you? Do you like to cook?'

'Yes, I do, believe it or not. Strange, but true.'

'Ah, so the famous Stewart Fletcher has some other hidden talents that I didn't know about. Speaking for myself though, I do in fact know, that you have some other, dare I say, secret talents that are guaranteed to drive a woman wild.'

'Is that right? So I drive you wild, do I? That's very interesting coming from a woman who knows precisely how to drive a man wild, too. That's if we are talking about the same skill here?'

'Oh, I think you know exactly what skill I'm referring to, but if I even start to imagine your secret skills working on me, I won't be able to get any sleep tonight and it'll be all your fault!'

'Well, you'll have to take some responsibility here for our conversation suddenly getting out of hand again, you know. I have an enormous hard-on again, thanks to you. I think I suppose I'll have to get used to this kind of, shall we say, *awkward* challenge every time I speak to you on the phone. Wicked woman!'

'I'm wicked? Speak for yourself!' Peta scoffed, loving this cheeky banter between them. 'Anyway, lover boy, I guess I'll have to forego our phone sex for now. It's time for me to sign off.'

'Yes, you do need to get some sleep. I will call you again tomorrow night, okay? Pleasant dreams, lover! I'll have you know, my dreams are probably going to be wet dreams tonight and it's all your fault!'

Peta laughed uproariously down the line, delighted to know she was affecting him this much and not feeling guilty in the least. 'You'll survive! Until tomorrow night then, erotic dreams to you!' Peta hung up quickly before Stewart could think of a comeback.

In a dreamy daze, Peta lay back on her comfy sofa, propping her back against some piled-up cushions. She replayed Stewart's every word over and over in her head, smiling about how one's life can change so dramatically in the blink of an eye. Suddenly, apart from the deliciously secret thrill of being Stewart's lover, she just knew her life was about to get a whole lot more interesting from now on. She made a promise to herself to stick around for whatever lay ahead of her.

If I'm still employed come Monday, that is.

CHAPTER FOURTEEN

Peta slept deeply to start with, but then awoke in the early hours before dawn, with a million erratic thoughts spinning around inside her head. After an useless hour or so of tossing and turning, stretching and even some deep breathing lying on her back, she finally gave up any thoughts of going back to sleep. After a quick shower to revive her and to hopefully steam out all the lingering kinks in her still-aching body from her most recent horizontal activity, she was almost ready for anything today.

As a working girl, Peta was required to keep a tight schedule of getting from A to B and then back to A again by her day's end. From Monday to Friday, she caught the water ferry to and from work, within a mad, hectic workplace. Regardless of her hectic weekly schedule, she could never really begrudge the daily challenges of her job. Not at all. She really loved her job. Sometimes, though, she just wished for more of an acceptable level of a more cruisy, stress-free balance, between both work *and* home.

After keeping up with her breakneck schedule throughout her working week, her free and easy weekend mornings were her time to kick back and relax. Saturday mornings were also her clean-up mornings, though. A quick cup of tea and toast was the only allocation of time she allowed herself before cleaning her whole place from top to bottom. Even though this set routine took a good couple of hours to complete, it always gave Peta a sense of satisfaction afterwards to know that, by doing so, there would be less to do from Monday to Friday. Once her tasks were completed, she was free to wander leisurely around her local area, to check out a few local street markets to pick up some fresh fruit and stir-fry vegetables, to restock her fridge for the week, then later on a Saturday night, catch a concert in the park, or maybe even some catch-up time with a fun group of work colleagues who lived close enough nearby at McMahon's Point.

With her laundry already underway, Peta unpacked the last fiddly items from her suitcase before storing it away. Still happily energised, the vacuuming, dusting and mopping followed in double-quick time. She was on a roll! Last but not least; her washing—which she pegged out to dry in the fresh air on the pull-out clothesline, just beyond the seating area of her garden.

Phew! Enough of these household duties for now. I definitely need a caffeine break right about now.

Still in a dreamy state of mind from talking with Stewart last night, Peta snapped out of her wild fantasies long enough to find her gaze had been absently fixed on a wind chime tinkling nearby. She smiled wickedly at the memory of Stewart slowly trailing a path of deliciousness with his ever-exploring fingertips, a devilish gleam of naughty intent in his eyes. She chuckled with delight at catching herself wantonly fantasising about Stewart within her pint-sized cottage garden. Normally, she'd be delighted to observe the colourful butterflies flitting happily about from flower to flower, but just not today. This morning her thoughts were elsewhere, and with good reason, too.

It's not every day a girl dreams of a tall, handsome stranger coming into her life, then have that very same dream turn into reality. This sort of thing only ever happens in movies, doesn't it?

I mean, come on! What are the chances of that happening in real life?

With a strong cappuccino—ready made for her from a foil sachet plus a warmed-up blueberry danish she pulled out of the freezer, she took advantage of the morning sunshine beaming down on her. Peta could hear the usual Saturday morning traffic off in the distance but, thankfully, it was blissfully quiet in her own little corner of the world.

Even with the intention of keeping herself extra busy this weekend, Peta struggled to make sense of her changing moods this morning. One minute she'd be caught up in some fantasy of Stewart turning up on her doorstep and carrying her off to her bed for the rest of the day, the next minute, she'd be bolted out of her delicious fantasy at the horrifying image of sitting meekly in Tess' office while Dominic rubbed his hands together with malicious glee. He'd smirk at her while Tess, with a disapproving look on her face, berated Peta for her unprofessional behaviour with their client before ordering Peta to leave her office and never come back.

At some point this past week, her whole life had become a total contradiction of all the goals she'd set out to achieve with her career. Two of her major career goals—forget the minor ones for now—included; remain professional at all times, and always keep your romantic life and your work life separate. No exceptions.

She was suddenly horrified to realise she had, in fact, already broken two of her hard and fast rules—all in one week, too. How could she have allowed that to happen anyway?

Never mind! I already know the answers. I swear my willpower is null and void lately.

Peta juggled her ever-revolving thoughts and stared off into space until a familiar voice jolted her back to reality.

'Peta? Are you home?' Alison opened the teak wood gate, which served as a private entrance to Peta's granny flat at the back of Alison's stately home at Lavender Bay. She searched Peta's courtyard for some sign her tenant was home and found her exactly where she expected her to be. 'Peta, you're back! How lovely to see you again. I've missed you.'

'Come on in, Alison!' she called out to her elderly landlady from the bedroom. 'I was hoping you would come by today and now here you are!'

'And why wouldn't I?' Alison answered in her quietly spoken, cultural way. Alison smiled as she hugged Peta back and affectionately planted a kiss on each side of her face. 'I wasn't sure if you would be back this weekend or not, but I am so happy to know you are home safe and sound again,'

Alison's face was one of pure serenity. With her unlined, English complexion, her elegant upright frame and soft wavy hair, always styled into a neat bun at the back of her head, the colour always reminding Peta of golden molasses, was obviously carefully mainted by some loving hairdresser. Alison's cultured appearance belied her years. Peta didn't know how she did it but, somehow, her landlady seemed to defy logic as to how a ninety-something-year-old woman is supposed to look, but Peta could pretty much guarantee Alison could most likely put a roomful of fifty-year-old women to shame.

So far, Peta's new accommodation proved to be a real blessing for both her and Alison so she couldn't have wished for a better landlady and really loved living here in this peaceful setting.

It certainly was a complete and happy contrast to her former lodgings of sharing a more upmarket rental house with three other people. Much to Peta's disappointment, no lasting friendships had ever developed between her and the other renters during their one full year together under the same roof. This was no doubt due to the erratic work hours they all kept.

Peta and Alison soon formed a strong bond and an easygoing friendship they'd both craved, regardless of the age difference. In fact, Alison had somehow become more like a doting grandmother to Peta than she had never experienced firsthand. Peta could barely remember her own mother, let alone either of her two grandmothers. If the family albums were anything to go by, though, her beloved Aunt Ruby looked very much like her mother, with the same skin and hair colouring, along with the statuesque beauty of a fashion model.

A special quality Peta loved most about her landlady, though, was the fact Alison never once attempted to interfere in her private life. They mostly kept to themselves Monday to Friday, but when Saturday or Sunday morning rolled around, they loved to enjoy several cups of tea and chat together happily for hours. They'd sit in either Peta's sunlit, leafy courtyard, weather permitting, or under the shade of Alison's expansive front veranda.

'How are you, young lady? I've bought some date and nut loaf for us to enjoy together, seeing that it's your turn to put on the kettle this weekend. Fair exchange I would say.' Alison chuckled.

'I will always make you as many cups of tea or coffee as you want, Alison, *especially* when you bring along such wonderful, home-baked goodies to go with them. Mmm! Date and nut loaf. My Aunt Ruby used to make this too. Delicious! Thanks, Alison. I must admit I'm not much of a cook myself. Being a full-time working girl, I don't really have time to spend in the kitchen.'

'You don't like cooking? Why is that, Peta?'

Peta stopped for a moment to think about it. 'I never really took the time to learn any real culinary skills, I guess. I can cook myself simple meals of course, but anything complicated, forget it! It was my Aunt Ruby, my late mother's sister, who helped to raise me whenever my father had to work overseas during my school years. Thankfully, she is an excellent cook like you.'

'I'm surprised your aunt didn't try to teach you to cook then,' Alison wondered.

'Oh, she did try to teach me, believe me, but I didn't seem to have the same skill for the art of cooking as she did,' Peta lamented. 'Even if she might have despaired of my many culinary disasters at times, she never tried to push me in that direction. When I lived with her, I was much more interested in writing, reading, or studying. She insisted on teaching me some basics of cooking, though. Well, enough to make a decent meal for myself, at least.'

Alison couldn't help asking, 'So, what sort of meals do you usually cook for yourself at the end of your working day then?'

'Oh, lots of stir-fries and quick pasta dishes seem to be my entire forte these days. Stir-fries are my favourite thing most of all, though. To me, it's no effort at all to throw together some fresh mixed vegetables into a pan and toss it around with lots of tasty sauces or seasonings. The quicker, the better, I say! Don't ask me to cook you a full roast dinner, beef stroganoff or even a light-as-air soufflé though!' Peta scoffed. 'Forget it. It's not going to happen,' she declared with no apology forthcoming.

'Ah, well! You are a career girl. To do that these days, you'd have to study all the time to stay ahead of the competition. Is that right?'

'Yes, that's so true. Well, it was for me anyway. What about you ? How do you feel about today's modern career women?'

'Learning to be a seamstress in my teenage years became a career choice for me. During my younger years, careers for women weren't considered all that important at all. Our options involved the inevitable choice of cooking, sewing or homemaking.'

'Good heavens! That'd be like a slow death for me. Not much of a choice at all, is it?'

'To tell you the truth, I hated it. I would have much preferred to study woodwork or even fixing bikes like my two older brothers, who were encouraged by my parents to become whoever they wanted to be.'

'Life certainly was restrictive for women back in those days.' Peta agreed. 'You're obviously an excellent seamstress judging by the beautiful stylish dresses you wear, even at home.'

'Oh, I don't regret being a seamstress all that much, really. After all, wedding dresses and evening wear helped to put a roof over our heads when I was married to my darling Teddy.' Alison then added wistfully, 'We were a team, Eddie and I.'

Peta and Alison continued to chat away as Peta tipped tea leaves into her one and only teapot while Alison cut slices of her cake offering for today.

After having morning tea with Alison for the very first time in Alison's sitting room, with a proper tea setting, Peta rushed out later that day to a nearby antique store, in search of a teapot, cups and saucers with matching cake plates and milk jug as a kind of celebration for her very own kitchen. She'd realised just how much she missed the same tea making ritual with her aunt and her father whenever he was back in Sydney.

Once Peta had set up their morning tea tray, she quickly excused herself. 'I just need to make a quick pit stop to the bathroom first. Go ahead and make yourself comfortable outside, Alison.'

'That's quite alright, dear girl, I'll take the cake out with me then, shall I?'

'Good idea! I'll be back in a jiffy.'

Once Peta had disappeared into the bathroom, Alison smiled to herself at Peta's admission of not being interested in cooking at all. *I must admit, it's a complete mystery to me why Peta doesn't seem to like cooking much at all. To Peta, the art of cooking is merely a means to an end. A sort of survival*

skill for the modern woman of today, I suppose. I can well imagine what my own mother would have to say about that!'

Peta rushed back into the kitchen to boil the jug again and fill up her coffee plunger—since they had already decided on coffee today—and carried it out the back to sit next to Alison.

After a few careful sips of their deliciously hot coffee, Alison spoke first. 'I don't know about you, Peta, but I've been so looking forward to catching up with you over our morning coffee.' Alison smiled, before affectionately covering Peta's hand with her own. 'Since I was away with my son Terry last weekend, I haven't seen you for two weeks now. I can't wait to hear how you went with your first major interview up at Cairns. So! How did it all go for you?'

'Well, to tell you the truth, Alison, I was very apprehensive at first,' Peta admitted. 'Apart from the interview I was sent up there to do, there was also a tropical cyclone brewing in the area. *And* if that wasn't enough to make life interesting, my client was very testy to start with.'

'Good heavens! Why was that?'

Peta didn't think Alison needed to know about everything that happened up north, so she glossed over most of it as best she could. 'Oh, it's a long story. Let's just say that, despite his ongoing popularity, Stewart Fletcher has always been very media-shy. When it comes down to talking about his private life, he's notorious for avoiding interviews every single time, so when I turned up at his front door, he wasn't too impressed about me being there at all.'

'I can imagine. So what happened next? Did you get to do the interview with him after all?'

'I did indeed, but before that, there was a tropical cyclone to get through.'

Alison relished hearing about Peta's experience with the famous author and could barely wait to hear more. 'You certainly have had a few challenges this time around. A raging cyclone *and* a stroppy author, all at the same time. So how did you handle it?'

'Well, I'll give you the short version. With me being an annoying journalist after all, I was reluctantly invited into a Stewart's house to take cover from the cyclone which, I must say, was pretty horrendous at the time. Terrifying, in fact.'

Alison smiled before commenting, 'Well, you did get to call him by his first name at least.'

Peta grinned, aware Alison had already caught on to her efforts to underplay her time spent with Stewart. 'Anyway, during the worst moments of the cyclone, we were forced to literally lay low in his old claw-footed bathtub, of all places, with a blanket over our heads to protect us from any flying debris.'

'Let me get this straight,' Alison interrupted again. 'You were forced to spend all of those harrowing moments squashed up close together in a bathtub, with this stroppy Mr. Fletcher, while those fierce cyclonic winds outside threatened to blow you both away? My-my!' Alison said innocently. 'If you don't mind me asking, did anything else happen in the bathtub, then?'

'Alison!' Peta exclaimed in shock, her face quickly turning beetroot red with embarrassment. 'I can't believe you just asked me that!'

'I may be an old lady, but I can still remember what real passion feels like. My darling Eddie knew how to keep me happy in more ways than one—if you get my meaning?'

'I absolutely do.' Peta grinned. 'But to answer your question, nothing happened in the bathtub. Not in that way, at least. Besides, it really was extremely uncomfortable with the two of us cramped together like that, so any horizontal activity was out of the question, anyway.'

'Yes, I suppose it would have been.' Alison agreed with a rather devilish grin. 'A real shame, though.'

Peta was a bit shocked to hear Alison talk so openly with her about sex, but when she was able to look Alison in the eye, red-faced and all, she exclaimed, 'Alison! I can't believe you just said that!' That's when Peta spotted the wicked knowing gleam in Alison's own eyes and burst out laughing. 'Alison, you make me laugh with what you come out with sometimes!'

'Well I may be a woman with an old body, but that doesn't everything has shrivelled up.'

'Alison! Now I really am shocked. What a wicked woman you turned out to be!'

'So,' Alison's smile, obviously delighted with her own cheekiness, couldn't wait to question Peta some more. 'All jokes aside, what is the famous Mr. Stewart Fletcher really like? What I mean is, did you become friends at least? I can't help but be intrigued now.'

'Yes, we did by the time I left there. The real Stewart Fletcher surprised me by being funny and smart, and not a grouch at all.'

Should I tell Alison about us? I'm pretty sure I can trust her by now.

'I'm going to tell you a little secret now. You'll be the first person to know that Stewart Fletcher and myself did become more than just friends by the end of our fateful night together. In fact, I believe I may have fallen head over heels in love with him. The best part is that I truly believe he loves me, too.'

'I thought so!' Alison blurted out. 'How wonderful! You have a definite glow about you that you never had before. I, myself, have only ever loved one man, and he loved me so completely in return too. Somehow, without you even telling me, I've intuitively picked up on this powerful new love between you and the dashing Mr. Fletcher.' Alison paused to take a sip of tea. 'You know, I can't help thinking his very own name itself sounds like it belongs in a romance novel too, doesn't it? A bit like how the simple name of Mr. Darcy from *Pride and Prejudice* provokes a kind of intrigue about him, just from his name alone. Wouldn't you agree?'

'Yes, most definitely,' Peta chuckled. 'More coffee?'

'Yes, thank you. Who can ever stop at one cup? Besides, I simply can't leave now, can I? I'll have to stay around a little longer to hear some more.' Peta lifted the plunger again to pour them another cup each, but realised it was close to empty already. 'How about I slip into the kitchen first and make us a fresh brew before I continue?'

'Oh yes, please do, Peta. Do you need any assistance?'

'No! Not at all. You just sit here and enjoy this lovely morning light. I'll be right back.'

Before long, Peta was back outside, replenishing their cups with the freshly made steaming, aromatic coffee.

'So, where do you go from here? In other words, what's next for you two?' Alison asked.

'Well, our affair will have to be kept hush-hush for now and I'm sure you understand why. Stewart has already started a new book recently, so he needs to knuckle down and concentrate on that for now. And I have my own work in Sydney, so we've agreed to keep our affair under wraps. After all, he lives up at Cairns and I live all the way down here in Sydney. I've often read about long-distance relationships being difficult enough to maintain as it is. We both thought it would be better to take it slow for a few months. Hopefully, after some time spent apart from each other, we'll know where to go from there.'

'Yes, I think you're both wise to do that,' Alison said. 'I've always been a true romantic. I truly believe that if your love story is destined to be, any complications along the way will sort themselves out in their own way and in their own time.'

'Yes, you're absolutely right. You always give me such good advice. Thank you!'

'Happy to help. You're a smart girl though, and I am sure you'll figure it out as you go along. One small piece of advice for you—that's if you don't mind me saying this?'

'No, not at all. I'd appreciate any advice from you right now. I trust you completely.'

'That's lovely to know. Thank you, my dear. My advice to you is: Whatever you and Stewart decide to do, please be true to yourselves above all else.'

'Oh yes! I certainly will remember that.' Peta rushed over to hug her elderly friend. 'Thank you so much, Alison. I also want you to know how much I value and appreciate you as my friend. I could never have asked for a better landlady than you, that's for certain.'

'I'm thrilled to have you in my life, too. You came into my life like a breath of fresh air and took my loneliness away. I believe God bought us together for a reason, don't you?'

'He sure has! Whatever happens from this moment on, is all in the hands of God and fate! I just wish I could have met Stewart a long time ago, that's all. It's frustrating to finally meet the man of my dreams, only to have to say goodbye to him so soon.'

'That may appear to be so, but if there's one thing I've learnt myself over the years, is that problems always have a way of sorting themselves out without any help from us at all. Trust an old lady on this one. By this time next year, you'll be asking yourself why you ever doubted this. In the meantime, it's time for me to leave you and let you get in with your weekend chores.'

Peta sighed. 'Is it time to say goodbye already? Time seems to fly by so quickly when we spend time together, doesn't it?'

'It certainly does!' Alison agreed as she stretched her hands out to hug Peta goodbye. 'Same time next week then?'

'Most definitely!' Peta embraced Alison with loving affection once more. 'By the way, thanks again for your wise advice in regard to a certain new romance, too. You've also helped me to forget some other work issues I need to sort out with my boss come Monday morning. Wish me luck.'

'Anytime, Peta dear. Bye for now!'

Alison turned and headed off along the side passageway. Peta watched her until her elderly landlady turned left onto the front footpath and out of sight, marvelling again over Alison's agility and sense of purpose.

CHAPTER FIFTEEN

This is it! The moment of truth. There's no turning back now. Peta prompted herself one last time as she stepped out of the lift in front of Tess' office on the second floor. She took one more deep breath for good luck as she opened the glass door into Tess' exclusive business domain.

'Good morning, Peta! Good to see you're back home safe and sound.' Beth, personal secretary to Tess, greeted her as Peta entered the reception area. 'Please take a seat. Tess is on a call now, but will be with you shortly.'

'Thanks Beth.'

As instructed, Peta seated herself outside Tess' office to await her summons into the official inner sanctum.

As to Peta, Tess was an exceptional boss who never expected her staff to do any more than she would herself. She also inspired dedication and loyalty from her staff, because she never once boasted of her promotion as the editor-in-chief of Australia's newest glossy magazine, *Today's Voice,* claiming to promise its readers the real truth behind the latest controversial headlines.

Tess was tough but fair, but Peta also knew if she was to push Tess too far, she would be fired in an instant with no second chances.

She flicked through the pages of a *Time Life* magazine from a neatly stacked pile of reading matter, more to distract herself than to actually read. What she was really needed to do was concentrate now on projecting an image of calm poise towards Beth, sitting at her lofty command post, outside Tess' office. On the inside, though, Peta's whole body was wound up tight into a bundle of raw nerve endings, threatening to trip her tongue up any moment now. If that wasn't enough, her inner thoughts were heading past the point of no return—a bizarre state of disordered mess and straight into an inevitable danger zone within sixty seconds. The magazine print in front of her blurred, only to be replaced by a thousand what-if images, spinning around in front of her eyes, instead of the peace and calm she craved right now.

Peta still had no idea what excuse she could come up with to justify her actions to Tess. Hopefully something will come to her if put on the spot. Undoubtably, it will all depend on the kind of reception she receives when she walks into Tess' office. With a bit of miraculous luck too, Dominic will still be down in Canberra, so she won't have to look into his smug face this morning. Heavens knows what lies he has up his sleeves.

Shit! What might Dominic already have told Tess about her unprofessionalism with Stewart? What could she put forward in her own defence, then? If Tess were to ask her if Dominic's accusations were true, what could she say? Maybe, as Stewart suggested, she should deny having any sort of relationship with him at all. Yes, I think Stewart is right. *I should just deny everything and stick to it—at this early stage, anyway. Well, let's hope it works on Tess.*

It was as if Beth picked up on Peta's turmoil as she broke into Peta's thoughts.

'By the way, Peta, I've been told by Tess that your interview with Stewart Fletcher went very well. I believe congratulations are in order for both you and Dominic.'

Congratulations? Peta stared at Beth in a daze, wondering if she'd heard her right.

'Well, Tess has told me that you have both done a great job with the Fletcher interview. She sounded ecstatic about it, in fact. Great work, Peta!'

'Really? She's happy about what we did, then?'

'Absolutely! But I think it's best that she tells you this personally. Just a sec. I can see she's finished with her call. I'll just buzz through to her now to let her know you're here.'

While Beth spoke to Tess on the intercom, Peta took a moment to digest Beth's words. So all of her stressing this past weekend may have been unfounded after all? Thank goodness! This meant Dominic couldn't have told Tess about any of his vindictive suspicions then. Surely he must have attempted to plant the seed of doubt in Tess' mind, at least?

Hell! Dominic might have something even more destructive in mind to get back at me for my rejection of him.

'Peta? Peta! Are you okay?' Beth's concerned voice suddenly broke into her erratic thoughts at last.

'Sorry Beth. I must have been miles away,' Peta apologised.

'That's quite alright. Tess will see you now. Go right on in.'

'Thanks. I'll see you on the way out.'

Despite Peta feeling more composed with her new resolve to stay strong in the face of opposition, she was still somewhat nervous anyway as she entered Tess' office.

'Ah! There she is! Clever girl! Welcome back! How are you Peta?'

'I'm good thanks, Tess. Happy to be back home. And you?'

'I'm great Peta. Thanks for asking. Please come in and sit down.' Tess motioned with an elegantly manicured hand. 'I've been waiting to hear everything about your trip to Cairns. Firstly though, would you fancy some coffee? I have a new, nifty little coffee machine in my office, so I can make myself a cup of lifesaving caffeine whenever I want to now.'

'Yes, I would thanks, Tess.'

'How do you like it? Black? White? Strong? Weak? You name it, I can do it.' Tess offered with an obviously excited lift to the tone of her voice.

'White and two, oh and rather strong too, thanks,' Peta responded, not wanting to spoil Tess' enthusiasm by telling her she'd finished her morning coffee ten minutes ago.

As Tess busied herself with her newly acquired toy, they chatted easily about other inconsequential matters. All the while, Peta knew she'd still have to tell Tess about staying at Stewart's with no Dominic around to act as a sort of unofficial chaperone. Just her and the sexiest man alive, alone together on the night of a raging cyclone; forced to lay cramped together for hours in an old-fashioned bathtub. Must've forgotten to add that bit of drama.

'Come and sit over here on the sofa with me. It's much more comfortable to chat here away from my desk.'

Peta nodded her head in agreement as she moved on over to the sofa and sat beside Tess, who immediately handed Peta a rather impressive, frothed-up mug of cappuccino.

'Wow! This looks just like a professionally made coffee to me.'

'Nothing to it! You really can't go wrong with these new fangle-dangle appliances these days. You just hit the button and *voila!* It practically does it all for you. It's certainly not rocket science. Would you like something to go with the coffee? A danish or a biscuit, maybe?'

'No, I'm good for now, thanks.' Peta sipped at her coffee, trying not to get any froth around her mouth in the process. 'Delicious!'

'Why, thank you, Peta. It's all in the way you press the button, really.'

Tess laughed and Peta joined in, relaxing at last with Tess' usual easy-going sense of fun. For now, they were like two old friends relaxing on Tess' soft leather sofa, sharing a lighthearted moment together.

The calm before another kind of storm! Peta fought to squash down her inner turmoil.

'Now, let's get into what we are here to talk about. I have been dying to know how you went with the interview, with your own personal slant on it, of course. I particularly want to know how you got along with the prickly, intensely private Stewart Fletcher. I must say, you seem to have handled the whole Cairns assignment very well and I am very proud of you.'

'Are you really, Tess?'

Peta could hardly believe she was receiving a pat on the back from Tess, rather than the images from her ongoing nightmare—of her boss kicking her out the door.

'I most certainly am. I was also very relieved to hear how you managed to survive that nasty cyclone with your body still intact. Let me tell you, you're much braver than me. I think I would've probably been out of there in a flash! Story or no story. It must've been terrifying to go through such a scary experience. I must confess, too, Peta, I felt rather horrified afterwards when I realised just how serious the cyclone warning was. I never should've sent you up there in the first place. I guess it just goes to show how blasé we Southerners can be. What perils those crazy—but tough—North Queenslanders must endure every cyclone season? There is no way I would want to live up there permanently. Not even if you paid me.'

'It *was* rather scary at the time. It was the howling winds I hated the most. You feel like you're going to be physically swept away at any time. Now I understand what it's like to suddenly feel so vulnerable and at the complete mercy of Mother Nature's unpredictable moods. As you just said, Tess, you have to wonder how the locals up there manage to survive these cyclones, season after season, with their sanity still intact.'

'That must be why we Southerners often joke about the North Queenslanders going troppo,' Tess added with a laugh. 'Over time, their carefree lifestyle must eventually catch up with them, resulting in some kind of tropical madness. It's also probably why they appear to be bliss-fully oblivious to everything going on south of their own border. Even the rest of the world for that matter. If the heat or the cyclones don't get them in the end, the drink will. Bloody crazy lot!'

'Amen to that!' Peta chuckled. 'The locals sure do seem like a happy bunch of people, though.'

'I'm rather curious now.' Tess added, studying a Peta's face the whole time. 'Where were you during the worst of the cyclone? Were you still holed up at the hotel resort, or where you caught in the middle of it, somewhere between Cairns and Stewart Fletcher's place? I'm aware that Fletcher lives a fair distance away from the city. I found myself worrying about how you could have possibly survived such an experience out in the open.'

Here comes the moment of truth! I must be very careful about how I answer her questions from now on.

'Thank you for your concern. I was perfectly okay, though. Stewart Fletcher lives about sixty kilometres from Cairns itself, completely enclosed within a lush rainforest area. Just after I'd arrived at the Ocean Breeze Resort Hotel, Dominic rang to tell me he was still in Sydney and he couldn't get up to Cairns until the following day. His airline and all the others had cancelled all flights to Cairns because of the cyclone. We came to the same conclusion that it was best for me, rather than waste a whole day, to continue on to Stewart Fletcher's place and at least try to secure the interview with him out of the way first. Just in case Mr. Fletcher used the cyclone as an excuse to back out of it. Our plan was for a Dominic to follow up with the photo shoot when he could get out there.'

'Great idea! That's using your heads. A wise and practical move! So what happened when you arrived out there all alone? I mean with Fletcher's uncooperative reputation and his dislike of women in general. Was he mean to you at all?'

'Well, he wasn't too impressed at first when I came knocking on his door.' Peta recalled with a smirk. 'Because of my first name, he told me he was, in fact, expecting a Mr. Peter McKenna.'

'Oh no! So when you turned out to be this beautiful blonde knocking on his door instead, the alarm bells would have gone off in his head. Oh my! So, how did you handle it?'

'Predictably, he was all fire and brimstone at first.' Peta laughed at the memory. 'He was dead set against letting me into his place at all and he even slammed his front door in my face *twice*!'

'What? He slammed the door in your face? What a bastard! Sorry, Peta.'

'I sat down on his veranda steps and refused to leave. I told him I was sent here to do a job, and I wasn't going to leave until I got what I came for.'

'You did?' Tess laughed uproariously. 'I bet that went down well.'

'Like the proverbial lead balloon but by then, the big, scary cyclone was also starting to make its presence known in a big way. I must admit, I was feeling more than a little scared by this stage and ready to drive away empty-handed. But then he finally relented and let me come inside.'

'Ha! That was big of him!' Tess scoffed. 'So how did he treat you once you were inside?'

'At the time, to be honest, we didn't really have time for any social niceties because he was rushing around making sure the windows and doors were all secure. After that was done, he actually behaved like a perfect gentleman from then onwards. He gave me something to eat, and he also offered me the sofa in his lounge room to sleep for the night.'

Well, technically, that's not a lie. Stewart really did offer me the sofa to start with.

'So what happened during the cyclone? Were you scared? Was any part of his house blown away at all, like a part of the roof, perhaps?'

'His house is more or less an old country shack really, which was built in the1930s, he told me. It had already survived many a cyclone over the years, even before he bought it. Stewart said houses were built to last back in those days and his is still solid as a rock.'

'Stewart? You call him Stewart now? How come?' Tess questioned with a gleam in her eye.

'He asked me to. Since we'd be sharing his house during a cyclone, he didn't think it was appropriate to stick to any formalities under the circumstances. He did the same with Dominic, too.'

'Fair enough. So, I gather by this stage, after he let you stay that is, he was finally agreeable to you doing the interview after all?'

'Well, not exactly, Tess. When Stewart let me into his place, the agreement between us, at the time, was that I not mention the interview at all whilst I was inside his home. I readily agreed to his terms and conditions because I so desperately needed to be safe inside, away from those howling winds screaming around me outside his shack. As you can imagine, it was totally terrifying at the time, so I had no choice but to accept his conditions of entry. I figured I could talk him around to the idea later. Once the cyclone had blown over, that is.'

'I can certainly understand that. I would have done the same thing. Go on.'

'Anyway, when Dominic turned up the next morning, I think Stewart realised then he had no choice but to go ahead with his scheduled interview, after all. At the beginning, he wasn't at all happy about either of us being there, but once we eased his mind about my relaxed way of doing things, he didn't seem so threatened by us anymore. Stewart actually opened up and gave us what we came for, so it all worked out beautifully in the end.'

'Great work! To both of you, in fact. I must say, I am very relieved to know that you and Dominic have a good working relationship with each other, too. Unfortunately, it's not always the case with some of the journalist and photographer teams I send out on assignments. It can be very difficult to get the right combination in regard to compatibility or personalities within some teams.'

Without sharing her own reservations regarding ever working with

Dominic again, Peta decided intuitively to not let on to Tess about his inappropriate behaviour.

'Up until now, I've only worked with Dominic a few times around Sydney, but each time, I have observed that Dominic is usually totally focused and professional with his work, just as I am. We both take pride in getting the job done to your satisfaction, Tess.'

'That's what I like to hear, Peta. So you won't mind working with Dominic again?'

'Sure.' Peta agreed. *Once I remind Dominic of his boundaries first, that is.*

'Wonderful! Anyway, I hate to push you out of here, but I have a very important meeting to go to and I can't be late. When I hear of any work you can do together in the near future, I'll be in touch with you via Beth of course. Once again, I'm super proud of the way you've handled your first major assignment. You've done us all proud. We'll talk again soon.'

Peta smiled at Beth as she left Tess' office, so much more relieved than when she entered a little under an hour ago. At least her career was still intact. *For now!*

As for Dominic, Peta understood that for the sake of her career, she'd still have to work with him on future assignments. There was no escaping this fact, especially where Tess was concerned, who always expected her staff to get along with each other, regardless of any ill feelings. Peta felt confident enough she could deal with Dominic's deluded ego trips about himself, if and when the time came. Next time, she'd be more prepared and not so willing to accept his bullshit anymore.

So as to avoid any misunderstandings with Dominic in the future, her time spent with him from now on has to remain strictly business.

CHAPTER SIXTEEN

It was almost a week since Peta left for Sydney, but already the once-prized sanctuary of his private bedroom was a sad and lonely place. He had a book to write and no amount of procrastinating would alter that fact. No-one would step forward to offer to write it for him. But here he was, mooning about with thoughts of Peta, his excuse of constant yearnings to devour her scrumptious body stealing his precious writing time.

He swore he caught a lingering drift of her exotic perfume. He could still sense her body lying beside him. He savoured her delightful responses to his touch and even the taste of her teasing lips piquing his desire again and again.

Let's face it, she literally has you screwed, man!

Professionally, though, Stewart knew he needed to start on his next book by the end of the day. He took some satisfaction in knowing once this latest addition to his *Tyler Jackson* series was done and dusted, he'd finally have time to explore new possibilities. Which included frolicking under the sheets with a certain beautiful lady, too.

To distract him from his reawakened libido, he'd an excellent excuse for stalling once again. Every second week, Stewart escaped his humble abode and his creative pursuits, for a few hours, to take off to Cairns. He'd travel for the essential task of restocking his almost-depleted fridge and pantry, plus various other essential items he needed to keep him going for the next fortnight.

After an hour or two spent at a local shopping centre, a trip to his bank and lastly, to the post office to pay some bills, Stewart headed home, grateful to leave the city behind once again. It was good to escape his enforced isolation and get back to civilisation most of the time, but it was bloody marvellous to head home again, too. Stewart drove past numerous sugar cane properties with their simple, weatherboard farmhouses positioned at the front of each property, along with their rusty sheds close by, shading their equally rusty tractors from the steamy midday sun. On both sides of the road, massive irrigation watering frames snaked their way throughout the far-reaching cane fields. For some crazy reason, these gawky irrigation frames always reminded Stewart of giant praying mantises with their long, gangly arms outstretched. Much like the insects waited patiently for their prey, the frames waited for the farmer to give them the go-ahead to shower the cane fields with their essential, thirst-quenching water and nutrients.

Back home, Stewart unpacked the items from the Rover, then stored everything away in its rightful place. He knew from habit that Oscar was now perched on the back of a barstool, looking for attention.

'Hello! Hello! Stu's back! Stu's back!' he squawked.

'Hello, my fine feathered friend.' Stewart scratched Oscar's top feathers. 'Yes, I'm back from that steamy city at last. Believe me Oscar, you're far better off staying here in the shade, mate.' When Stewart stopped scratching Oscar to finish his task, Oscar moved closer to Stewart and dipped his head for some more of those blissful scratches. After a few minutes, though, Stewart finally had to reject any further nudging from his persistent, narcissistic parrot.

'You're not going to like hearing this, Oscar, but I'm going to have to call it quits on this whole head scratching thing of yours, but if it's okay with you, Oscar, I promise you that when I've finished storing away the last of these bags, we can then go out on the veranda together, just you and me—to share an ice-cold beer together, okay?' Oscar bobbed his head a few times to let Stewart know he didn't believe him.

'Oscar's got an itch! Oscar's got an itch!'

'Well, tough! Don't look at me like that. It won't do you any good. You need to fly away now and leave me to finish up here. Go! Please!' Oscar predictably squawked in protest at Stewart's firm order to leave his kitchen, but Oscar, as persistent as he can be, finally took the hint to fly back to his shady perch on the veranda.

'Bloody stubborn bird!' Stewart muttered. 'I have to wonder who's the real boss around this old shack!'

Since Oscar was already sulking, he didn't really expect an answer.

While Stewart finished off his household tasks, he continued to switch from one persistent thought to another. Once he'd ticked off his domestic to-do list, he allowed loving thoughts of Peta to settle happily back into place. This time, however, his thoughts are now of the overactive kind.

He wondered how Peta was managing on her first morning back at work. Hopefully, he'd hear from her tonight, otherwise he'd be still worrying about her all through the week, wondering if she can manage to keep her job. Even worse; what repercussions might occur if Dominic should still happen to submit a formal complaint about her lack of professionalism while she was out here with him. Let's hope that arse Dominic doesn't make life too difficult for her.

Hell! Maybe she'll even lose her job over this, and it'll all be because of me. She could even be hiding out in some lonely bar somewhere in Sydney right now, drowning her sorrows.

Stewart put a stop to his maudlin thoughts.

What in the hell is wrong with me? This kind of thinking is not even funny. Of course Peta wouldn't do something like that. She has way too many brains to even think such a thing. At least, I trust she isn't really like this.

Which gave him cause to wonder as to why he should have to ask himself this question in the first place? To be honest, he didn't know much about the *real* Peta McKenna, did he? What he did know, though, was that he was crazy in love with her, and that's all he needed to know for now. Those other details will eventually come to light later.

Let's hope so, anyway.

One other thing he knew was his urgent need to concentrate on his own work and let everything else take care of itself. Besides, there was more than enough work to keep him out of mischief for the next few months.

Stewart was just about to send Tyler into a remote roadside cafe and into a roomful of rough, burly bikers in tattered leather jackets. Right at that extremely tense moment when Tyler was completely surrounded, Stewart's phone rang, breaking his concentration. He jumped, startled.

Damn! I forgot to take the phone off the hook this time.

Stewart tried to ignore the persistent distraction, but the damn phone kept right on ringing.

'Don't answer it!' Tyler Jackson begged Stewart. 'I need you to extricate me out of this sticky mess you've got me into!'

But it was too late. The spell was already broken. Stewart hesitated too long and his incoming call automatically transferred over to the answering machine after the set number of rings.

'Stewart? Are you there, bro? I guess you're still in the middle of writing, otherwise you would have answered my call by now, you slacker! I'm sorry to bother you at this time of the day, but I need you to pick up.

Please. It's really important … Okay, I get it! You're obviously not there. When you do get this message, please call me back immediate—'

'Matt! What's wrong? Why are you calling me in the middle of the day? Is Mum okay?' Stewart snatched up the phone.

'Relax! Bloody hell! Questions, questions! All is well. Mum sends her love, by the way.'

'Very relieved to hear that. You don't normally call me in the middle of the day. What's up?'

'Yeah well, like I said, I'm sorry, but you know damn well I wouldn't be calling you unless it was really important.'

'Okay, okay! I get it! Sorry to bite your head off. I do tend to get a bit caught up in my writing process sometimes. So, tell me, little brother. What's this urgent problem then?'

'I have some good news and some bad news. Which do you want first?'

'I sort of guessed there'd be some bad news tucked away in there somewhere. You choose.'

'Okay, the good news first, then. It seems our father didn't hate you as much as you once thought. The probate for Father's will has only just been settled, which also means that all of our father's assets are to be divided evenly between us all—Mum, me and you.'

'What do you mean? Come on, spit it out, Matt! Anytime today would be good.'

'Okay! Jeez! Such impatience! Well Father, as you well know, was a very astute businessman. He had his fingers in a lot of highly profitable pies it seems, which is why it has taken so long for all of his financial affairs to be finalised.'

'We all know how smart Father was when it came to organising his financial matters. But what does our father's latest financial affairs have to do with me? When I left Melbourne after he and I exchanged those last angry words, he told me, in no uncertain terms, I am no longer his son and I was to be written out of his will. End of story!'

'That's what I've been trying to tell you. You haven't been written out of his will. Maybe he did write you out at some point way back then. But according to Bernard, it appears he had a change of heart sometime within the past year, and you are very much included, after all.'

'I don't understand. Why do you think he changed his mind?'

'You know how Father was, Stu. When it came to backing down from any fight, he was stubborn as all hell! Just like somebody else I know! Not mentioning any names of course.'

Stewart grunted good-naturedly, by way of responding to Matt's stirring him about he and their father being so much alike with their stubbornness. However, he deliberately chose to ignore Matt's teasing just the same.

Once Matt realised Stewart wasn't going to respond to his gibe, Matt had no choice but to continue, 'Well, Stu, I think the years just slipped by way too quickly for him—for all of us, really. Before we knew it, he was gone. Bernard also told me Father has left a private letter for you too, but has been given strict instructions to give it to you, and only you, if anything should ever happen to him. No doubt in the event he'd never get to tell you how he felt himself. Anyway, you can collect it personally when you come down to Melbourne next week. You can also pick up the deeds to our Pittwater holiday house, too. After you sign everything off legally, of course.'

Matthew said the last part quickly, right at the end of the good news, waiting for the penny to drop. He didn't have to wait too long.

'Hang on a minute. Whoa! Back up a minute, will you? Are you telling me that Father has left me our family's holiday house at Pittwater? You're kidding me, right?'

'I kid you not. Father left me his share of his law business in Melbourne. To Mother, he has left her our family home in Melbourne, plus a generous amount of money for her to live on. Your good news for today though, he has left you the Pittwater property. How about that? He always understood how you loved that place just as much as he did.'

In shocked response to this latest news, Stewart leaned right back in his office chair, with an instant flash of happier memories flooding his busy mind. It was a rather distracted Stewart who attempted to answer Matt this time.

'Yes, I certainly do have a lot of happy memories of going fishing with Father at Pittwater. I guess I already had it in my head that he must have sold it years ago.'

'No, he still hung onto it, even though he hadn't been down that way since you left home.'

'Wow! You have blown me away with this news. I can hardly believe this.'

'Being a solicitor myself certainly has its advantages, which is why I am privy to this particular confidential information directly from Bernard. He wanted to make sure you will be down here in Melbourne, Stu, in person, by next Tuesday.'

'Do you mean this coming Tuesday? As in the Tuesday of next week? Bloody hell!'

'Yep! You got it! This is the only reason I've been allowed to tell you this now, before the reading of the will, Stu. As you know, Bernard has been Father's solicitor, like, forever. While it's true Bernard could just send a copy of the will to you via Australia Post, but given the fact that you live all the bloody way up north and out in the middle of nowhere, too, he didn't like his chances of you receiving them any time soon. Bernard also feels—as do I—that it's important that you be here in person—as a way of letting the past go once and for all.

'I'm happy to say, though, that's the only bad news I have for you. I'm happy to report everything else is good down south of the Victorian border. Look, bro, I do understand that coming back home is going to be a huge challenge for you, but I really can't stress enough to you, that you absolutely *must* be here by next Tuesday to sign off on these legal papers with Bernard. Unless you really don't want any part of your inheritance at all. Or even the letter from Father.'

'Naturally, I'm excited about the house at Pittwater, Matt, but Father's letter is also important to me, too. You already know that, though, otherwise you wouldn't be ringing me in the first place … Am I right?'

'Perceptive as always.' Matt waited for Stewart to gather his thoughts together. 'So to answer my question then, Stu, do you think you might be able to make it down this way for Tuesday perhaps?'

'The answer is yes, of course, Matt. Hopefully this trip back home will mean some kind of closure for me at last. Besides, I can't wait to see you and Mother too. But that goes without saying.'

'I'm glad you added that last bit. I was beginning to feel neglected for a bit there.'

'Very funny!' Stewart scoffed. 'You're overdue for a good thrashing from me when I get down that way, little bro. Seriously though, the fact that our father has even acknowledged me at all, has lightened my heavy heart enormously. Especially considering the way I left Melbourne under such a murky cloud of anger and regret.'

'I have a feeling this is going to be a real turning point for you, but only you can know that for sure.' Matt waited now for Stewart to gather his thoughts together. 'So, I'll go ahead and let Bernard know he can expect you in this office next week then. Is that acceptable for you, Stu?'

'Hell yes! I'll look on the computer now and book a flight for next Monday. I'll call you back with the flight details as soon as I know for sure.'

'Good man! I'll hold off on making an appointment with him, though, until I get some flight details from you. I'll also ask Mother to open up your room, shall I? She did say something to me about turning it into a sewing room sometime soon.'

'Ha! You're hilarious! By the way, Matt, in case I've failed to tell you this before, thank you for taking the time to arrange all of this! You're a legend!'

'You're welcome!'

Matt brushed off Stewart's gratitude as no big deal, but Stewart could still tell by Matt's voice that it meant a lot to him to know Stewart acknowledged his help anyway.

'Well, since you have expressed such gratitude to me now, I might even consider opening my wallet to buy you lunch and a beer in the city when you get down this way.'

'Deal! In the meantime, though, I still have some urgent work to do. I suppose I should go easy on poor Tyler this time and extradite him somehow from the bikies' cafe still in one piece.'

'Tyler? Bikies' cafe? What in the hell are you talking about? Ah!' The penny finally dropped. '*The* Tyler Jackson from your action stories, right?' Matt laughed.

'How quickly you forget. Tyler Jackson is my alter ego of, course.'

'Oh man! I will never understand where all of your crazy characters come from. You definitely take after our mother when it comes to all of this literary mumbo jumbo. But for now, Stu, I must get back to work too. I'll look forward to catching up with you next week. Please don't forget to send me those flight details ASAP so I can lock in that appointment for next Tuesday.'

'Okay, okay! As soon as I get off this call from you, I'll get online and book my flight right now. I promise to I'll ring you back within the hour. Thanks again, Squirt! Bye for now!'

'Squirt? Wow! You haven't called me that in a long while.' Matt chuckled.

'Well, you may be all grown up now, Matt, but you'll always be Squirt to me. Bye mate!'

CHAPTER SEVENTEEN

Peta was fully committed to finishing off the last of her paperwork close to knock-off time on Friday afternoon. She'd only been back at work in Sydney for a week, but already it was beginning to feel like she'd never left.

Argh! When is this ever going to end? Unbelievable! Will somebody please remind me why I chose to become a journalist in the first place?

What she wouldn't give to be back in Cairns with Stewart instead. Peta found herself in a constant dreamy state of mind since returning home. It was hard to believe she'd only known him for a week. How was that even possible? True, she knew *of* him, but not the man behind the image. Her time spent alone with him seemed like some crazy fantasy now.

Ah, but what a lovely fantasy, though.

For the next twenty minutes, Peta managed to push the distraction of Stewart doing things to her body she couldn't have imagined a week ago.

Her long list of emails from her inbox were slowly and systematically being moved to her sent folder, with still about a dozen to go.

Somebody—anybody—please save me from this drudgery!

As if on cue, her phone extension buzzed. The call was coming from Tess' office.

Strange! It's Friday and nearly time to go home. Why would Tess be calling me now? Well, there's only way to find out.

'Hello, Peta speaking.'

'Hi Peta. It's Beth. Tess would like you to pop into her office for a minute, please?'

'Right now?'

'Yes. Tess requested for you come immediately!'

'On my way,' Peta answered casually, but she was worried. Maybe Dominic told Tess of his suspicions about her affair with Stewart, after all.

Oh hell!

Tess greeted Peta at her office door with a smile. No frown, at least.

A good sign, perhaps?

'Hello Peta. Thanks for coming to see me so promptly, especially on a Friday afternoon, too.' Tess turned to Beth as she prepared to pack up her desk for the weekend break.

'Beth, I just need to talk to Peta about the new assignment we talked about for next week, so it shouldn't take too long. I can lock up, so there's no need for you to hang around. You just go and enjoy your weekend.'

'Thanks Tess, I will. You enjoy your weekend, too.'

'Thanks for all your help this past week, as always. Especially with the meeting this morning.'

'My pleasure. Bye! See you Monday. Bye to you too, Peta.'

'Thanks Beth. You too.'

As soon as the lift doors closed on Beth, Tess got down to business.

'Sorry for the late summons to my office. I am sure you must have thought I was calling you in here with some bad news. Especially on a Friday afternoon when most of the staff are itching to get away for the weekend.'

'Well, I must admit the thought did cross my mind for a minute or two,' Peta replied honestly, then laughed. 'I thought maybe you might be laying me off or something.'

'Not a chance! Besides, you're one of our best journalists. I'd be crazy to let you go.'

'Thanks Tess. It's reassuring to know you feel that way.' The tension at the back of Peta's neck relaxed.

'Sorry for such short notice, but a newsworthy story has been bought to my attention today. You and Dominic will be going on an assignment together next week. I will need you and Dominic to be in Melbourne for an interview for Tuesday of next week.'

'Melbourne?' Peta asked nervously, then found herself laughing openly. 'Sorry, Tess, but I can't help finding this kind of funny in a way. Dominic and I seem to be going from one end of Australia to the other lately.'

'Not intentionally, I assure you.' Tess smiled, seeing the funny side of it too. 'It sure does seem that way, doesn't it?'

'So what's happening in Melbourne?' Peta asked.

The thought of working with Dominic again so soon doesn't exactly thrill me at all.

'There's an organisation in Melbourne called The New Hope Foundation. You may have noticed it's been featured in the news a lot recently.'

'Yes, come to think of it, I did hear something about them. They use classical music to help autistic children, don't they?'

'Yes, that is correct. This sort of research into autism started off in the United States and has also been researched in Europe, too. I only just found out yesterday their work has been extended to Melbourne as well. The woman behind all the research is now based in Australia. Her name is Doctor Alora Stansky and she has agreed to be interviewed by you next Tuesday. I thought this particular assignment would be right up your alley.'

'Tuesday? You mean this coming Tuesday?' Peta bolted upright in her chair.

'I'm afraid so. Next Tuesday is the only day we can catch Dr. Stansky for an interview. Her schedule is all booked up for the rest of this month unfortunately, so it's this Tuesday or not at all. Which means you will be flying out Monday night to allow plenty of time for you to be in Melbourne by Tuesday morning, hopefully with no delays along the way. Would that be okay be with you? I know this trip, like Cairns, is also on such short notice for you.'

'It's okay, Tess. I'm good to go. I just wasn't expecting anything else quite so soon, that's all.'

'Yes, I quite understand. It is a lot to lay at your feet so soon after your trip to Cairns. Anyway, moving on. You will, of course, be required to interview Dr. Stansky as arranged. At least you should feel more welcome this time around! You'll be relieved to know there will be no stroppy Mr. Fletcher locking you out this time.' Tess raised a perfectly shaped eyebrow a few times now to emphasise her point. Peta and Tess looked at each other for a moment, then laughed uproariously together.

'No more scary cyclones, either!' Peta threw in, which made them laugh even more.

Once their moment of spontaneous hilarity had passed, Tess grabbed a tissue to wipe her eyes.

'I tell you, Peta, we must have both needed this moment of sheer silliness to wipe away the sometimes-tedious routines of our working week. Anyway, back to the business at hand! Dominic will be going along with you. His job will be to take photos in and around the Foundation's headquarters in Melbourne and, of course, the children. I have a nephew who is autistic, so naturally, I have a personal interest in this research. Apart from that, though, I think it'll make a wonderful human-interest story for our next month's magazine. What do you think, Peta?'

'It sounds really interesting. Especially regarding this new research into autism, combined with the benefits of classical music as well. Do you have any printed information about the Foundation?'

'Yes, of course. I anticipated you asking me that very same question. I would never send you off into the unknown, without some essential information to back you up.' Tess reached over and grabbed a thick folder and handed it to Peta. 'This should answer all of your questions and more. A bit of light reading matter for your flight to Melbourne,' Tess joked.

'Light reading matter?' Peta questioned as she grabbed the folder from Tess and flicked through the pages. Her eyes immediately glazed over as she tried to take in the detailed information at a glance. 'Gee thanks, I don't know what to say.'

Peta tried to be lighthearted despite her inner trepidation. 'I promise I won't you down, Tess. Like I said before, I'll be sure to familiarise myself with this all of this paperwork over the weekend. As you know by now, I don't like to go into any job without getting all of my facts straight first.'

'That's what I love about you. Your unfailing attention to detail. That's why I know you'll nail this interview.'

'Thanks again, Tess. Your faith in me means a lot.'

'I do have absolute faith in you, sweetie. If your interview with Stewart Fletcher is anything to go by, then I know you will do really well this time, too.' Tess leaned forward. 'I took the liberty of asking Beth to book your flight for you on Monday.' Tess handed a rather bulky cardboard envelope over to Peta. 'Here is your ticket for your flight. Beth has asked me to tell you that, as with Cairns, your flight details and the name of the airline are enclosed in this envelope. She also said to tell you this package includes the necessary documentation for the use of a hire car if you should need one while you're down that way.'

'Two more questions before I go. Will Dominic be on the same flight as me on Monday, and how long will I be down in Melbourne for?'

'Dominic is already down in Melbourne as we speak. He's doing a fashion shoot this weekend I believe. Anyway, I will leave it up to you to touch base with him sometime on Monday after you arrive. I'll also leave it up to the both of you to organise a meet-up as to a time and place that's convenient for the both of you. As for your overall stay in Melbourne, I will be giving you most of next week to cover everything you have to do down there.' She smiled. 'I've decided to give you a bit of extra free time down in Melbourne to make up for me putting you in danger on your last assignment. Besides, you could always take advantage of some Melbourne's fabulous fashion houses while you're down that way,' Tess suggested in a woman-to-woman kind of way, but then, typical of Tess, she was all business again. 'As always, the only thing I ask from you in return is for you to email me the transcript of the interview with Alora Stansky by Friday morning of next week at the very latest.'

'Don't worry, Tess. I will, I promise. Okay—I'll be off then. Enjoy your weekend!'

'You too! Oh, and good luck, Peta. I do hope all goes well, with some good weather thrown in as part of the deal. As I've said before, I have a lot of faith in you. You know that, don't you?'

'Yes, I do know that. Thank you also, by the way, for the extra time in Melbourne. I might just check out all the new fashions in Melbourne, as you've suggested.'

'Enjoy!' Tess agreed with a smile. 'Bye Peta!'

'Bye! Talk to you again soon!'

Once Peta was in the lift and on her way home for the weekend, reality began to sink in. She was all too aware of the thick folder still tucked under her arm. A little light reading? More like cramming for an exam. Luckily for Peta, she had never completely forgotten her Girl Guide motto from her childhood: Be prepared!

CHAPTER EIGHTEEN

eta rushed to answer her mobile, nearly spilling her steaming cup of tea in the process. It must be Stewart! She was just about to call him. Great minds think alike.

'Hello! Peta McKenna speaking.'

'Hello, my darlin' girl! It's your dear old Dad here.'

'Dad? How lovely! I haven't heard from you for months. What have you been up to?'

'I've just returned to Australia a week ago. I've been over in Washington covering the Presidential elections. What a crazy time that was. I'm glad it's all for over now, at least my part in it all, anyway. So what have you been up to, young lady?'

'Well! I've been very busy this past month as well, I might add. I don't know if I told you this at all, but I was recently given the opportunity to interview one of Australia's top authors for *Today's Voice*. Stewart Fletcher no less. Since he lives up in Far North Queensland, I had to head up that way to do it and I'm relieved to say it all went very well in the end.'

'Stewart Fletcher, huh? I hear he's difficult to pin down for any interview. Two separate observations I've heard about him were "downright testy" and "cantankerous". Ah, but I'd imagine your good looks and charm would have won him over, though.'

'He *was* very prickly at first, but thankfully, quite cooperative in the end. It all went much better than I expected, thank goodness! I've received some good reviews so far, which is always a positive thing, isn't it? You would, of course, know all about good and bad reviews, right Dad?'

'Oh to be sure! In my early days as a journalist, I sweated over every single one of them. Twenty-four-hour deodorant became my new best friend.

Peta's laugh tinkling down the phone never failed to warm her father's heart. He missed not talking to his only child more often these past few months. To Lucas McKenna, absolutely nobody could ever match the magical laugh of his precious daughter. He also missed the warmth of her loving hugs reserved especially for her old man too.

'Ah, precious girl, your laugh is like sweet music to my ears, it is. It does your old man's heart good just to hear you laugh at any time. It even brings a tear to me eye, it does.'

'There you go, waxing lyrical again, Father dear.' Peta exaggerated her suffering-daughter groan perfectly over the phone line, but she loved him for his silliness, anyway. 'Let's not get too carried away, shall we? So Dad, where are you right now? Back in Sydney, I presume?'

'No, I'm afraid not. I am down in Melbourne right now and will be until the end of the month at least. I was hoping to get down to Sydney to see you soon, but this particular story is taking much longer than I had anticipated.'

'You're kidding, right?' Peta squealed over the phone. 'You're not going to believe this, but I will also be down in Melbourne next week to do another interview. Wow! Amazing timing, huh?'

'This is indeed wonderful news!' Lucas happily agreed. 'So, can you give me some details right now, if you please? For starters, what day and time will you be arriving? Maybe I could even pick you up from the airport, if you'd like me to.'

'Not sure yet. I still have the airline ticket in my bag since I've only just arrived home about half an hour ago. I haven't even checked the details myself yet, but I do believe I should be down in Melbourne sometime around midmorning on Monday. I was going to check all the details after I've made myself a cup of tea.'

'Well, what are you waiting for then? Have a quick check now for me, if you could be so kind, so I can make some plans at this end as well.'

'Hold on for a sec while I drag the travel folder out of my bag.' Peta put her phone down on top of a nearby cushion on the sofa, while she dug deep into her roomy bag for the folder with the travel details inside. 'Ah, found it at last!' Peta declared triumphantly.

'You women and your handbags!' chuckled Lucas. 'Your mother was the same. She always had to have her bag with her at all times. I tell you; the contents of a woman's bag will always remain a mystery to me. Why can't you be like us men and just carry a wallet, keys and a handkerchief in your pockets. It's a no-brainer really and so much less complicated, I always say.'

'Maybe so, Father dear, but contrary to popular belief, women don't always wear pants and we certainly don't have deep pockets like you guys do. Besides, today's modern woman must always be prepared for all sorts of emergencies when she leaves home for the day,' Peta counter-challenged with a familiar smug tone to her voice, while acknowledging at the same time, how easily they fell into their familiar father-daughter banter.

'Oh really!' Lucas scoffed. 'Please enlighten me then if you will. What sort of emergency supplies do you speak of?'

'Oh, the usual feminine things of course,' Peta said, unable to resist the challenge of teasing him. 'But if you insist; apart from the usual prerequisite make-up, safety pins for broken bra straps, a small sewing kit for loose buttons or even for occasional loose hems, spare panties, tissues, cough drops, eye drops, Band-Aids, sticky tape, notebook and pen. Then there's my money purse, mobile phone and sunglasses. I could go on if you like?'

'Spare me, please!' Lucas groaned dramatically. 'I know when I'm beaten. Now for those flight details if you have them ready.'

'Yes, of course I do. The airline is National Airways. The flight number is NA207, and it gets into Melbourne at 9:40 am, next Monday morning. Don't worry about picking me up from the airport, though Dad. A shuttle bus has already been organised to take me to the Azure Hotel.'

'Will you be working on your own down in Melbourne then?' Lucas asked.

'No Dad, the same photographer who I worked with in Cairns will be with me again.'

'He won't be sharing a room with you at the hotel, will he?'

'Dad! Don't be ridiculous! Dominic is just a colleague. I assure you, there's nothing romantic between us at all and besides, he's already down in Melbourne on some photo shoot.' She smiled into the mouthpiece. Although her beloved father is known as Lucas McKenna, a tough, intrepid, international news correspondent, he is above all, a hopeless softie when it came to his only daughter.

'Okay, that's alright then.' Lucas backed down immediately. 'Anyway, if you call me after you've settled into your room at the hotel, I'll come to you. When do you have to start work down here?'

'Tuesday morning, so I'll have most of Monday to catch up with you.'

'Wonderful! We'll get to spend some quality time together. We can start by sharing a quick lunch somewhere within Melbourne's CBD. Afterwards, we could perhaps spend some leisurely hours window shopping up and down Collins Street. For dinner, I know of a great restaurant down by the Yarra. Whatever we do though, we'll have fun together as we always do. How's that sound?'

'Sounds wonderful! I can't wait to see you again, Dad! It's been too long, hasn't it?'

'Indeed it has! I'm so looking forward to hugging my precious girl again. In the meantime, I will leave you to your cup of tea and give you a chance to settle in.'

'Thanks, Dad. I must admit it has been a hectic week back at work after my trip up north.'

'I must say, me darlin' girl, you have indeed made your old man very happy with your news today. Things couldn't have worked out better if we tried. Bye now! Love you, sweetheart!'

'Yes, I'm very excited too. Bye Dad! See you Monday. Love you too!'

Peta's phone rang again right on cue. She knew exactly who it was this time.

'Hello, beautiful lady! Have you missed me?' came Stewart's voice down the line.

'Hey yourself, sexy man. Do I miss you? Now, let me think about it for a minute.' Peta anticipated his comeback.

'How cruel thou art! How could you carelessly crush me like this? I'm a broken man now.'

'Yes, I'm heartless I know. Okay, okay, I tell a lie. I miss you so much it hurts.'

'Where does it hurt? Come on up here then, gorgeous. I promise to make the hurting go away again and again. What you really need, sexy lady, is a massive dose of sexual healing and lucky for you, I'm just the man to do it for you.'

Stewart's low husky voice immediately prompted an electrified charge of tingles to zap her most erotic core. Her newly awakened body responded with an expressive sigh of anticipation.

'Believe me, Stewart, if I could be up there with you right now, I would be in a heartbeat. My mind has been struggling, since I've returned home, to stay focused on any work tasks at all this week. Perhaps it could have something to do with a certain guy I met up in Cairns last week.' Peta chuckled. 'Has it really been only last week since I first met the *real* Stewart Fletcher? Seems like you've already been part of my life forever. How on earth could these intense yearnings for you have happened so quickly?'

'I feel the same. If you cast your mind back to before I met you, I was sworn off women forever. Then you come along and turn my life upside down. All in just one day, too. We can always blame it on the cyclone. If it wasn't for that *little bit of wind,* as you called it, I might have been able to keep you at a distance forever. But no, thanks to your stubbornness to get your job done, I had no choice but to rescue you from being dangerously swept far away from my veranda steps and into oblivion.'

Stewart and Peta laughed together at a memory that would forever be a joke between them now.

'So, instead of me literally being swept away by those nasty winds at the time, you swept me into your arms and left me totally defenceless to your dangerous sexual moves instead. I didn't see that coming at all. What about you, Stewart? I guess I caught you unawares in the same way.'

'Damn right! To me, you were like some unmovable force I'd never encountered before. You stormed into my life without any warning at all and, ultimately, into my heart forever. Now I can't stop thinking about you! During the day, I ask myself all the time: I wonder what Peta would think of this? Or I'll remind myself to tell you about some music I'd like to share with you, or I'd remember some silly joke to tell you next time we talk. You are so very much part of me now, like breathing.'

'Same here. So, when are we going to see each other again, do you think?'

'Hopefully as soon as we can organise some time together alone. Obviously, I am all for seeing you, plus touching and kissing you all over, sooner rather than later. We'll just have to work on that idea together and see what we can come up with, right?'

'Interesting choice of words there. We'll have to see what "comes up"?'

'Ha! What a cheeky woman you turned out to be, Ms. McKenna.' Stewart growled. 'I never realised just how naughty you can be until now! I love it, though! You're a woman after my own heart—and lately my runaway libido—when you say things like that. Please don't ever stop!'

'Better get used to it!' Peta whispered down the phone line. 'There's more where that came from and I'm thinking some really naughty thoughts about you right now.'

'Ahem. I think we had better change the subject for now. My friend down below is raring to go again, thanks to you! Even just the very thought of you makes him instantly pop up, you wretched woman!'

'Where were we? Oh yeah, that's right. Unfortunately, my sexy lover, with you down there and me up here, there will be absolutely no chance of any real loving with you anytime soon. Anyway, I really think perhaps we should change the subject for now. Speaking of other subjects, how did you go with your boss on your first day back at work? Have there been further problems with *Monsieur* Dominic this week?'

'I'm happy to say, not as much as I thought there might be, but it's all sorted for now though. Dominic apparently didn't say anything to Tess at all of his suspicions about us, thank goodness! He was probably more worried about me reporting him for sexual harassment in retaliation. Anyway, how are things going for you with your new book?'

'Coming along nicely, but first, before I forget, I do have some good news to share with you tonight. Unbelievable in fact. As far as my book is going, though, it will have to go on hold until the following week at least.'

'Sounds intriguing! You did say good news though, so tell me more, please?'

'Do you remember asking me, during our very first meal together, to share with you my childhood years in Melbourne, just before the cyclone hit?'

'Yes, I do. I do recall you were very reluctant to tell me anything personal about yourself at all. You probably thought I was secretly recording you at the time.' Peta laughed.

'I did!' Stewart admitted sheepishly. 'That's probably because I have been taken advantage of by unscrupulous professionals too many times before. So yes, I was very wary of your motives at the time.'

'I understand what you're saying, but anyway, please continue.'

'I don't know if you remember me telling you back then, about how my father and I became somewhat estranged before I left home for good.'

'Yes, I remember that. How you and your father were never able to put things right between you before he died last year.'

'Yes, that's right. We were both very stubborn with each of us refusing to back down at all, which I'm ashamed to admit now. I had kept in touch with my mother and my brother, Matt, but my father always refused point blank to even acknowledge his eldest son existed anymore.'

'Oh Stewart. My heart aches for both you and your father. To me, it is just so sad that you were never able to put things right with him before he passed away. I could never imagine, not even in a million years, not ever talking to my father again. It must have been so emotionally devastating for you both at the time.'

'Up until now, I honestly believed my father hated me but it turns out he didn't after all.'

'He didn't? So, what's happened to change that, then?'

'My brother called me this morning, telling me my father's estate has finally been settled after nearly a year. I don't really know the full details of Father's will yet, but it seems I was included in his will after all.'

'Really? You're kidding? Oh Stewart, that's so wonderful. Not just because your father has acknowledged you again, but because you realise now he really did care about you after all.'

'I know of two certainties of the will though. Matt will inherit Father's law firm in Melbourne, which makes perfect sense to me, since Matt is the only solicitor left in our family now. My father's biggest issue with me as his firstborn son, was that I wasn't interested in being a solicitor at all.'

'Well, we're all different,' Peta defended Stewart's decision to go it alone at the time. 'I don't believe any parent has the right to make their children carry on with family traditions if their heart's not in it. I'm sure all of your loyal fans would agree with me on that one. It's good for Matt to inherit the family firm then, especially a well-established and respected firm such as it is. So where do you fit into the equation, then?'

'When Matt and I were still young, my father purchased a holiday house at Pittwater in Sydney. He loved that area down south as much as I did. That's probably the main thing we had in common at least. During our summer school holidays, we as a family, would fly to Sydney and stay at our holiday house at Pittwater. It's right on the water too. Close enough to throw a fishing line into the river. It's always been my favourite place in the whole world. So long story short, as it turns out, I have inherited that holiday house at Pittwater.'

Stewart stopped talking and everything went quiet. Peta could almost hear the unmistakable wonder in his voice.

'Oh Stewart! I am so happy for you! I can tell just by listening to you, this house holds some very special family memories for you. It's even more wonderful to know your father has openly acknowledged it too. To me, it's the ultimate expression of his deep, unconditional love for you.' Peta sniffed, letting her tears flow freely.

'Don't you go getting all weepy on me now. You'll also have me blubbering soon too and you know it's not supposed to be cool for a grown man to cry.'

'Well I happen to believe it's rubbish when people say a man shouldn't cry.' Peta scoffed, blowing on a tissue. 'My father cries all the time. He's worse than me when it comes to sad movies, but to look at him, he's the most masculine-looking man you could ever meet.'

'Yes, I suppose you're right. Believe it or not, I can be a bit of a soppy male too at times too, although, you would be the only person I would ever admit that too. I trust you now, to never to print that, though, because if you ever do, naturally I will strongly deny it.'

'Tempting, but I'll try to resist.' Peta snickered. 'Anyway, back to your good news please.'

'Yes, ma'am. The reason why I have to forgo my writing next week is because I have to fly down to Melbourne to sign the deed to the Pittwater property by the end of next week.'

Stewart's news bolted Peta upright from lounging back on her comfy sofa. 'Let me get this straight. You're telling me now that you'll be down in Melbourne next week?'

'Yes, afraid so. It means a delay in starting my new book, but it'll be worth it.'

'I don't believe this!' Peta squealed excitedly. 'Unbelievable! Talk about synchronicity!'

'Peta! Have you gone mad?' Stewart questioned, sounding totally baffled now with Peta's sudden excitement. 'What has gotten into you all of a sudden?'

'You're not going to believe this, but I will also be in Melbourne next week too!'

'What! No way! You're kidding me, right? How come?'

'Would you believe, I have another interview already for next Tuesday and guess which city I am flying to next week for this new interview?

'Melbourne? I don't believe this!'

'Yep! Go to the top of the class! Here I am, flying from one end of Australia to the other. How lucky am I to have a job like this?

'Very lucky, I would say. How come? What I mean is, who will you be interviewing this time? I do hope this interview isn't going to be with some other Aussie author as well?'

'Ha! Very funny! You seriously don't think I'd be telling you this if that was the case, now would I?'

'No, I guess not. You'd better not, anyway! For a minute there, a little green monster called Jealousy was about to rear his ugly head,' Stewart admitted but with a happy smile in his voice.

'Not a chance! Besides, there's only room for one sexy author in my life at any one time.'

'Whew, that's a relief then, but do you realise you failed to answer my question before, Ms. McKenna. Just out of curiosity, mind you, who *will* you be interviewing this time?'

'It's a new Foundation recently established in Melbourne, who uses classical music to help children with autism.'

'I've heard something about that. Is it with The New Hope Foundation, by any chance?'

'Yes, that's it!' Peta responded excitedly. 'I imagine it should be really interesting to visit their headquarters down in Melbourne. I'm very much looking forward to the challenge of it anyway and since I've already completed my first major interview with you, this should be a piece of cake, really.' Peta teased him, waiting for the expected reaction and she got it.

'Oh? So you're implying that I'm difficult then?' Stewart questioned with equal jest.

'At the start maybe, but then, well, you did allow me to come inside your home, I suppose.'

'You should be thanking me, you know. You've been initiated by cyclonic gale force winds and my wrath from the onset.' He chuckled. 'Things can only get easier from here on.'

'That's true. I can't deny it. You did initiate me extremely well, I must say.'

They burst out laughing again, both enjoying the easygoing interaction between them.

'Oh man, I haven't laughed this much for quite a while. You're so very good for me. If I'd known this at the time, I might even have let you in a lot sooner.'

'Is that right? That's good to know. Well, I'm glad I stayed outside your front door then. By the way, do you realise that your veranda steps can be extremely uncomfortable to sit on after a while?'

'Most wooden steps are, you know. So, getting back to Melbourne again, how are we going to manage some time together? I mean, I know you have your interview to do on Tuesday and I have my legal session with Matt and our father's solicitor on Tuesday morning, as well. My flight to Melbourne is already booked for Monday, but I could perhaps change it to a time that suits both of us.'

'Mmm. To tell you the truth, Stewart, I think it might be better to leave things as they are for now. I haven't had a chance to tell you yet, but my father will also be in Melbourne next week. I spoke to him on the phone just before you rang. We've already arranged to be catch up on Monday—for lunch and dinner. It's been quite a while since we've seen each other, so I don't think he'd appreciate it if I suddenly cancel out on him.'

'No, I don't imagine he would.' Stewart acknowledged thoughtfully. 'So, your father would be *the* Lucas McKenna, news correspondent to the world, that we are talking about, right? I'm not sure if it's such a good idea for me to meet him at this stage, considering our affair is supposed to be hush-hush for now.'

'I don't think you'll be able to avoid meeting him.' Peta sighed. 'Anyway, we'll both be busy with our own stuff throughout the day on Monday and Tuesday. Maybe it will be best to just wait and see what eventuates once we're down there. What are your feelings?'

'Yes, I think you're right. There's no point in changing our plans just yet. I'm sure everything will fall into place in its own way. I am willing to go along with anything as long as I get to spend some private time with you. Overnight at least, if we can manage it. Which brings me to my next question. How long do you think you'll need to complete your work in Melbourne?'

'Tess has generously given me most of the week down there. She feels bad about putting me in danger with the cyclone up at Cairns. With my father being down in Melbourne at the same time, I'm sure Tess won't mind me taking a few hours off here and there to spend some time with him as well. Besides, she has a lot of respect for my father, so I'm sure it won't be a problem.'

'So, how do we handle this somewhat tricky situation of you and me spending this alone time together in Melbourne, then? I am quite sure you won't be able to fool your father for long.'

'Yes, I know it won't be easy fooling him. He's pretty sharp when it comes to sniffing out the truth, especially when it comes to his only daughter. When I was growing up, he always seemed to know what I was about to get up to, even before I thought of it myself!' Peta chuckled. 'Parents are intuitively sneaky in that way.'

Stewart responded with enthusiasm anyway, 'But as the saying goes, "Where there's a will, there's a way." I am sure we can work something out. Even though I'm about to start my new book. Just between you and me, I seriously think this might be the very last escapade for Tyler. Just lately, I've had this strong desire to work on something completely different.'

'Always reinventing yourself as a professional author makes perfect sense to me.'

'I agree. But for now, I'm excited! AND very horny! This time next week, I hope to be horizontal with you between the sheets. Shall I go on?' He growled, with an obvious huskiness to his voice.

'Stop torturing me! I miss you so much, Stewart! You do realise that, don't you?'

'I miss you too, my love. I can't wait to be with you again.'

'Oh, me too. Well, I guess we had better say goodbye for now. I should tell you to try to get some sleep, but I don't think either of us will be able to sleep much tonight. I'm so excited!'

'Likewise, but we have been talking for a while now. Apart from you, I'm also hungry for some food. Let's not say goodbye, though. We should say, "Until we meet again."'

'Can't wait to see you and feel you again!'

'Oh, me too! Somehow, we'll find a way to be alone together. In the meantime, we both need to come up with come creative ideas to make our time alone together count. Until next week then.'

'Yes, for sure! Sweet dreams—or should I say sexy dreams tonight. Farewell, my love!'

Ah! Time to kick back and relax, at last! Peta stretched out on her comfy sofa with lots of squishy cushions supporting her back and a half-finished glass of cab sav beside her. A gentle breeze drifted in through her wide-open doorway. With both of her French doors opened wide, the outside gentle breezes were invited freely into her living room to caress her face and her hair softly as she laid back into the sofa cushions. She lazily sipped her favourite wine, whilst allowing herself the freedom to listen to music and just think.

Thanks to her father's influence, Peta was also passionate about the superior sound quality from her collection of vinyl records. Soft, melodic music from her retro turntable took over the room, allowing uplifting waves of calming notes to seep unimpeded into every open pore of her fully stretched-out body, effectively releasing any residual tensions left over from her oftentimes gruelling work week. This harmonious effect worked on most parts of her body, *almost* doing a fair job of caressing her scattered mind. It wasn't really working completely just yet, but was slowly getting there just the same. Despite her best intentions to chill out before going to bed, so many mixed, erratic thoughts continued to jostle each other inside her head, madly fighting for attention.

Argh! Why can't I just relax and let go tonight? Music usually always works.

One part of her was very excited about seeing both Stewart and her father again, but something was still chipping away at her peace of mind. There was something important she'd obviously forgotten to figure into this whole scenario.

So why not tonight? For the life of me, I just can't think of what it is, though.

Peta stayed on the sofa, willing her body to cooperate with her mind's inner commands to relax. Try as she might, though, worrisome thoughts still persisted on stirring her scattered brain. What was it she desperately needed to remember?

Peta bolted upright on the sofa in panic, before leaping off like her pants were on fire. As always, in moments of stress, Peta started pacing around the room. Round and round the dining table, then for good measure, round and round the sofa.

Of course!—Dominic!

That's what's been niggling at her stressed brain all this time! What will happen when he finds out Stewart is going to be in Melbourne at the same time as her next week? If Dominic needs any proof of his suspicions about Stewart and herself, this would be it!

Oh shit! How did I ever manage to get myself into this situation? I fell in love, that's how!

Peta wasn't sure how to work this problem out, but hopefully a solution would present itself to her real bloody soon.

Hell's Bells! Think, dammit! Think!

After unsuccessfully trying to come up with a solution, Peta finally understood pacing the floor just isn't working for her anymore. As Aunt Ruby always says, 'When a difficult decision refuses to present itself, it's time to go and sleep on it.' She's absolutely right, as always!

Peta was tired before she started mulling over all this, but now she was downright exhausted. Maybe by tomorrow morning she'd think more clearly. After all, she got herself into this mess, so she'd just have to figure out a way to get out of it. Tomorrow could take care of itself. Tonight she needed to rest her weary head. Never mind about Stewart's action hero, Tyler Jackson, always getting himself into dangerous waters on his many hair-raising escapades. She had this niggling feeling she'd be facing a few escapades of her own any day now.

CHAPTER NINETEEN

here was an empty seat between herself and another woman around her own age, seated by the window. As soon as the seatbelt sign was off and the minimum niceties had been exchanged between them, her fellow passenger seemed to lose herself immediately in an extra thick, current bestseller she had at the ready. Peta was relieved to know this passenger wasn't all that fond either of the longwinded or polite getting-to-know-you conversations between fellow passengers.

What Peta couldn't understand, though, was why her fellow passenger even bothered to book a window seat if she'd planned to read a book during the entire flight? Even though Peta preferred a window seat, it *would* be easier to access the loo from her aisle seat, especially with her nervous bladder retaliating lately.

The difference between this flight and her last one, Peta quickly realised, was that she hadn't even known Stewart back then. Yes, she knew *of* him, but hadn't yet met the man himself. So much has changed in her life since that fateful trip. Who would have thought she'd end up falling in love with Stewart?

Go figure! Fate can certainly throw some interesting curveballs sometimes! She hoped they'd spend some time alone together during this coming week. Perhaps when she saw him again, she'd know for sure her feelings were real and not some obsessive, impossible infatuation after all. Peta gave pause to wonder, though, what would happen if and when Stewart and her intuitive father should happen to meet while down in Melbourne? What are the chances of them meeting up? What if, despite her best intentions to keep them apart, they still end up meeting anyway? How will they relate to each other?

Hell! I can't get my head around this right now!

As her flight touched down, Peta said a silent prayer for nothing *sticky* to go wrong this week. As she followed the other passengers off the aircraft, she squared her shoulders and breathed deeply a few times in an attempt to shut out her inner voice nagging her again.

It's time to get your act together, Peta! It's showtime!

As if in a dream, Peta watched as the shuttle bus merged with Melbourne's increasingly busy morning traffic, before wheeling her luggage in through the doors of the Azure Hotel.

Wow! This hotel is aptly named!

Peta glanced around the reception area, really loving the restful azure colours throughout the foyer. In fact, the whole reception area and the dining room beyond was decked out in a stunning nautical theme.

Who would have thought such a tropical-looking hotel even existed in cold old Melbourne? It works, though.

Once checked in, Peta headed for the lift and the seventh floor as directed by the hotel concierge. She was delighted to note that even the interior of the lift stayed true to the azure nautical theme. The interior walls of the lift featured a seaside mural. This hotel must be one of Melbourne's little secrets. Peta had never even heard of it before. On the way up to her floor, she made a mental note to thank Beth for booking her into this quaint little treasure, especially since she usually preferred quiet, out-of-the-way places. This place fitted the bill perfectly.

After sliding her key through the slot of her private suite for the next few days, Peta gratefully wheeled her luggage along with her into her room. On the way to the ensuite, Peta took a moment to look around her and sighed with a deep satisfaction. As in keeping with the theme of this charming little hotel, the azure theme was also featured throughout her entire suite. There were shiny dolphin taps over the spa bath, shell soaps and matching bathroom accessories. To Peta, there seemed to be such a serene balance between the vibrant turquoise floral cushions on the chairs of the bamboo dining setting, bar stools and the matching bed covers. The walls even seemed to glow with a soft pearly, off-white vibrancy.

Well, if I'm going to worry myself sick over things I can't control, then at least I can fit these recent unavoidable injections of chaos into my life in absolute style.

The first order of the day would be to open up the heavily lined curtains to allow her room to be infused with Melbourne's still, misty, late-morning light.

First things first, to really claim this suite as my own for the week, I need to make myself a cup of coffee. Then I'll sit down by the window and let Dad know I'm here and ready to spend the day with him.

'Hey Dad! It's me! My flight landed in Melbourne about an hour ago. I'm ready to catch up with you today. If you're still able to, that is. Call me back when you get this message. Love you!'

With that done, Peta made herself a cup of coffee from a selected capsule she popped into an efficient little coffee machine in the little kitchen. Very similar to the one Tess had bought for her office just recently. Once the gurgling and hissing from the coffee maker was done, she wandered back out onto her private balcony beyond the glazed double glass doors to await her father's call. While she sipped her steaming, frothy hazelnut latte, her thoughts turned to their day ahead, wondering what activities her father had in mind for their day spent together.

As Peta gazed out over Melbourne's city landscape, she was reminded of special times spent with her father during each of her school holidays. Right back from preschool, and each year after that, through until her graduation day. Her father wasn't always able to get back home to Australia for every school holiday, but it was never really about the amount of time he spent with her. To Peta, it was more about their quality time together when he could be with her.

Her school friends often told her after each school holiday, that apart from just one day as a family on Christmas Day, their parents never really wanted to spend any time alone with their children. What with their numerous scheduled business meetings, their never-ending social engagements and sucking up to their high-profile superiors, any one on one family time spent with their offspring were never on the agendas. Peta observed during her school years that for a good number of her school friends, boarding school soon became their whole way of life.

At least with her own father, he was home with her in every sense of the word. She remembered always travelling around and exploring new places with him all the time as well as their evenings together playing chess, scrabble, or taking part in some lively debate with each other. What Peta especially enjoyed the most, though, was to listen to her father's deep melodic voice as he enthralled her with his real-life adventures overseas to some far-flung country. He never hesitated to satisfy her inquisitive mind about life's mysteries, with her endless questions either.

Although Peta could recall only too well her father wisely leaving any delicate womanly discussions to his sister-in-law. Peta laughed now at his awkwardness in answering some of her more persistent questions.

'Er, you'd best ask your Aunt Ruby about that one!'

Peta's mobile phone buzzed beside her, sending her happy childhood memories back into safekeeping to relive at some other time.

'Morning! It's your old man returning your call at last. Sorry! I was on another call about a reliable lead to a story I've been chasing for some time, so I couldn't let it go. Please forgive me for making you wait so long. How are you anyway, darling girl?'

'I'm good thanks, Dad. Don't apologise for making me wait. I know the nature of the beast and those all-important story leads! Don't you just love 'em?' Peta heard her father's deep chuckle of agreement on the other end of the line. 'Anyway, my time hasn't been wasted at all. I've been sitting here, sipping delicious coffee and reminiscing about our happy times together during my school holidays in Sydney. I sure miss those days, Dad. What about you?'

'I most certainly do agree!' Lucas sighed deeply. 'What wouldn't I give to have those days back again?'

'You sound exhausted. Are things not going well with your work lately?'

'It's not so much work really, sweetheart. I guess I'm just feeling my age lately. I think it's time for me to retire. You know—to put my roots down permanently back in Sydney again.'

'You're kidding! I never thought I would hear you actually admit you don't want to travel overseas anymore. So, what's happened to make you feel this way?'

'I can't even tell you exactly when things started to shift for me really, but I guess it's crunch time for me now. Yes, you're right, I have always loved to travel as you well know, just as your dear mother did. The truth is that I just don't seem to have the inclination to go global trekking anymore. I'm tired of continually fighting off other younger correspondents for top stories as well. I am truly over it! I am actually thinking of buying myself a good-sized boat with my hard-earned savings, so I can spend my retirement years fishing every single day.'

'Wow! That's fantastic! Well I, for one, would certainly love to have my dad living somewhere closer to Sydney full-time. So, where do you think you might want to settle down then? Any ideas?'

'Yes of course I do. Lots of them! But I'd rather wait until later to do that. I'd already planned to tell you all about my new future ideas over dinner later tonight if you're up for it?'

'Yes of course I'm up for it. Did you seriously think I would miss out an opportunity to spend some catch-up time with my most favourite dad in the whole world?

'Favourite dad, huh? You have another father stashed away that I don't know about?' Lucas questioned lightheartedly.

'No of course not, you silly man!' Peta laughed. 'You are my one and only father. But you should already know that anyway. Well, at least I hope you do. Rest assured, though, nobody could ever replace you in my heart.'

'Thank you, precious girl. The feeling is mutual. Nobody could ever replace you either.'

'So tell me, what exactly did you have in mind for our dinner tonight?'

'I have a really special little place in mind. Right on the Yarra River too. I always make a point of going there whenever I come to Melbourne. It's the whole atmosphere of the place that pulls you in and, of course, the food isn't half bad either. Plus, I know how you adore your seafood.'

'Sounds amazing! So, can I expect you soon, then? Time is a-wasting you know! I'm looking forward to us having a quick lunch first, if possible. Catching an early flight meant I didn't have much breakfast this morning, so I am absolutely starving.'

'Why does that not surprise me?' Lucas couldn't help commenting. 'I can't ever remember a time when you weren't hungry. Come to think of it, your mother certainly had a healthy appetite. She could eat like a horse and never gain an ounce. Exactly like you really.'

'Good metabolism. Maybe even some good Irish genes too, perhaps?'

'Ha! Lucky you! Wish I could say the same. I only have to look at food these days, for me to start wearing it all over my entire body soon after.' Lucas chuckled, before changing the subject. 'So, you're staying at the Azure, right?'

'That's right, Dad. Do you know where it is?'

'Yes, indeed I do. After we talked on the weekend, I keyed it into my GPS straight away. I'll pick you up in the foyer by the reception desk, in about one hour. If that's okay with you?'

'Perfect! I'll meet you at the reception desk in the foyer. One hour. Got it! Love ya, Dad! '

'Love you too, sweetheart. I'll be there before you know it. Bye for now.'

Before heading down to meet her father, Peta decided now would be the perfect time to touch base with Dominic. Best to get it over with while she was still in a good mood.

'Hello? Dominic Marseilles speaking.'

'Dominic, it's Peta. I'm now in Melbourne, I arrived about an hour ago.'

'Ah, Peta! What a pleasure it is to hear from you again! I trust you had a pleasant flight this morning?'

At least he seems happy to move on from our last disastrous encounter in Cairns.

'I did, thank you. Tess asked me to check in with you upon arriving in Melbourne. So you're free now to proceed with our new assignment tomorrow?'

'Oui! I am indeed, but before that, I was hoping we could perhaps meet for a leisurely lunch today to go over our notes for tomorrow. I trust you will be agreeable to this?'

'Sorry, but I'm afraid I can't. My father is also working here in Melbourne until the end of this month. I've already promised I'd spend most of today with him. We haven't seen each other for quite a while now. I'm sure you understand. My father would indeed be extremely disappointed if I cancelled on him.'

'*Oui!* You mustn't hurt your father's feelings. Of course I understand,' Dominic answered after a marked hesitation.

Peta could tell he was not happy with her answer at all. *Tough!*

Peta's unwelcome answer did little to stop Dominic's persistence. 'I do have to ask though, *chérie*. Do you think perhaps, we could share a few drinks later on tonight?'

'No, sorry, but that won't be possible at all. We could catch up tomorrow morning, over coffee to go through our notes before we head off to The New Hope Foundation, though.'

'*Oui!* I guess that will have to do then.'

Peta could hear a groan of obvious frustration in Dominic's voice over the phone but chose to ignore it.

Too bad!

'I must admit,' Dominic couldn't resist adding, 'I am rather disappointed that I won't get to see you today. We haven't really had a chance to talk to each other since you walked out on me at the restaurant in Cairns. I do hope there are no hard feelings between us?'

'Well I must say, you did catch me off guard at the time.' Peta decided that if they were ever going to work together again with no more misunderstandings between them, she really did need to finally set things straight with Dominic, and to hell with the consequences. 'Look, Dominic, I'm sorry if I ever gave you the impression I was interested in anything more than friendship with you. For some reason, you must've imagined the champagne and good food would somehow loosen me up. You should know by now that I never become involved with any of my work colleagues. Ever!'

'Well, I *was* hopeful, but it doesn't really matter now. You've made your feelings perfectly clear to me, but that does not mean I am able to switch off my feelings for you just like that.'

'You and I will always be friends, but you have to realise, Dominic, that's all we'll ever be.'

'Yes, I do know that now, but I thought that someday, just maybe …'

'Please try to understand right now, that there will *NEVER* be any "maybes" where you and I are concerned. I just don't feel that way about you. End of story.'

'Okay, I'll back off for now. But well, I just can't help myself where you are concerned.'

'Oh for heaven's sake, GET OVER YOURSELF, DOMINIC!' Peta raised her voice with exasperation.

After a predictable silence on the other end of the phone, Peta took a few deep breaths now and continued.

'Besides, we have a job to do this week, so let's not let any bad feelings get in the way of that, shall we? Now, to change to subject, where shall we meet tomorrow then?'

Dominic tucked his ego away long enough to answer Peta, but with a definite coolness in his voice. 'I know of a very good cafe in the heart of the city centre. I have the use of a hire car, so I can pick you up at your hotel, if you are happy for me to do that, *chérie.'*

So you'll know where I'm staying, Dominic. Uh-uh! That's not going to happen.

'No, it's okay thank you. I appreciate the offer, though. I could meet you there at around 8:30 since the interview is at 9:30. That will give us enough time to go over our notes beforehand. That okay with you?'

'*Oui,* we can do that.'

'*AND,* if it's all the same to you, I'd really appreciate you not calling me "*chérie*" anymore either. Let's just concentrate on getting the job done, shall we? In regard to you picking me up, though, I do appreciate the offer Dominic, but I usually prefer to move around as freely as possible on my own.'

'Of course, Peta.' Dominic's voice sounded both peeved and dejected.

'Well, I guess I shall see you at The Hot Bean on Collins Street at 8:30 sharp then? It's just a few doors up from the post office.'

'Yes, 8:30 at The Hot Bean, Collins Street, near the post office. Got it! Sorry, but I really do have to go now. I'm supposed to be meeting my father downstairs any minute now. See you tomorrow!' Peta hung up before Dominic could say another word.

That man just won't take the hint! And it's not like I've been leading him on either.

Despite any professional repercussions that might happen because of her rejection of Dominic, Peta was determined to push all thoughts of Dominic out of her head. She checked her overall casual look in the full-length mirror one last time before quickly heading out of her room to catch a lift down to the hotel lobby.

All the more reason, Peta decided, for Stewart and herself to keep their love affair strictly private. Especially where Dominic's amorous thoughts were concerned.

Peta waited close by the reception desk at the hotel foyer as arranged, with still five minutes to spare, knowing full well her father's strict adherence to punctuality over the years. Predictably, he was five minutes early too. She spotted him through the glass-fronted entrance as he locked his car, parked in a five-minute pickup zone, just under the covered front foyer. He headed towards the hotel's automatic front door without a moment's hesitation. You could pretty much set your clock by Lucas McKenna.

Peta observed her father with loving affection as he entered the hotel and headed straight for the reception desk. Her father was an impressive man indeed. His towering height, broad shoulders, and barrel chest gave him an undeniably charismatic presence. With his ready smile and a pair of twinkling eyes, one could not help but be impressed by his powerful presence. When he smiled, the world literally smiled with him. His booming voice perfectly matched the size of the man, as well as his deep, resonant chuckles. Very few people could resist her father's infectious charms for long. Peta could well understand why her father was still in demand to give motivational talks to hundreds of fledging journalists, and why an impressive list of prestigious universities and upmarket colleges still vied for his attention all the time.

Her beloved father always reminded Peta of a great big cuddly bear. She imagined he could easily pass for one of those American mountain men from those re-runs of old TV shows she watched years ago. Grizzly Adams was one such character who instantly popped into her head when prompted to recall her father's image. His thick head of hair, the colour of molasses, was now generously streaked with silvery strands of grey all over his head and sideburns, but to Peta, he still presented himself as an impressive figure.

Seeing him now, Peta was immediately taken aback by how much he'd aged since she saw him last. Peta couldn't help but notice the dark rings under his eyes and how tired he looked. To Peta's sharp observation, his shoulders were stooped, like the weight of world was pulling him down, cruelly exposing his emerging vulnerability for all to see.

How could this have happened so quickly to him in such a short space of time? He was actually slowing down right before her very eyes.

I can't let him see my reaction to his sudden ageing. Absolutely not! That will never do. He'll pick up on it straight away. Perhaps it's time for a show of blissful ignorance from me now.

'Ah, here she is!' Lucas grabbed his daughter and despite Peta being almost as tall as her father, he easily lifted her up into a crushing, but affectionate, bear hug. 'It warms my heart, it does, to hug you and see you again.' Lucas shamelessly clung to his daughter for the longest time. Peta returned his hug with equal affection.

'I'm just so happy to see you too, Dad. I've really missed you.'

Peta held onto her father like she was afraid to let him go. A few unleashed, traitorous tears rolled freely down her cheeks.

'Ah! I have missed you too! You surely are a sight for your old man's baggy eyes, darlin' girl.' Lucas' laugh bellowed with gusto. 'Come on, turn around now and let me look at you.'

Lucas spun her around as he carried out his fatherly inspection every time they caught up with each other. Peta had given up, a long time ago, with feeling embarrassed about her father's time-honoured ritual. Not like when she was an awkward, gangly teenager and he openly inspected her in his usual boisterous fashion, in front of her school friends, totally mortifying her back then.

Peta now twirled around for him dramatically and imitated some snapshot poses for full effect, with a happy, cheeky grin on her face.

Lucas McKenna's heart practically thumped out of his chest with love and pride for his only daughter, every time she indulged his fatherly pride in this way.

With Peta looking so much like his beautiful vibrant wife, so much so, that, even after all these years, he still missed her sorely. In a flash, she had been taken from him, far too quickly, to a drunk driver running into her car as she was driving home from her occasional modelling work. Despite his grieving, Lucas never ceased to be grateful his little girl was home safe with Ruby at the time, otherwise Peta would have been killed too. If it hadn't been for Ruby stepping in to help him raise his little daughter, he might have fallen into an emotional heap of despair at the time.

Lucas had only ever loved one woman in his life and even after all these years, he still missed her terribly.

'I don't know how you do it, sweetheart, but every time I see you after a long break, you seem to look more and more beautiful every time. Why, if I didn't know any better, I'd say you're even glowing. I couldn't quite put my finger on it when I spoke to you the other day, but I do declare that there is definitely something different about you. Rest assured, daughter dear, by the end of today, I will have figured it out though.'

'Just good clean living, Dad. That's all.' Peta laughed, trying to hedge away from his usual penetrating observation of her. The deep, private part of Peta knew something had definitely changed within her lately, but it wasn't just some*thing* though, but rather some*one*. With this secret acknowledgement locked away inside her heart, she flashed what she hoped was an innocent enough smile for her father.

Lucas eyed his daughter again, his eyes narrowed with obvious parental suspicion, then shook his head, 'Sorry kiddo, but I'm not buying it.'

'Kiddo? You haven't called me that for years. You only ever call me that when you're trying to wheedle some confession out of me. Well it won't work!'

'You're right. I haven't called you kiddo in a long time, but I am now.' Lucas continued to study her face for any clue at all. 'Something is most definitely different about you since I saw you last, and you know full well, don't you, my dear girl, that I will eventually figure out what it is?'

'Oh Dad, really! You can psychoanalysis me as much as you like, but you'll be wasting your time.' Peta linked her arm under her father's elbow. 'Now, are we going out for the day or not?'

'Of course we are, but this conversation isn't over yet, not by a long shot. Okay, let's go!'

To Peta, her father's love for her was completely evident by his wide grin, as he led the way out through the double glass doors of Peta's hotel.

'So, tell me one more time, Father, what exactly is planned for our father-daughter day out?'

'Well for starters, some lunch first, followed by some leisurely retail therapy up and down Collins Street, essential to my well-thought-out plan for our time together today. Then, when we've had our fill of our daylight activities, at sunset, I'll be taking you to a special place for dinner. Like I said on the phone earlier, it's down by the Yarra. Trust me, you're gonna love it!'

'I do trust you, always! So, let us not waste a minute of our day then. Lead the way.'

Lucas opened the front passenger door of his earlier model Holden Commodore for her, waving his arm before her in a mock chivalrous gesture. 'Jump into my chariot, if you please, my lady, and we shall be on our way.'

'Lovely! Don't mind if I do. Drive on please, Mr. McKenna, and don't spare the horsepower.'

'Right away, milady!' Lucas grinned as he carefully merged with the crazy oncoming, midday traffic.

It was like old times again. Two wandering adventurers together, where age never mattered in pursuit of fun and happiness as they set about creating many more happy memories together. And while the old adage might be true that time stood still for no-one, Peta smiled at the thought that for this father-daughter team, it did for now.

CHAPTER TWENTY

'I *don't know about you,* Stu, but if that's lunch, then I've just scoffed down my full quota.'

After finishing his roast lamb kebab, Matt wiped his mouth with a napkin, sighed a deep satisfied sigh and gulped down the last of his beer, signalling to Stewart he was ready to leave.

After Matt collected Stewart at Tullamarine Airport a few hours ago, they enjoyed lunch at a popular Turkish restaurant just off Collins Street. After a rather active and exploratory partaking of several items on the menu, they were ready to head back home to catch up with their mother. Before leaving the restaurant, Stewart seized a few moments to glance around the packed restaurant, noting the stylish presence of other happy diners all around them. *Typical of Melbourne's city people,* he mused, *to always be so immaculately attired and seemingly living a full and active life.* Even though Stewart had grown up in Melbourne, he has never really embraced the climatic elements of his home territory and for the life of him, he could never really understand why most Victorians never really cross over their border into the much sunnier state of New South Wales. Better still, the *much* warmer state of Queensland.

Why stay here year after year, only to freeze your bloody arse off? Stupid!

Stewart couldn't help but remark, 'I swear this city hasn't changed at all, really. I mean, it's been close on ten years since I left Melbourne, but looking around me now, it seems like it was only yesterday. I feel like I'm stuck in some kind of time warp. Melbourne's unpredictable weather seems to remain constant, doesn't it? Still as chilly as I remember too.'

'Well any place south of steamy old Cairns would be chilly to you, Stu. Take heart. After all, you're here for only a week. It takes at least two weeks to get used to our chilly weather again.'

'Two weeks? Ha!' Stewart shot back with his retort. 'More like two decades if you ask me.'

'Jeez, Stu! You're back here for only five minutes and already you're complaining about our fair city. Suck it up, bro!' Matt scoffed in his usual teasing way. 'Anyway, I think maybe we should head on home to see Mother before we do anything else at this stage. You right to go?'

'Sure am. First though, if we have enough time that is, I would really like to call into a florist shop somewhere around here and buy Mother a bouquet. That okay with you?'

'So that's the way it has to be huh, Stu?' Matt questioned, a serious tone to his voice.

Stewart turned back towards Matt with a puzzled frown. 'What do you mean? What is the way what has to be?'

'Well I mean to say, you've only been down in Melbourne for an hour or so, and already you're vying for our mother's affection. And to make matters worse, here you are trying to make me look bad now by buying her flowers?' Matt took a deep breath and lowered his head in misery. 'Don't think I don't know what you're up to. You just want to have Mother all to yourself now.'

Stewart stared at Matt, totally perplexed, until he caught Matt's grin breaking through.

'Oh you bastard!' Stewart laughed. 'You had me going for a minute there. I can see I'm going to have to be very careful with what I say around you while I'm here. You really have grown up, it seems.'

Stewart leaned over and ruffled Matt's immaculately groomed tawny hair with affection. 'So Squirt, why don't you ever buy our mother flowers then? What a cheapskate!'

'Ha! I resent that! I'll have you know, I *do* buy her flowers for Mother's Day. Once a year is enough, isn't it?' Matt shrugged his shoulders, as if to say 'what did I do?' then gave his big brother a boyish grin in defence.

'Like I said—cheapskate! So to answer my question, will it be okay to stop for flowers?'

'Sure. All jokes aside, that won't be a problem. Take all the time you need. I'm sure Mother will appreciate the thought.' Matt grinned at Stewart. 'Besides, you can't go wrong with flowers when it comes to grovelling to one's mother, or with any woman really.'

'Amen to that, bro! Works most of the time at least. I've just realised, you probably have to head back into work for a few hours soon. I do appreciate you taking the time out of your busy schedule to pick me up this morning, though. I'm sure it must have impacted your appointments for today, even if you won't admit it.'

'One of the perks of being a boss is not having to stress about a few unproductive hours now and again. Besides, appointments can be shuffled around most of the time. I know I should feel guilty, but I rarely ever take time off usually. Trust me, a few hours isn't going to matter all that much. I wouldn't want to miss spending some one on one time with my long-lost, big brother now, would I?'

'Point taken! Let's hit the road then.'

'I just have to make a pit stop first. You know, point Percy to the porcelain. Be back soon.'

Stewart observed Matt with undisguised affection now as he watched his younger brother head off to the men's room. It came as a bit of a shock to realise Matt was no longer that gawky boy he'd grown up with.

In a blink of the eye, Matt had became a fully grown man while his back was turned. Stewart also realised that while Matt wasn't as tall as him, what he lacked in height he made up for with a stocky, solid build, along with a well-proportioned chest. Just like their father, really. Stewart inherited his height from his mother's side of the family and his thick, ebony hair directly from his mother. Matt had obviously inherited their father's golden tawny tones.

Stewart realised even though he and Matt might not look anything alike, they were still brothers in ways that counted. They both possessed the same offbeat sense of humour and thankfully the same resilience to bounce back from the tough challenges life tended to throw at them. He was so proud of the way Matt turned out, with no inflated ego at all. Thankfully, Matt didn't take himself too seriously either.

Stewart also appreciated the fact Matt was always steadfast with his loyalty and discretion in protecting his family, too. He never once betrayed Stewart to the press during his highly publicised divorce to Felicity. It must have caused a lot of embarrassment to Matt and their parents at the time, but Matt never complained about Stewart's highly over-exposed marital scandal.

Man oh man! He sure has grown up! To look at him now in his classy, three-piece, midnight blue suit, his fancy blue and white striped shirt with its white collar and cuffs, Stewart could well imagine Matt impressing both clients and courtroom judges alike. Even his vibrant yellow tie made a bold statement of its own.

He looks so professional! It's hard to believe Matt was ever that rough and tumble kid I used to wrestle with.

Stewart snapped out of his reverie when he noticed Matt returning to their table, dodging other seated customers with a smile and a few friendly hellos along the way.

'I'll just fix up our account, then we can go find a nearby florist for you.'

'Come on, Matt. Let me pay for lunch. I don't feel right about you paying for it.'

'Stop! I don't want to hear any arguments about this, Stu,' Matt said. 'That's what expense accounts are for. When I'm not wearing a suit and tie, then you can pay. Just not today.'

Matt pulled out his wallet as he stepped up to the front service counter and extracted his credit card. With that done, he was handed a printed copy of his credit card receipt. 'Let's go, bro!' Matt said as he moved quickly toward the wide-open doorway of the open plan restaurant, leaving Stewart to trail close behind. As soon as they'd reached Matt's parked car, they both climbed in and buckled up.

'Let's go find those flowers. I know just the place. It's not too far from here either. Trust me, she'll love 'em!'

With that said, Matt pulled out into the busy midday traffic and headed straight for Collins Street. Stewart relaxed into the plush seats of Matt's prestige car, happy to be driven around his old childhood stomping ground.

First up for Peta and Lucas was a quick lunch of a scrumptious savoury muffin and a delicious mango smoothie for Peta. For Lucas, it was a thick slice of quiche with a side salad and a black coffee. After devouring absolutely everything, there was nary a crumb left over for the tiny ravenous swallows hovering around the tables. They waited for any tasty morsels of food to fall to the ground or to be left behind on the tables by all the well-fed humans.

With lunch out of the way, an extended stroll up and down Collins Street was required to work off all they'd just eaten. Peta and Lucas ducked into practically every boutique shop along the way. This famous street, as remembered by Peta from previous visits to Melbourne, was constantly alive with activity, colour and ultra-fashionable people. When in Melbourne, Peta knew one simply must visit Collins Street or miss out on being part of the famous fashion capital of Australia. Even though Peta accepted Melbourne's well-earned pride of claiming to be the undisputed fashion mecca of Australia, Peta found Sydney to be just as wonderful too. Especially for a working girl. Anyway, when in Melbourne, why bother arguing against the fashion statistics? Just bring lots of money with you and do as the locals do.

To the uninitiated, Collins Street features an endless variety of boutique shops loaded to the max with originally designed clothes which can be purchased from the designers themselves—with a hefty price tag to go with it. She was only too aware, as well, that the Collins Street shop windows were cleverly laid out to attract the most discerning shopper through their elegant glass doors.

Peta couldn't wait to check out all the latest fashions Melbourne was famous for and even allowed herself to get caught up in the whole rich scene of Collins Street. Being a practical girl, though, she was content to merely browse today. When shopping for clothes, Peta often found the smaller city boutiques offered the same new fashion promises, but without the inflated prices for a city-based working girl such as herself.

Lucas noticed Peta eyeing off a particular dress in one shop window they passed by. 'What do you think of that dress, sweetheart?'

'It's gorgeous, Dad. I just love the whole style of it, especially with those silvery swirls starting at the waist all the way down to its cleverly designed layered hem. So amazing!

'Why don't you let me buy it for you, please?'

'No thanks, Dad. I love that you want to please me in this way, but I am much too practical. Besides, I would probably only ever wear such a dress like this once in a blue moon. I can pretty much guarantee the price will be exorbitant too.'

'Okay, if you insist. Well at least let me buy you something else, then. Something that is useful for you, but without the price tag. Think of it as a special memory of our time in Melbourne together.'

'Well, since you put it that way. It certainly would be a lovely to have a memento of our day spent together. Let me see.' Peta looked around to get her bearings. 'Now, if I remember rightly from my last trip to Melbourne, there is a little shop in an arcade just up ahead. I'd like to check it out again if you don't mind.'

'I don't mind at all. Lead the way, my dear.'

Peta looped her arm through Lucas' again. She almost skipped in anticipation of choosing just one special item of significance of this day spent solely in her father's company. As was her habit, Peta always liked to think carefully about every purchase she made. She found the store she was looking for and with a happy grin, she dragged her father inside with her. After spending a good fifteen minutes of looking through a wide selection of colourful scarves, handbags, gift-wrapped body washes and hand creams, Peta made her decision.

'I just love this scarf, Dad! I find myself coming back to it repeatedly, so that's a good sign for me.' She quickly found a nearby mirror and looped it in various ways around her neck. 'I think this soft caramel colour will match most of my winter wardrobe perfectly. Yes! This is definitely it, Dad. What do you think?'

'Looks great! It goes well with the autumn patterned blouse you're wearing today, too. I think you're absolutely right. It has the kind of colour mix you could wear with most clothes. It really does have a real vibrancy about it, too. Good choice.' Lucas reached his hand over towards Peta. 'Take it off for me for a moment if you would, so I can go pay for it. Then you'll be able to wear it whenever you like. You certainly need it down south. There's a definite nip in the air today.'

'Thanks so much, Dad!' Peta kissed her father's cheek and hugged him before she unwrapped the scarf from around her neck and handed it to him. 'I'll treasure this gift forever, because it will always remind me of this magic day spent with you.'

'Oh, you're very welcome, sweetheart! I rarely get to buy special things for you these days, so you make me happy when you do allow me to indulge you from time to time.'

Peta and Lucas exited the little shop and joined the steady rhythm of foot traffic along the way, their arms linked as always with their deep affection for each other and life itself. Despite having to continually dodge hordes of people coming towards them, they were in complete harmony with each other.

Lucas particularly enjoyed escorting his beautiful daughter around. He impulsively gave a profound smile to everyone who passed them. Today, people couldn't fail to notice the full effect of Peta's natural beauty with her long flowing hair that was finally freed from her usual practical ponytail, thereby framing her happy, expressive face with a lively bounce.

Lucas suddenly squeezed Peta's hand. 'You know, darlin' girl, you look like you've always belonged within this whole elaborate fashion scene of Melbourne. I have seen many beautiful women here in the past few weeks, but they all pale in comparison to your beauty.'

Peta squeezed his hand. 'You always say the sweetest things, Dad. Thank you!'

'Well I mean it! You know, you look more like your mother every day.' Lucas went quiet for a moment, no doubt savouring the memory of his late wife. 'I loved your dear mother very much, as you know, and even after all this time, my heart still aches whenever I think of her. She was such a passionate woman too. I fell in love with her at first sight. Did you know that?'

Peta shook her head slowly in acknowledgement to his question.

'I was never able to look at any other woman in the same way after she came along.'

'I know, Dad.' Peta gave her father's hand a gentle squeeze. 'I know you and Mum loved each other very much. I just wish I could have gotten to know her when I was growing up. Aunt Ruby looked a lot like Mum, didn't she?'

'Absolutely! The two sisters were similar in lots of ways, especially with their height and obvious beauty and that easygoing way about them. So gentle and kind natured to everyone they met, too. Full of fun as well, as you probably already know from your aunt. I don't know what I would have done if she didn't step in to help me raise you after your mother was taken so cruelly because of that drunk driver. Speaking of your aunt, have you heard from her lately?'

'Sure, I get to talk to her by phone whenever I can. Sometimes we FaceTime each other too. She amazes me with her energy and she shows no sign of ever slowing down either. Always flitting around, helping with the various mercy missions she's always involved with.'

'That's our Ruby, alright.' Lucas agreed. 'I often wondered, though, why Ruby never married, especially when she broke off her engagement a week before her wedding. Her romantic heart seemed to shrink up inside after that. I guess we will never know what happened either. She's a closed book when it comes to discussing anything private about herself. That is one way in which she and your mother differed. Your mother always wore her emotions on her face.'

'Yes, I know what you mean. Aunt Ruby has deliberately pushed romance aside all these years. But having said that, I have seen another side of her too. I'd sometimes catch her admiring herself in the mirror when she thought I was in another room. She was definitely wearing a romantic, secretive smile as she stared intently back at her reflexion, obviously re-calling some special memory from long ago. Intriguing to say the least.'

'Yes, I agree! She can be a rather mysterious lady sometimes.' Lucas smiled. 'But we love her all the more for it, don't we?'

'Yes, indeed we do.' They happily lapsed into silence for a while. 'So what's next, Dad?'

'I was thinking maybe we could drive around for a bit and check out a few more places, then gradually make our way to the wharf area for dinner. What do you think? More shopping or is it time to leave these city streets for now?'

'Sounds good to me. I think I've had enough retail therapy for now.' Peta checked her phone. 'I can't believe it's nearly 2:30 already.'

'How about we start working our way back to the car then?'

'Yes, let's please do that. I think I'm all shopped out for today.' Peta looked up and down the street from where they were standing. 'It might be easier if we cross this road at the next pedestrian crossing since your car is on the other side of the street. The traffic is way too heavy for us to even try to cross here.'

'Smart girl! You must have inherited some of your brains from your old man at least.'

'Of course I did. There's no point in denying it. Well, let's make tracks, shall we?'

Just as they were crossing the street at the lights, Peta could have sworn she heard her name being called out behind her.

'Peta! Wait up!'

This time the voice behind her was much louder and way more persistent.

CHAPTER TWENTY-ONE

ithout needing to turn around, she recognised the voice from a familiar resonance deep within her heart. It shocked her just the same to hear him calling her name in the middle of Collins Street. Peta turned and stared at him with disbelieving eyes.

'Stewart? I can't believe it! What are you doing here?' Peta blubbered, suddenly lost for the right words, completely oblivious of her father standing close by.

All she could think of at this very moment, was Stewart walking toward her, with his eyes totally fixed on her and *only* her. To Peta, it instantly reminded her of a well-known song, attached to a love scene in some romantic movie. In this case it was Sonny and Cher singing *I've Got You, Babe.*

As far as Peta was concerned, Stewart definitely did have her, too. It had only been about two weeks since they last parted at Cairns airport, but for Peta, it may as well have been only yesterday, such was the impact he had over her whole body. *Especially* her body. Suddenly, right here in the middle of Collins Street, Stewart was the *only* person she could see in front of her and behind her. She never even seemed to register as to why all of these people were now having to side-step this frozen person, right in the middle of them, who now happened to blocking their intended path through the crowded lunchtime foot traffic. Even her own beloved father, still standing beside her, immediately appeared to have faded away into the background as well.

Wearing a silly grin, Stewart continued walking towards her and, just like Peta, he was also completely oblivious to anyone else around him.

Maybe his mind was merely playing tricks on him and this was all just some cruel joke after all. She wasn't really standing right there at all, and any second now she was going to go POOF and disappear, back into the treasured store of his most wild and persistent fantasies.

But no, she was really was here, looking absolutely gorgeous. His ever-ready libido thought so too.

How is it that she can take away his breath so damn easily? No other woman has been able to have such an immediate effect on him—ever! Not even Felicity, and most people considered her beauty to be flawless.

Taking in the intoxicating proximity of Peta's beauty up close and personal, Stewart was forced to keep his rampant libido on a leash for now.

'What am I doing here, you ask? Why, picking up some flowers for my mother, of course. I am led to believe that a good son must never return home without flowers for his mother—especially if he has been away for too long.' Stewart's sexy baby blues twinkled back at her ... 'Wouldn't you agree?'

'Good move! I understand, too, that most little boys always want to please their m-m-other. Jeez! Here I am tripping over my words with you already.' Peta laughed, but at the same time, using this deceptively lighthearted greeting to restore her usual self-composure, especially after being thrown by Stewart's sudden appearance just now.

It was not lost on Peta, as to how the fickle finger of fate can have such a strange sense of humour at times. What are the chances of them both running into each other on busy old Collins Street like this under normal everyday circumstances?

All the time, while they attempted their broken conversation, they were both totally mesmerised with each other. As they looked deeply into each other's eyes, they smiled at each other, spontaneously remembering another time, another place, not so very long ago, when right at the very beginning, they couldn't even stand each other.

Thank goodness that's not the case anymore. Sneaky tentacles of wanton desire sprung forth to work its magic on their ordered lives once again. There was no denying it!

Without further ado, Stewart pulled Peta into his arms and kissed her deeply. Peta responded by wrapping her arms around him and returned his kiss with equal fervour, wondering at the same time how she could ever have imagined her future without him in her life. This one kiss confirmed what she already knew. There was no denying it anymore; the heart knows what the heart wants. She was truly and deeply in love with Stewart. In effect, she had fallen in love at first sight with this contradictory but intriguing man, just like her own parents had with each other. Even if she failed to realise it until just now.

For some mystical reason, time stood still for both of them, as everything and everyone around them disappeared, just like in some old-fashioned '40s movie fade-out. It really was just the two of them for a serendipitous moment in time.

Peta and Stewart resurfaced from their spontaneous kiss when they were abruptly forced to acknowledge a rather loud and deeply resonant voice nearby.

'AHEM! Don't mind me!'

'Oh dear! Sorry, Dad!' Peta now smiled sheepishly at her father. She felt shy and even embarrassed.

Stewart, on the other hand, couldn't help but sense the piercing glare directed his way by this mountain-of-a-man, now standing between Peta and himself, the man's thunderous voice matching his imposing stature perfectly. 'If you don't mind me asking you, *Sir*, I would really like to know why you were kissing my daughter just now?'

Peta knew that look of her father's all to well. Even if her father appeared to be jovial and obliging *most* of the time, it still wasn't a good idea to attempt to try and dismiss him out of hand, *ever!* Many people have learnt at their peril—including herself sometimes, as a wayward teenager—over the years, but Lucas McKenna's easygoing nature had its limits and could only stretch so far.

To her father, Stewart was still a total stranger and now here Peta was, his only child too, kissing this stranger so openly.

Peta recovered her composure quickly. She grabbed Stewart's hand to enclose it within her own for a bit of extra support. The trick now was to pacify her deceptively calm father, who was now looking her way with his bushy eyebrows raised, waiting for an explanation from her. Not good, but it was obvious; there was no escaping the truth …

'Dad! I would like you to meet Stewart Fletcher. Author extraordinaire!'

Lucas stared Stewart down, but with a reluctant acceptance to who this stranger really was, despite Fletcher's questionable past. It would appear this so-called 'author extraordinaire' as Peta had referred to him, was now obviously coming after his daughter next and now his hackles were standing up with distrust for the man, especially after this very tall stranger—albeit a ruggedly handsome stranger at that—was actually kissing his only child—indeed, his only daughter—ever so boldly in bloody Collins Street, for God's sake!

Despite his distrust for the man, he knew he would have to tread very carefully when it came to revealing his true opinion of the suave Stewart Fletcher to Peta herself. Especially since Peta has always been very reserved up until now, even with her own father, when it came to talking to him about her most private feelings. He quickly realised, he was actually seeing real evidence of his daughter's maturity for another type of love for a man who wasn't her father. His little girl was indeed grown up.

Lucas instinctively decided to put his judgment of Fletcher aside for now, or risk losing his daughter's trust forever, with spoken words that can never be taken back.

Lucas moved closer towards Stewart to shake his hand, but was still determined to be on guard with him anyway.

Lucas extended his hand to shake Stewart's. 'So I am finally getting to meet the famous Stewart Fletcher!'

'Likewise. I am indeed very honoured to meet you, Mr. McKenna. Your reputation precedes you, Sir,' Stewart offered Lucas a friendly grin, but somehow still sensed a undefinable reserve coming from Peta's famous father just the same.

'Mr. McKenna? Sir?' Lucas scoffed. 'Such unnecessary formality! It's Lucas, please! You must be mistaking me for my father. I haven't been called Mister for … well, since forever!' Lucas guffawed. Stewart laughed nervously, along with Peta, at Lucas' attempt to ease his awkwardness of using such ridiculous formality with Peta's old man.

Despite a sense of some residual hackles still emulating from Lucas, Stewart took to Lucas immediately. The three chatted away for a few minutes, mostly with Lucas and Stewart silently sussing each other out, while trying not to appear to be doing so, while Peta, on her part, attempted to keep the conversation going on an even keel. That is until a car horn right beside them suddenly jolted Stewart into awareness that Matt was now illegally parked in the fifteen-minute zone nearby. He also realised, too late by now, that it just wasn't possible for Matt to park his car anywhere else close by so he could come and talk with them.

'Peta. Lucas. That man in the car next to us is my brother Matt, who I have just remembered has been patiently waiting for me all this time. I must be going!'

Peta and Lucas leaned forward a bit to give Matt a friendly wave. He returned their wave in the same friendly manner.

Dammit! I can't see what Matt's brother looks like inside his car.
Unfortunately, introductions with Matt would have to wait for now.
How much alike are they, I wonder?

'Matt shouted me lunch after picking me up from the airport. We had only planned to just pull over for a few minutes, so I could duck into that florist over there. I think Matt's car horn is my cue to leave you both—for now.' Stewart gently took hold of Peta's hand, with an overwhelming reluctance to let her out of his sight again. 'If I don't leave with Matt right now, he'll end up with a traffic fine because of me. By the way, where were you two heading just now? Before I stopped you, that is?' Stewart locked eyes with Peta again, signalling to her to be extra careful what she says to her father once they leave here. He was well aware that her father is probably still very much indecisive as to whether Stewart was even worthy of his daughter's affections or not. Probably not, judging by the prickly vibes Lucas was sending his way.

'We were just on our way back to where we parked the car,' Lucas volunteered first off.

'Then we were planning to head down to the Yarra for dinner tonight,' Peta added.

'You and Matt are welcome to join us if you like.'

Lucas extended the invitation in good faith, but was desperately hoping Stewart would decline this time. Deep down, though, Lucas admitted to himself that he really just wanted to have some one on one time with *only* his precious daughter tonight. Surely, there was nothing selfish or rude about that, was there? For the sake of good manners, though, Lucas still went through the motions of asking Stewart and his brother Matt to join them anyway.

'The place is called The Seafood Den. Have you heard of it?'

'Yes, I do know which place you mean. They've been in Melbourne for … well … forever. Unfortunately I can't, though. My mother has organised a welcome-home dinner for me tonight, so I shouldn't even think about skipping out on that—I'd be in big trouble for sure if I did!'

'Of course! We completely understand.' Peta gave his hand a reassuring squeeze. 'You go and enjoy your family time with Matt and your mother. Particularly your mother. She must be so excited to see you again I'm sure.'

'Yes, I do believe so. She's probably waiting by the door as we speak.' Stewart agreed with Peta, but still held onto her hand as if his life depended on it. It was almost as if he was afraid to let her out of his sight for even one second, despite the guarded daggers Lucas was sending his way.

'Look Peta, I really do need to spend some quality time with my mother, but I was thinking,' he paused, and his grip on her hand tightened. 'Maybe I could catch up with you both at your hotel later tonight for a drink or two? This is merely a suggestion, mind you. I'm open to any other ideas, though.'

'Sounds like a good plan to me.' Peta's eyes sparkled even brighter at the thought of seeing and hopefully touching Stewart tonight, even if their time spent together would be in the company of her father. 'You happy with Stewart's suggestion, Dad?'

'Yes, by all means. We shall see you later then, Stewart.'

Even though Lucas agreed to meet Stewart later at Peta's hotel, Peta already knew her father will probably try to worm his way out of it at the last minute. When it came down to late nights these days, her father loved his bed more.

'About tonight then. My mother usually retreats to her bedroom to read a book or write in her journal at around eightish. If it's not too late for you both, I should be there over at your hotel at around 8:30 or thereabouts. So, your hotel is the …?'

'The Azure. Just one block away from Collins Street,' Peta said with a happy smile, never taking her eyes off Stewart for even one second.

'The Azure! That's right. I know where it is. We'd better go! I can see a parking inspector heading this way right now.' Stewart leaned over to give Peta one last kiss, but with Stewart's awareness of Lucas watching his every move, he kissed Peta with much more reserve this time.

Stewart made a point then of formally shaking Lucas' hand before opening the car door and adding, 'Catch you both later!'

'Indeed you will!' Peta whispered softly as she watched Matt's sleek silver BMW merge into the busy afternoon traffic.

Matt could wait no longer to bring up the subject of what just happened. Never mind Stewart's obviously distracted silence, he had to know *now!* 'So Stu, just to satisfy my extreme curiosity, who was that gorgeous woman you just kissed right in the middle of Collins Street? And who is the older guy with her?'

'Long story, Matt, but I'll give you the shorter version for now. Peta is the journalist who interviewed me for the magazine story featured in *Today's Voice* nearly two weeks ago now. The big guy with her is her father, Lucas McKenna, who is a well-known overseas news correspondent. Peta didn't realise when they gave her this latest assignment that her father would also be working down here as well. It's also the first time they've been in the same place together for over six months now.'

'Ah yes! I thought I'd heard the name of Lucas McKenna before. Of course! Matt nodded as his memory clicked back into gear. 'I see his name heading many of the top significant news stories all the time. You realise you've only answered one part of my two questions. What is your *real* connection to the gorgeous Peta, then? Is there anything going on with her that I should know about?' Matt queried with definite interest and a sideways grin. 'I mean. What's with the passionate greeting back there? I tell you, man. There should have been a full orchestra playing when you kissed her like that! Come to think of it, the beautiful lady didn't exactly reject your romantic advances either.'

Stewart paused before answering Matt. 'Well, to tell you the truth, I've been wondering the same thing myself lately. In-between the interview with Peta back at Cairns, and well—up until just now, I didn't know for sure. I think, Matt, that I have fallen madly, crazy in love with her. I am now completely and utterly convinced that she feels the same way about me, too.'

'So, what's the problem then? I never thought you would want to be with another woman again after Felicity. She really took you for a ride, didn't she? Personally, I couldn't stand the woman!' Matt's hands gripped the steering wheel for a moment, before continuing, 'There, I said it! Man! It feels so good to be able to admit that to you at last, Stu.' Matt sighed deeply and continued. 'Even though I never actually met Felicity in person, since for publicity's sake, she slyly insisted it would be so much more romantic for you to elope, leaving her gullible fans even more obsessed with her. I could see for myself how she ruthlessly manipulated you with the media and played on your love and devotion for her too. She even convinced you not to invite your own family to your wedding. What a bitch! I always had my suspicions about her and was even tempted to warn you, but I honestly didn't think you would've listened to me, anyway.'

'That's true. I wouldn't have listened. But I assure you, I'm well and truly over Felicity. Do you know she tried to come back to me again? This was at the same time that Peta was up in Cairns. Felicity wanted us to make a fresh start together, but I finally realised she'd just run out of money again. By this time, I was more than happy to send her on her way forever. My heart is closed to her at last. As the saying goes, "love is blind" and I certainly had blinders on where Felicity was concerned. But, that's all ancient history now. Thank goodness!'

'Do you see a future with Peta, then?'

'Believe me, I've asked myself that same question a million times this past few weeks, with no easy answer forthcoming. How can we ever be together permanently? I mean, Peta is Sydney-based with a developing career as a journalist. I live way up at Cairns and I spend a lot of my working days in front of a computer, writing for hours on end. What sort of relationship would that be? Peta would have to fly up to Cairns to be with me each time. When she can manage to get away from her own work, that is. The only other alternative would be for me to fly down to Sydney in-between writing my books and try to fit in with her own full-time career as well. Hell's bells!'

'Boy, I see what you mean! You've certainly chosen to travel the hard road at times. If you want my advice, you should try to take a step back for a moment and look at your situation realistically. Samantha has always been a strong, motivated woman, who runs her own successful art gallery, both in Sydney and overseas. She certainly wasn't about to leave her exciting art world behind to move up to some old shack in North Queensland to be with you. Then there's Felicity, another strong-minded woman who also just wanted to be married, but still with her career, along with the fame and glory that goes with it. Both selfish, self-absorbed women if you ask me, only out for themselves. Never mind their husband—as in you—they swore they'd love forever. Now you've fallen for another career-minded woman. Are you really prepared to put yourself through all of that again? Is she really worth it?'

'Yes, I do believe she is! I really do love this woman, bro. In every way possible. Peta told me she had been in a relationship for a while and, like me, she's been burned too. But since we've met, she has opened up her heart again. Neither of us were looking for love at the time. Despite our initial resistance and believe me, there was tons of that!' Stewart chuckled. 'We still fell in love. Who knows, maybe it will be third time lucky this time?'

'I don't know what to say, Stu. This is something you'll have to decide for yourself, but if it was me, I would walk away while you still can, before you get in too deep with her. I would really hate to see you get your heart broken all over again.'

'I know, I know! You're right. Why do I always fall for impossible women?' Stewart stopped talking for a moment. 'Enough about me for now, bro. How's your own love life going?'

'Love life? What love life? Work keeps me pretty busy, as you know. There is a woman I've been seeing for the last year or so. Leila is her name, and she comes from a well-to-do family from Toorak. What can I say about her? Beautiful, smart, funny and extremely patient! I'm sure Mother, and even Leila's mother, would love it if we tied the knot sooner rather than later. According to Leila's mother, it'll be a "profitable match made in heaven for all concerned". Mother keeps saying to me that I must decide for myself, but then the next minute, she's reminding me that Leila isn't going to wait for me forever. Lately, she's been dropping some not-so-subtle hints too. Frankly, Stu, she's starting to drive me crazy.' He released another heartfelt sigh. 'Anyway, I'm in no rush to marry, and Leila isn't either. Even though her family is filthy rich, Leila doesn't need to work at all really, but she still keeps herself busy with her various charities and causes. I'm just not sure how I feel about the whole marriage bit, that's all. The jury is still out on this hesitant decision of mine. The opposing argument rests for now.'

'Spoken like a true man of the law. Women are such funny creatures, aren't they? As the saying goes, "You can't live with them and you can't live without them." God bless 'em all!'

'Amen to that, brother!' Matt agreed, as they slapped their palms together in solidarity.

'Anyway, regardless of what I decide to do about Peta, I just hope Mother doesn't ask me too many questions about my love life. Or rather the lack of it up until now, that is.' Stewart paused for a moment. 'Though if she starts to probe me for the answers she seeks, follow my lead and back me up. *Please!* We know how sneaky she can be when it comes to admitting to something against our will.'

'Don't worry. I shall do my best to divert the course of maternal justice in your case, and mine, too, if need be. Anyway, our street's coming up now. Speaking of Mother, I'm sure she'll be waiting outside the front door the minute she hears the car.'

'It'll seem strange sleeping in my old room again—for this week at least.'

'Ah, mate, I hate to have remind you again, but Mother has turned your old bedroom into a sewing room.'

'Oh, you are just so hilarious!' but Stewart still laughed anyway at Matt stirring him.

CHAPTER TWENTY-TWO

As *matt drove through* the massive wrought-iron gates at the entrance of the Fletcher family home, Stewart's eyes took in everything around him with poignant familiarity. After all these years of living away from home, it felt so good to acknowledge some things stayed the same.

Throughout all of his growing-up years of living here, Stewart's romantic soul always imagined his family home had transported itself from Italy, to gracefully plonk down slap-bang in the middle of a classically designed renaissance garden.

On the upstairs level of his family home, double, curved glass doors opened out onto balconies, encased with wrought-iron edging. Each balcony was ablaze with pots of brightly coloured geraniums in tones of tangerine, cherry red and creamy white. In-between each balcony, trellises of creeping vines cloaked maroon brick walls. To complete this grand statement of 'old money', lush, verdant, immaculately manicured lawns rolled away in every direction towards vast, distant boundaries.

As predicted, Elizabeth Fletcher was indeed waiting at the bottom of the paved entrance for her sons to come home.

'Stewart, darling! It's so wonderful to have you back with us again, even if it is only for a short time. Come and give your mother a hug!'

Stewart happily obliged. He couldn't help noticing how much happier and healthier his mother looked these days. Her shiny ebony hair was now streaked with silver, but her skin was clear and her eyes shone with a fresh sparkle. Stewart thought her new chin-length bob really suited her high cheek bones and wide, smiling mouth, rather than the tight French twist she always wore. He was delighted to note the worrying frown his mother always tried so hard to hide from her two sons was nowhere to be seen.

Tension had always been an insidious presence in the family home, long before Stewart decided to give himself, his mother and little brother a hard-earned break by leaving home for good. He remembered his beautiful, gentle mother trying hard to calm the ongoing family tensions between her stubborn husband and eldest son. She even tried hard to protect Matt, the innocent participant in this carefully hidden family drama. But nothing short of a major climatic disaster could have stopped the all-too-predictable tirade of anger that inevitably exploded between his father and himself on that fateful day.

'Hello Mother! Oh, I have missed you!' Stewart happily accepted his mother's welcoming arms to enfold him. 'I must say, it's great to be back at the old humble homestead again.'

'He still has the same quirky sense of humour, doesn't he, Matthew?' Elizabeth chuckled as if Stewart wasn't even there. Tears of happiness ran unrestrained down her cheeks.

'Thank God for that!' Matt agreed. 'We wouldn't want you to become all serious now, Stu.'

'Well, now that we have the first part of our reunion out of the way, let's head inside, shall we?' Elizabeth suggested, back to her usual efficient self. She led the way up the precisely cut stone steps, which circled both sides of the front entrance.

'Stewart, maybe you might like to pop your belongings upstairs? After that's done, you can join Matthew and myself in the sunroom for a spot of tea. I'll have Helena put the kettle on right away.' Elizabeth chattered on, blissfully happy to be fussing over both her sons again.

'Will do! Don't bother to show me the way. I still remember where my old room is.' Stewart stole a glance towards Matt and grinned. 'That is, unless my room really has been turned into a sewing room like Matt said?'

'Sewing room?' Elizabeth looked a bit confused at first, then immediately picked up on the joke between her two sons. 'Yes, well, you know how it is. I suddenly have a new passion to create all sorts of things with my hands these days. Your old room was absolutely perfect for me, too. After all, it has been just unused space for years. Anyway, darling, you can just push the sewing table over towards the wall and we can toss the mattress down on the floor for you later.'

'Oh, you two are just too much! I'll be right back!' As Stewart left the room, he overheard Matt as he laughed along with Elizabeth. 'I didn't think he would believe me. Dammit! Ah well, I'll just have to try harder next time I guess.'

Stewart smiled as he raced up the stairs like a kid again, taking two steps at a time. For the hundredth time he realised how much he'd missed his family during all the years of his own self-imposed isolation in the wilderness. Not that he'd ever want to return to Melbourne full-time. It was too bloody cold these days for his warm, tropical heart.

Stewart lazed away the rest of afternoon in the glassed-in sunroom, happy to relive childhood memories with Elizabeth and Matt. Now and then, a twinge of guilt would resurface in his mind, admonishing him yet again for not returning sooner. At times, he drifted too far away to be reached by anyone.

'More tea, Stewart? Stewart? Are you still with us?' Elizabeth touched his arm gently to prompt him for a response.

'What? You're talking to me? My apologies. There I go, lost in thought again. No, I don't think I shall have any more tea, thank you. I think I've drunk enough tea this afternoon to kickstart another high tea at the Hilton. It was all so delicious though, the tea and those moreish pastries, too, I might add. Even though you and I had lunch earlier today, Matt, I guess I must be still a bit peckish.'

'A bit peckish?' Matt scoffed. 'You've just about eaten all the pastries and you've had not just one cup of tea, but three! What a pig!'

Stewart's sheepish grin warmed Elizabeth's heart. Despite the time span of her eldest son being away from his family home for so long, some things never change. Stewart's voracious appetite was still intact, at least.

'Mother, please ignore Matt's unjust comments just now. He's just jealous because he wasn't quick enough to grab that last pastry.'

'Am not jealous!'

'Are too. You great big toad!'

'Lizard breath!'

Stewart and Matt played along with their childish banter in jest until Elizabeth laughingly put a stop to it. 'Enough, you two! My sides are splitting!' Elizabeth pleaded. 'I don't know when I've laughed so much. Not for a long, long time. It seems some things *do* stay the same and you two aren't nearly as grown up as you think you are.' Elizabeth's smile contradicted her observation.

The two brothers protested jokingly that they *were* grown up, even as they threw one more bunched-up napkin at each other. Elizabeth sighed out loud this time for dramatic effect.

'What are your plans for the rest of the day?' Elizabeth asked after the last remanent of their afternoon treats had been cleared away. Elizabeth's loyal housekeeper placed their tea things onto a nearby trolley before discreetly leaving them to enjoy their long overdue family time, completely uninterrupted.

'I regret to say you will both have to excuse me for a few hours,' Matt said. 'I have to head in to work for a bit to tidy up a few important cases I am responsible for. Besides, the sooner I finish, the sooner I can get back here for our family dinner tonight. Right?'

'Your brother works much too hard, Stewart,' Elizabeth explained unnecessarily. 'He starts early and finishes late most days.' She gave Matthew a pointed stare. 'Don't you, Matthew?'

'You of all people should know by now that with running one's own law firm, you can't always stick to regular, nine-to-five work hours. If you don't put the time in for your clients, there is always some other law firm that's ready to take them away from you without any qualms at all.'

'Yes, I *do* understand how it works,' Elizabeth sympathised. 'But as your mother, I worry about you just the same. Besides, you can't expect Leila to wait forever. I think that lovely girl has been more than patient to wait this long. Really Matt, she deserves better from you.'

Matt said nothing in his defence, but Stewart could see his hands clenching in frustration.

'Hey, Matt!' Stewart interjected diplomatically. 'Thanks again for picking me up at the airport today. Oh, and the lunch too. So, we shall see you back here later today then? I'm sure Mother and I will be able to amuse ourselves for a while until you return. Right, Mother?' Stewart stretched his arm around Elizabeth, who stiffly nodded her head. No verbal response from Elizabeth was necessary when her body language was enough to portray her obvious displeasure.

'You're very welcome, Stu.' Matt threw Stewart a grateful look as thanks that his big brother made it possible for him to make a quick escape. 'I assure you, I wouldn't have missed this afternoon with you and Mother for anything.' Matt quickly kissed Elizabeth on the cheek, hugged Stewart, then headed toward the door. 'Have a good catch up, you two. See you both later!' he yelled, bolting out the front door towards his car.

Stewart couldn't help smiling to himself at Matt's extra-speedy exit.

In the past, Stewart could discuss anything with his mother, but now he found himself in unfamiliar territory. He could fool some people some of the time, but with his own mother, he couldn't fool her at all usually. Despite their closeness, he instinctively knew when utmost caution was called for.

Elizabeth called out to Stewart from the sitting room. 'In here, Stewart darling.'

Stewart entered the sitting room to find his mother seated on a comfy, delicately patterned floral settee. Despite the years of family heartache and her obvious signs of ageing, his mother still looked serenely beautiful and always oh so elegant.

'I thought we should move in here now. The afternoon sun is fading fast. Once the evening chill sets in, my sunroom won't be quite so sunny anymore. You don't mind do you, darling?'

'No, of course not. Any room is okay with me if I get to spend some quality time with you.'

'It has been a while, hasn't it? Far too long if you ask me.' Elizabeth looked around her now and smiled. 'I imagine this room must bring back some mixed emotions for you, darling?'

'It certainly does, Mother.' Stewart looked around the familiar family room as though he'd only just left yesterday. Everything still looked the same to him. The large picture window closest to them still afforded a calming view of well-placed garden beds, with their leafy shrubs, bordered by a flowering ground cover. Inside, at the far end of the spacious room, a huge mahogany writing desk took pride of place. A full-length bookcase directly behind the writing desk took over a whole wall, packed tightly with an impressive collection of rare literary works, along with some other more sophisticated, philosophical titles. The red-bound law books along the whole of the bottom row had originally belonged to Henry and now Matthew. A duplicate set of law books also lined the wall of their office at their legal place of business. The focal point of the family end of the room was a classically carved stone fireplace.

Stewart remembered spending many cosy nights in here during Melbourne's most unforgiving winter nights, playing various board games with Matt. Or listening to his parents discussing current events over a glass of tawny port or golden muscat. Unfortunately, just as his mother had hinted at, this room also contained a long-held painful memory for Stewart too. This was the same room where he and his father had exchanged those last angry, hurtful words all those years ago, which ultimately resulted in Stewart storming out, vowing never to return.

Stewart settled himself onto a sofa directly opposite Elizabeth. The recent autumn nights of Melbourne heralded the promise of another sharp, chilly winter just around the corner. For now, the fireplace remained unlit. Stewart could guarantee that within another week, the neatly stacked wood pieces beside the fireplace would soon be ablaze every night until winter's end. During this time, Stewart remembered, with winter's icy breath all around, the setting sun down here in Melbourne seemed to be almost relieved to escape this city's dismal foggy horizon for another warmer side of the world.

'Can I get you anything, Stewart?'

'I think I'd fancy a nip of sherry right about now. Even if it might be considered to be the wrong hour of the day to be partaking of liquor, I just don't care what the general masses dictate right now.' Stewart put out his hand gently to stop Elizabeth from getting out of her chair. 'Please don't get up. I still remember where it's kept, you know. Would you like a glass, too?'

'Yes, why not! Don't mind if I do. Thank you, darling.'

While Stewart poured their drinks, mother and son discussed snippets of gossip and more recent news about people Stewart once knew. Those who still live in Melbourne, of neighbours and of some old friends that Stewart went to school with. Elizabeth also filled Stewart in on some of the local politicians, misbehaving again in their usual predictable manner, especially with their local council elections already underway.

'So what else is new?' Stewart laughed along with Elizabeth. 'Most of them can't even run our bloody country, let alone a country fete. Bloody hopeless, the whole damn lot of them! It doesn't matter what political party they are affiliated with, they're all out to line their own pockets in the end.'

'Hear, hear! Couldn't have said it better myself.'

Elizabeth and Stewart clinked glasses together in mock seriousness.

'Here's to the Australian public taking their revenge in the polls!' Stewart toasted.

'Indeed! And here's to all the male politicians being kicked out and women taking over the country instead.' Elizabeth threw in for good measure.

'Not so sure about that idea. Is there any reason why men and woman can't work together? I mean look at Julia Gillard. She thought she would be "The One" to get this country back on track, but she ended up getting herself into a whole heap of trouble in the process.'

'Maybe so, but let's not forget, Stewart darling, that she was blocked at every turn by quite a few backstabbing egotistical male members of parliament too.'

'Yes, well, you're probably right. So another toast to the power of women in politics then!'

After a few more mocking, half-hearted toasts, Elizabeth suddenly became serious. 'Okay, let's leave politics and everything else aside for now, darling. Let's talk about you.'

Uh-oh. Here comes the maternal inquisition!

'What about me?'

'I'm going to ask you straight out, darling. What's happening in your love life these days? I suppose what I'm really asking is; is there anyone special in your life?'

'Yes, there might be someone in my life right now, but there are some obvious logistics we need to work out together first, but that's all I can really tell you at this stage.'

'Well, can't you at least tell me something about her?' Elizabeth prompted him, knowing full well Stewart's reluctance to talk about his private life. Even to his own mother.

'She lives in Sydney, but I met her up in Cairns slightly more than a week ago now.'

'So, what's she like then? You can tell me this, surely?' Elizabeth prompted her son again.

'Well, she's funny and smart, stylish, easygoing, and she is definitely no drama queen. Let me see. What else can I tell you about her? Oh, did I happen to mention that she's also absolutely gorgeous! I hope you can understand that's all I am prepared to say about her at this stage.'

'So, do you now care for this woman more than Felicity? Maybe more than Samantha too?'

'Much, much more. I can see where you're coming from, Mother. You seem to forget that when I met Samantha, I had only just left Melbourne, and I realised later, that time in my life was all about my rebellion against Father. In the end though, I only ended up hurting myself.'

Stewart sighed and shook his head.

'I honestly didn't plan to fall in love with Samantha. When I think about it now, it wasn't what I would call true love. We were young and reckless. Back then, I just wanted to write books. Nothing more. No pressure, no commitment. Samantha, being the talented, free-spirited, visionary that she is, tirelessly set out to change the art world in her own way. Eventually, our ideals of living the perfect life together weren't working anymore. In fact, our deluded, no-substance relationship became all terribly sad and drab at the end.'

'I couldn't help but notice that Samantha had no qualms at all, about using the ex-Mrs. Stewart Fletcher title to promote her art business either?' Elizabeth said.

'Yes, well, that's Samantha for you. She's all for promoting her business however she can.'

'And Felicity? What happened there?' Elizabeth asked.

'Felicity? What can I say? She came into my life like a whirlwind. I'd never met anybody like her before. She was so beautiful and sexy and I really thought she loved me for me. I foolishly believed she must really love me to give up her glamorous lifestyle to live way up north with me as my wife. It was all about the challenge of the chase for Felicity, though. Her dream of living up in the tropics was just like some romantic Hollywood movie to her. The true reality didn't take long to sink in for Felicity, though. Just the two of us alone together forever in some quaint little shack up in the steamy, mosquito-infested tropics. Not happening at all. Anyway, you know the rest.' Stewart sighed.

'Yes, I do darling.' Elizabeth reached over and squeezed Stewart's hand. 'You know, I never realised what it was like for you personally. I'd heard so many false stories in the papers about how mean you were to Felicity. I was beginning to feel I didn't really know who my son was anymore.'

'I've always been me, Mother. I may have changed my thinking at times, but not about who I am.'

'So, do you think this new lady in your life will be lucky number three for you?'

'I'm not sure yet, but I certainly hope so.' Stewart smiled, feeling more at ease.

'Please do! I'd really like to meet this mystery woman someday. In the meantime, I do need to ask you about something else that has been niggling at me for years. If you don't mind?'

'Sure, fire away. Obviously, whatever it is worries you still.'

'Thank you! I'll just come right out with it then. Why did you take off the way you did, darling? Your father refused to ever speak about that terrible day. Henry's only way of dealing with it was to just push it all down. Out of sight, out of mind, like nothing ever happened. Despite this foolish strategy, I knew his heart was breaking, but there no way he was ever going back down. You and your father are very much alike in that way I'm afraid. Stubborn until the end.'

'Yes, I know we are.' Stewart took a deep gulp of his sherry before continuing. 'At the time, though, it was either leave or have the life sucked out of me day by day. After I left here, for the first time in my life, I felt completely free from the pressure Father kept heaping on me. I know I hurt him and yes, you and Matt too, but I finally had to accept I could never be who Father wanted me to be. He wanted me to follow in his footsteps and study law at university. But the idea of being stuck in a drab office as some trapped, suited-up solicitor for the rest of my life, just wasn't for me, Mother, and you know it.'

'Yes, I do know it, darling. You and I are a lot alike in this way. Your father, God rest his soul, also wanted me to give up my studies in art and classical literature to stay home, to just be a wife and mother. I too, rebelled against him at the beginning of our marriage and I'm so glad I did. Back in those days, I was far too high-spirited to just stay at home, or to be expected to help out with various charity causes to further my husband's career. So, I fought hard for my independence.' Elizabeth walked over to the buffet to replenish their sherry glasses. She handed Stewart's refilled glass back to him and sat down again.

'The thing is, darling, what you probably don't realise is, your father had to toe the line with his own father, too. Your grandfather was so much stricter that your father ever was with you. Nobody would ever dare say "NO" to George Fletcher. Oh no! With his big booming voice, he overpowered everyone in the room, even Grandmother Fletcher, the gentle soul that she was. You might not remember this, son, but your father also loved our holiday house at Pittwater as much as you did. He always felt totally alive there. He just loved to be out on the water with his family. You do remember how relaxed he was there with us, don't you?'

'Yes, I do, now that you mention it. Once he was stripped of his business suit, it was like he was a different man altogether. A more lenient father too, come to think of it. Just out of curiosity, though, Mother, why did you both pick the Pittwater area to invest in property? Why not somewhere along the Great Ocean Road in Victoria? It would've been a lot closer for a start.'

'Believe it or not, your father hated the cold too. He dreaded the winters in Victoria, but never really expressed that to many people. When Grandfather Fletcher demanded your father take on the family business, any arguments from your father were strongly discouraged. So, here he stayed. But later, when he visited a client who he was fond of, who had already moved to Pittwater permanently, Henry fell in love with the area immediately. Before he flew back home, he'd already bought our holiday house.'

'Ah! I never knew Father hated the cold as much as I do. It explains a lot now. Maybe he even envied me when I set off on my own. He must have longed many times to escape his own father's strict obligations, too. I never realised until now just how much alike we are after all.' Stewart stared deep into his crystal sherry glass, lost in thought. 'I've judged Father far too harshly, haven't I?'

'Despite the stubbornness in the two of you, I know you both held a grudging respect for each other.' Elizabeth broke into his troubled thoughts. 'Underneath all of his anger and bluster, Henry really did understand your decision to leave and to find your own way in life. I think that's why he wrote you back into his will and bequeathed the Pittwater property to you. He always knew how much you loved that place too. When you accept his gift of the property tomorrow, spare a thought for your father whenever you stay there, darling. He really did love you very much.'

'Yes I know that now. Thanks for telling me all of these things, Mother, and do you know why? Because now that I know more of Henry Fletcher—the man, not the father—I can finally let go of my long-held resentment and anger towards him too.'

Elizabeth wiped tears from her eyes. 'You will never realise what it means to me to hear you say that, darling. I just wish you two could have had this kind of talk together when your father was alive. It might have saved you both a lot of unnecessary heartache over the years, don't you think?'

'True! There's been too much wasted time between us. I've been such an idiot at times.'

'Well, you can still keep beating yourself up over it, darling, or you can remember what you just said yourself earlier. You are who you are and nobody can change that. I think we each have a purpose in life. The one thing I do know for sure, though; you were never meant to be a solicitor.' Elizabeth stopped talking for a moment. 'Let's get away from this subject for now, if you don't mind. Just out of curiosity though, darling, what do you plan to do with Pittwater property? Will you rent it out or will you sell it?'

'No, Mother. I've been thinking about it a lot since Matt rang me about it. I plan to live in it!'

'Really? What about your house up in Cairns then?'

'That one I plan to sell as soon as possible. I think I need a whole new fresh start in my life, in more ways than one. Anyway, I will be merely changing one paradise for another.' Stewart grinned. 'What more could any man ask for?'

'Well you certainly will be a lot closer to us than Cairns is now. It was much too hot up there for me to visit you. Matt will love the idea of you moving to Pittwater too, I'm sure. He missed you very much after you left, you know.'

'I've missed him too. Speaking of Matt, I think you need to ease up in trying to push Matt into marrying Leila. The more you try to push him in that direction, the more he will resist you.'

'Yes, I know. I just want him to be happy, that's all. It worries me that he has to work so hard. It would be lovely for him to have Leila to come home to. I think they could be so happy together.'

'Really Mother, that's Matt and Leila's decision to make, isn't it? Matt is a big boy now, and he's more than capable of making his own decisions. Seriously! Just back off and leave him be.'

Elizabeth let out a frustrated sigh. 'Yes, perhaps you're right, darling. I promise I'll try.'

Despite his mother's promise to leave well enough alone, Stewart knew with a hidden smile her promise wouldn't last. She loved her sons very much. Sometimes a bit too much, maybe.

'It's still another hour or so until Matt comes back home. Do you mind if I just pop up to my room and relax for a bit, darling?'

'Not at all. Please, go ahead. I might stretch out right here on this sofa for a while. I left Cairns really early this morning, so I think some catch-up time will be good for me, too.'

'Good idea!' Elizabeth walked around the glass coffee table to hug her son. Elizabeth's height had always been most impressive. Even though his mother had inevitably aged, and her shoulders had stooped a bit over the years, Elizabeth Fletcher could still look almost directly into Stewart's eyes.

'Oh, Stewart darling! We shall have a marvellous dinner tonight. You, Matthew and I. It will be just like old times. Now if you will excuse me for a little while, I shall head on upstairs now. See you soon, darling.'

'I'll still be here, I promise!'

CHAPTER TWENTY-THREE

Peta and Lucas tucked into their meal with gusto. To Peta, this meal by the sea bore no resemblance to the simple fish and chips she remembered as a child. She recalled being served her meal steaming hot and all wrapped up tight in a large sheet of white paper, covered over by several sheets of newspaper.

Peta's greasy hands and happy grin said it all. Their choice of freshly caught fish was made after much careful consideration by Lucas, then grilled to absolute perfection, so it simply melted in their mouths. Along with the tossed salad, crusty bread and a chilled glass of riesling, their meal was more like a gourmet feast.

'What sort of fish is this? I don't think you told me the name of it when you selected it.'

'It's Tasmanian striped trumpeter. I particularly chose this type of fish because of its fine texture, soft flesh and its excellent flavour. Wouldn't you agree?'

'Mmm definitely! It's all so delicious! Everything I've tasted has the "ahhh factor" for me.'

'The "ahhh factor"?'

'You've never heard of the "ahhh factor"? No, of course you wouldn't have. It's something I made up myself a while back. It's my own way to judge any sort of food or drink to be really, really good,' Peta said with an excited gleam in her eyes.

'Is that so? Okay, I'm all ears. Please enlighten me on the "ahhh factor", if you please?' prompted Lucas, grinning.

'Well, you know when you take that first sip of some tea or coffee for example and it instantly ticks all the right boxes? Do you know what I mean? It has the right amount of heat. Not too hot that it burns your mouth, but not lukewarm either—which I absolutely detest, by the way. It has just the right amount of sweetness with just a dash of milk. None of that watery skim milk either! Oh, and the aroma! Don't get me started on that! But really, the "ahhh factor" comes into play when you first sip it. Your taste buds send off a message to your brain letting you know you are going to enjoy it, right to the very last mouthful, so you have no choice but to follow up with an "Ahhh!" It just hits the spot when all of your tastebuds come together in agreement. In other words, it's really is all about the perfection of taste, isn't it?'

'Mmm. Good theory!' Lucas agreed. 'Well, my dear, I have to admit, regardless of whether anything I eat or drink after today has the "ahhh factor" as you say, I'll probably just eat it anyway!' Lucas guffawed. 'So according to your personally proven theory, this meal *does* have the "ahhh factor" for you. Is that correct?'

'Absolutely! It just happens to tick all the right boxes for me. This theory of mine goes for any sort of food or beverage. But you already knew that, right?'

'Yes, yes! You're right of course!' Lucas agreed.

Peta grinned at Lucas, realising she was getting a bit carried away with her subject matter.

'Do you know what I've enjoyed most about this meal, though, Dad? Sitting here, talking to you, and spending some time alone with you at last. That's really the best part about tonight.'

'I couldn't agree with you more, sweetheart!' Lucas squeezed Peta's hand with his usual fatherly affection. 'Speaking of coffee, would you like a cup now? I do particularly enjoy a cup of coffee whenever I dine out.'

'Yes, I would. Flat white with one sugar, thanks, Dad.'

'Coming up!' Lucas spotted the owner of The Seafood Den over by the counter and yelled out to him. 'Hey, Harry! Can we get two coffees over this way when it's convenient for you?'

The man in question took no offence at all to Lucas' familiar insults. He sauntered on over to their table with a broad grin, flicking his tea towel over his shoulder in a no-nonsense manner. With his neatly trimmed grey beard, his huge head covered by a cap turned backwards and an oversized black apron covering his expansive waistline, Harry reminded Peta of an old sea-dog—albeit a cleaned-up one—not the fully trained chef he really was. According to Lucas, The Seafood Den topped the list for the best seafood restaurant to eat at in Melbourne again this year and she could understand why.

'Lucas, you old bastard! You think I don't have other customers to serve, but you? I'm a busy man, you know. I catch fish in the mornings, then I have to serve ungrateful customers like you at night.'

'At least I keep coming back even if I can't get any decent service around here.'

'For the life of me, I don't know why I put up with such a stroppy Irishman as yourself. Must be because I like you anyway despite the usual crap you dish out to me every time you visit my fine establishment. Bloody hell!'

Harry let loose with a raucous, uninhibited belly laugh just like her father's. Peta could tell straight away that, despite all of their sarcastic wisecracks and insults, her father and Harry enjoyed each other's company. They obviously respected each other too.

'So Lucas, may I ask who your beautiful companion is this evening?'

'Harry, I do apologise. This beautiful woman you see before you is, in fact, Peta, my daughter. By the way, Harry, Peta is also a journalist just like her old man,' Lucas added proudly.

'Blimey, Lucas! How could an ugly Irishman such as yourself manage to produce such a lovely vision as I see before me? Unbelievable!'

'I know Harry. I often wonder the same thing myself.' Lucas squeezed his daughter's hand again to which Peta returned with equal affection. 'Peta is my greatest achievement in life so far—bar none.'

'Don't mind me, gentlemen! I do have a voice you know. Why are you both talking about me like I'm not even here?' Peta asked with a pointed stare at both men.

Harry laughed heartily in response. 'Ah! The beautiful lady has a voice—and such a lovely voice it is, too.'

⸎

Lucas couldn't help smiling to himself as he watched Harry enjoying himself immensely, by harmlessly flirting with Peta. That's if Harry's silly, over-attentive grin was anything to go by. But then again, Lucas was used to most men openly ogling his beautiful daughter wherever they went. He used to get the same reaction when his late wife was alive, too.

⸎

'Don't take any notice of him, sweetheart. Harry is notorious for being an impossible flirt,' Lucas whispered to Peta, but loud enough to be heard by Harry. 'Be warned; he does this with all of his customers of the female persuasion. Can't help himself.'

'Well, I wouldn't be a red-blooded male if I didn't notice the obvious beauty of your daughter.' Harry turned to speak to a Peta now. 'Are you sure Old Man Lucas here is your father?'

Peta nodded her head and laughed delightedly at the continuous banter between her father and Harry.

'He is indeed. By the way Harry, I was just saying to my father what a superb meal this has been. I used to think fish and chips was something we Aussies usually enjoyed from a wrapped paper parcel, but you've just proved me wrong.'

Harry responded to Peta's praise by placing his hand over his heart in mock seriousness, before dragging a scrunched up handkerchief from his apron pocket to wipe away a non-existent tear from his eye. 'Ah! You have indeed touched my heart tonight, kind lady!'

Harry followed up his over-the-top declaration of gratitude to Peta by turning to Lucas to slap him on the back in jest. 'I tell you, Lucas, my man, this daughter of yours is not only beautiful, but she has proven herself to be an appreciative customer, too. I thank you from the bottom of my heart, Peta, you have made an old man very happy tonight..' Harry leaned forward and gallantly kissed Peta's hand. 'Pity all of my customers can't be more like you.'

'Before I get the shotgun out of my car Harry, you can now redeem yourself by getting us some coffee. Sometime tonight would be good … If it's not too much trouble?'

'Grrr! Don't push your luck, McKenna. You're cruisin' for a bruisin'! But rather than be shot in the bum by some over-protective father, two coffees coming up. Will that be with or without a wee tipple of the Baileys?"

'Yes, why not? By all means let's have a tipple or two. Thank you Harry … Peta, do you fancy a wee Baileys?' Peta merely smiled in response, thereby giving Harry her enthusiastic nod of approval, before Lucas butted in to confirm their order, 'So, that will be one black and one flat white, both with a wee tipple of some Irish health elixir, thank you, Harry.'

'Health elixir? Huh! You Irish will use any excuse for a tipple or two. I'll get right onto it then, shall I?!'

Once Peta and Lucas received their coffees from one of Harry's wait-staff, Peta released an exaggerated 'Ahhh!' for her father's amusement. They both gave their thumbs up in approval to Harry standing over by the counter. He waved in return before turning his attention back to his sizzling grill plates.

Lucas sipped slowly on his coffee for several minutes, but Peta wasn't fooled. It was when her father suddenly went all quiet, she knew all too well his sharp, observant brain was busy ticking over. Soon a whole barrage of questions is going to shoot forward from his mouth. Judging by the sharp look he was directing her way from across the chunky wooden table, Peta knew it was bound to be any minute now. She was right.

'Forgive me if I speak out of turn here, dear girl, but I couldn't help observing some mighty powerful, hot steaming love coming from you and this Stewart Fletcher out onto the crowded streets of Melbourne this afternoon. Correct me if I'm wrong, of course. I mean, you can tell me to mind my own business, but I know what I saw. Even Blind Freddy could see that you two definitely have something going on between you. If this should be true, and if he should happen to break your heart one day, though, please be aware that I won't be too impressed with the esteemed Mr. Stewart Fletcher. No, not at all.'

'Yes, you're right, Dad, and I get the strong feeling that you don't really like Stewart all that much so far. What is it about him that is worrying you already, Dad?

'Well to be honest, it could have something to do with those two ex-wives he's left behind in his past. He doesn't seem to have a very good track record as a long-term relationship option, does he? But by all means, correct me if I'm wrong. Are you really sure you want to become Mrs. Fletcher the Third in a few years from now?'

'I know where you are coming from, Dad. I also know that as my father, you don't want to see me be hurt, but you are so wrong about him. You really are. Please trust my judgement on this, Dad.'

'Unfortunately, because of his high-profile marriage to Felicity Cambria, he has been labelled by the press as some kind of monster, but believe me, he is not at all like that at all. Once you get to know him, you'll realise that I'm right. 'But, to be perfectly honest, Dad, up until today, I too was having my doubts about the possibility of any long-term commitment with Stewart. After seeing him again today though, I know deep in my heart that I am completely in love with him and no doubt can ever change that feeling for me now.' Peta finished.

'I don't understand, sweetheart. If you really are so in love with him as you say you are, what are the doubts you *were* having, then?'

'We seem to be at some sort of crossroad in our relationship right now, so some serious decisions will have to be made very soon.' Peta sighed deeply.

'What sort of decisions do you mean?'

'Well, our individual lifestyles for a start. As you already know, Stewart is a full-time author and has already written heaps of books. For him to write those books, though, it means he must spend most of his working hours within his own self-imposed, solitary existence. Oh, and did I also mention, he still lives all the way up in North Queensland?'

'Yes, you may have mentioned this before, I believe, but please do carry on.' Lucas prompted his daughter.

'As for me, it's true I also write for a living. As fate will have it though, I also happen to live all the way down in Sydney, which of course, is a bloody long way from Cairns! Like you, Dad, for me to do my job professionally, I need to be all over the place in search of good stories, so I'm never in one place for long. I suppose I can't complain. I did choose this career for myself and I know all too well we journalists must accept this part of our careers as the addictive nature of the beast.'

Peta took another sip of her coffee.

'Stewart needs a peaceful and quiet environment in which to write, whilst I live a chaotic life in the noisy, hectic city of Sydney. He values his secluded lifestyle up north and while it does work for him, I, on the other hand, love the hustle and bustle of Sydney, which works for me too. Yes, Dad, I am fully aware Stewart has been married twice before and will probably want to remain this way for a long time to come.'

'Well, to tell you the truth now, sweetheart, that's not the feeling I got when I watched you two together. Seems to me he is totally in love with you as well and his whole past commitment issue no longer applies where you are concerned. I could be wrong, but I don't think so.'

'Do you really think so, Dad?' Peta stared into the depths of her glass coffee mug, deep in thought. 'The thing is, I've had one serious relationship before Stewart and up until now, my career always took precedence over getting seriously involved with anyone at all. That is until Stewart literally came storming into my life and captured my heart completely.' Awareness hit Peta just at the mention of Stewart's name.

'So what you're saying is that, deep down, you're worried your career will have to take second place if you and Stewart ever seriously decide to become a couple?'

'No! I mean, yes! Of course my career is important to me, Dad, but I also know for sure that I love Stewart as I have never completely loved any other man before. After I returned home to Sydney, I missed him so much immediately! It was like I'd left a big part of myself behind with him. I used to think I'd never let anything or anyone stand in the way of my career, but now I'm not so sure. I find myself desperately wanting to be with him all the time. On the other hand, though, Dad, I don't want my own dreams and aspirations to be pushed aside either.'

'Life doesn't have to be as complicated as you are making it out to be, darlin' girl. Any woman these days can still have a long-term relationship or even a successful marriage and still have her own career, too. Besides, a lot of writers work from home these days. You would already be aware of this, I'm sure. Apart from your work with *Today's Voice*, you write your own blogs and you also do freelance work for other publications. Just like I've had to do over the years. You must admit, apart from our careers in general, though, we *still* crave some sort of normal life, don't we?'

Peta smiled at her father when she realised what he was trying to tell her. 'So you think I can be with Stewart every day and still have my career, too?'

'That's entirely up to the both of you. If there really is such a forever kind of feeling between you, then with a little bit—or sometimes a lot—of compromise, you can somehow make it work. There'll be many day-to-day challenges for sure, but if it was me, I know what I'd choose. Even though I've always had you in my life to fill my lonely days, I still miss your mother very much. If I could have that magical time with her again, I would hold on to it with both hands and never let go.'

Lucas, the big softie that Peta loved the most, pulled out a handkerchief to wipe his weepy eyes and blow his sniffly nose. 'If it really is true love, then don't you think he's worth the effort?'

'Yes, you're right, of course!' Peta stood up and rushed around the wooden bench table to hug her father. 'Thanks, Dad. You've helped to put things into perspective for me, as you always do.'

'My pleasure! Now! It's my turn for some advice from you. I want to talk to you tonight about my idea to retire and go fishing!'

'So you think after all of your tripping around the world you'll be content to retire now and just fish all day?'

'Damn right, I'm ready! I have been since the middle of last year. I am so over "tripping around" as you put it. I'm not as young as I used to be. This past year alone has meant endless travel delays, plus sitting around airports on uncomfortable plastic chairs, lost paperwork, and some questionable internet connections to send off my stories. The list goes on. Like I've already said, I'm over it!' Lucas sighed deeply. 'In the past I took on all of these not-so-glamorous challenges of endless travel in my stride and nary a complaint would pass my lips.'

'I must admit, Dad, you do seem to be looking a bit peaked this time. Is your health okay?'

'That's another thing that's influenced my decision to retire. According to my last health check-up, my cholesterol levels are way up and my blood pressure has increased dramatically too. It's definitely time for me to call it quits. Right after I wrap up my last story in Melbourne, that is. There will be no more global travelling for me anymore, darlin'. The only travelling I want to do now is to cruise up and down the Pittwater waterways in my own boat in search of the biggest fish I can find.'

Did Dad just say Pittwater? Of all the places he should pick. I don't believe it!

'Sounds wonderful, Dad. It's time for you to do what you want to do now. You've earned it.'

'So I have your approval for my future plans then?'

'Yes, absolutely! I think the Pittwater area would be the perfect place for you to retire to. I know you've always loved that area.'

To be on the safe side, Peta decided not to tell her father anything about Stewart's inheritance of the Pittwater property at this stage and even the possibility of them perhaps staying there sometimes, too.

I don't want to get Dad's hopes up. Just in case things don't work out between Stewart and me after all.

'I'm so glad you are happy with my decision, sweetheart. As I said before, once I finish up this story in Melbourne, I will be going in search of a fishing boat. Nothing fancy mind you, but it will have to be big enough so I can live on it most of the time. Later on, I might even buy myself a little shack down by the water so I can throw my fishing line off the jetty where my boat will be moored.' Lucas sighed happily. 'Ah, I can almost smell the place in my head now.'

'You mean the fish heads, don't you, Dad?' Peta laughed. Despite her teasing Lucas, she was thrilled for him for his future retirement.

'Jest if you must, my girl.' Lucas chuckled. 'Mark my words, though, by this time next year, Pittwater will be a reality for me. That I promise you!'

'Don't think I'm knocking your idea, Dad. I'm really excited about your retirement plans and it'll be lovely to know you'll only be a one-hour drive from Sydney so I can come and see you on weekends.'

'It will be great, won't it? So, do you think you and Stewart might move into together?'

'What I'm thinking is that, while we're both here in Melbourne at the same time, we need to sit down and talk about it together before we decide on anything further. Call me a worrywart if you will, but there're still a few decisions we need to make before we even get that far.'

'Wise decision. You always did have a mature way of looking at life, even as a little girl.'

Peta checked the time on her mobile phone. 'Speaking of Stewart, we are supposed to be meeting up with him soon. Perhaps we should make a move then?'

'Would you mind if I catch up with Stewart sometime later this week instead?' Lucas yawned loudly for effect. 'I'm afraid I'm all done in for tonight. I need my sleep!'

Peta eyed Lucas suspiciously across the table. 'You wouldn't be trying to avoid Stewart tonight, would you, Father dear?'

'No, not at all!' Lucas denied. 'No, honestly, I am absolutely ready to head off to my comfy bed right now. There's no reason why you two can't still catch up, though. Besides, I can almost guarantee Stewart isn't going to mind too much if I cop out tonight.'

'Well okay, Dad, but don't think I don't see when you're trying to get out of something.' Peta smiled with a knowing look. 'I guess we really should head back to my hotel, though. Besides, I wouldn't want you to miss your sleep now, would I?'

'Well, at least one of us will be getting some sleep tonight.' Lucas smirked.

'Dad! You're terrible!' Peta laughed in spite of her embarrassed flush. 'What on earth are you implying?'

'Well if you don't know by now, I didn't explain about the birds and bees very well, did I?'

'Honestly, Dad! You're really embarrassing me now. Yes, we definitely do have to go *NOW!*' Peta headed quickly towards the exit while Lucas laughed uproariously at his daughter's shocked expression. On the way out the door, he made a quick detour over towards the front counter.

'Hey Harry!' Lucas yelled out to catch Harry's attention over by the searingly hot, triple cast iron grill plates. 'See ya next time, though why I keep coming back, I'll never know.'

Harry came storming over to the counter with a feigned look of indignation and flicked a tea towel in the air towards Lucas. 'Get outta here, ya bum! And don't come back neither! Oh, what the hell, McKenna! Well, at least until you're working down in our fair city again.'

'That could be quite a while, Harry. As of next month, I will be retiring to my fishing boat, which I still have yet to buy. So if you are ever down Pittwater way, come and spend a week or two with me. Then I can feed *you* some fish for a change. Maybe even some Baileys too.'

'You're on, mate! I'll be there. With a carton of rum too for us old sea dogs.' Harry came from around the counter to hug his good friend, with a tear in his eye despite his gruffness. 'Geez, McKenna. After all this time I've been trying to kick you out of my restaurant and now, I've finally done it. Even so, this place won't be the same without you. Even if you do insult me all the time.'

'I love ya, Harry. Just remember, if I didn't like you, I'd be so much more polite to you.'

'I get your meaning, Lucas! Likewise for me too.' Harry grinned, then turned towards Peta and hugged her. 'Bye, beautiful! Struth! I still can't believe he's your old man. Anyway, it's been a real pleasure meeting you.'

'Same for me, Harry. Thanks again for a wonderful meal! I'll never forget it. Bye, Harry!'

'You're welcome! Bye, gorgeous! As for you, McKenna, I'll see you down by the river and by jeez, you'd better have a fishing line in your hands and a carton of rum already in the galley.'

'You're on!' Lucas raised a chunky thumb in agreement. 'See ya, mate!'

'Thanks so much for spending the day with me, Dad. This whole day has been so very special for me what with the shopping, especially the beautiful scarf you bought me and let's not forget that fantastic food we've just eaten at Harry's. Even though I know it's called The Seafood Den, I will always think of it as just Harry's.'

'Yes, I agree. To me, the Den will always be one of Melbourne's true cultural treasures. It *has* been a great day, hasn't it? Spending any day with you, though, darlin' girl, is always a special day for me.' Lucas reached over and squeezed Peta's hand with loving affection.

As Lucas and Peta headed back to her hotel, Peta's mobile trilled inside her bag. 'Your hotel is just up ahead, but you still have time to answer his call. Well, go ahead and answer it, then! Don't keep your man waiting,' Lucas prompted her.

Peta dove deep, rushing to answer it before it stops ringing. 'Excuse me, Dad. I'll only be a minute.'

'Take all the time you need, sweetheart.' Lucas answered with a knowing grin.

'Hello, Peta speaking.'

'Good evening, beautiful! Do you know who this is?'

'I most certainly do!' Peta's heartbeat started jumping erratically merely from the sound of his voice.

How does he do that and why does it happen every single time I hear his voice?

She knew her father would probably pick up on her excitement and even tease her about it later, but what the heck. She may be in tune with her father on most levels, but not so much when it comes down to sharing her most private, intimate feelings about Stewart. Peta focused on staying cool as she spoke to Stewart, very much aware her father was sitting right beside her in the car.

'So, what's happening at your end? Will you still be coming over to the hotel tonight?'

'Yes, for sure, but it might have to be a bit later than we planned, if Matt doesn't get back from his office soon. He probably had a lot of work to catch up on, since he took some time away from his office to be with his big brother today. I'll keep you posted, though. What about your father? Will he still want to wait around for me to get there? Perhaps you should check with him first. Is he still there with you?'

'Yes, he is, but he says he's already bushed and wants to head off to his bed. He says that maybe he could catch up you one other night this week before you head back to Cairns—if you're agreeable to that?'

'Yes of course! Tell him I'm very agreeable to that idea. We'll have much to talk about I'm sure … What about you, though? Are you still happy to see me later tonight?'

'Well, I don't know Stewart. I'll have to think about it. Let's see … Yes, I suppose so,' Peta teased, knowing full well the reaction she'd be sure to entice from him.

'You suppose so? Ha! You're really asking for trouble now,' Stewart threatened with a deep growl. 'I will deal with you appropriately, in exactly the right way, later tonight. Mark my words, Peta, you'll begging for mercy and that's a promise!'

'Is that so? I'll take that under advisement then, shall I?' Peta laughed delightedly, but then just in time remembered she wasn't alone. 'Okay, Stewart. Dad and I are still in the car on our way back to the hotel as we speak. I will see you when you get here.'

Thankfully, Stewart picked up on the hint about Lucas still being close by. 'You will indeed, my love. I'll see you soon!'

'Yes, you will! Oh, before you go, would you mind sending me a quick text when you're on your way?'

'Will do. Say goodnight to Lucas for me, please. I'll be there as soon as I can. I promise.'

'I know. Anytime at all is good for me.' Hopefully he'd also get her drift on that one.

'I *do* get the message. So, until we meet again, sexy lady …' he whispered his soft, loaded words full of sensual yearnings.

Sleep will not be required tonight. At least not until the early morning light is on its way.

CHAPTER TWENTY-FOUR

'*Oh man! I haven't* eaten lasagne this good for a long, long time. Please be sure to thank Helena for me, for remembering my favourite. She always makes it just the way I like it.'

'Yes, Helena is a real treasure, isn't she?' Elizabeth agreed with Stewart. 'I don't know what I'd do without her. It was Helena who suggested lasagne for you tonight and she was right again. Lasagne or macaroni cheese, right? Whenever I'd ask you what you'd like for dinner when you were still a growing boy, those two dishes is what you'd request every single time.' Elizabeth chuckled.

'Dead right!' Stewart agreed wholeheartedly. 'Since I've been living up in Cairns, though, I don't eat pasta much at all now. Hot, heavy pasta dishes are the last thing you feel like eating at any time. No thanks! It's usually anything that can be grilled on a skillet or the cast iron barbie out on my veranda. Any excuse, really, to escape my hot, sweaty kitchen up in the tropics.'

'So it's true! You really have turned troppo, Stu.' Matt interjected. 'So what do you do when you're thirsty up there? What's your poison these days, bro? Is it beer? Wine? Or just iced water?'

'All three. Cool water during the day and lots of it! Although, I have been known to knock back a beer or two out on my veranda as the sun sets on another day. Of course a good drop of red before retiring to my bed is just fine with me, too.' Stewart raised his wine glass to his mother now. 'Speaking of wine, good choice, Mother. Really smooth.'

'It is rather smooth, isn't it? It actually comes from a smaller South Australian vineyard. One of my favourites actually.'

'What about you, Matt? What's your personal choice of beverages these days?'

'Same as you, really. I do enjoy light beers, especially ones made at a microbrewery close to here. I also enjoy a good red at dinner, too. Oh, and like you, Stu, a port or sherry before bed, of course.'

'Would you both like some sherry now?' Elizabeth offered. 'We can retire to the sitting room, if you like?'

'No, not tonight, thanks. I must confess I had to bring some work home with me tonight. I have a court hearing to prepare for Wednesday, and I can't fob that one off onto my other partners. As both of you are well aware, we also have the reading of Father's will in the morning as well. So as you can understand, I'll need to catch up on some last-minute briefs before tomorrow.'

'Oh really, Matthew! Do you really have to work while Stewart is here? Honestly!' Elizabeth effected a drawn-out sigh, just to make sure Matt didn't miss her disapproval.

'You know I do, Mother, so there is no point in making an issue out of it. I'm sure Stu understands, don't you, bro?' Matt threw Stewart a desperate look.

'Mother! Leave him be!' Stewart reminded her with a direct look about her earlier promise to back off with her ill-placed interference in his life.

'Yes, I know what you're saying, but I find it hard to understand why your brother can't find more time for you.' Elizabeth pushed her maternal boundaries. 'After all, you'll be leaving Melbourne again soon.'

'It doesn't matter.' Stewart attempted to pacify his mother. 'Why,

Mother, just today alone, Matt and I have had lunch and afternoon tea together and now dinner, too.' Stewart tried to reason with her on Matthew's behalf. 'That's more than most adult brothers get to spend together in one day. Besides, did you not notice tonight how he always hogs all the garlic bread?' Stewart threw in some humour in a feeble attempt to lighten his mother's rapidly changing mood, but she wasn't buying it.

Elizabeth turned to address Matt directly now, 'Well, I just worry about you all the time, Matthew darling. You must know I only ever have your best interests at heart. You work far too hard these days. Just like your father used to.' With that said, Elizabeth finished up with a few more dramatic sighs, and just for good measure, some not-so-subtle sniffles into a dainty hanky.

Matt rolled his eyes towards Stewart, but he still came around the table to hug their mother.

'Yes, I know you love me and I love you too, but you have to let me live my own life. I am all grown up now, Mother. If I work too hard or if I end up one day as an exhausted old hermit with no social contacts to speak of, then it will be my own fault, not yours.' Matt took a deep breath before continuing. 'Please, I don't need any extra pressure from you right now.'

Stewart intuitively observed an ongoing, emotional tug of war going on between Matt and their mother, he wasn't aware of before. After a brief moment of strained silence, Matt was the first to speak.

'Anyway, if you will both excuse me, I really do have some work to do.' Matt moved around the table to give Stewart a hug. Stewart obliged by standing up to save Matt leaning over. 'Stu, please don't wait up for me. I will hopefully catch you at breakfast tomorrow morning.' He threw Stewart a sly grin and whispered ever so quietly, 'If you're still around, that is … If you get my drift?'

'I promise I'll be here, Matt.' Stewart winked, no cheeky comeback required. 'What time is our appointment with Father's solicitor again?'

'The appointment is at ten, but we will need to leave here by 9:15 at least, taking the heavy morning traffic into consideration.'

'Gotcha! I promise that no matter what, I'll be here and ready to leave at 9:15.'

'Good man!' Matthew thumped Stewart on the back in his usual affectionate, brotherly way. 'Mother, I will say goodnight to you now, but I shall see you in the morning as always. Love you!'

'Love you too, Matthew darling.' Elizabeth seemed to have regained her composure while Stewart and Matt were saying their goodnights. After Matthew left the dining room, Elizabeth moved away from the dining table. 'If you don't mind, Stewart darling, I think I will retire for the night. I'm feeling a bit below par at the moment. But what are you going to do now? I imagine you must be feeling somewhat exhausted yourself by now. It's been a long day for you, hasn't it?'

'Please don't worry about me.' Stewart reassured her. 'I'm not really sleepy just yet, but I'm sure I'll be able to amuse myself somehow. I guess I'm still feeling a bit wired up, despite the heavy meal. I think I might just slip out for a little while—if you don't mind, that is?'

'Really? And how do you plan on getting around Melbourne, darling?'

'I can just catch a taxi into the city area. I'll be fine.'

'Don't be silly, darling. You don't need to catch a taxi. Take my car in the garage. It's the small white car parked in there. I find it a zippy little thing in the traffic. The keys are in the bowl by the front door. Since I don't drive it very much these days, the battery needs turning over anyway.'

'Well, since you put it that way, I will make use of it tonight then. Thank you, Mother. I really do appreciate your thoughtfulness.' Stewart hugged her. 'In fact, I think I will head off right now and let you settle in for the night. I guess I'll see you in the morning, then.'

'Goodnight, darling! Don't be too late back. Believe it or not, we all need our sleep.'

'Yes, you're absolutely right.' Stewart kissed his mother on the cheek. 'Goodnight!'

With the car key in hand, Stewart quietly closed the front door behind him.

Stewart did feel guilty about not being completely honest with his mother, especially about Peta being in Melbourne all this week, or that he was about to be with her now. Despite his inner guilt, Stewart's instincts screamed at him not to let on to his mother at this stage just how serious he was about Peta. Especially if she should start to grill him in the same way she grilled Matt earlier tonight. The less said, the better.

With his niggling guilt tucked away for now, Stewart hurried out towards the garage with a spring in his step. As he drove out the front gate and hit the gas, he smiled wickedly to himself.

Yes, we all need our sleep, but I must confess, sleep is the last thing on my mind tonight.

CHAPTER TWENTY-FIVE

'I *think that's Stewart at* the door now, Dad. Anyway, I'll touch base with you by phone sometime tomorrow after I'm finished with the interview. I mainly just want to thank you again for the lovely time I had today.'

'My pleasure! Go on, don't keep him waiting now. Talk soon. Love you!'

'Love you too, Dad. Bye!' they ended the call.

Excited at the thought of spending tonight alone with Stewart, before ringing her father, Peta had freshened up with a leisurely shower, taking time to shave her legs so they were silky smooth.

Let's see now. Mmm. What to wear?

Not that she'd much to choose from since she'd only bought minimal clothes with her. *Ah!* But she did have her turquoise silk pants and matching robe to fall back on. This outfit was one of Peta's favourites and never left home without it. Wherever and whenever she travelled, she always took it with her, regardless of the season. This particular silky set was deliciously soft and lightweight with an added magical touch of luxury.

What more could a girl ask for? Yes, they definitely work. They always make me feel oh-so-sexy too, so it's a no-brainer, girl!'

Peta smiled at her reflection in the ensuite mirror as she applied her make-up.

Why concern yourself about what clothes you wear tonight? You won't be wearing anything for long anyway. Besides, it's not your clothes he's coming to see, right?

So true! Peta wickedly conceded. She threw the bathrobe onto the bed before sliding the slinky turquoise pants up over her ultra-smooth legs. Then she added a matching belt around her small waist to finish off the whole look of a woman ready for a full night of loving. Her long golden tresses flowed freely and sensuously down her back in soft waves, alive with bursts of golden lights from a softly-lit lamp nearby. Her cleverly applied make-up gave her a more natural, glowing look she always favoured. She took one last look in the full-length mirror on the wall before hovering near the door, ready for Stewart's arrival. She was deliciously and unashamedly dressed to kill and owning the feeling completely.

But that's the whole idea, isn't it?

With the soft anticipated knock on the door, Peta checked her appearance one last time before opening the door a crack just in case it was one of the hotel porters instead.

'Ah! You're here at last!' Peta gave Stewart a tentative smile as she opened her hotel door even wider for him to step through. Suddenly shy with him, she attempted to make conversation. 'Did your mother mind—'

She never got a chance to finish what she was about to say. Without hesitation, Stewart pulled her towards him and kissed her with such a mind-numbing passion, she couldn't even think straight anymore, let alone discuss his mother.

'Ah Stewart. Do you think maybe we should go inside now?'

Peta asked when she could finally draw breath. Not that she was complaining.

'Yes, you could be right there.' Stewart looked around, suddenly aware they were still outside the door to Peta's room. He grinned, completely unabashed, then waved his hand towards her hotel room in a chivalrous fashion. 'Let's do that, shall we? After you, please, my lady.'

'Why thank you, kind sir. What a true gentleman you are!'

'All the better to watch your sexy posterior moving so sensuously before me, my dear.'

'What a cheeky wolf you turned out to be!' Peta chuckled. 'And here I was thinking you were merely being chivalrous. How wrong I was.' Despite her half-hearted admonishment, she enticed him in further with an exaggerated shimmy of her hips as he followed her back over the threshold.

Once they were inside the room and the door closed, Stewart came in for the kill, with Peta in complete agreement of his fast-track, amorous pursuit of her body. In fact, she even cooperated by stripping off his shirt, undoing his belt and opening his pants zipper without fumbling before pulling down his pants. All in one effortless movement to floor level, covering his shoes completely. All actions, Stewart noted, completed in double-quick time too.

'Holy cow! You pretty much managed to strip me of my clothes without even breaking a sweat. I must say I am very impressed, Ms. McKenna!'

Peta chuckled at his sex-craved response to her, immediately igniting her hunger for him even further.

'I'd forgotten how much of a devil-woman you can be. Not that I'm complaining.'

'Do shut up and kiss me again, Fletcher!' Peta's inner fire needed quenching right NOW!

'Happy to oblige, but first things first, my dear, I just happen to have with me a full packet of those little close-fitting protective raincoats … if you get my drift. Can't be too careful, can we?'

'Ah! What a clever man you are! I've even bought a packet myself—just in case. Now we have twice the protection and the opportunity for twice as much sex, too.'

'Oh, what a wicked woman you are! So, you'd best not keep me waiting then.'

After much more deep kissing and a lot of tongue and lip exploration, Stewart pulled away first. 'I think it's time for me to undress you now, don't you think? I mean, here I am already half-naked with my pants around my ankles and you're still fully dressed. That won't do at all.'

'Just do it quickly, Stewart. I want you so badly.' Peta managed in-between kissing his responding lips with an insatiable fervour.

'Oh, mercy, Peta! I want you too. I knew I wouldn't have slept without coming to see you tonight. You've had me all tied up in knots inside, ever since I saw you in the city earlier today.'

'Me too!' Peta admitted. They kissed again, with each kiss more demanding that the last. 'Go on, then! What are you waiting for? Undress me. Please!'

Stewart looked deep into her pleading eyes with a smoky glint of his own. He took his time in unwrapping her silky robe with exaggerated slowness, at last revealing her full, creamy breasts, stoking her fever even higher. He leaned down and sucked first one nipple then the other, knowing full well, he was about to tip Peta over the edge. She moaned softly at first, then louder as her desire for him nearly drove her insane. She arched her back as the torment of his lips edged her towards sweet ecstasy.

Her silky pants were stripped from her body even faster than her robe was. Stewart's undies and pants quickly followed, leaving the lovers with no more annoying distractions to worry about.

'Let us be horizontal immediately!' Peta demanded as she grabbed Stewart's hand and dragged him towards the bed. This was the moment! The very cue Stewart had been waiting for; to unwrap the first of many little foil packages for the night.

Stewart followed her willingly, his erection now fully engorged, seeking its own explosive release at exactly the right time. They both landed on the bed together, in a tangle of arms and legs deliciously entwined, both seeking the ultimate touch and feel of each other to the infinite degree. For a few tingling hours at least, with their sensory responses on full alert, everything else seemed to fade away into oblivion for them. The infinitesimal beauty of their lovemaking moulded them together perfectly as they moved in unison. They responded to an undefinable primal need, which for them, reawakened the memories of yesterday. From a totally unplanned and spontaneous sexual encounter at the top end, right down to a sneaky, totally planned one at the bottom end of Australia, geography played no real part in igniting their passions at all. This exquisite re-ignited memory of their bodies once again melded together as one, heightening the memory of their first night together, forever more.

'Stewart? Are you awake?' Peta ran her fingers over his smooth, muscular chest as she spooned her body close behind him.

'Barely!' Stewart laughed. 'Oh man! I think you've done me in, for sure. How on earth will I ever be able walk out of here upright?'

'Ah, so it's my fault, is it? What about me? I have an interview to do tomorrow morning. How am I supposed to be serious when I just want to giggle with happiness instead? Oh Stewart! I hope what I am about to say next won't frighten you off, but I think I have in fallen in love with you. No I don't think—I *know* I have fallen in love with you.'

Stewart turned around to look lovingly into Peta's luminous eyes. He brushed a strand of hair away from her face, then caressed her cheek.

'Well, that certainly is a coincidence, because I know I have definitely fallen head over heels in love with you, too. How about that? And here I was thinking that maybe I probably shouldn't be feeling this way about you at all. I realise now I must have fallen in love with you that day you came knocking on my door. Since then, part of me was intent on denying it. "It's too soon," I kept telling myself. I didn't want to rush you either, in case I might scare you off.'

'I can assure you, my love, you'll never be rid of me now. You're going to be stuck with me forever.' She reached up and kissed his mouth. 'Could it be possible for us to fall in love with each other so fast and so strongly? This feeling that I have for you has my head and my heart spinning into overdrive right now.'

'I don't think anyone really wakes up in the morning and suddenly says; "Okay, this is the day I'm going to fall in love!" I think that's all part of the magic though. You just never know when it's going to happen. Maybe Cupid really does shoot us with his little arrows, just like that old '60s song.' Stewart chuckled, his hand all the while working its way down to her breasts in ever-circling, light-as-a-feather caresses, sending delicious shivers up and down Peta's body.

'You're absolutely right! It is all Cupid's fault!' Peta agreed happily.

Peta teased Stewart's lips with light feathery kisses followed by some more sensuous explorations. Her kisses were initially light enough to make him want more, but increasingly forceful enough to send a not-so-subtle message to reawaken his ever-ready libido yet again. Her lips didn't linger on his own for too long this time. Indeed not. They were needed elsewhere now. Her lips explored the contours of his chest and his firm stomach, all the way down until they found what they were searching for. Once they reached their intended destination, her busy tongue ran rings around his manhood until Stewart had no choice but to release a guttural cry for mercy.

'Oh man! What are you doing to me? That is such sweet torture. Please don't ever stop!' He groaned. Peta didn't stop either. Not until Stewart begged her to. When she ceased, he surprised her by moving down her body to give her a taste of her own delicious medicine. His lips and fingers inflicted sweet revenge on her throbbing, hidden button until, like Stewart, Peta found herself begging for mercy too.

'Oh Stewart! I give up! You win!' Peta arched her back for what seemed like the hundredth time. 'Please, please, take me now!'

'I will too! With much pleasure, I might add.' Stewart lowered himself over her willing body.

It didn't take too long at all for their united passions to crescendo to its ultimate peak, until they finally fell back onto the mattress together, in an exhausted heap, panting heavily, completely sated.

The lovers faced each other now, both with silly grins, their eyes taking in every little detail of each other's faces, while their minds attempted to absorb at a deeper level what had happened between them. Even if something should eventually tear them apart, this one night alone would become an everlasting, irreplaceable memory, to be stored away for the rest of their lives, each time spent together more powerful that the last.

Sated at last, the lovers drifted off into a blissful slumber together until the early morning light stirred them. After laying peacefully in each other's arms for a few moments, Stewart suddenly jolted awake.

'Hell! What time is it?' He looked around for a clock and finding it with disbelieving eyes. 'It's 6:30 in the morning already! I really will have to get going, my sexy, gorgeous lover.'

Stewart kissed the back of Peta's head. Peta rolled over and somehow lifted her head up with great effort. She opened just one eye first and looked around the room, not quite sure where she was. When her gaze came to rest on Stewart beside her, she smiled at him and stretched her body languorously. Stewart couldn't help smiling at the sight of her glorious hair, all messed up now and spread out around her naked body.

'Look at you, you shameful wench! And here you are now, grinning like the proverbial cat who has just licked the cream!'

'Ahh! Perhaps that is true, my love,' she put her hand out to tug on his arm. 'Come a little closer so we can start all over again.'

'Oh no you don't!' Stewart reluctantly moved out of reach and grinned at her, his mood light and happy. 'I never realised what a shameless hussy you were until now. You know what, though?' Stewart whispered as he leaned forward to kiss her already swollen lips.

'No, but please tell me what's on your mind, my horny lover?'

'I love the way you want me just as much as I want you. Please don't ever change?'

'Well, if you also promise to keep making love to me the way you did last night, I think I can pretty much guarantee that I'll never stop loving you or wanting you either. Which reminds me. I seem to remember I just asked you to come closer! Why do you continue to resist me?'

'Why? Because you're a dangerous woman, that's why. If I do come closer, I know I won't ever want to leave you and I really do have to go now, my lovely. Besides, you have an interview today and as you already know, I have an appointment with my father's solicitor this morning.'

'Yes, of course! I forgot about your appointment. I guess I must have my mind on other things.' Peta smirked. 'Would you like some breakfast? I have some fresh fruit and some yoghurt in the fridge. I even have a coffee machine over there. You know the ones that take those cute little capsules?'

'Well, I will have a quick cup of coffee with you to wake me up a bit more, but I think I will pass on breakfast, though.' Stewart threw on his clothes on and wandered over to the coffee machine. 'Are you having a cup too?'

'I think I would prefer a cup of tea this morning, if you don't mind. There is supposed to be some tea bags over there, right next to the coffee capsules, I think.'

'Found them! English Breakfast, Irish Breakfast or Earl Grey? Let me guess; Irish Breakfast, right?'

'Huh! Wrong! Earl Grey will be my choice this morning, my good man. Just because I'm of Irish descent, doesn't mean I prefer everything Irish, you know,' Peta stated primly.

'Oops! My apologies. You're right. I shouldn't make assumptions, should I?'

'Well, you're partly right. I do adore Irish Breakfast, but I also love Earl Grey too.'

'Earl Grey it is then. So tea for the lady and coffee for me. I need a kickstart this morning.'

'Aww! Hard night last night?' Peta questioned with a not-so-innocent gleam in her eye.

'Very cheeky!' Stewart laughed. 'When you put it that way, yes it was a very hard night and it'll be even harder, too, if you keep giving me any more cheek.'

'Promises, promises.'

'What are you doing tonight? I can at least deliver on that promise if you're up for it.'

'Don't you mean if *you're* up for it?'

'Oh man! I can't get any sense out of you this morning, can I?' Stewart shook his head in mock frustration. 'You'd better watch out! You're really asking for trouble, you know.'

'Well, in case you don't already know by now, I can handle your kind of trouble anytime.'

'Yes, you can! You definitely can!' Stewart admitted defeat with a grin. 'What have I got myself into with you? Getting back to my question, though. What are you really doing tonight?'

'Not really sure yet. What would you like to do? Did you have something in mind?' Peta cautiously sips her steaming tea.

'Not at this stage. I guess it will depend on how the day pans out for each of us. Why don't we just play it by ear for now?' Stewart suggests.

'Good thinking! Maybe we can agree to touch base with each other around lunchtime after we're both finished with our own agendas. We could even meet up later tonight for some dinner?'

'I agree. Whatever happens, though, I might need to talk to you in private about an idea I have that definitely includes you. Do you think we might be able to manage that?'

'What sort of plans? You've got me intrigued now. Can you give me a hint?'

'No, not yet, but you'll love it, I promise.' Stewart swallowed the last of his coffee, then leaned over to kiss Peta's warmed lips from sipping her tea. 'I can tell you one thing though, beautiful. Whatever plans I make for the future will always include you. That's a promise!'

Stewart backed away quickly now before Peta could drill him for more detailed answers.

'I know you're up to something! Come on, what is it?' Peta prodded.

'We'll talk later, I promise. In the meantime, I have to go! No doubt Mother will be wanting to know why I didn't return home last night. She hates secrets, so I really do have to go or accept the consequences of my actions.'

'Yes, you will!' Peta kissed Stewart one last time. 'In the meantime, I'm going to miss you heaps. Love you!'

'Love you too! By the way, I do hope the interview goes well for you!'

'Me too!' Peta agreed. 'Should be interesting, I'm sure. Good luck to you too, my love!'

Stewart kissed her one more time, moving away from her before the temptress could lure him back to bed for the rest of the day. Not that it would take much effort for him to do that either.

CHAPTER TWENTY-SIX

'*Well, here's the man* himself.' Elizabeth looked up from her breakfast as Stewart entered the sunlit morning room. 'Where did you get to last night? I was just asking Matthew if he'd seen you this morning, but he has just assured me that he hadn't.' Elizabeth now threw Matt a questioning look.

'No need to worry, Mother. I was just catching up with a good friend of mine. Sorry if I worried you both. What's for breakfast by the way? I'm starving!' Stewart avoided his mother's disbelieving stare whilst Matt remained silent, offering no conversation as of yet. On the other hand, Matt did offer a cheeky smirk to Stewart from behind his morning paper.

Stewart guessed this was no doubt because Matt was trying to avoid one of their mother's familiar I-know-what-you've-been-up-to looks, directed not just at Matt, but both of her sons this morning.

'Help yourself to whatever's on the buffet, bro,' Matt offered helpfully. 'There's fresh coffee in the plunger and there are also some warm Danish rolls or some slices of toast over there too.'

Stewart wandered over towards the buffet as directed. 'Let me see! Ah! Creamed mushrooms in that delicious garlic sauce I've always loved.' Stewart lifted the lids on each of the stainless steel servers. 'Mmm, there's also scrambled eggs, crispy bacon, and grilled tomatoes, too! Man, what a feast! Back home, I usually only ever settle for a few slices of toast with cheese in the morning, but at least two coffees to wake me up. Perhaps I should just take it a bit slower this morning. I do have to admit, though, these mushrooms are just too hard to resist. I might even have some grilled tomatoes and toast, too. Ah, what the heck! It would be a shame for all this delicious food go to waste, wouldn't it?'

Stewart threw a few slices of toast onto an empty plate, spooned a generous serving of mushrooms on top, and added some grilled herbed tomatoes on the side. With his fully loaded plate in one hand and a mug of coffee in the other, Stewart sat himself down at the bamboo and glass morning table, with his mother to his right and Matt to his left.

'Go for it, Stu! Worked up an appetite, have we?' Matt snickered, totally ignoring the warning flicker of caution directed his way from Stewart. Matt grinned before continuing, 'I'm glad you made it back in time, though, Stu. I was beginning to wonder if you may have forgotten our appointment this morning.'

'Not a chance, Matt, but I still have time for some breakfast, don't I?' Stewart looked from Matt to his mother, then back to Matt with a frown. 'Well, do I have time or not?'

Matt burst out laughing, 'Of course you do, bro. I was just messing with you, that's all. We still have an hour to go yet. So enjoy! Come to think of it, you do look a bit scrawny these days.'

'Gee, thanks very much.' Stewart relaxed again, his happy mood restored. 'You'll keep!'

'So, where were you last night, Stewart?' Elizabeth broke into their conversation now, determined not to be ignored. 'For some reason, you don't even want to tell me your friend's name. Big secret is it?'

Stewart realised he might be in a bit of trouble with his mother this morning. She didn't even laugh at their teasing each other like she usually did. She hadn't even called him darling yet, either.

Holy shit! I think my mother's wrath is about to rain down on me.

'I really am sorry, Mother, I didn't let you know I might be back later than I planned. Time just seemed to slip away so quickly, but I have been very inconsiderate, I know, Mother.' Stewart attempted to pacify Elizabeth but soon realised mere words were useless at this stage. She was beyond gentle reasoning and was now into being really pissed off.

'Yes well, you must know that as a mother,' Elizabeth huffed with indignation, 'I still worry about *both* of my sons. Yes, even if you are both fully grown men. When you're staying under my roof, I would just like to know that you're safe, that's all. Call me old-fashioned, if you must, but that's the way I am. Take it or leave it!'

Stewart got up and walked around the dining table to hug his mother. 'We don't mind you being old-fashioned, mother. Isn't that right, Matt?' But his younger brother appeared to be completely engrossed in the finance section of his morning newspaper. Either that or he just preferred not to react to any friction at this point in time. Stewart was on his own for now.

'Anyway, Mother,' Stewart covered Elizabeth's hand with both of his and looked her in the eye with contrition, which always used to work whenever he found himself in trouble. Well, when he was still growing up, anyway.

Bloody hell! It's not going to work this time, though. I can already tell; more grovelling may be called for here.

'I do appreciate the fact that you were worried about me, Mother, but I am back home safe now, so there's no need for you to to worry anymore. Love you!' Stewart hoped his mother was mollified enough now for him to enjoy his breakfast guilt-free at last, but he was wrong.

'So, when do you plan to tell me who was this good friend you were catching up with? Was it perhaps an old school friend, or a really close friend, perhaps?' Elizabeth questioned with a suspicious glint in her eye.

'No, nobody you know, Mother.' Stewart was prepared to leave it at that.

Easy man! Hold your tongue here.

'Oh man, this breakfast tastes really good. I never realised just how hungry I was until now.'

Stewart quickly grew tired of his mother's third-degree tactics about where he'd been last night. He was beginning to understand why Matt was so frustrated with her prying into his life these days and now it is his turn it seems. *Jeez! She was never this bad this before when I grew up here. Was she? Maybe her behaviour is due to some kind of feminine insecurity or change of life thing? Well, bad news, Mother—I'm not your little boy anymore!*

Matt came to the rescue, sensing Stewart's sudden quietness as a warning sign. His temper was about to explode if their mother didn't back off with her persistent questions soon.

'How are you going there, Stu? Nearly finished?' Stewart merely nodded with his head down.

Their mother eventually took the hint and went back to sipping her coffee, deceptively quiet for now, but Stewart could imagine her brain still ticking over. She'd wait for as long as necessary to pursue the subject a bit later, no doubt.

'If you're finished, Stu,' Matt intervened again for the sake of peace. 'I really could use your help with some necessary details I need from you before we head off, which will be in about thirty minutes from now.' Matt didn't wait for an answer as he headed off to retrieve his briefcase over by the front door. Thankfully, the simmering tension in the morning was broken for now.

'I'm ready, Matt.' Stewart was suddenly standing beside him. 'Do you mind if I just pop upstairs for a quick shower and a change of clothes first?'

Matt turned towards Stewart. 'Sure go ahead. I'll be in the sitting room when you come down.' Matt spoke briskly to Elizabeth now. 'Mother, will you be ready to leave soon?'

'Absolutely! I'll shall return momentarily. See you both soon.'

Elizabeth arose from her seat and walked past Matthew with her chin set firmly in place. He recognised that look for what it was. To their mother, nothing was over until she said so.

'Stewart, you remember Bernard, don't you?' Matt asked Stewart. They'd just entered Bernard Singleton's well-established law practice at the business end of Melbourne.

'Yes, of course! How are you, Bernard?' Stewart greeted Bernard and shook his hand.

'Couldn't be better, Stewart. It's been a long time since you've returned to our chilly city, hasn't it?'

'Chilly city is right!' Stewart laughed. 'A bloody lot colder than Cairns, that's for sure. I can assure you, Bernard, right here, right now—that's *never* going to happen! Not in a million years. You Melbournites would have to be crazy to live down here by choice.'

'Oh, it isn't so bad really.' Bernard chuckled, expecting such a response from Stewart. 'I do love to visit the northern states each year, but I'm always glad to get back home again. Anyway, please come on in and make yourself comfortable.'

Bernard left greeting Elizabeth until last. 'Elizabeth! Always a pleasure! How are you, my dear?' Bernard clasped Elizabeth's hand warmly, then gave her a lingering kiss on each cheek. Bernard, like Stewart, stood half a head taller than Elizabeth's own above-average womanly height.

'Hello Bernard. It's always lovely to see you again, too, although I'd prefer to see you under different circumstances. How are things with you these days?'

'Oh, busy as usual, but then you understand what a solicitor's life is all about, Elizabeth.'

'Indeed I do, Bernard. Indeed I do.'

Elizabeth gave him a warm smile of understanding. For some reason, she couldn't help noticing what a handsome man Bernard Singleton was. With his disarming smile and thick head of silvery hair, Bernard immediately reminded Elizabeth of the Hollywood actor Richard Gere. How come she had never noticed him in this way before?

Good Lord, Elizabeth! Where is this coming from? Mmm … Come to think of it, why is he still single, too, after his divorce two years ago? I thought he would have been snapped up by now. Elizabeth blushed over her hidden thoughts now, but allowed herself a secret smile anyway, before questioning her naughty wayward thoughts. *Do behave yourself, Elizabeth, and for heaven's sake, why are you even thinking such a thing in the first place? … Interesting!*

'I'm sorry, Elizabeth, forgive me for my tardiness. Here I am blocking the doorway.' Bernard gallantly stepped to the side to allow Elizabeth to enter his office. 'Please, do come in!'

With his greetings completed, Bernard was all efficiency again. He sat at his massive teak desk and grabbed a thick folder he placed over his blotter, opened it, and handed three stapled, itemised copies of Henry Fletcher's will for Elizabeth, Matt and Stewart.

'I requested a copy of the will for each of you, for your individual records. I'm sure it must be a relief to finally have the long drawn-out legalities of Henry's estate settled. I'll be reading my copy aloud, so each of you can follow along. You all happy, so far?'

Elizabeth, Matt, and Stewart all murmured in agreement for Bernard to continue.

'As I told you before, Matthew, you will inherit the family law firm, as well as the family home upon your mother's passing. Elizabeth, as you can see, you have been given a very generous monthly personal allowance to keep you financially comfortable for a very long time. You'll notice there will be also a separate allowance Henry has generously allocated to be used specifically for the ongoing maintenance of the family property. Upon your death, the maintenance allowance will naturally pass on to Matthew for its ongoing care.' Bernard paused to take a sip of water. 'Any questions so far?'

'Not so far, Bernard. Please continue,' Matt prompted him.

'Stewart, you're next. As Matthew has already informed you, you are to inherit the family holiday property at Pittwater near Sydney. Once I hand you the deed for the property today, you'll be the sole legal owner. What you do with it from this day onwards is entirely up to you.'

'I already know what I want to do with it,' Stewart declared. 'I've been thinking about it a lot this past week. I want to move down to Pittwater and live there permanently.'

Elizabeth smiled, but didn't comment. She'd known that's what Henry had in mind for him all along.

'Really, Stu?' Matt interrupted. 'You'd actually leave Cairns for good? I don't believe it!'

'Well, you can believe it, little brother. I want to be a lot closer to the people I love.'

'So, this means I'll be able to visit you at Pittwater. It's a bloody lot closer for me, too, I might add!'

'You'd better visit me, Matt, or else.' Stewart laughed then, affectionately punching Matt's arm.

Bernard interrupted the brothers' excited conversation. 'Let's continue, shall we? So, Stewart, when do you think you will be making your intended move to Pittwater?

'I'm not really sure yet, Bernard. I still have the first draft of my next book to finish first. At a rough guess, I would have to say within the next six months, maybe.'

'I had to ask you this, because the Pittwater real estate company look-ing after it has been renting it out, on and off, for quite a few years now. I'll need to advise them you plan to live there yourself, so they can keep it vacant from now on. Are you happy for me to tell them this?'

'Yes, please do. I will, of course, keep you up to date on exactly when I plan to make my move permanent.'

'Very well. I'll make sure I do that today. Now, Stewart, there is one more important thing I need to give you now.' Bernard reached inside a folder and pulled out a plain white sealed envelope. He held onto it briefly before passing it over to Stewart.

'Stewart, this is a private letter your father left in safekeeping with me, along with his last revised will. I was to give it to you only after his passing. He stipulated it was meant for your eyes only, Stewart. You are therefore requested to read it private, at a time of your own choosing.'

Stewart studied the sealed envelope with trepidation. He nodded to Bernard and accepted it without a word to Matt or Elizabeth. Stewart somehow knew that they already both understood why. Bernard picked up one more sealed envelope on his desk and handed it over to Stewart with no ceremony required.

'Stewart Aaron Fletcher, I hereby entrust you with the deed to your new Pittwater property. The keys to this property will be handed over to you by the real estate at Pittwater once the current tenants have officially moved out. I trust this arrangement will be acceptable to you?'

As Stewart held the deed, printed on crisp, thrice-folded white paper with the official Government seal on it, in his hands, he couldn't help but stare at it in wonder. It took a brief moment for him to respond to Bernard's question. 'Yes Bernard! Of course these arrangements are acceptable to me. Like I just said, it'll be at least six months before I can make my move down south, but as soon as the present tenants have vacated the premises, I will then—and only then—set things in motion to gradually move everything all the way from Cairns to literally south of the border.'

Stewart gathered his wits together and looked around the huge desk. First at his mother, studying him with a smile, Matt grinning at him, before finally settling on Bernard's smiling face. Stewart laughed at himself. 'I suddenly find myself speechless, for a change.'

'About bloody time, too! Peace and quiet at last,' Matt quipped good-naturedly.

Elizabeth, her eyes moistened with happy tears, moved closer to Stewart, and pulled him into her arms.

'Congratulations, Stewart darling. I feel quite certain your father is here with us today, too.'

'Ahem!' Bernard had to reluctantly interrupt the Fletcher family again to get this meeting back on track. 'Sorry to break into this happy occasion, but there is still one more thing I need to tell you, Matthew and Stewart, before our business is finally concluded for today. Your father has also left you both $500,000 each for you to do with what you wish.'

'Unbelievable!' Stewart shook his head in total disbelief and looked over towards Matt. 'Did you know about this, Matt?'

'No way, bro. I swear I had no idea!' Matt turned back to Bernard now with a shocked look on his face. 'Wow Bernard! I didn't see that one coming! I don't know what to say either.'

The awestruck brothers looked at each other. Stewart spoke first, 'Can you believe all this Matt? I don't know about you, but I am suddenly blown away by the depth of our father's generosity. I mean, the house at Pittwater, *plus* this very generous amount of money. Unbelievable!

'It certainly is a lot to take in all at once.' Matt agreed.

'I must say to you all now,' Stewart admitted. 'The realisation that Father didn't really hate me after all, is worth way more to me than this generous amount of money or even the Pittwater property ever could.'

'Yes, I know, and I for one, am thrilled to bits for you, Stu.' Matt shook Stewart's hand warmly. 'You can finally move forward into a whole new life and leave the sadness behind once and for all.'

'Amen to that!' Elizabeth agreed before giving her eldest son a motherly hug, the earlier tension between them now forgotten. 'Your father always loved you, darling, but a piece of advice from me now. Don't let foolish pride or stubbornness rule your life anymore. It's just not worth it.'

'Thank you, Mother.' Stewart hugged her back. 'I'll try to remember that from now on.'

'Well, I think that concludes our business for this morning,' Bernard had to reinforce again. 'Sorry everyone, but unfortunately I have another appointment shortly. Elizabeth, Stewart and Matthew, if you could each sign these papers in front of you, the legal side of our meeting will be all finalised at last.'

After they signed the papers as instructed, Stewart and Matt shook Bernard's hand. They both took a moment to thank Bernard warmly for the way he handled their father's affairs so efficiently over the years, before saying their goodbyes and heading out the door, talking animatedly together.

As Elizabeth started to follow her sons out of the room, Bernard quickly stepped in front of her, blocking her path.

'If you don't mind, Elizabeth, I was hoping to catch you for a quiet moment after this meeting was finished.'

'Oh! Why is that?' Elizabeth queried with a frown. 'There's nothing wrong, I hope?'

'No, not at all I assure you. I was just wondering if you'd be interested in having dinner with me sometime?'

'Yes, I believe I would, Bernard.' Elizabeth clasped his hand warmly. 'Give me a call soon.'

Bernard kissed her cheek, almost like a caress. 'You can count on it, my dear! Bye for now!'

Stewart found a quiet corner back at home and settled down to read his father's letter uninterrupted.

To my eldest son, Stewart.

If you are reading this, then it means I am already dead and buried and all you have left of me is this letter from me to you. As I write this, I can only imagine the look of surprise on your face when Bernard is finally permitted to hand it to you.

Your mother always said, you and I were much too stubborn for our own good and she's right. There were many times after you left when my heart literally ached to pick up the phone and call you. I always knew your mother was in touch with you and she had your phone number, but my stubborn pride always stopped me from reaching out to you every time. I know she would have happily given me your number without even asking why.

Emotion filled Stewart's body, but he kept on reading.

I wish I could have told you when I was alive, son, just how very proud I am of you. Yes, I was angry and disappointed you never wanted to follow in my footsteps, but I am also intensely proud of you for the way you stood up to me. I sorely wish I could have stood up to my father too, when I was your age. I often felt cowered by your grandfather, just like you were with me. Too late, I realised how unforgivable it was of me to repeat that same pattern of rigid control over you. I still find it hard to forgive myself for that.

I know you always loved our holiday property at Pittwater as much as I did. We had some really good family times there, didn't we? I always felt truly free and happy when I was there. I would love to live there one day when I retire, but perhaps it's not to be. But it can be for you, son. That's why I want you to have it after I'm gone.

That place was never meant to be about any monetary value, but more about the memories of many happy family times spent there together. For you, and indeed for myself, this was always its true value overall.

So when you are down that way fishing, please spare a thought for me, a foolish old man, sometimes.

Now the emotion really caught in Stewart's throat. By this stage of reading his father's letter, he gave up trying to roughly wipe away the tears streaming down his face, but still he read on.

When you eventually do have a family of your own, you'll be able to take them there for holidays too. You can picture me right there beside you, probably as some restless spirit, itching to go fishing with you one more time.

We've have so many wasted years apart, son, and for what? If I could offer you any advice now, it would be to try not to make the same mistakes with your own children as I did. Let them be themselves, but most of all, tell them you love them every single day.

I love you, son. I always have. Please remember that.

Your loving Father,

Henry Paul Fletcher.

The tears came easily for Stewart now. He no longer struggled to hold them and no longer cared about what other people thought of seeing a grown man cry. Not that anyone was here to witness his tears. At the same time, his tears helped to wash away the hurts of the past. True, he can't ever go back to put things right with his father, but he was heartened to know the connection between him and his father had never really been irretrievably broken. Not by his spiritual connection to his father, anyway.

CHAPTER TWENTY-SEVEN

'*Ah! Peta, it is* so wonderful to see you,' Dominic declared as he rushed over to give Peta an effusive hug, as if nothing out of place had ever happened between them. Even with Peta side-stepping his intended hug, Dominic still chose to ignore Peta's obvious rejection. Instead of accepting Peta's rebuff, he merely stepped back to openly admire her now.

'Let me look at you. Perhaps I am imagining it, but you seem to be simply glowing this morning. Could there be any reason for this?' Dominic questioned with a sly look. 'Perhaps it's because you are happy to see me again. *Oui?*'

'Dominic! How are you?' Peta completely ignored Dominic's effusive greeting, offering him only the briefest of handshakes at the entrance to The Hot Bean Cafe.

For all outward appearances, Peta's voice was friendly enough, but Dominic couldn't fail to sense some hidden undercurrents in Peta's reserved response to him anyway.

Even if Dominic felt a little peeved by Peta's reluctance to return his welcoming hug, he never let on. When it came to his work, he was easily distracted by talking about his never-ending passion for photography.

Dominic admired Peta's obvious skill for avoiding any unwanted attention about herself, by cleverly asking him about his work instead. Works for him every time.

'Tess tells me you've been working down here over the weekend. How's it going?'

'Oh, the usual delays and hassles with outdoor shoots, but that assignment is finished now. But enough about me now. When did you arrive in Melbourne?' Dominic asked.

'I arrived here Monday morning. Which of course is yesterday now. But you already know that since I told you on the phone at the end of last week.'

'*Oui*, of course. I do remember you telling me now. So yesterday, you spent all day here in Melbourne with your father then?'

'Yes, I did spend pretty much all of yesterday with my father.' Peta ignored his questioning look. 'Naturally, I was thrilled to find out he's going to be down here in Melbourne until the end of the month. It's been quite a while since Dad and I have even been in the same city together.'

'That's good then,' Dominic said, but with none of his usual enthusiasm.

'Yes, it certainly was, Dominic.'

Peta could tell by the sudden surly look on Dominic's face that this super-polite conversation wasn't thrilling him one little bit. *Well, too bad, Dominic, because that's all you're going to get from me today.*

Once they'd stepped inside, Peta looked towards the back of the cafe, immediately finding what she needed. 'Sorry Dominic, but I desperately need to make a pit stop before we place our order.'

'Yes, of course! I'll just grab us table, shall I?' Dominic offered.

'Good idea. I won't be long.' Peta headed for the ladies' towards the back of the cafe, sensing Dominic watching her as she walked away.

Inside the ladies' room, Peta attended to her immediate needs and as she freshened her make-up, her busy thoughts suddenly tipped into overdrive. It was just as well that Dominic decided to let go of their disastrous dinner scene back in Cairns. Knowing him as she did, though, she could guarantee he hadn't forgotten it completely. He wouldn't be able to resist flirting with her again. Although, when he did, she'd be ready for him this time. Unfortunately for Dominic, his huge ego would always win out over common sense.

Peta emerged from the ladies' a few minutes later. 'Let's order those coffees, please. We've a lot to cover this morning, so let's make it count.'

She gave Dominic no choice but to follow her lead, making sure he knew she was at her professional best. Nothing was going to come between her and her work ethic. Not even him. She met his gaze and observed the moment when Dominic realised his amorous pursuit of her probably was going to be a lost cause this morning.

Good! Doesn't mean he'll give up entirely, though.

'I think that all went well, don't you?'

Peta and Dominic stood by their hire vehicles in the car park of The New Hope Foundation's headquarters.

'Yes, I do believe so. The children were amazing, weren't they? I especially loved to watch them dance with such free expression to the music. They seemed to open right up to everything around them. Judging by their happy laughter, anyway. You could just tell they were really enjoying themselves and it wasn't all staged for our benefit.'

Peta smiled at the memory now of watching them earlier this morning.

'By the way, how do you feel about your photo shoot today? Are you happy with what you've captured, Dominic.'

Peta and Dominic were thankfully back on a professional footing. *If only we could stay this way.* Despite Dominic thinking he was God's gift to women, he was always good to work with.

'*Oui*, I am most certainly am. I thought you handled yourself very well in there too, Peta. Not that I ever doubted it for a minute. I am sure Tess will be very happy with our efforts today. I do believe she was very pleased with our last assignment together. By the way, I was just curious about our last subject matter. Have you heard from Stewart Fletcher since then? After all, you did spend some time together all alone?'

Peta's temper bristled when she noticed Dominic slyly studying her reaction. It was clear Dominic couldn't help himself when it involved women who he came in contact with on a daily basis. *He's probably still peeved with me too because I dared to resist his advances.*

'Tess told me Stewart was very happy with the interview and the way we both handled the whole process along the way. He also told Tess the story we did for him helped to win back the full support of his devoted followers, especially in regard to Felicity Cambria's lies about him.'

Although pleased Fletcher liked the story and the photos, Dominic was still unsatisfied with her answers. He wasn't entirely convinced Fletcher was out of the picture where Peta was concerned, so he decided to ask one more question. 'But have you heard from him privately?'

Huge mistake!

'Really, Dominic!' Peta fixed him with a withering glare before answering. 'Frankly, it's none of your business either way, is it? In fact, you shouldn't even be asking me such a question in the first place. I am a professional just like you. And I shouldn't have to justify to you, who I talk to.'

'I'm sorry, Peta!' Dominic at least had the grace to own up to his mistake and to even look guilty this time. 'Yes, you're absolutely right and I accept now, my questions have been totally uncalled for. I don't want to ruin my good working relationship with you, either. Please, can you ever forgive me?'

Peta took a deep breath before continuing. 'Yes, of course, I forgive you. But enough is enough, Dominic. Let's just put all this behind us and move on, shall we? Anyway, it's time for me to go.' Peta extended her hand to shake his. 'So, until we cross paths *professionally* again, Dominic, stay well and be happy.'

'*Oui*, Peta.' Dominic sighed. 'I do hope we'll have the opportunity to work together again someday. *Au revoir!*'

CHAPTER TWENTY-EIGHT

'*Hello! Peta speaking.*' Peta knew who it would be, but pretended otherwise. Here she was, all alone, stretched out and totally relaxed in her hotel suite, anticipating Stewart joining her later tonight.

'Hi, gorgeous! Guess who?'

Stewart also sounded lighthearted and happy to Peta. Without even trying, the deep sexy tone in his voice sent delicious shivers throughout her body, especially down into her most responsive secret parts, which had already become as natural as breathing. Because of their buoyant moods, Peta couldn't resist having some lighthearted fun with him now.

'Gee, I have no idea. Wait, I know! It's Tyler Jackson, right?' Peta teased him.

'Tyler Jackson? I'll have you know, babe, that Tyler is merely a figment of my imagination. However, if you're happy to speak to his alter ego instead, then that would also be me.'

'I suppose I'll have to, then. I really did want to speak to Tyler though.'

'Oh boy! Mark my words.' Stewart snickered. 'You're asking for trouble, lady!'

'I'll look forward to it!' Peta countered. 'Seriously though, how was your day?'

'You know that old saying; "Some days you win and some days you lose"?'

'Yes, of course I do.'

'Well today, I've actually won more than I could have ever imagined, my love.'

'Really? How so?'

'If you don't mind me saying, I would much rather tell you about it all while we're sitting somewhere quiet together. Besides, it's going to take too long over the phone and I can't wait to look into those mesmerising emerald eyes of yours, when I tell you what I have to tell you.'

'Sounds intriguing! So how soon do you think you can get here?'

'At a rough estimate, I would have to say about two to five minutes should do it.'

'Two to five minutes? You must be very close by then. Where are you exactly?'

'Would you believe me if I told you I'm downstairs in the lobby?' Stewart laughed. 'How do you feel about coming down here right now, so we can go out together for a while? Just you and me, on a real date?'

'You don't want to come up here instead?'

'Ah-ah! No way! You're way too dangerous for me to concentrate on anything, especially with that great big bed beckoning us close by as well. One whiff of that exotic perfume of yours and I'll be a goner. No, I think we would be much better off being somewhere else for now. By the way, have you eaten yet?'

'No, I haven't. I was waiting to hear from you before deciding where to eat.'

'I'm sure there must be some great places around here where we can go. You interested?'

'Absolutely! Give me ten!'

'I'll be waiting down by the reception desk. Okay?'

'Gotcha! By the way, handsome, have I told you today that I love you?'

'Love you too, gorgeous. I will await your sublime presence in about ten minutes then. Any longer and I will be coming up to get you. Then if I must, I shall drag you away with me!'

'Ah, so you like to play rough, do you?' Peta giggled. 'See you soon, lover!' Peta hung up her phone with a definite bounce in her step.

Peta stood waiting by the reception desk as promised. There was no sign of Stewart, though. At that very moment, one of the reception staff came over.

'Excuse me, but would you be Ms. Peta McKenna?'

'Yes, that's me,' Peta answered, still looking around for Stewart.

'A gentleman asked me to give you this note.'

With that done, the young man smiled as he headed back to the reception desk. Peta thanked him and opened the note to read it, totally intrigued now.

Meet me over at the big palm by the front entrance, and please don't tell Stewart.

The note was signed: *Your Secret Admirer, TJ.*

Peta laughed out loud, then looked over towards the double glass doors at the entrance to the hotel. There was indeed a rather oversized indoor potted palm near the entrance.

This is so much fun.

Peta smirked and headed for the potted plant as instructed.

So he likes to act out, does he? I could get used to this.

Now in position beside the palm, Peta suddenly heard a not-so-quiet, 'Psst!' behind her.

'No! Don't turn around! Stewart will see me. He doesn't want me to meet you because he thinks I'll steal you away from him. Keep looking the other way!'

Peta was more than happy to play along with this crazy game of Stewart's. In fact, she was rather enjoying herself.

'And you would be Tyler Jackson, I presume? As per the initials TJ,' Peta whispered back.

'That's right, I am. Stewart never stops talking about you, so I just had to meet you for myself. Even if it has to be incognito for now. He's right, though. you know. You are very beautiful.'

'Why thank you, kind sir. Come out from behind that palm now. Let me see your face!'

'No! I can't! Stewart will be back any minute, so it has to be this way for now, fair lady.'

'Oh, what a shame! I was so looking forward to meeting you. I've heard so much about you.'

'Of course you have! Who hasn't? I must away! If I'm discovered, I'll be in big trouble!'

'It was lovely almost meeting you, Tyler. Some other time, perhaps? I promise not to tell Stewart.'

Someone grabbed Peta from behind. 'You promise not to tell me what?'

'Stewart, you startled me!' Peta giggled and half-heartedly tried to squirm out of his arms.

'Who were you talking to just now? Anybody I know?'

'You might know him, but it doesn't matter. Just a bit of harmless flirting, that's all.'

'Some other man has been flirting with my woman! Where is he? I'll kill him!'

'You're totally crazy, you know!' Peta declared, shaking her head.

Her playful squirming away from Stewart predictably turned into a fumbling kind of discreet groping behind the potted plant. Before long, they were right into some breathless kisses to finish off their playful game.

'I think I could really get into this quirky but fun side of you more and more, Mr. Fletcher!'

'Is that right, Ms. McKenna? The very fact that you played along with my craziness proves to me that you and I are really two of a kind … Would I be correct about this assumption?'

'You know, I think you might be right! Anyway, enough games for now. I'm starving! Besides, I'm incapable of acting out any more on an empty stomach! Let's go!'

'Yes, I most certainly am, too. What do you feel like? Any ideas?'

They linked hands as they wandered outside together. They stood in one spot now and looked around in both directions.

'I think I feel like some Italian tonight. Maybe a pizza to share? What do you think?' Peta asked.

'Italian works for me, too. In fact, I can see one just across the road. What a coincidence!'

'Yes, I know.' Peta chuckled. 'I confess I spotted it earlier today. Nice and close too.'

'Let's do it, then! I'm glad you like Italian too. It's always been one of my favourite cuisines.'

'Do you realise there is so much we are yet to learn about each other? The list seems endless.' Peta stopped for a minute and stared at Stewart in wonder. They gazed into each other's eyes.

Stewart covered her hand with both of his. 'Even if it takes a whole lifetime to get to know you, I'll be more than happy to make that journey with you—and that's a promise.'

Peta squeezed his hand in mutual agreement before they attempted to cross four busy lanes of traffic to the other side of the street.

After devouring every single slice of an extra-large seafood pizza with a creamy marinara sauce, they finally declared themselves to be no longer hungry. The generous topping of prawns, scallops, calamari and red onion rings smothered with loads of melted mozzarella were delicious. After nearly draining a whole bottle of lambrusco, the dregs of which clung stubbornly to the bottom of their glasses, Peta leaned back and patted her stomach.

'Oh man, I am so full!' Stewart groaned, forced now to loosen his belt just one notch. 'In hindsight, I really shouldn't have finished off that last slice.'

'Me too! I don't think I could eat another mouthful. To quote one of my father's favourite sayings: "I'm full as a goog!" Whatever a goog is.'

'Here's a bit of trivia for you; a googie egg means a cooked boiled egg, I believe. Anyway, this has been an excellent meal, I must say. Remind me to thank the chef before we leave. He's only young, too. No more than thirty I would say, and this place is a real credit to him. Wouldn't you agree with that?'

'I most definitely do agree with your excellent review of this restaurant. A fine chef for certain. To be sure, to be sure.' Peta clinked her glass against Stewart's with a satisfied, cheeky glint from her one open eye.

'What the hell!' Stewart burst out laughing at her silly expression. 'Are you drunk?'

'I could very well be! But on the other hand, maybe I'm just drunk because I'm happy.'

'Amen to that.' Stewart clinked his glass against hers in complete agreement.

'No more stalling. You have things to tell me. I want to know everything!'

'Yes, gorgeous, I was just about to. I promise to tell you absolutely everything.'

'What're you waiting for? Spill the beans, Fletcher!' Peta raised her glass.

Stewart narrowed his gaze. 'I believe you really are tipsy, Ms. McKenna. Am I right?'

'Whatever! Quit your stalling! Out with it and don't leave out any details either!'

'Yes ma'am! I already told you about inheriting the house at Pittwater, didn't I?'

'Yes, you did!' Hearing the serious tone in Stewart's voice at last, Peta sobered up instantly. 'That's so wonderful, Stewart. I know this place is very special to you.'

'Yes, it sure is. I have a lot of childhood memories of that place. It was also the one place I was able to spend quality time with my father. We both loved to fish together. It was the one thing we could enjoy together where words weren't required. We'd sit quietly for hours. But do you remember that song *You Don't Know What You've Got (Till It's Gone)?* Well, that's so true.'

Stewart's face reflected his troubled thoughts. Peta said nothing as she waited for him to continue, mostly out of respect for his deep-seated regrets threatening to resurface against his will.

'My father also left me a private letter with the solicitor in the event of his death. I'll share it with you one day. Basically, he told me in the letter how sorry he was for our regrettable estrangement from each other and how much he loved me.'

With soft tears misting her eyes, Peta reached over and put her hand over Stewart's. 'Oh Stewart! Despite the emotions his letter must have roused in you today, you still must be feeling somewhat relieved and happy after reading it.' Peta grabbed a spare napkin laying on their table and sniffled into it a bit. 'Damn! I've gone all teary-eyed now. I think we need to move on from here with our conversation, otherwise I'll need extra napkins from our young chef to sop up all my tears.'

'Me too, I think.' Stewart chuckled. 'But you're right, let's move on with the rest of my news.' Stewart reached into his sports coat pocket and pulled out a few folded sheets of white paper. 'These crumpled papers are, in fact, the deeds to my newly acquired Pittwater house.'

'Wow! So it's all official then.' Peta accepted the printed deed from Stewart and held it almost reverently in her hands. She opened out the folded sheets of paper and read the line where Stewart's name was printed towards the top of the page. 'Aha! So your middle name is Aaron. I did wonder about that. So what do you plan to do with the house then? I mean, will you rent it or maybe sell it later?'

'I can tell you now, I will never sell it! When I die, this place will be passed down to the next Fletcher generation and so on and so forth. In the meantime, my love,' Stewart paused for a more dramatic effect. 'I plan to live in it.'

Peta's eyes practically popped out of her head. With no words forthcoming, Stewart grinned at her stunned mullet expression.

'Did I just hear you right? You plan to live in it? As in permanently? What about your house in Cairns? What about Oscar? And what about writing your books?'

'What's with all these endless questions?' Stewart smirked. 'I'll try my best to answer all of your questions, but please, one at a time if you don't mind. In the meantime, it might be a good idea for you to close your mouth for now, so no more persistent questions can escape!' Stewart couldn't resist teasing her.

Peta closed her mouth as she gave him the evil eye. Her silence didn't last long, though.

'Stewart, I swear if you don't answer my questions real soon, I will literally keel over from too much excitement. Come on! Don't torture me anymore. Tell me all and don't spare any details either because I'll know when you're holding out on me,' Peta threatened with a cheeky smile.

'I will attempt to answer your questions in the right order if I can remember them all, that is. Yes, I do plan to move down to Pittwater to live in my newly acquired property. No, I don't intend moving from

Cairns immediately. I figure on a period of at least six months because, a) I have to finish my current book first; and b) not until I am able to get someone to either rent it or buy it, whichever comes first. As for Oscar, my fine feathered friend, we're best buddies really, so could I ever think of leaving him behind? Of course he will move down south with me. Matt has warned me to check with the wildlife people first, just to make sure that I can relocate a wild bird from one state to another legally. He thinks there might be some yearly licence fee I might have to pay, to keep him down in New South Wales. Anyway, he says he'll be happy to look into that for me. He has even jokingly offered to waive the legal fee, too.'

'Well, it *would* be a shame to leave Oscar behind.' Peta agreed then grinned, as she thought of another reason to take Oscar with him. 'Not only that, Stewart, but who else but you would be understanding enough to supply him with his wine dregs every night?'

'That's true!' Stewart laughed. 'Besides, I also think he'll enjoy the soothing tranquillity of water all around him. As will I,' Stewart declared.

'By the way, who's looking after him while you are away? I'm sure he misses you when you're not around. Especially with no wine to steal. I still can't get over that. What a crazy bird!'

'He is that.' Stewart chuckled. 'Whenever I have to go away, my neighbour, Jan, looks after him. She also cleans my old shack once a week too. Of course, it helps that she loves Oscar as much as I do.'

'A good neighbour to have around.' She asked her next question with care. 'I need to ask you something important now and I would like an honest answer, okay?'

Stewart took Peta's hand and looked deep into her eyes. 'I think I know what you're about to ask me. You want to know is there any special reason for me wanting to move house, right?'

'So, you're a mind reader and a kick-arse author too.' Peta smiled and squeezed his hand. 'That's exactly what I was going to ask you. It's just that I got the impression when I first met you in Cairns, that you'd never leave there. I guess that's why I am so surprised by your sudden decision tonight.' Peta paused before speaking again. 'So apart from your recent inheritance, I'm thinking maybe there's some other reason why you want to move south of the border?'

'Yes, there is, and I think you already know the answer to that question, don't you?'

'Are you saying that you are moving because of me?'

Could he be? I sure hope I'm right.

'That is exactly the reason, and you know it! Since you have come into my life, I no longer want to be closed off from love anymore. You have calmed the raging storm inside of me, Ms. Peta McKenna, and I will thank you every day of the rest of my life for it. Despite your rather annoying stubbornness on the day we met, I really did fall in love with you the first moment I saw you. I just didn't know it at the time.'

'Oh, you think?' Peta laughed. 'What with you strutting around, all filled with indignation and bluster. You were certainly very determined to be rid of me. You almost had me convinced for a while there that you hated me with a passion.'

'So, what gave me away then?' Stewart laughed, recalling his stroppy behaviour at the time.

'I should have realised this was your way of protecting yourself from further heartache. Your rather bizarre behaviour at the time was merely a preconditioned response you'd put in place for yourself to push *all* women away—not just me. But I know better now. I also know that when Stewart Aaron Fletcher gives his heart to someone, he gives it unconditionally, which unfortunately leaves you somewhat vulnerable at times, and sadly, taken advantage of, too. Am I right?'

Stewart stared at Peta in wonder. 'I think you must have seen through me right from the start. Yes, that's exactly what I was trying to do the day you came into my life. I was madly attracted to you from the start, but was determined not to show it. My first marriage to Samantha was just a stupid rebellion against my father really. My second marriage to Felicity was equally impulsive too. I'd never met anybody like Felicity before and for a while there, I even allowed myself to be caught up in her glamorous world. In the end, I realised my dreams for any future with her was only about Felicity, but never me.'

'She is very beautiful, though, Stewart. I can certainly understand why you fell for her. Unfortunately, though, that kind of lifestyle, in the public eye all the time, rarely lasts forever.'

'Yes! That's exactly what I mean. Don't you see, Peta? That's why I tried so hard to resist you. You are part of the media world that seemed hell-bent on destroying me, so I wanted no part of it anymore.'

'I do understand what you're saying. But all of your past heartache shouldn't matter anymore. You should know by now I'm here to stay! I was never out to get you. I just want to take your pain away now if I can. You should know for sure, too, that I mostly just want to love you, Stewart, and make you happy. Just as you do with me.'

Stewart reached for Peta and kissed her soft responsive lips. 'I love you so much and I want that too!'

'Ah, Stewart.' As much as she loved his warm kisses, Peta realised people were now staring at them. 'I think we've hogged this table long enough. People are starting to stare at us.'

'Mmm, I do believe you are right! Let's get out of here and go some other place that's quiet, so we can continue what we've started here. Plus, we still have much to discuss yet.'

'Would you like to come up to my room? I can make us a hot drink so we can talk quietly.'

'It could be very dangerous, but still the best offer so far, my sweet Irish lady. Let's go!'

They stopped by the counter to pay their bill, then headed off across the road, hand in hand.

Back in Peta's room, Stewart held on to her hand as she attempted to head off to her kitchenette.

'Ah. Not so fast, beautiful lady. Give me a kiss first!' Stewart whispered as he pulled Peta closer to him and Peta willingly obliged before coming to her senses.

I can't let him distract me from what I have to say to him now. It's the only way. He might hate me now, but I think in time, he will see it was the only solution in the long run. It really is the only solution. I must be strong for both of us.

She slipped out of his arms again. 'Ah, so that's why you agreed to come up to my room. You just wanted to seduce me!' Peta acted all indignant and Stewart laughed with glee of the challenge ahead. 'The very nerve of you!' Peta sidestepped his groping arms one more time.

'I must confess, this is indeed true. So what are you going to do about it? Kick me out?'

'No I won't kick you out just yet. Besides, I might be the one to take advantage of you later if I have a mind to,' she saucily warned him as she headed for the kitchenette. 'In the meantime, though, I think I should make us some coffee so we can finish our little talk first. After all, that's the real reason why we came back to my room. Right?'

'Yeah, I know! As much as I hate to admit it. What with you being a mere female and all, but yes, you are absolutely right. Milk and one sugar please and don't forget to stir my coffee anticlockwise if you don't mind!'

'Don't push it, Fletcher!' Peta turned and gave him a warning look, ignoring his cheeky grin.

'I'll just take a seat at the table, shall I? Or maybe I should help you make the coffee.'

'Oh no you don't! Don't think I don't know what you're up to. You stay right where you are!' Peta warned him half-heartedly. 'Besides, I'm nearly finished anyway.'

Peta placed two cups of steaming coffee on the small table over by the glass doors.

'Now that we have our coffee, let's continue with our discussion, shall we?' Peta said. 'Where were we, anyway? Oh, that's right! Your plans to move south of the Queensland border, I believe. So, tell me quick, when were you planning to make this move?'

'I figure in about six months should do it. This should give me enough time to finish off my current book and at the same time, make a serious start at some packing. In the meantime, I'll put my old shack on the market and see what nibbles I get. Failing that, I can always rent it out to some seasonal workers during the sugar cane season. That's only until I can sell it, of course.'

'So you really don't mind leaving the tropics? I know you love it up there?'

Stewart thought about his answer. 'Yes, of course I love it, but I love you more, so there's no contest. Apart from Oscar, this past year, to be completely honest with myself—and you—I have never felt lonelier.' Stewart reached across the table and squeezed her hand. 'Up until now, my life has been in a kind of limbo, just waiting for you to come into my life. Now that you have, I want to be so much closer to you in every way possible. But here is a very important question for you to answer now, Peta.'

Stewart suddenly got down on his knees in front of Peta and looked deep into her now-glistening eyes.

'Would you perhaps want to spend the rest of your life with me? And would you perhaps, even consider marrying me, too?' Stewart held his breath, waiting for her answer.

Peta stared at Stewart realising what he'd just asked her. Her heart wanted her to say 'YES!' This time, though, her more logical, more down-to-earth side, reared up, forcing her to hesitate with her answer. The reality of their future together began to sink in. She realised with a jolt, that true love can never be this simple. Some serious compromises will have to be made. Right here, right now. She needed to extra careful, too, how she handled this tender moment with Stewart. She also needed to openly express her reservations and why. After all, their very first meeting was fraught with a whole heap of miscommunication. If there is to be any hope of a future together, there can only be clear communication between them from now onwards.

'Stewart, please don't take this the wrong way, but I can't marry you.'

Witnessing the pain on Stewart's face now, almost made her think twice about her decision. Stewart's only reaction was to stand up, walk towards the nearest window and to stare out over the city, not really seeing anything at all.

This can't be happening! After Felicity, Stewart swore he'd never allow himself to feel this dejected and miserable merciless pain ever again. Surely not with Peta, too? He was a fool to even think Peta could ever love him for himself.

Women really are all the bloody same. To hell with them all!

'Stewart, will you please come back here and talk to me? It's very important that you hear what I have to say—for both of our sakes.'

'I should've known you were too good to be true. Now I know I was right!'

Stewart's words were loaded with such abject misery. Just looking at him now made Peta want to cry, but somehow, she held back her tears, determined to see this through to the end.

'No! You are definitely not right!' Peta spoke forcefully now, determined to get his attention. And it did.

Stewart turned to shoot daggers at her, his dark mood unmistakable.

Peta almost faltered.

Oh shit! He's suddenly morphed back into that brooding, dark creature again. Well, girl, looks like it's going to have to be in for a penny, in for a pound.

She may as well get it over with. *Here goes!*

'In fact, you couldn't be more wrong and if you could just sit down and hear me out, you'll realise that what I'm suggesting is the only way to protect *both* of our futures right now.'

Despite Stewart's inner turmoil, he finally turned away from the city view to face her again. He dared to hope that maybe, just maybe, Peta did have a way to save their fragile relationship, after all. He was willing to hear anything Peta had to say for now at least, rather than sink back into that deep, dark hole of his own making, he had hollowed out for himself too many years ago.

'Okay, I'm listening.' Stewart returned to his chair and clutched his coffee cup with both hands like it was some sort of lifeline he desperately needed to hang on to, to survive this empty feeling threatening to take over his soul any second now. 'Please do continue with your grand plan then. I'm all ears!'

'I think we can both agree we want a long-term relationship together, Stewart. And I understand why you're all excited about moving down to Pittwater. I totally get that, I really do. Plus, the thought of us being together forever, is also part of that excitement for you. I truly believe, too, that I will never have to question your love for me and you shouldn't have to question my love for you either, despite your past hurts that are obviously impacting you right now, especially with my negative answer to your marriage proposal tonight. I imagine most men would feel challenged by such an answer from the woman they love. To my mind, though, that's exactly where those hurts should remain now, Stewart. In the past!'

She gazed at him, trying to gauge his reaction.

'Deep down, Stewart, surely even you must realise that getting married and living happily ever after, really is just a fairytale after all. Especially in this day and age. There are so many factors we need to consider for any future for us. If we are both serious enough to make it work, that is.'

'I'm listening,' Stewart said, much calmer now. 'Which particular factors do you refer to then?'

'Well, your two past marriages for a start. I bet at the beginning of either of your marriages, you'd never imagined in a million years being divorced from either of them, did you?'

'No, I must admit, I didn't,' Stewart conceded. 'Each time I thought it was for real. Funny how our best intentions go astray sometimes.'

'Well then, please also imagine for a moment if I'd said yes to you just now. How long do you think it would be before our honeymoon bliss wears off? When those old doubts and insecurities start to niggle at you again? Six months? One year? I have to confess, I'm a bit old-fashioned when it comes to marriage. I, for one, envision my marriage to you, of us growing old together. And I couldn't bear it if, after a year or two, we were to walk away from each other, after too many sad, unexpressed delusions have already torn us apart.'

'I must admit I'm confused. You say you can't marry me, but I also get the feeling that you don't really want to split up with me either.' As is his habit under extreme stress, Stewart ran the fingers of both hands through his hair in utter frustration. 'So, what in the hell do you want then, Peta?'

'It's all perfectly simple. Why can't we just live together for six months at least? This way, we'll both, ideally, be able to tell for sure if we can get along together in the same house on a daily basis. I truly believe, this way, we'll soon be able to sort out if our love is real or just some romantic delusion.' Peta moved closer to Stewart now to take his hand. Thankfully he didn't move his hand away as she expected he might.

'After six months, if you were to ask me again to marry you, then you will know for sure, I really do love you for you! Not for what I can take away from you. Wouldn't you agree?'

Peta stopped talking and waited patiently for Stewart's answer. It was like he'd an entire jury panel taking up space inside his head telling him what to do. She could almost see the cogs of his brain struggling to process his answer to her. This could take a while after all. Peta looked away from him, not knowing what to expect. There was one thing in her favour. At least he hadn't made a move to walk out the door yet. That's a positive thing, surely? Maybe, the longer his inner jury takes to decide its final verdict, the better it might be for both of them in the long run.

At that moment, Peta felt his hand cover hers.

'I have to agree with you, my darling.' Stewart reached over to stroke her face tenderly. 'You are absolutely right. It must have taken a lot of guts for you to reject my marriage proposal like you just did, then to back up your decision with some very valid points. You have obviously thought this out very carefully, about our long-term future, which is more than I can say for myself. To be perfectly honest, I didn't give my marriage proposal much thought at all, really. Just like in all of those classic romantic movies, I sort of expected you to immediately jump in with the answer I anticipated—which would have been a resounding "YES!" of course.'

Peta was finally able to let go of a deep breath she didn't realise she had been hanging on to all this time. In effect, by letting go of this inner tension, it also allowed her body to relax instantly. Now she was able to state her case to Stewart and sum up her arguments more clearly, with no fear of rejection, from her own point of view as well.

She squeezed his hand back. 'I can honestly say that was one of the hardest decisions I've ever had to make in my life.' Her hand reached up and lovingly stroked his face too. 'I love you so much, Stewart, and if you don't know that by now, you never will. Luckily for both of us, you must feel the same way as I do, otherwise I think you would've already left here by now. Am I right?'

'Yes, right again! I felt for a moment or two there, my heart would be wounded forever, but thank goodness, it was just my inflated ego instead.'

They both laughed together, then looked deeply into each other's eyes. Without any unnecessary spoken words, Peta knew they were both fully aware just how close they'd come to walking away from each other forever.

It was the turning point they needed. After a significant pause, Stewart was the one to speak first.

'I would love for you to come and live with me. As long as I can have you with me every day, I won't care about damaging my delicate moral fibre permanently. At least for now, anyway.' Stewart grinned. A sudden thought jolted Stewart forward. 'Oh hell! What about your father? He won't come after with me with a shotgun for leading you astray, will he?'

'Don't worry about Dad. I'll talk to him about it. He'll be happy as long as I'm happy. As far as I know, he doesn't even own a shotgun. He might have a very sharp throwing knife tucked away in his sock drawer, but as far as I know, no shotgun. Lucky for you!'

Stewart wiped his brow in mock relief. 'Whew! I'm sure glad you clarified that for me. You had me a bit worried there for a minute.' Stewart chuckled. 'Well, in that case then, Ms. McKenna, I'll be very happy to live in sin with you for however long.'

'Oh Stewart! You won't regret it, I promise you.' Peta jumped up onto his lap and kissed him deeply.

Stewart was only too happy to oblige—at least until he forced himself to withdraw first.

'If you keep that up, babe, something else will come between us. If you know what I mean?'

'I'm counting on it!' Peta teased him. 'But in the meantime, lover boy, there is one more thing we need to decide on. Could I have your full attention for a little while longer please?'

'Well, you'd better get off my lap then or I won't be responsible for what happens next.'

'Point taken and felt!' Peta chuckled, but she did as she was told and moved over to the settee.

'Now, where were we?' Stewart moved to a nearby chair but kept a safe distance from Peta. 'If you have anything more to discuss with me, then you'd best do it now. Otherwise you're literally mine for the taking!'

'Yes, I am definitely all yours. But for now, we still need to discuss when and how we're going to do this whole moving-in-together bit. I have this new idea that has just popped into my head and it could actually work for us! Feel free to correct me if I'm wrong. Okay?'

'Oh believe me, I will be feeling you all over later, but please do continue … Anytime tonight would be good,' Stewart prompted with mock impatience.

'Don't rush me!' Peta quipped with a grin. 'Okay, here goes! You head on back to Cairns and sort out all you need to do in order to get yourself down south as soon as possible. In the meantime, I'll be heading back to Sydney late tomorrow afternoon as planned, to sort out my own stuff. I will then be ready to move to Pittwater to join you within, say, a time frame of five to six months. How does that sound to you?'

'Not only are you beautiful and extremely sexy, but you are also absolutely brilliant too. I think that should work out splendidly for both of us. Ah, but there's just one big problem I can foresee now.'

'Really?' Peta frowned. 'I thought I'd covered everything. What did I miss then?'

'What are you going to do about your own work? Up until now, you've lived the life of a very busy journalist. Sorry, but I just can't see you retiring to live blissfully by the water for the rest of your life. How do you intend to occupy yourself when I'm intensely self-absorbed with my various writing projects? What happens to your own career now?'

'Is that all you're worried about?' Peta scoffed out of hand. 'Not a problem, I can assure you. A lot of journalists work from home these days, silly! I can still be out and about, covering and researching stories for Tess. This way I can also be out of your hair while you're busy writing too. *Plus*, I am already doing other freelance writing jobs on the side. How do you think my father survived financially all these years? It pays to have more than one boss these days. Just like my father, one day I want to have my clients come to me … So, does that answer your question satisfactorily? Are there any other problems you can foresee that I can't?'

'Nope! I think you've pretty much covered everything. Speaking of your father again, though. Please apologise to him for me, will you? I know we had planned to get together again before I head back home tomorrow. Time has just slipped away so quickly this week.'

'Not a problem.' Peta smiled. 'You'll probably be seeing a lot of him at Pittwater anyway. I haven't had a chance to tell you this before, but my father plans to buy himself a fishing boat and retire to the Pittwater area within the next couple of months too.'

That got Stewart's attention. 'You're kidding right? Do you mean your old man is also going to living around the Pittwater area as well? I can't believe it! Man! How's that for a coincidence? Please tell your father that he will always be most welcome to come and stay with us. I think I'm really going to enjoy getting to know your dad a lot more in the very near future.'

'I think, in time, he's going to love getting to know you, too. When I say in time, though, I just mean that what you'll have to remember, Stewart, is that I am his only daughter—his only child, really—so if he seems a bit strained with you at first, it's only because he's thinking he might not see me so much anymore once you and I are living together full-time, or he might be in the way, perhaps.'

'Are you kidding? I'll be more than happy to have him nearby. Plus, it looks like I'm going to have a permanent fishing buddy too. What more could any man ask for?'

Peta had this sudden image of Stewart and her father, in full fishing gear, reeling in a fish together, even larger than both of their imaginations combined. Happy times ahead!

'Well, to be perfectly honest, after seeing him this past week, I've realised just how exhausted he looks to me since the last time I saw him. For his current health's sake, he really does need to take life a lot easier from now on.'

'Well, I personally don't think he could have picked a better place to retire to. He'll feel like a new man in no time. You're going to love it there too, my love. I swear, that river has the power to totally relax anyone within just five minutes of arriving there. Personally speaking, the water never fails to calm me as it irons out the kinks in me. Your father will find this out for himself, though.'

'I'm sure he will. Being around a body of water like that calms my wandering soul, too.' As Peta raised herself from the sofa with the sultry intent of capturing Stewart's full attention. She started by slowly untying her silky robe and slowly lowering it one shoulder at a time. In one swift sexy movement, she tossed the robe onto the bed, before standing before him stark-naked, her hand touching herself in her most secret place, locking her cat eyes with his baby blues.

'So, my love, now, if all the details regarding our future life together are finally sorted,' Peta slowly lowered herself down onto his lap, wriggling her hips seductively on the way down. 'I have a very urgent request to ask of you.'

'You do?' Stewart groaned with the sweet intoxicating pleasure of her closeness. 'And what would that be?'

'Take me back to bed! Right this minute! Let's seal this deal of ours between the sheets.'

'Or we could even do it on top of the sheets. I think my cheeky friend down below agrees with your idea too. Due to the closeness of your body, he's rearing and ready to go! So let's oblige him, shall we, but with a little protection along the way—At least until we are finally wed, of course.'

'Before we do head back to that big beautiful bed over there, I really do need to tell you first, Stewart. I love you so very much. So, there, I've said it! I've been so wanting to say that before now, but well … This moment with you all to myself, definitely feels like the perfect time for me to declare my love, openly and honestly, for you, Stewart.'

'Oh darling! I feel exactly the same way. I love you too! You've made me a very happy man. You know that, don't you?'

'Oh I do! I do! Now do stop talking, Fletcher. Just keep touching me in that special way of yours and I will be yours forever! That's a promise!'

354

ONE YEAR LATER

'*Quick, pass me the* basket, will you?' Lucas yelled to Stewart. 'I think I've finally got this big sucker in the bag this time. What a beauty he is, too!'

'Well done! At a rough guess, I would have to say he would have to weigh forty kilos and he's most likely close-on a metre long at least. What do you think?'

'Oh, at least. Probably even more. He's definitely the biggest jewfish I've caught in these waters, to be sure.' Lucas proudly held his prize catch up high so Stewart could snap a photo of proof with his mobile phone. 'Ha! Eat your heart out, darlin' girl! Your wife foolishly challenged me to be the first to catch the biggest fish this summer and, by Jove, I think I've done it!'

'Well, she won't be able to knock you now. This photo will prove it,' Stewart declared, excited now for Lucas. 'She wouldn't dare knock you again after this one.'

'Damn right! But I really do enjoy us teasing each other all the time. That's half the fun of it.' Lucas smiled with affection. His love for his only child knew no bounds. 'Ah, Stu! Have I ever told you how happy you and Peta have made me since you've moved to Pittwater?'

'Only about a million times, especially after a few scotch whiskies,' Stewart quipped.

Lucas' laugh bellowed loud enough to disturb the fish darting around his gleaming pride and joy—his six-metre fishing boat. He'd bought it almost brand new after his retirement just under a year ago now and he'd never looked back. Lucas was indeed a happy man these days and much healthier too—an obvious fact that Peta reminded her father of constantly.

'Well, Stu, my boy, maybe it's time for us to head on back to the old homestead by the water and cook the smaller fish we've caught this morning for breakfast. What do you say?'

'An excellent idea indeed, Lucas, my man! I'll raise the anchor so we old seadogs can sail back to our home shores. I think we might have to cook the fish this morning ourselves, though. Peta still has that upset tummy again. She's had it for more than a week now, so between you and me, I'm rather worried about her now. It's just not like her to be sick at any time, usually.' Stewart frowned. 'But as her father, you would already know this … Right?'

Instead of answering Stewart, Lucas pretended not to have heard him, by whistling happily over the top of Stewart's worried question. He set about storing their combined catch together into his onboard freezer to be filleted on his thick wooden block close to the river's edge, when they reached shore again. Lucas waited until Stewart's back was turned before smiling to himself. He suspected Peta's ailing stomach was much more than just a tummy ache, but he wasn't about to say this to his son-in-law just yet. That was Peta's job.

'Oh, I am pretty sure she's going to be just fine. You'll see!'

Peta poked her head outside the kitchen door to listen for her men to return home for breakfast. She could hear the distant but familiar motorised rumble of her father's boat returning to their private jetty. She sat at their picnic table on their newly stained and renovated wooden deck. Her inner nervous system felt a bit jolted in anticipation of this morning's important discussion she couldn't put off any longer. While she waited, she sat chatting happily away to Oscar who was, as usual, busy preening himself on the railing. Peta could understand now why Stewart referred to Oscar as his best friend. Peta talked calmly to Oscar, whilst attempting to calm herself inside. Her rambling chitchat to Oscar, in effect, allowed her mind to drift back over the past year.

'I can't believe it, Oscar. Where has the time gone? Such a happy year, too.' By way of an answer, Oscar merely bobbed his head a few times, before concentrating on his grooming task again. Peta left him to it, as she wandered over closer to the smooth wooden railing, to look out over the expansive tranquil waters of Pittwater.

The move she and Stewart made here together was such an exciting, happy time for both of them. They still tended to their own careers, but they made absolutely sure they always allowed plenty of time for each other, too. Time for relaxing, but most of all, time for loving! Peta's smile broadened again with the memories of just these past twelve months alone. Every day had been ecstatically happy for Peta and, if all went well, even more so for the following years ahead. If Stewart doesn't react badly to what she was about to tell him, that is.

Peta spared a thought for Stewart now. His self-imposed, isolated lifestyle up in Far North Queensland was a thing of the past. If he ever imagined his blissfully quiet life here on the river would stay the same, well, he's in for a shock. Their life is about to change real fast and become even more complicated too, she feared. Since they made their decision back in Melbourne to live here permanently, despite the logistics and challenges of bringing their plans to fruition, their deep feelings for each other never faltered. In fact, their lovemaking intensified even more, if that was even possible. When she had first met Stewart under such tense circumstances, she could never have imagined one day being married to him. Never in a billion years! While Peta still worked for Tess, the bulk of her work was mostly home-based these days.

Speaking of Tess, Peta thought Tess might be angry when Peta told her about her secret love affair with Stewart, but she'd already guessed that's what might have happened. Her sentimental, easygoing boss was actually delighted to hear she was instrumental in getting them together in the first place. Even Dominic came to accept Peta's deception with a shrug of his shoulders and good-natured *c'est la vie* to go with it. Yes, that is how life goes, Dominic!

Peta looked back at the house in which she'd spent so much of the past year. Successful freelancing and blogging meant she could balance her workload throughout the week and spend many blissful hours with Stewart and Lucas out on the river most early mornings. Stewart had been busy too. He'd finished his last Tyler Jackson book and was now writing the second book of his new series—inspired by Lucas, as Sebastian Goldstein, a retired, but well-to-do gentleman travelling the open seas on his boat and getting himself in and out of all sorts of trouble. He had even written in Harry from The Seafood Den as Harry Limestone, Sebastian's sidekick and intrepid fellow adventurer and business partner, helping him to catch all sorts of global criminals together. So far, all his reviews were promising and, most of all, his fans had finally accepted Tyler riding off into the sunset, forever searching for more adventures further afield.

What a magical wedding they had too! Right here with a marriage celebrant in attendance, and generously catered by Harry's restaurant. Their wedding was just six months ago now and it would be hard for Peta to ever a imagine a wedding more perfect or more beautiful. Her beaming father walked her down the flowered aisle Aunt Ruby had expertly perfected along the length of their newly renovated back deck. As she and her father walked towards Stewart, Peta was intensely aware that each tiny step she took bought her closer to her true soulmate in life. Body to body forever. Their small gathering of guests all looked on, delighted for them to have made this pivotal, highly anticipated step into a marriage built on mutual trust and true love.

Peta wore a strapless, close-fitting, stunningly sequinned cream dress, emphasising her full bosom and statuesque height. A lacy bolero and cream deck shoes, decorated for the occasion with delicate white flowers, completed her wedding attire. Fresh frangipani blossoms threaded throughout her golden French plait only enhanced her natural radiance. On her walk to the altar, with her arm looped through Lucas', Peta grinned at each of her guests along the way. Aunt Ruby, her dear friend and former landlady Alison, plus Matt's fiancé Leila, and even Elizabeth, who seem to tower over Leila's petite size. There they all were, happily bunched up like a living, breathing floral bouquet, sharing a huge box of tissues together. Matt, Alison's son Terry, and Elizabeth's new husband Bernard, were next along the line. The men held tall steins of beer in their hands. Last but not least, stood Harry, Lucas' fishing buddy, with an enthusiastic, thumbs-up approval for Lucas and Peta. Even Oscar, all freshly plumed and deliriously happy with his new life by the river, bobbed up and down from his lofty perch nearby.

Stewart's mother shocked her two sons by falling in love with Bernard Singleton and marrying him secretly, followed by a honeymoon on a six-week cruise to Europe. Despite Stewart and Matt's initial shock, they were happy for her. Busy with her own happy life now, Elizabeth didn't have as much time to interfere in her sons' lives anymore. Peta loved Elizabeth, though, and couldn't have wished for a better mother-in-law.

Aunt Ruby and Alison hit it off immediately. So much so that Ruby invited Alison to come and live with her permanently. A move that suited them both since Peta was no longer living in Alison's home. The two grand dames, as Peta liked to think of them, spent many happy hours together on her aunt's covered veranda, profusely surrounded by gentle sunlight and flowers everywhere they looked. They constantly regaled each other with their memories over endless cups of tea, walnut and date cake, and other fresh-baked cakes and scones—using Alison's best china setting and teapot, of course.

With her father also living on the river and a regular guest to their home, Peta's happiness was complete. To Peta, he looked so happy and healthy these days. It warmed her heart to see him and Stewart getting along so well together, despite her father's initial testy acceptance of Stewart competing with him for his daughter's affections. They have certainly become great fishing buddies too. Co-conspirators is more like it. Peta laughed. These days, her ever-competitive father seems to get great pleasure out of trying to beat even his own daughter, with the biggest catch, each of them with their own ideas of what real fishing expertise is. As for Stewart, he never claimed to be a man worthy of competing against his wife or his father-in-law, but he is always happy to support either one of them. Which was whoever he happened to be with at the time. To play it safe, he preferred to listen, but never *EVER* did he interrupt or disagree with either one of them during any intense fishing competition.

Peta loved to tease her father, though. She never missed a chance to go out on the boat with them whenever she could. Although just lately, any excessive rocking of the boat might give away her little secret much too soon.

The thump, thump, thump of Lucas' boat moving ever closer towards their private pier broke into Peta's reverie.

Ah, they're back at last! Time to face the music! Will today become a symphony or a soap opera I wonder?

'Good morning, you two! How did you go this morning? Did you manage to catch the fish of your dreams, Dad?'

'Laugh at me if you will, but darling girl, you are going to be eating your words in a minute when you see what we caught this morning.'

'Oh really!' Peta laughed. 'I'll believe it when I see it! Come on then, Father dear, I can't wait to see this big beauty then.'

After the boat was tied down, Stewart grabbed his wife and greeted her in his usual way with his promising kisses, always loaded with sensual overtones to Peta.

'When you two have quite finished!' Lucas chided them good-naturedly. 'Stewart, you might want to bring your wife over here, if you please, so I can gloat some more to her.'

Peta leaned over to look into the oversized esky, trying not to let the smell of the fresh fish sent her tummy into its usual gut-churning motion lately.

'Holy cow, Dad! I think you really did catch the biggest fish this morning, just like you said. I'm very impressed! He's a real beauty, isn't he?'

'And you didn't think I could do it, did you?' Lucas' grin broadened even more. 'Ye of little faith, oh daughter of mine.'

'Yeah, whatever!' Peta threw back at him as she and Stewart walked off the boat together, hugging each other. 'Come up for breakfast when you're ready, Dad.'

'I just have a few things to check on first. I'll be about thirty minutes tops. In the meantime, it'll give you two a chance to talk about things. I'm sure you're got *lots* to talk about. Right, darlin' girl?'

Peta turned to look back at her father, but he'd already disappeared from view.

Dammit! How does he do that?

Her father always seemed to know when she was keeping a secret from him. Come to think of it, the way Stewart has been studying her extra closely lately, it's like he's also picked up on something different about her.

I guess it really is time to put him out of his misery.

'Stewart, please, can you sit down here a minute? I've got something to tell you.'

'Are you okay?' Stewart immediately looked concerned. 'I couldn't help noticing that you've been feeling a bit off lately. Where's your normal healthy appetite? Please, darling, tell me what's wrong.'

'Nothing is wrong with my health, I can assure you. Most women, I believe, feel some kind of nausea at the beginning of each pregnancy.'

That should do the trick!

'Whoa! Back up a minute, will you? Did I just hear you right? You're pregnant?'

'Yes, I am indeed. Eight weeks along, I'm told. You're not mad at me, are you?' Apprehensive now, she watched Stewart carefully as he attempted to process her news.

'Mad at you! How could I ever be mad at you about something as wonderful as this?' Stewart rubbed her tummy gently in disbelief. 'We're really going to have a baby? I'm going to be a father!' He grabbed Peta and kissed her deeply. 'I never thought I could be any happier than I have been this past year, but you've just proved me wrong. I love you so much.'

Peta laughed with happy tears streaming down her face. 'Well, you might have had a hand in making this tiny little person growing inside me. I couldn't have done it without you, really. Well, not with as much fun anyway,' Peta quipped.

'True!' Stewart stared at her in wonder. 'I can't believe it! Stewart eased Peta into his arms as if she was fragile and kissed her again before yelling out to his father-in-law. 'Hey Lucas! Can you hear me?'

'I'm here, I'm here!' Lucas yelled back from the wheelhouse. 'Faith and begorrah! What's all the shouting about, son?'

'I just thought you might want to know that you're going to become a grandfather, you handsome Irish devil!'

'Well, I sort of guessed that for myself with Peta's nausea lately. Wonderful news, though! I'm going to have a grandson or a granddaughter, now, to take fishing one day. 'Tis surely a blessing, for sure. This, indeed, will be a day to remember. I've just caught my biggest fish ever this morning *and* I'm about to become a grandfather, to boot. I believe this occasion calls for a celebration. What do you say, Stu?'

'Absolutely! I'll even bring out the good whiskey! Hurry on up here, Lucas!'

'Well I never!' Peta affected a shocked look for the fun of it, but was more than willing to celebrate too—but with something non-alcoholic for her, though. 'You two are actually going to drink whisky this morning? At breakfast, too, no less?' Peta protested half-heartedly.

'Well, it's not every day I find out I'm going to be a father.' Stewart defended his actions with a huge grin just the same. 'That's celebration enough, don't you think you sweet Mama? So, will you be partaking of a wee drop of whisky too, my darling wife?'

'I'm afraid not. I won't be drinking any alcohol for the next seven months. But you two can go ahead and have a drink for me.'

'Oh, we will, I assure you! This could be a long breakfast, me thinks!' Stewart laughed.

Sometime later, after a full, hearty breakfast of grilled freshly caught fish, grilled tomatoes, mushrooms and lots of buttery toast, Stewart and Lucas clinked their whisky glasses together. Peta joined in happily with a clink from her glass of chilled, lemon-infused sparkling water.

'Here's to our newest family member and to his or her beautiful mother!' Lucas toasted his future grandchild.

'And here's to a future heir to the ownership of our river paradise, be it boy or girl!' before Stewart added with a protective arm around Peta. 'One last toast from me, to my father, Henry Fletcher, for making our happy new life here at beautiful Pittwater even possible.'

Peta joined in too with her own toast. 'And here's to many more babies to follow—to a home filled with a never-ending bounty of love!'

Stewart looked worried. 'Mm, Peta darling, just how many babies are we talking about here?'

'Not sure yet. Maybe six or maybe even a full dozen. What do you think, darling?' No words were audibly forthcoming from her husband yet. The look on his face, though, was enough to prompt Peta to put him at ease at last.

'Gotcha on that one.' Peta moved to hug him from behind. 'You should have seen the look in your face just now. Don't worry, I only mean one other baby, maybe even two. What do you think?'

'Hear, hear!' Her two favourite men in the whole world chorused happily together with several generous nips of their best whisky to fuel their excited words.

Peta smiled, recalling the expression on Stewart's shell-shocked face when she mentioned them having not just six children, but another six too.

It didn't matter how many children they were destined to have really, as long as each one of them knew they were loved. Right from the very moment of conception. At least they'd have lots more fun, making even more babies to love.

THE END

ACKNOWLEDGEMENTS

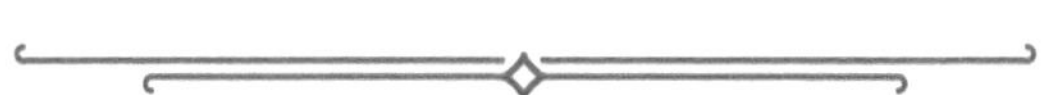

How does one begin to count the ways I have been helped by others with my writing journey?

For a start, my English teacher back in primary school was the very first person who really inspired my passion for the written word. After I was given an assignment by her to write a one-page story about a haunted house, she had essentially ignited a fire in my belly. Three pages later, she finally had to say to me, 'Toni, I said one page—not three!'

Next, a big THANK YOU must go to Gerard Traub for opening the door for me, into the wonderful world of publishing. I have been in awe, for many years now, of Gerard's all-inspiring talent as a published poet (*Reflections*) and as an author of his recently-published children's book (*Lily the Lotus*). Gerard is a wonderful mentor to me too, always encouraging me to, 'Get on out there.'

Next, I would like to thank Karen McDermott for having the faith in me to take me onboard and, most of all, trusting me enough to deliver the 'goods' for her. I absolutely know I am in good hands with Karen's hands-on, just-do-it approach to everything she does. Not only that, Karen's unique brand of professionalism, along with her exceptional publishing team, have wrapped their ever-supportive wings around me, their brand-new fledging author. All the way from faraway Western Australia, too!

Speaking of MMH Press, how could I not thank Dylan Ingram, for his unconditional support and endless patience (oh, and his gorgeous Irish accent, too) since I first became part of MMH Press. He has, without a doubt, become my number-one contact and go-to guy within my tentative journey into the publishing world. I couldn't ask for a better support system than Dylan.

Also at MMH Press, I wish to thank Ida Jansson a million times over for her amazing cover design of *Calm the Raging Storm*. I was blown away when I first laid eyes on it and I am STILL blown away by what she has created for me. She is truly a genius!

Last, but not least, I wish to thank Danielle Line for her structural edits of my manuscript. Like Dylan, Danielle was also very supportive, especially when my 'original' written ideas or plots didn't always match the avid reader's concept of what a good romance must always include.

Where would I be too, without the ongoing support of my awesome writing friends within our Alumni Brisbane FM Masterclass Group? I'd probably still be wandering around aimlessly, trying to get those elusive ideas and words down on paper. There are too many of us now to list all of our members, but you know who you all are. Their ongoing support, friendship and endless enthusiasm for each other's writing projects has been so uplifting! Every time I leave our monthly meets, I feel their inspiration and encouragement follow me home.

Last but not least, I want to express special acknowledgement for my best friend and soulmate, Gary Enzweiler, who has always encouraged my writing journey. I marvel at his acceptance as to why I've needed to stick to my early-morning writing schedules for the past five years as a full-time writer. He's been there for me, not only for my writing-sucks! days, but also for all of my I'm-gonna-do-this! days too. I also thank him for his creative inputs, helpful ideas, cooked meals (for a distracted writer) and the invaluable propping-up of my fragile writer's ego when necessary.

Apart from acknowledging people connected with my writing journey, I never want to dismiss the importance of love from my whole family including Gary's two sisters, Pam, Bev, and Steve (who have been with me all the way), our awesome neighbours, and all of my special long-time friends (you know who you all are). All of my new friends too—Plus, all the girls of The-Loop-Group (love you, ladies!).

Thank you one and all! You're as much a part of this book as each one of my characters are.

ABOUT THE AUTHOR

*T*oni *has always been* a writer, even if she didn't always realise it. Her rampant imagination lit a fire in her belly at the age of ten and all from just a simple one-page story for English class, which somehow turned into a three-page adventure instead. As well as dabbling in short stories and stage plays, Toni has also been a poet for over twenty years, prompting her to self-publish her own poetry book back in 2009—essentially, the contents of a shoebox collection of neglected poems. Toni has entered short stories and stage plays in various competitions over the years, which was never really about the prize money, but more of a excuse to spread her creative wings each time.

Toni has had a varied working life experience. Firstly as an office junior at an ambulance station, a bank clerk, disability support worker, child care worker, seasonal strawberry picker, barmaid, waitress, telephonist and telemarketer, as well as various other occupations throughout the years. All of these varied career choices have helped to enrich her overall view of the world, putting her in touch with many interesting characters to fuel enough creative ideas for years to come.

She has been working on *Calm the Raging Storm* since 2017. Her second book is due to be published in 2022. This is a historical romance titled *Isabella's Moon* which she wrote in 2018, and is based on the true life memoirs of an Australian war bride, during the tumultuous World War II years.

This year, Toni has been busy researching her third book, based on the true adventure story of her paternal grandmother, covering a period from 1880 to the early 1970s—and is mostly based around her hometown of Walgett, a small town up in the north-west corner of New South Wales, close to Lightning Ridge.

On a personal note, Toni has lived on the Sunshine Coast in Queensland since the year 1999.